**Scapegrace** *n. arch.*: A mischie[...]
especially a young person or ch[...]

Jackie Gay was born in Birmingham and travelled in Europe,
Asia, the Far East and Africa before returning home to write.
She has worked as a teacher and editor and her stories have
been published in *London Magazine* and *Quality Women's
Fiction*. *Scapegrace* is her first novel.

# Scapegrace

Jackie Gay

TINDAL STREET PRESS

First published in 2000 by
Tindal Street Press, 16 Reddings Road,
Moseley, Birmingham B13 8LN
www.tindalstreet.org.uk

Copy-editing: Emma Hargrave
Typesetting: Penny Rendall

The extracts from *The Crucible* by Arthur Miller, Methuen 1953,
are quoted by kind permission of the publisher.

A CIP catalogue reference for this book is
available from the British Library.

ISBN 0 9535895 1 X

Printed and bound in Great Britain by
Biddles Ltd, Woodbridge Park, Guildford.

For Mum, as promised

# Acknowledgements

I would like to thank Lesley Glaister, Penny Rendall, Julia Bell, Joel Lane, Alan Beard, Alan Mahar and Emma Hargrave for their encouragement and support.

# The Shed

We were in the shed when it happened.

'Good job your mum's out,' whispered Gina. 'She might have seen green smoke coming off the roof.'

'Smelt a whiff of sulphur,' said Ellie.

'Or felt a shiver from nowhere,' said Rose, quivering; a little thrilled, 'like the holy spirit.'

We laughed, and felt immediately brighter. Our shoulders relaxed, errant locks of hair were looped behind ears, Cora casually lit a cigarette. 'D'you want one, Alice?' she said, waving a packet of ten No. 6 in front of me. 'Let's share it,' I said – and all five of us watched as the smoke curled out of her nostrils and settled under the dusty eaves. None of us dared move though; our yard was a tricky place at the best of times. The shed skulked in the far corner of it, behind my mum's secondhand shop, itself tacked on to the scruffy end of the High Street. Two suburbs out from the city centre, we were; two more to go before the road rolled off the plateau and down into the countryside. The traffic only lulled for an hour or two at night; when sleeping in our flat above the shop I was often woken by the silence: a gap when noise you weren't aware of is suddenly switched off.

My mum was in the right trade, we all agreed, because she could never bring herself to throw anything away. From the back alley behind the High Street we had to squeeze through the bars of the rusted-up gate, then pick our way through the hopeless congeries of corroding bicycle parts, warping tables, cracked pottery slopping with greenish water and vault over the broken twintub before reaching the shed. We were safe once we got there, though; it was the best bunking-off hidey-hole we'd ever found.

That day we'd escaped the monotony of school to try and catch the travelling fair before it moved on, but the field where the stalls and rides had been was a rutted mess of tyre tracks; we just caught the last silver-sided lorry lumbering off the site, trailing fairground music. So we filled the afternoon by jumping on and off the back of the number eleven Outer Circle, two or three stops before the conductor got to us, hopscotching our way around the city until we finally got chased away at the bus station in Harborne. Then running home, taking the back routes, five girls a streak of blue down underpasses and over footbridges, cutting down to the canal bank where midges hung over the trickle of water; mudbanks still cracked from the summer's scorch. Over the tunnel where the witches lived; the air thick with the smell of chocolate from Cadbury's. Straight lines across the parks – always faster than the parkie – we knew holes in fences and alleys to hide in; weaving our way through the busy streets full of chip shops and mechanics in greasy boilersuits and leftover hippies with fur coats and bare feet. Then down the alley, across the yard and through the door into the cool, dim shed, stacked with boxes spilling out dressing-up clothes and salvaged toys – although we were too old for all that really and pinned photos of ourselves in teenage poses around to prove it. Rose at the Mop, her red hair splayed out. Ellie's fourteenth birthday party where I wore a denim waistcoat and Cora snogged every boy over twelve; Gina in dungarees outside the *Lazy Fox* trying to cajole some lads to go in and buy us lagers.

It was my idea to try levitation. For our first attempt Cora had volunteered and lay rigid across two desks while the rest of us puffed around her. She didn't move, not even a millimetre. 'We have to think together,' I said, 'then it'll work.'

'How are we supposed to do that?' said Ellie, red creeping up her face.

'I don't know. Chant or something. Focus our minds.'

'I've got no chance then,' said Gina.

'You concentrate well enough if you've got to come up with a quick excuse,' said Rose.

'Yeah, your mind comes into focus then,' said Cora.

'What's that to you?'

'Nothing. Just saying.'

'It's not like concentrating on physics, you know,' said Cora. She was languid, gazing out of the window. A layer of mist clung to the damp grass of the playing field; the hockey-players' legs faded out below the second stripe of their socks. It was chilly, but the sky was bright and held the promise of sunshine, as if it could burst through any moment to flood the classroom and lift Ellie – the next subject – clean up to the ceiling, where she would hover and shimmer like the autumn light.

'We can do it,' said Rose, suddenly convinced. 'We will.'

We met on our first day at Rock Hill Comprehensive, standing in the queue for the nit nurse. Still awed by the size and smell and bewildering rules of this new world, the whole class had been ordered to line up by height in the gym. Us five had only an inch or so difference between us and scrabbled, stretched, stood back to back and chopped the backs of each other's heads with our hands. Cora was tallest even after we made her take her platforms off, then Gina, although I thought her hair springing vertically out of her scalp didn't count. Then me, the middle one; then Rose, anxiously raking her fingers across her scalp, examining her fingernails; then Ellie who was telling Rose how nits only like clean hair anyway, they're not anything personal.

'I shouldn't worry about it anyway,' said Cora. 'After that ruck if one of us has got them we all have.'

'Looks like we're all in this together,' said Gina. And that was it, we were a group, until this year barely distinguishable from the other knots of schoolgirls and boys that made up the school, excited that our initials made up a word: G-R-A-C-E. We did have other people in our lives – Rose's big Catholic family and series of penpals, for instance; and Gina sometimes slipped off to mess with the rougher, tougher gangs dodging the wag-van on the streets. She was dragging the rest of us down, we kept being told, but they'd got her all wrong, we knew that for certain. Anyway, it was the group that mattered, that was real, despite our occasional bickering. Gina would growl Dylan songs down Rose's ear just to irritate her and Cora rankled us all by growing a bra size practically every week. Because we'd had to choose options we'd been split up during lesson time – Cora casually brilliant at art, me in my lab coat laced with chemical burns – so we became even closer during breaks; gravitating towards each other in the dinner queue to gripe about the teachers and shake off the unfamiliarity of being apart.

'I wish one of you were in geography with me,' sighed Ellie. 'I hate sitting there on my own.'

'They don't want us to be together, do they?' said Cora, flicking through a copy of *Jackie*. 'Do you think my hair would suit a perm?'

'You'd look like Robert Plant,' I said, dodging the cuff I knew Cora would throw.

'Bugger him,' said Gina. 'Give me Dylan's boot heels any day.'

'But he's so old,' said Rose. 'How you can stand his voice?'

'I love it,' said Gina.

'He's brilliant,' I said. 'What's for dinner? Smells like puke pie again.'

There was one class that we were all together in, though; English. The teacher, Mr McGeady – new that term and already thought of as a bit weird – was our favourite, mainly because of his eccentric clothing, which he wore without a flicker of embarrassment. The boys thought he was definitely a poof. On the first day of our 'O' Level English Lit. class he burst into the room dressed in a wide-striped gangster suit, yellow bow-tie and enormous oval glasses and announced breathlessly that

10

now, now boys and girls, you are standing on the rim of a bottomless canyon. Gina glanced round the classroom mouthing 'canyon?', which set ripples of giggling off in Ellie and Rose. 'Oh yes!' continued Mr McGeady, undeterred. 'Some will mock – they always do – but some, some –' his eyes swept around the class '– will take a step today, a step that will transform their whole lives, this step –' he paused to shush a pair of squirming boys '– is that into the eternal and everlasting world of lit-er-a-ture.'

'Blimey,' whispered Gina. 'I thought he was talking about at least God.'

'He could be,' I said, 'the Bible's full of stories, isn't it?'

'They're not stories,' said Rose, 'the Bible is true.'

'Good point,' said Mr McGeady, who, we were about to learn, had ears as sharp as a hare's and a little meter inside his head that buzzed the second you stopped concentrating. 'Truth and fiction, a subtle and complicated business. Perhaps here you'll learn something of the ways fiction can throw new light on essential truths. Which does lead me rather neatly on to introducing the text for this term.' Wide-grinned, he reached behind the desk for a pile of books and started to pass them round the class.

'What the hell's he on about?' said Gina.

'Oh stop it,' said Cora, shifting around under the too-small desk. 'You just pretend not to understand books.'

'How peculiar,' said Mr McGeady, slapping a slim volume in front of Gina. 'Here. *The Crucible*. A play. Let me see if I can bring this world to life for you, Georgina. Quiet everyone!'

'Gina,' she muttered. 'Not Georgina; Gina.'

'Listen!' Mr McGeady took a deep breath. He seemed to be holding it in, and for some reason the class did too. '*Salem, Massachusetts, Spring 1692 . . .*' His voice boomed around the stilled classroom – it sounded different somehow, as if it was coming from somewhere else, 'Like God,' as Rose said later. 'You think God is everywhere,' said Gina. 'I know what she means though,' said Cora.

'*No one can really know what their lives were like . . .*' Mr

11

McGeady continued, the low afternoon sun bouncing off his back as he paced around the classroom.

We exchanged glances. Hadn't we been saying the same thing only the previous day? That our parents and teachers seemed to have no clue about our lives, which were daily intruded on by such strange vividness that it seemed impossible that we were brushed off as just troublesome schoolgirls. Even the TV programmes, radio stations and magazines which were supposed to be for teenagers felt like a girdle, a constraint to us; as if by swallowing all 'that guff' – as Gina called it – about Donny Osmond's chihuahua and how to make our eyes look bigger, we would be accepting something much larger, which we didn't want to take on, but somehow would, if not careful. Reading *Jackie* was like cracking a code – this *Crucible* thing about seventeenth-century Salem had more relevance by the looks of it. We would examine, bemused, the photo stories resolving in weddings – as if weddings were the *end* of life; and the fashion photographs of young girls.

'Does being beautiful,' Cora drawled, examining the pictures minutely, crossing and uncrossing her legs in a parody of the models' poses, 'mean I have to look like this?' We flitted around in front of mirrors pulling faces; crowded into the photo booths at Woolies, pinned up our hair, pushed out our chests and pouted; moving from gorgeous to absurd to ugly and back again and then peering at the strip of pictures, wondering if the pictures we saw were really *it*, were really us. We'd swap clothes to see if anyone noticed; Cora could wear anything – and did, much to the teachers' annoyance – but still looked aloof, something the teenage mags most definitely didn't promote. The boys gave her a wide berth, but their eyes followed her; she would turn and catch them out with a disdainful 'Ha!'

'*The edge of the wilderness was close by* . . .' Mr McGeady was still reading from the introduction to the play, accompanied by an unprecedented hush. We were hot and itched from the sunlight that poured into the classroom. '. . . *and was full of mystery for them*,' he continued.

'What's this play about?' Gina whispered.

'Dunno,' said Rose. 'I've got goose pimples all up my arms.'

'Witchcraft,' said Cora, 'a group of girls that get into witchcraft.'

'It is not!' exclaimed Ellie.

'Not just that,' I said.

Mr McGeady broke off from his reading. The class relaxed; chairs were shifted, throats cleared, scuffles broke out. 'You can finish the rest of the introduction for homework,' he said. 'Now, let's read the first few pages of the actual play. Who wants to take a part?'

The hands of us five girls shot straight into the air.

By the time we came out of English, we knew we could do it, our doubts rinsed away by the strange voices that leapt from our mouths as we read out parts from the play. '*How high did she fly?*' said Cora, just before the bell rang. The words crackled in the air. Even Mr McGeady seemed a little startled.

Taz Turvey must have noticed us sneaking off because he caught up with us just as we were squeezing between the bars of the school fence to find the fair. 'Where are you lot going?' he said. 'I'll come with you –' We turned as one creature and Gina stared at Taz with her dark eyes – black and bottomless now – and a visible shiver ran through him, from the top of his spine right down to his toes. 'Maybe I'll not bother,' he said.

'I could have done it!' Gina said, when we were at last safe in the shed. 'I could have lifted him clean off the floor.'

'Lifted who?' said Rose.

'Taz. Back there in school. I felt the power. I *did*.'

'Oh you and that Taz,' said Rose. 'Why do you always have to go on about him?'

'You started it.'

'Never mind Taz,' said Cora, 'this is about us.'

We decided that we would try and lift Ellie, as she was the smallest and youngest of the group and also confessed that she was a little scared and would be better off lying down.

'I might wobble halfway up,' she said, 'I've got an awful funny feeling in my stomach.' We dragged a bench out of the yard into the shed and Ellie lay down and closed her eyes. A stray cat settled on to the window ledge and watched.

'She looks like the Virgin Mary,' said Rose, her voice trembling.

'I bet the Virgin Mary never got levitated,' said Gina.

The group gathered around Ellie – me and Cora at the shoulders, Rose and Gina at the hips – and each slipped two fingers underneath Ellie's body.

'Two fingers?' said Gina. 'Is that enough?'

'We're not going to lift her,' I said, 'we're just . . . what's that word?'

'Vessels,' said Rose, 'for something that's bigger than all of us.'

The dim light in the shed puckered, like the beginning of an old film, and the dust on the floor seemed to swirl around our feet. 'It'll start without us if we're not careful,' said Cora, swaying.

We closed our eyes and tried to forget everything else; it only ever seemed possible in the shed somehow. We felt light, as if we were suspended, and stood motionless, attached to Ellie only by the tips of our fingers. Traffic rumbled constantly and other noises encroached; a child's cry, a door slamming.

'We need quiet,' muttered Cora.

'Shush,' Rose gasped, 'she's going to move, I can feel it!'

'Keep your fingers in contact!' I said, and we bent our heads in time to catch our hands – unbidden – following Ellie's body as it rose a few inches up from the bench. She settled back down gently and opened her eyes.

'You OK?' whispered Rose.

'Yes,' said Ellie, slightly surprised.

'We did it!' whooped Gina, eyes flashing in the darkening shed, igniting the rest of us with her excitement. 'Yes! What does it feel like, Ellie? Can I be next?'

We lit the shared cigarette, chattering in hushed voices. Ellie was quiet. Suddenly she sat up, looking even more ghostly than she had during the floating.

'Alice, can I borrow some of your clothes?' she said.

'Of course . . . but why?'

Ellie held out the back of her skirt. It was marked with dark splotches of blood.

'Ouch,' said Gina.

Ellie's arm curved protectively over her stomach. A last, low beam of sunshine filtered through to the shed and cast an amber, shadowy light on us. Our faces came back into focus.

'Come on,' I said. 'Let's get up to the flat and find some clothes.'

'What time is it?' said Rose. 'I've got to go.'

'Me too,' said Gina, shaking her head as if to try and clear it.

'Tara then.'

'Tara.'

'The pain goes, Ellie.'

Ellie pushed her hair back and grimaced. She was sweating, the cramps coming in waves. I felt an echo of them myself as I nudged her towards the door.

'Bye.'

While Ellie was getting cleaned up I crept back down to the yard, unable to resist. Cora was still there, sitting on the step of the shed. We sat together, watching the yard's shapes merge as the darkness thickened around us, listening to the rumbling of the city.

'That's it then,' said Cora. 'We're all grown-up women now.'

# Fire

'Fires?' said Ellie. 'I haven't seen any fires.'

We were standing around outside school, reading the letters we'd been given in sealed envelopes. Packed buses rumbled past, kids jumping on and off the open back deck, the
windows upstairs steamed from breath and wet wool. The
pavement was crowded with people, mothers with pushchairs,

old folk shrunk into overcoats, who stood unsteadily as schoolkids dodged around them. Dogs barked, a Chopper bike ran over Rose's toes, its owner a blur of denim and hair. The city hummed all around us.

'Let's go to the park,' I said.

'Not the shed?' said Gina.

'We can't get near it. Mum's having a clearout and the yard's out of bounds.'

'*My* mum's not going to like this note,' said Ellie. 'She already thinks Rock Hill's too rough for me. If she finds out there's *fires* . . .'

'Too rough?' said Gina. 'She should come down our estate if she thinks school is rough.'

'The less Ellie's mum knows about you the better,' said Cora.

We came to a halt next to a large weeping willow and pushed back its heavy branches, letting them drop down behind Gina, enclosing us in a makeshift den.

'She'll try and move me, I know it,' said Ellie. 'She's convinced I'll turn into a right dropout if I stay at Rock Hill.'

'Bullshit,' said Cora, stretching her legs out and admiring her new – strictly against school regulations – two-tone shoes. 'How could anyone think you'll turn out bad?'

'Well, none of us really know how we'll turn out,' I said, peering out through the acned leaves. It bothered me this, that we couldn't even predict what might happen tomorrow, let alone in the future, which was as mottled as the autumn leaves around our feet.

'Oh, *very* helpful, Alice,' said Rose. 'We can't have Ellie leaving us.'

It was on the cards, though. Ellie's mum was just looking for an excuse to take her away from Rock Hill. 'She thinks she can just lock me away from it all,' said Ellie. 'She won't even buy me a bra.' Previous letters about graffiti and smoking in the toilets had been bad enough, now there were these fires.

Rose – religious and from a respectable family, and me – studious-looking, good reports, had been delegated to go round to try and convince Mrs Allen that it was just a school, not a place of festering evil, which was the impression you'd

17

get if you listened to Ellie's mum talking to her relatives on the phone; but Mrs Allen couldn't be convinced that we were safe at Rock Hill, because we had each other. She didn't see that by staying steadfast, together, we had *power*. 'They've got no direction, Elinor,' she'd said once, appearing alongside us in the Saturday morning queue outside Silver Blades and dragging her daughter away. 'Why don't you get yourself some proper friends?'

No direction, we could take, but proper friends? She might as well have said we weren't proper people.

'What if the fires stop?' said Gina, stripping back a willow leaf.

'Might help,' said Ellie, 'might be too late.'

'Beside the point, I'd say,' I said.

'You *know* something,' said Cora to Gina, who squirmed around to the other side of the tree trunk, yellow dust from the bark smearing all over her school skirt.

'Gina?'

'*Gina!*'

She slithered up the tree trunk and flexed on a branch above us. 'OK,' said Gina. 'It's Kenny Marshall and his gang from our estate who've been lighting the fires. 'He's got this massive grudge against Wills-Masterson; swears he'll see her finished one way or another. They've gone nuts, the lot of them, necking cough medicine and sniffing fire extinguishers –'

'Fire extinguishers?' said Ellie, her head tipped up towards Gina.

'You don't want to know, Ellie, honest. Kenny'll have the whole school down, if you believe the way he goes on. You know what his family are like.'

We did. It was part of Rock Hill legend that Kenny's older brother, Mark 'Magpie' Marshall, had been the first to challenge Wills-Masterson's new regime. Everyone from first years to caretakers talked of how lucky she'd been when Magpie was finally locked up for vandalizing a signal box. Just in the nick of time, everyone said, close shave for that teacher of yours. Little brother Kenny then had to take on the family grievance. Little brother was also Gina's cousin.

'*Your* family,' said Rose.

'I can't help that,' snapped Gina.

'What's going on, Gina?' I said. 'You'll have to tell us sometime.'

'No quarter,' muttered Cora, more to herself than Gina. It was a group rule. We had to explain ourselves, no excuses. It was tough, but it worked. Like when Rose was convinced she could live on a carrot a day, we managed to keep her from joining her sister in ward eight of the General because she couldn't lie to us about how much she'd eaten. We went to the loo with her too; no one can keep an eye on a girl like her friends, that was something else adults didn't understand. So now Gina had to tell.

I scrambled up the tree to coax her – sometimes Gina just closed up, took herself away from us. Divided loyalties, Cora said. But there was more to it than that; she took herself off physically, roaming from one end of Birmingham to the other. From our perch on the tree branch we looked out over the muddled patchwork of the city; a bird's view of the alleyways, lock-ups, railway embankments.

'Come on, Gina,' I said, 'you can tell us.'

A narrowboat chugged up the reddish-brown canal that weaved through the layers of Birmingham's urban spread. The smoke from the boat's stove joined a few other thin lines rising in the still evening air from gardens, chimneys, allotments. That was what had done for her, she said, staring out; the fire. She knew that cousin Kenny and the rest of his gang were up to something but had kept away until she saw them come back to the estate one night with blackened faces and firework eyes. They had this buzz about them – irresistible, Gina said, like sneaking into town at night when it's all neon and noise – and so she followed the boys one night and watched from behind a hedge as they scurried around collecting sticks and undergrowth and then – the magical moment – struck a match, which fizzed and flared, lighting up the lampless school grounds. The boys had dashed off once the fire was going, but Gina stayed, nurtured it until it was a glorious blaze tearing into the black

19

night sky. She had stayed all night, dozing and rocking on her heels and then woke into a soft dawn blanketed in grey flakes like snow, or feathers. 'It was incredible,' she said, dreamily, 'I opened my eyes and I could feel *everything*.'

'You stayed out all night?' said Rose. 'What did your dad say?'

'They don't always have to know,' muttered Cora. I swung my head sharply in her direction, but she was staring at Gina. 'Sounds amazing,' said Cora, louder.

'I don't think Ellie's mum would agree,' said Rose.

'Can you get them to stop?' said Ellie.

'Put it this way,' said Gina, as we clambered down from the branch to join the others, 'asking them nicely isn't going to do much good.'

'Get your mum to sign something else,' I said to Ellie. 'Anything – permission for swimming – and then I'll forge her signature on the slip.'

'What if you get caught?' said Rose.

'Better than Ellie getting sent away.'

We just made it out of the park gates before they were locked and chained for the night, fence spikes silhouetted against the reddening sky. We were scruffy and tired, shoes scuffed, hair escaping from bands and frosted with tree-moss. We brushed each other down as best as we could, spat on grubby palms and slicked down plaits, then split off for our homes with only two things certain. One, Gina would keep away from the Marshall gang – damage limitation, Cora said; and two, that something had shifted. Knowing about the fires shifted things.

'Quiet everyone,' said Mr McGeady, pressing his hands down on an invisible cushion of air as if this would somehow calm the noisy and excited class.

Backsides refused to stay on chairs, hands fiddled with books, rumour and hearsay and gossip poured out of mouths and into ears and straight back out again. *Someone set the sports pavilion on fire! Burnt to the ground!* Fortunately, the blaze was spotted by a passer-by and quickly extinguished but Wills-Masterson was reported to be not only scarily livid but so pained by the letdown that no one, not even the teachers, could look her in the eye without feeling somehow guilty. According to the school bush telegraph, she was hauling suspects – including Kenny, no doubt – into her office for an audition with the police at that very moment.

'Did you know the pavilion was set on fire last night, sir?'

'Is it true that the cricket stuff all got burnt up?'

'I bet it was one of those Marshalls.'

Hands shot up and quivered for attention. Kids perched on desks, some were moving towards the front of the class, to hang around Mr McGeady and snatch up any juicy drops of information he might inadvertently release. The classroom windows were splattered with charred flakes, stirred up by the wind that whistled around the school grounds. Doors banged, paper skittered up the corridors.

'Look, sir, there's bits of fire on the windows!'

'Everything stinks of smoke.'

'Yeah, sir, I need a letter to take home. Otherwise my dad'll batter me for being back on the fags.'

'Yes, sir, we need letters.'

'Quiet!'

'But, sir, we need letters.'

'No letters. No discussion of the fire. *Quiet!*' Mr McGeady looked slightly surprised that he'd succeeded in hushing the class. 'Open your *Crucible*s please. Today we're going to discuss Abigail.'

That caught our attention. Cora, Rose, Ellie and I had been ignoring the clamour up until then, worried instead about Gina, who – disconcertingly – had not shown up for school that morning. And we weren't willing to condemn Kenny either, even though most people seemed to have already made up their minds. The character of Abigail, then, was a welcome distraction. As leader of the play's forest-dancing, spirit-conjuring girls, we agreed, she must be the one in touch with the power.

'You mean like you?' Ellie turned towards me.

'Like you wish you were,' Rose needled.

'Like we all wish we were,' said Cora.

'Abigail.' Mr McGeady's voice had an edge of desperation to it. 'Would anyone like to comment on her character?'

'She's a cow,' muttered Taz Turvey. The boys around him curled into sniggers. 'She's just leading them all on.'

'Leading on, possibly,' said Mr McGeady. 'But would you kindly expand upon exactly what you mean by "a cow"?'

It was the rest of the class's turn to snigger. Taz wriggled up straight in his seat. 'Everyone knows what that means,' he said. 'Abigail's shagged that Proctor bloke – not that he was complaining much. Anyway she wants more but he's feeling guilty because of his wife and so she's been mucking about trying to put a spell or something on the wife and got all her mates in on it and they got caught and now she's trying to worm her way out of it by making out something spooky is going on. Like I said, a cow.'

Mr McGeady sat down with a thump at his desk. Sunlight poured through the streaky windows; I was sweating, smeared my palms on my thighs. 'Right,' Mr McGeady said after a while. 'I fail to see where your vehemence comes from though, Richard; it's not a personal insult that Abigail behaved in the way she did.'

'But it's just cack. Why didn't they just knock off together and be done with it? Why all that fuss with witchcraft and guilt and morals?'

'I can see we are going to have to do some work on historical context,' said Mr McGeady, sharp again. 'Now, who else has got something to say about Abigail?'

'They're all ready to have a go at her, aren't they?' said Cora.

'And it's not as if the rest of the village are pure white,' I said. 'She's only trying to protect herself . . .' I trailed off, confused about where my sentence was leading me.

'Good, good,' said Mr McGeady. 'Interesting ideas – including yours, Richard,' he added hastily, 'if a little roughly expressed. Now I want you all to write something about Abigail – her character, motivations – maybe do an imaginative piece about her life up to date. Anything you like as

22

long as it shows that you've read act one. You can finish it off for homework. Questions? Settle down now.'

No one settled very well though. We sat and scratched, shuffled, flicked through our *Crucible*s. The room was simmering from sunshine and radiators. Someone was playing with marbles behind me, I could hear the glass balls clicking in the runnels of the desks, but Mr McGeady either didn't notice or didn't care, he was marking books, his face a running commentary on the content.

'Sir?' said Cora, after what seemed like hours.

'Yes, Cora.'

'Can we write *anything*?'

'Yes, as long as it's relevant.' He had started to pack his neat leather briefcase and half the class followed cue, shoving books into their bags, hissing coded messages across the room.

'Even about sex?' She threw the word casually into the growing heat of the classroom.

'Pardon?'

Cora leant back on her chair until it rested on the gritty window. Sunlight blazed from behind her but she appeared cool, composed, not prickly and flushed as the rest of us were, including Mr McGeady who wiped his hand across his forehead. 'Taz's right,' she said. 'And Alice. It's all about hypocrisy. Historical context has got nothing to do with it. No one wants to admit that teenagers – teenage girls – might want sex. What's so different now?'

Mr McGeady only managed to mutter something about 'next time' before he fled from the pungent classroom – thirty adolescent bodies in the refracted heat – where the class was just realizing that by teenagers, Cora meant *us*.

23

# Echoes Down the Track

Us. GinaRoseAliceCoraEllie. Our teenage faces jerk through my head. GinaRoseAliceCoraEllie. Cora was always the tallest. No one ever caught up with her.

I'm on a train. On my way back. Though there's no 'us' now; the group scattered long ago. But the city will still be there and I try to picture it – buildings, landscape – always more manageable than faces; people. The Post Office Tower and the HP Sauce factory and more canals than Venice and a tree stump on the bank of the Birmingham & Worcester with a carving of my name. Spaghetti Junction – it had just been built back then; a miracle of modernity, they used to say on TV, urban myths of people getting lost for hours on its loops and curves. Now it's twenty-one; the flyover that came of age. My memories seep upwards as the train skims the countryside. Streets and canals and people always teeming and chattering; a hotchpotch of family-owned factories and small engineering lots, warehouses and pubs; curry-chips stalls and markets overflowing with shimmering fabrics. Where I've been living – the place that I've left – it's quiet; a peaceful country village where the years slipped past, like the slow-moving stream at the end of our road. I've had a few reports from Mum, of course. 'That nice grocer's two doors down has closed. There's a chain one there now. Apples all sealed up in plastic.'

She tried to get me to go back, my mum. 'Just for Christmas.'

'What's the point in us squeezing ourselves into a tiny flat when we can all be comfortable in the house?' said Dan; my husband Dan.

'How do you know it's small?' said Mum, bristling. 'You don't know anything about it.' It's not that she really dislikes Dan, I don't think, it's just that she can't quite get a handle on him. 'Anyway, it's Alice that should come back, not you,' she said. She always thought my estrangement from the city was unnecessary.

'It messes up my head, being there,' I'd say, and she'd eye me suspiciously, trying to cut through my words with a sharp look, to catch me unawares. She never managed it until now, with this letter.

It wasn't just the letter though. I shift around in my seat, the miles rolling away beneath me, trying to work out what it was that made me leave him, leave my life. What's driven me on to this train that's heading straight for New Street. Dan probably won't even notice I've gone until the fridge empties out; working late, he'll think, she probably told me. Maybe she's at a conference. That's how it's been lately. Sitting opposite each other in the kitchen, knives scraping on the plates, Dan shaking the bad news out of the paper. I didn't say much – now it feels like I haven't said much for years.

Dan's friends had started commenting on it: 'Quiet, your missus, isn't she?'

'She's got hidden depths,' Dan would say, sliding his arm around my waist. 'You never quite know what's going on with Alice.'

But you did with Dan. I'd started testing him, digging up rosebushes in the garden when he was away and moving them a couple of feet; rearranging photographs and pictures in the house to expose patches of unfaded wallpaper. Dan still had his briefcase in his hand, rain wet on his shoulders when he commented. 'I'll have to move those roses back,' he said. 'Look, I'll show you why . . .' We stood at the window while he sketched shapes with his hands – foregrounds

25

and backgrounds and the Leylandii he'd recently planted down the end, blocking off the view over the common land below us. 'You see how that bed's all cluttered now,' he said. 'You do see that, don't you?'

'How about getting some pots for the patio then?'

'Oh no. We've always liked things tidy, haven't we, Alice?' It was an appeal, the nearest thing to eye contact for weeks. 'We've always agreed on that.'

I try to picture his face when he finds my note. *The truth is that I don't want to go and live in America, Dan. I know it's what we planned and I understand it's the right move for you. But it's just not for me. I need to do some thinking, so I've decided to go home.* He might even be relieved that I've found a reason, something that we can hang the failure of our marriage on; neat, blameless. I nearly wrote *take Lucy instead* but managed to resist throwing spurious guilt into the melting pot. I've never minded too much about his girlfriends; didn't marry for love. It was a domestic arrangement, a mutually beneficial partnership. And now I'm chucking it all over my shoulder like a crumpled-up paper – yesterday's news – and not even looking back. The practical parts are amazingly easy. Pack a bag; buy a ticket.

The train rides smoothly over the tracks, a faint rhythm to its progress. GinaRoseAliceCoraEllie. Out of the window I can see fields, flashes of acid yellow, villages snug into hillsides screened by trees. The sun beats through the window, the train's rhythm lulls me, my head lolls on my shoulders but then I'm jerked awake by the click of the door behind me; open, closed, open, closed. My stomach is curdled, my skin alive to the heat and the breeze whistling through the window. The train is pushing on, intruding between fields and woods, splitting roads and canals, scattering houses unevenly up hillsides. Even if I got off at the next stop and straight on to another train back to the village, to Dan, nothing can be the same now. I can't reel in that moment, that flash, which powered my hands to write notes, to pack, propelled my feet down the drive and on to the platform. In an hour or so I'll arrive at New Street, lurking under the hub of the city; get in a taxi to the flat above the secondhand shop at the scruffy end of the High Street. Where my mum will be waiting; always there.

Her letter came a week ago. *Dear Alice, I just had the most peculiar dream about you. You were sitting at the edge of a forest staring into it and all those girls you knew at school were dancing around you, teasing and mocking. And you just sat there, on the edge of this wilderness. I so much wished you would move. When I woke up the flat seemed empty without you. I went over to the baker's and old Len in there asked after you. 'How's your Alice?' he said, and I said, 'How should I know?' He looked at me ever so peculiarly, patted flour on to my shoulder.* Here her handwriting fades, smudged by coffee and her sleeve. I try again to pick out what has been wiped off but can only read one more line, at the bottom of the page, *It's time for you to come home. I just know it is. You can look after yourself, Alice. You always could.*

I rang her up. 'Mum, are you OK?' But that was the wrong thing to say. 'Everyone keeps asking me that. Why are you asking me that?'

I showed the letter to Dan but he passed it off as just the way she is. 'How can the flat still be empty without you?' he said. 'You've been gone more than fifteen years.' He was disturbed by it though, as if Mum's scattiness had edged over into eccentricity and that could be dangerous – possibly even hereditary – if the looks he snatched at me were anything to go by. Dan turns away from anything even slightly offbeat; inside the lines is where he wants to be. A fully paid-up member of society; badges earned and displayed. Perhaps that's why I married him. An easy passage to the inside.

But I've left all that now; I'm making my way back to the city, the place where I grew up. And the only thing I know for certain about it is that Gina Marshall won't be there.

# Growing Pains

'It wasn't me!' said Gina, eyes wide. 'I was ill. Look, I've even got a sick note from Dad.'

To Whom it May Concern
Last Friday, 12 October, my daughter Gina Marshall was too ill to come to school. She had the raging shits and didn't leave the bathroom all day.
Sincerely,
N. Marshall, Father

I laughed. 'That's your dad all over.'

'Doesn't mince his words, does he?'

'You can't give that to school.'

'Why not? It's the real thing.'

'Anyway, they can't blame you for the sports pavilion fire now.'

'You want to put money on that?'

Gina was twitchy; her legs swinging underneath the bench, scudding the earth floor, disturbing an arc of dust each time. Weak sunlight filtered through the grubby windows of the shed and caught the motes, enveloping us in a soft, earthy haze. We'd slipped out of library study to be there, to hang around among the broken-down furniture and boxes of jumble that seemed half alive; shifting around on the edge of our vision. It felt as if something might have made its home there; elves, maybe, or imps. More like rats, Gina scoffed. From the outside the shed looked small and grey and insignificant, a battered garden shed in the corner of a convoluted jungle of scrap. We had to squeeze ourselves through the door one by one but once we were in there it expanded like a Tardis, and the mess was ours – even Mum's junk didn't migrate this far. We liked to sift through the boxes, finding cracked mirrors and battered teapots and pictures of clowns with crosses for eyes to decorate the shed with, alongside our photos. We dressed old dolls in strings of plastic amber, made shrines out of bowls and mirrors, strung scarves around the eaves and our faces. Maybe we'll find something rare and precious in here, we thought, among the mouldering books, broken jewellery and bags of clothes that should have gone for jumble years ago.

'The fires won't stop,' said Gina. 'Marshall's gang have gone electric lately.'

'I bet your aunty's doing her nut,' I said.

'Wills-Masterson's out for blood,' said Rose. 'Trouble is she's got no one to sink her fangs into.'

We laughed. We'd nicknamed our headmistress Dracula as she had large, pointed incisors, which occasionally slipped outside her fleshy lips and sat there, glinting on her lower lip. Taz and his gang called her the Willie-Master, but Cora said no, that doesn't fit, it's the girls she's really after; so Dracula she stayed. Sometimes only one of her fangs slid out, which always seemed worse. Never mind her skein of sculpted candyfloss hair or her gold-buttoned suits; it was when the teeth came out that we knew there'd be trouble.

'She probably sharpens them every morning, just in case she comes across one of my family,' said Gina. 'At times like this I really wish I wasn't a Marshall.'

'She's got her fan club though,' said Cora. 'Bunches of first years trailing behind her, all dewy eyed.'

'She can't get you,' I said to Gina, 'you haven't done anything.'

'Haven't you noticed the way Rachel Williamson and her lot look at me now?'

29

'They do it in assembly,' said Ellie, 'when Dracula is preaching.'

'Well, who cares about Rachel?'

'She fits in so well she disappears,' said Cora. 'But Ellie's right; we're who everyone looks at when Dracula gets fired up.'

'And we're where they stop,' said Gina.

Gina kicked some more. There was a groove underneath her feet. None of us could keep still, but we couldn't bear to go back to school either, all those faces etched with disapproval. And for what? I wished we could just barricade the shed door and stay in there, with the dolls and the photos and the scrap.

Cora was sifting through a pile of rags; moth-eaten and ancient. 'I bet you'll miss the fires though, won't you, Gina?' she said, holding up a soiled corset with a daunting number of hooks and eyes.

'What?'

'Imagine getting that on and off in time for games,' I said, eyeing the corset. The musty smell of old clothes was extinguished momentarily by a sharp and disturbing body odour.

'Poo,' said Rose, holding her nose.

'The excitement of the fires,' said Cora.

'I told you, I didn't light them.'

'No, but you liked them.'

'Yeah, well,' said Gina. 'It was watching the boys that set me off. One minute they were boring podgy lads kicking a ball round the streets and next thing they were –'

'Electric,' said Cora.

'But that was nothing compared to the fire.'

I unpicked and rebraided my plait. Gina dug her groove deeper with an old tennis racket. The dusty air sagged on top of us.

'Let's levitate again,' said Gina.

We had done it a few times since Ellie's first floating – always in the shed – and it had become no stranger than any other part of our lives – bodies sprouting hair and flesh overnight, the sudden jumpiness of our parents, blood and

30

fire and unanswered questions. In fact it was a release, to escape and drift for a while, hover in the air touching nothing, complete for those few seconds.

'I keep having these weird dreams,' said Ellie, sunk in her corner of the shed, barely visible.

'I'm not surprised,' said Gina. 'Everything's weird right now.'

'I think they're . . . I think I . . . I wake up all hot, and can't quite remember what's gone on except . . .' Ellie's anxiety spidered out of her corner of the shed.

'Sounds like a wet dream to me, Ellie,' said Cora.

'Our Johnny has them all the time,' said Gina. 'I can hear him snuffling and moaning through the wall.' She groaned, long and wistful, and we half laughed.

'I feel like my body's running away with me,' said Ellie. 'I've never even kissed a boy.'

'Just ignore the dreams, Ellie,' said Rose. She was shifting about on the bench, sitting on one hand and then the other. 'You can't help what you do when you're asleep.'

'Yeah, but it doesn't go away when you're awake,' said Cora. 'The feeling.'

Rose stopped shifting and stood up, her body snapping straight. 'Come on,' she said. 'We've got to go.' Her decisiveness stirred us and we squeezed out of the shed door, shaking our limbs into action.

'Well,' said Cora, as we hurried down the alley. 'It doesn't go away, does it?'

Ten minutes late, we skidded into English. Mr McGeady was reading from the play.

'*Abigail, what sort of dancing were you doing with her in the forest?*' he questioned, his eyes flicking straight to us, the glint of challenge stopping us short.

'*Why – common dancing is all,*' said Rachel Williamson.

All eyes swivelled back towards the teacher, willing him to continue the drama, but he broke off – half smiling – to address us. 'Well, girls,' he said. We tried to straighten our clothes out. 'What sort of dancing have you been doing?'

'We had a free period,' lied Cora smoothly.

31

'Sorry we're late, sir,' puffed Rose.

'I wish we had been dancing,' muttered Gina.

'Sit down then, get your books out.'

Mr McGeady was intent on taking us to Salem. 'Imagine you're in church,' he said, 'with the whole town spying on each other through the sides of their eyes while the preacher thunders hell and damnation.'

It wasn't difficult. Rose shivered straight away, her sweat gone cold. Gina bristled. Every trace of our other worlds – schools, classrooms, homes, parents; even fashion, music, football – slipped away and we were in Puritan New England where spirits lived in the nearby woods, curdling milk, pinning men to their beds, stalling wagons and stealing souls.

'Think what it would be like to wear the clothes,' Mr McGeady said, 'long prickly dresses and every lock of hair tucked away under bonnets.'

'I'd be naked in the woods by now,' whispered Cora.

He told us how in Salem everyone's actions were watched; chalked up, misdeeds marked and judged, on earth as well as finally, by God. 'How do you think these circumstances would have affected people in the village?' said Mr McGeady, back in the twentieth century. I wriggled in my seat, trying to bring the classroom back into focus.

'It's horrible.' Cora shuddered. 'The church giving everyone an excuse to interfere.'

'John Proctor didn't even go to church, did he?' I said.

'All the more reason why they'd be talking about him,' said Rose.

'He just wants to get on with things in his own way,' said Gina.

'Too right,' said Taz Turvey. 'Why should he have to make himself like all the others?'

'Good question,' said Mr McGeady. 'Extremely apposite. App-o-site.' He chalked the word on the blackboard. 'Now, has anyone got work on Abigail to hand in yet?'

Rows of shaking heads said no; McGeady's response was to hand out more, on top of comprehension to do in class. We settled to work, chewing pencils, jiggling feet. The whole school was hushed; squirrels moved down from the trees outside, scavenged around the bins.

'Sir, what does apposite mean?' said Robbie, one of Taz's gang, after a while. It was nearly dinnertime, people were glancing at their watches, stretching and yawning.

'Look it up,' said Mr McGeady, without moving his head from a pile of marking. 'In fact, more homework – you can look up these words for next lesson and explain how they are important to the play. Dissembling. Contention. Calumny. Write them down. And find one more of your own. Class dismissed.'

'He's in a bossy mood today,' said Cora, as we watched the teacher slap together his books and click down the corridor on steel-tipped heels. He could have been whistling.

'That's what this literature stuff does to people. Gets them all puffed up above everyone else,' said Gina darkly.

'What's your problem today?' I said.

'Oh, I don't know.' Gina shook her frizzed hair. 'Things are bad at home. As if the whole school whispering about me isn't enough.'

'You can tell us you know.'

'I know. I will. Later.'

'Later then.'

'Tara.'


After school we drifted back to the shed. It was raining – thin, bitty strips of rain that seemed to be joined invisibly, pulling down more and more endless grey wetness. We slouched around, tugging at our ties, kicking our shoes off and letting our socks roll down to our ankles. The afternoon was quiet – muffled by the rain – and we could hear the pigeons from two yards down warbling and gossiping in scandalized tones.

'Even the pigeons can make more sense of things than us,' grumbled Gina.

'Are you really going to give that note in at school?' said Rose.

'Yeah, why not?'

'It'll wind them up,' I said.

'What else can I do? Dad's notes are always like that. I think he *wants* to upset people, sometimes.'

'Pass me something to lean on,' I said. 'I bet I can copy his writing.'

'There's an old games board or something down here,' said Gina, reaching behind me. 'What are you going to write?'

'The same as he did, except change "raging shits" into "sickness and diarrhoea".'

'I don't understand why your dad can't do that,' said Rose.

'Make sure it's different from the note you did for me,' said Ellie.

'OK.' I finished the note then hurried out of the shed into what was left of the daylight. The board slipped off my lap and flapped open on the powdery floor. As the door creaked behind us a last shaft of light sneaked through and glanced off the board. The word OUIJA lit up; like theatre neon, like a promise: OUIJA.

# A Father, a Brother

'Dad?'

Gina and I slammed her front door behind us – we were breathless from running, laughing, safe now from being caught on the wag – but then stopped short. The house was stripped. The curtains were gone; cushions, windowsill trinkets. Instead there was a pile of stuffed black binliners.

'Dad?' Gina looked inside one and pulled out clothes; new ones with the tickets still on, and underneath LPs – *Madrugada*, *Bringing It All Back Home* – tapes, leather jackets, all wrapped, all new, 'All nicked,' said Gina. I watched her face darken. 'Wait here a sec,' she said. 'Dad?' Her voice echoed around the bare walls. 'You said you'd keep out of all this . . . Where's Sandra? Where are *you*?'

'She's gone.' It came out in a muffled groan from the kitchen. Gina's dad was clamped to the kitchen table – hanging on as if that was the only solid object in the whole world. He looked ravaged, his black curls crushed on one side of his head and stiff springs on the other; his face bulbous and swollen. Gina went over and rubbed his shoulders, kissed the top of his head.

'What are you doing out of school anyway?' he grumbled.

'What are you doing with all that stuff in the house?'

'Loz had to get shot of it.'

'What's wrong with Loz's house?'

'Too hot.'

'Yeah but then again Loz doesn't look like a mugshot off of *Z-Cars*.'

Mr Marshall's face softened; he leant back on his daughter. 'You're a cheeky piece.' She kissed his head again. 'Just like your brother. He just asked me if he could have some of the jackets to sell.'

'Is that why Sandra left? Because of the stuff?'

He shrugged. 'Dunno. Gone to something better I expect.'

'Dad . . . Sandra's not like that.'

'Isn't she? She tell you she likes living with a loser, did she?'

'Well, she wouldn't have moved in in the first place if she didn't . . .' Gina jostled her dad, trying to make him smile; pulled her fingers through his flattened hair and I was jealous – despite everything – of her dad, of their closeness.

But something happened, Mr Marshall seemed to change a gear. He heaved himself upright to his full six-three and shrugged his daughter off like a coat on a hot day. Gina stepped away just in time. 'Don't you ever think I wanted to be like this,' he growled. 'A bloody doley. What am I supposed to do when every factory in Brum is turning away men? Sandra said we should leave, go to another town, another country even, but what would I do over there, eh? And there's always five kinds of busybodies breathing down my neck, whichever way I turn. And it rankles.' He towered above Gina, his body too big for the back kitchen. 'Understand? They *rile* me.'

Their breathing was loud in my ears. They stared at each other.

'I know, Dad,' said Gina eventually.

'I'm going out.'

Gina's dad forced his way through the kitchen until his bulk filled the back doorway; shoulders knotted, big hands hanging. 'Gina?'

'Yeah?'

'Don't give up on me, hey?'

We watched him lope down the garden and into the alley; Gina from the kitchen window, me from my perch on the stairs, peering round. 'Alice?' Gina said, once the sound of

36

his footsteps had faded. 'Now you can see how he is.'

Gina and I had just lugged the last of the black bags upstairs and out of sight when the rest of the group arrived, bursting free when the school bell rang and haring round the streets to find us.

'Hey Gina, are you all right?' said Ellie. 'We were worried about you.'

'You two shouldn't sneak off like that,' said Rose. 'We're your friends.'

'What's happened to the curtains?'

'Sandra's gone.'

It was bad news. We all liked Sandra, her big hair and runaway mouth; she was nothing like a teacher, or a parent. Gina had been pleased when her dad brought Sandra home because before that he'd always seemed a bit lost, so what did it matter that Sandra was totally over the top? Johnny said he was different before their mum died, but Gina couldn't remember anything of that. Sandra wore magnificent steel-toed cowboy boots and an even more magnificent Dolly Partonesque bust that mesmerized everyone who met her. Gina had come home one day to find the entire house cushioned and draped and her dad rapt, with his arm around this woman.

'I must admit the place does look odd without her stuff,' said Cora.

'I'm going to miss her,' said Gina, sinking into the sofa, 'but nowhere near as much as Dad is.'

'Is he OK?' said Ellie.

We had a soft spot for Gina's dad. He wasn't bothered by our bustle and noise and bickering and – in the days before Sandra – never objected when we trashed his kitchen for the sake of a few burnt scones. All of our cookery experiments took place at Gina's house. Most of our dressing-up experiments too, as Mr Marshall – unlike Rose's parents, or Ellie's – didn't make moral judgements on what we wore, but instead said what suited us, which was much more useful. And he didn't fake it. His eyes turned up at the corners at Rose's pretty frocks, widened at Cora's stacked heels.

Gina sparked the gas fire and we all huddled around its

orange glow. 'I'm really worried about him,' she said. 'You know what he said to me just now? "Don't give up on me." As if I would! But it's almost like he's given up . . .'

'Why *can't* he get a proper job?' said Rose.

'Mum says all blokes used to have to do round here was queue up outside the factories,' I said. 'I don't know what they do now.'

'It's enough to put you off growing up completely,' said Cora. 'Imagine being poor all your life.'

'Dad says all the jobs are slave labour and they expect you to keep signing on anyway,' said Gina.

'I don't understand it,' I said. 'He made me laugh even when I'd had those teeth pulled, remember? He should be given a job in a hospital or something.'

'What, looking like a police mugshot from *Z-Cars*?' said Gina.

We laughed. It was the only explanation of Gina's dad's situation that made any sense to us – that he was always in trouble because he looked so dodgy. Walk into the dole office with that bulk, that curled lip, the jagged scar down his nose (Gina swore it was from falling over a barbed-wire fence, but even we doubted that story), and everyone immediately thought he was working a scam. The local police picked him up routinely for any local misdemeanour, small or large, and he antagonized them further by refusing to be cowed by badges, officiousness, warrants or intimidation.

'I think he will be soon though,' said Gina.

'It doesn't bear thinking about,' said Cora.

'What are we going to do?' I said.

The door creaked and Mr Marshall stepped in. 'Hello girls,' he said, flatly. He smelt of wet wool; rain darted in between his legs.

Gina rushed to his side. 'Dad! Shut the door quick. What's the matter?'

'Johnny's been arrested.'

'Arrested?'

'Johnny?'

'Yes, your brother Johnny.' Mr Marshall was snappy, jerked his head like a dog after a wasp. The room darkened, as if a bulb had gone somewhere. Rose started to cry.

'What for, Dad?'

He examined the circle of faces around the fire. 'I'll tell you later.'

'We're not kids, Mr Marshall,' I said, trying to make my voice as grown-up as I could. 'And we'll find out sooner or later.'

'Johnny's our friend too,' said Ellie.

'He can't have done anything too bad,' said Cora. 'Everyone knows Johnny's only messing about.'

'Everyone except the police,' said Mr Marshall. He slumped down; we could hear the squelch of his wet clothes. 'Drugs,' he said. 'They say he's been selling drugs around the estate. Reckon they caught him with a big lump in his hand.'

Cold shock winded me. Johnny selling drugs? He might have got hold of a scrap, I thought, but not dealing.

'Johnny's not into that,' said Cora.

'Even my mum likes Johnny,' said Ellie. 'And she doesn't like anyone.'

Mr Marshall tried to smile. 'Do you think she'd tell that to the police?'

Silent tears were running down Gina's face. 'What are we going to do?'

'They'll let him out later. Then court I suppose. His life won't be worth living round here any more though.' His voice thickened. 'Now come on, you girls. Off you go home. Me and Gina need a bit of peace.' He herded us out of the door and we scurried off down the wet street, one dark silhouette blown against the orange city glow. The wind carried the sound of Mr Marshall's voice over too. 'Gina love,' he said. 'Get your thinking head on, girl, we've got to do something about those bags.'

'What was he talking about when he said bags?' asked Rose. We were nearly back at the High Street, back in a different world. Shops, lights, people; all glistening and shiny and soaked.

'Alice, why did you and Gina go off this afternoon?'

'She was sneaking through the fence and I couldn't persuade her to stay so I went with her.'

'You're going to be in such trouble.'

'I can talk my way out of it. It's Gina that's really in bother.'

'Yeah. Poor Gina.'

'Poor Mr Marshall.'

'Poor Johnny.'

We stood at the bus shelter and dripped, huddled together and watched the people in the street; for clues, I thought, all these people stepping assuredly off buses and into taxis and hurrying up the street – they were teenagers once. There were some women hanging around a pub doorway. 'Why don't they go inside?' I said. 'I wish we could go into pubs.' We all did. To us, always outside in parks and on streets and canal towpaths, the smoky yellow glow that leaked out from pub doors and filtered through beer-glass windows was loaded with promise. Rumour had it that the Bridge – a canal pub further down the road, which we often passed when roaming – was on a leyline, an ancient meeting place, so it was top of the list for when we could get away with being eighteen.

'Probably waiting for someone,' said Cora, glancing at the women.

'They look like complete tarts to me,' said Rose. 'Do you think Johnny's really in trouble?'

'I hope not,' said Ellie.

'I wish there was something we could *do*,' I said, for the zillionth time.

The rain had stopped and the wind was fading. We could see the reflection of an approaching bus in the glassy puddles, as it lumbered down the High Street. Ellie and Rose got on it, waved at us through the muggy windows. 'Will your bus be long?' I asked Cora.

'No. Anyway I can walk down to Moseley if one doesn't come.'

'I'll be off then.'

I plodded up the street. I could see Cora's bus making its way down. As I passed the pub doorway one of the women broke away from her huddle and clattered down to the bus stop. 'Cora!' I heard her say – the last breath of wind blew the words to me – 'Don't you look different in your school uniform!'

40

# Stalled

The train is stalled, at a junction in the middle of nowhere, flat fields spreading out all around it. It seems appropriate somehow. A bit of waiting time before the train snakes its way back into Birmingham, squeezing between railway and flyover and then under the city centre and into my past.

My mind slips back to what I've just left: the house, the job, the husband. That life seems like a purge, a scouring of all the messy bits, clearing up so I could find an adult space to live in. When we moved to the house, Dan and I bought shelving; racks of it. Storage boxes, chests, cupboards. Now it seems terrible, a tyranny. I'd come home from the lab leaden-footed and have to tidy, sort, clean. Otherwise I couldn't sleep, would have nightmares of mislaid boxes and lost letters. All those things and places to put them; a tidy life, no loose ends. It really seemed possible then, a sensible way to arrange things.

People always got this idea that I was sensible. My Aunty Gladys said it when I went to live there, 'I don't know how you got in with those girls, Alice, you're so sensible normally.' I couldn't articulate it then, that I didn't want to be sensible, even if I knew how to do it. We all did, I think; we knew what was expected of us, but squirmed underneath it. It was one of the things that Dan liked about me, that I knew when to visit great-aunts in nursing homes and which presents to send when babies were born. I know he expected me to accompany him last Christmas, down to the bottom of the garden where the brambles thickened; to the patch of common land where the travellers were spending their winter.

'Come on, Alice,' he said, waving his copy of the eviction order, grabbing his buckled green wellies. 'Now we can get rid of them for good.' I had a sudden vision of what he'd look like to them, with his trimmed beard and wax jacket. A maniac from the centrally heated house, ranting and waving a piece of paper that ordered them to dig their trucks out of the frozen mud.

'It's not up to us to tell them,' I said. 'The court will serve them notices.'

'Get your boots on, Alice,' he said.

Mum didn't come for Christmas that year, she hadn't been up for a while. I was exhausted from overwork – more and more responsibilities piled on me; on everyone, it seemed. People sitting on the evening train with another day's work in their briefcases, going hot and cold at the thought of mince pies and presents and visiting relatives. It made Dan boil. 'And there's that lot sitting in their trucks and bloody caravans doing nothing all day while we flog ourselves to death to pay for it. And at the end of *my* garden.'

'They've got kids to look after,' I said. 'Last Sunday the man with the ring through his nose chopped wood for four hours.'

'Have you been watching them?' said Dan. I didn't answer. 'A ring through his nose?' said Dan. 'What does he think he is, a bloody cow?'

I remember how my skin burnt as I watched him go off down there; to shout, to bang on people's doors. It was freezing, a sudden drop in temperature at dawn had frozen water around the tree branches. He crunched off down the lawn while the ice-trees tinkled and chimed in the wind, and I burnt.

They were gone within a day. Lashed wood on to their roofs and tinkered with engines, clouds of diesel smoke in the air and old ladders under the tyres. Dan came back from the site with a few tin cans and an empty whisky bottle. 'There's more rubbish than that in our front hedge,' I said. 'And we've got a cellar full of bottles.'

We were both glad to get back to work after the holidays. The house without any visitors had too much space in it, was chilly although Dan built up fires, using wood the travellers had collected and chopped. I looked out of the window and saw the empty space where they'd been and something stalled in me; their moving on, their quiet exit seemed like a lesson, but I couldn't quite grasp what. Dan joined the village forum and discovered that the post office was due for closure and that the pub was being taken over by a chain. Within weeks he was talking about America. I felt like a puppet; a doll with a cord you pulled for some set words to come out. *Nice day dear, what do you want for tea?* He got into a mess one morning – lost his phone, mislaid his car keys – and he turned to me, a plea in his voice. 'Alice . . .' he said, standing there with one arm through his overcoat. But I found I couldn't help him any more. Couldn't fake it. 'I'm late myself,' I said, pushing past him. 'Your phone's in the charger.'

People are getting restless, the train has been stopped for an hour or so now. They have places to be, deadlines to meet. I'm stuck here, suspended; the train could jerk into life at any moment or we could be waiting all night. Everything shelved for a few hours, out of our hands. It feels OK though, this pause, to take a breath. I buy a doughnut from the buffet and smile at the girl behind the counter; she starts, everyone has been snapping at her for hours.

Dan didn't believe me when I said I didn't want to go to America. 'But think of the lifestyle,' he said, 'the standard of living.'

'This is the man who wants to get out of the village because they're building a Wacky Warehouse,' I said.

'We'll go and live in the mountains, Alice.'

'Well, I hardly thought you'd choose a house in Compton.'

'Alice, what's got into you? You sound like Rupert on a bad day.' Rupert was Dan's adolescent nephew. I started laughing then because I'd only just stopped myself from crunching down on to the sofa with a grunt, just like Rupert did, his limbs flailing and twitching in disgust.

'I'm trying to talk seriously about this,' said Dan.

'I'm not going,' I said. My heels were dug in, earth rucked up in front of me. 'I won't like it there.'

'You can't know that, Alice.'

'I do.'

'How?'

'I just do.'

'Now you're being plain ridiculous.'

The train judders into life and we move on. The countryside is receding now, there are fewer gaps between villages, more motorways, factories; a long silverish ribbon of canal meanders alongside the railway, heading into the city with us. For me it's like going back in time, the blackened redbrick, the embankments and viaducts and arches, pigeons diving from the eaves. Road stacked on top of railway with canal in between. Trains snaking out of concrete and boats chugging through lead and graffiti. I finger the photograph in my pocket, the only photograph of Gina that I have. A Polaroid snap of her in a field in France or Spain, standing between rows of vines with a basket and some secateurs, taken by some transient friend and then sent to the shed. No letter, no message. Just Gina's sturdy brown legs in the clay and her hair escaping from a bright gypsy scarf. She must be about seventeen; we'd both left the city by then. I watch them, the people who still live here, as I go back in. Cycling, being walked by the dog, panel beating, welding in a mask, fluorescent sparks flying. Driving buses, pushing prams, darting between the traffic for a ball. A flash of them in shop doorways and at bus stops, smoking, raising an arm for the bus. Spaghetti Junction, its fat pillars all yellowed and dingy, but its shape still there, creaking under the traffic. As the train picks up speed for the last leg to the station it all rushes past me and through me and then sudden darkness. We're plunged into the blackness of the tunnel. When I see daylight again I'll be home.

# Ouija

'Ouija?' said Rose, stepping into the shed and turning over the board. 'What's this?'

It was the first chance we'd had to escape to the shed since Johnny's arrest and all of us were out of sorts. Gina spent most of her time picking at scabs on her knees, her eyes hooded by her thickening fringe; Ellie's mum had taken to leaving private-school brochures next to the cornflakes, open at glossy photos of tennis courts and girls in perfectly pleated whites.

'Who does she think I am?' said Ellie. 'Do I look like the *Mallory Towers* type?'

Additionally, one of the teachers – not Mr McGeady, we were sure of that, although Rose had clammed up about him for some reason – had been complaining to Wills-Masterson about us in the group being a bad influence on each other and we'd all been hauled in front of Dracula. 'Do you realize how important this year is in your studies? . . . You seem to be isolating yourselves from the other students . . . The time has come to toe the line.' It was coming at us from all sides and Gina, especially, was not conducting herself well. Wills-Masterson was convinced that the group were in some way responsible for the sports pavilion fire, and Gina didn't help herself by acting one hundred per cent hardcase; curt replies, insolent stares from her black eyes. There were letters to parents, endless detentions.

45

Rose had been to see Dracula and tried to explain, about our friendship, how it was a good thing, but she was dismissed with a flash of yellowing tooth and a warning that she was 'better off out of it'.

'Shall we levitate?' said Ellie. 'We've got to do *something*.'

'Ouija,' said Cora, picking up the board. 'I've heard of that.'

'Can't think where though,' I said. We all hunched around the board. In addition to the word OUIJA scrolled across the top, the letters of the alphabet were arranged in two arcs beneath it, with the numbers 1 to 9 and the words YES, NO and GOODBYE dotted around. There were symbols, too: a sun, a moon, what looked like a genie coming out of a lamp, five-pronged stars, and cackling imp-type creatures dancing around the edges. 'Imps!' I said. 'I told you there was something living in this shed.'

'Alice, they're just pictures on a board,' said Gina.

'Maybe they come to life when you play the game,' said Ellie.

'Yes, we can call up spirits or something,' said Cora.

'We join our fingers on a glass,' I said.

'You're supposed to ask it questions,' said Rose, 'but I don't think we should –'

'How do you know this stuff?' said Gina, interrupting us sharply. The atmosphere was very still; the board seemed to be pulsating. We glanced at each other; the board shifted.

'Don't you?' said Cora. 'Don't we all?'

I placed the board on a packing crate in the middle of the shed. Rose edged towards the door but seemed unable to leave. A quick 'bye' might have done it; then we could have given up on the idea, buried the board away for ever.

'We need a glass,' I said and we all rummaged in the junk, glancing back at the board and at each other and then back at the board. It just throbbed gently on the edge of our vision. I nearly said, 'Hey, let's do it tomorrow, I'll get a glass from the kitchen,' when Gina pulled a glass – clean and sparkling with a notched diamond pattern – out of a heap of rags. It caught the shed's meagre light and drew it – and us – in towards it.

I sat down and put two fingers on the glass. The others joined

46

me, even Rose's hand was reaching out, tugging her body with it. There was no noise. The bustle of the street outside subsided – cars were slung across the middle of the road and frozen – the pigeons hushed, the air stilled. My head cleared instantly and all I was aware of was my own breathing and our fingers joined in a star on the glass. Even the familiar musty smell of the shed seemed to have disappeared. We could have been anywhere.

'What do we do now?' whispered Ellie.

The glass moved. A–S–K

'Alice?' A voice came piercing through the walls of the shed. '*Alice!* Are you down in that shed?'

We all fell away from the Ouija board and blinked, trying to bring each other's faces back into focus. I rushed to the door just in time to block my mum's view.

'What are you lot doing in here?' she said, peering over my shoulders into the murk. Ellie slipped the glass under her jumper. Cora flicked the board closed.

'Nothing,' I said.

'That was really odd,' said Mum. 'I knew you were all down here but then I suddenly had this feeling you'd gone.'

'You've been reading too many freaky books, Mum.'

'Hmm. Anyway, it's time for tea, Alice. Come on in now.'

'We just need to tidy in here, Mrs Tracey,' said Ellie.

'OK, five minutes.'

We watched my mum's heels clip effortlessly through the yard, not daring to meet each other's eyes until she'd gone.

'She *felt* it,' said Rose.

'That is weird,' said Gina.

'She just seems to know things sometimes,' I said. 'We'll have to make sure she's out next time.'

Rose's head snapped up from the board. 'We're going to do it again?'

'Don't you want to see if it really moved?' I said.

'I don't know.'

'It is scary,' said Ellie.

'We're all together,' I said. 'As long as we're all together, we'll be fine.'

47

*

All through the next week we attempted to be normal; concentrate on lessons, avoid detention, pass the time by doing 'Is he the one for you?' quizzes in *Jackie* – Cora ripped the magazine up when her answer came out as 'No'. 'I bet Cathy & Claire have never even *heard* of an Ouija board,' she spat. By Friday her neck was strung with egg-sized hickeys. Ellie said the wait was a trial to see whether we were fit for the spirits; Gina – picking at a splinter on her desk – said more likely it was a test to see if we were up to life or not, which looked like a shit sandwich from where she was standing. We sat through lessons, drawing patterns in the desks and willing the bell to ring.

All our parents took us to one side and asked us what was the matter – except Gina's dad, who said she had good reason to be fed up with *him* for a father – and I realized that our moodiness was making everything worse. Mum would never be persuaded to go out if I was moping around. So we perked ourselves up, went around smiling and chirpy for a day or two and – abracadabra – Mum announced she was going to her sister's for the weekend.

In the shed Rose's eyes went straight to the board and she stopped dead.

'Have you ever known a week last so long?' said Gina.

Cora flipped open the board and the words swam into focus in front of us. OUIJA. YES, NO, GOODBYE.

Rose's eyes had already closed and her eyeballs twitched underneath them. Her face was pale and clammy. 'There's lots of ways to get in touch with God, you know,' she said, defensively.

'Rose, who are you talking to?' said Ellie.

'We haven't even started yet.'

The tips of my fingers and toes were tingling. 'They are here though,' I said. 'I can feel it.'

'Hang on,' said Gina. 'What are we going to ask them?'

'Let's just ask if they're friendly,' said Ellie.

At the centre of the board the glass appeared to be hovering. 'Is anybody there?' Gina whispered in a mock-scary

48

voice. The glass clattered down and wavered on its rim. For a second we thought it might shatter.

'Watch it, Gina!' I said.

'Prat,' said Cora.

'They must be nice spirits,' said Ellie, her voice sounding unconvinced. 'We'd know by now if they weren't.'

'They're trying to talk to us,' said Rose. She sounded shaky, her voice coming from a place way behind her.

'Are you sure you're not getting carried away with this?' said Cora.

The glass shifted. NO.

'It moved!'

'Did you do that?'

'Course not.'

'Who did then?'

M–E

The world stopped spinning. Like the fires, said Gina later, when the universe shrank and there was nothing but me and my face in the flames. We sat frozen, the only movement rapid glances between our five faces. I thought I felt the glass quiver.

'It wants to move,' I said, tautly. 'How do we make it move?'

A–S–K

The scrape of the glass on the board made us start.

'Of course! We have to ask it questions.'

'Be careful,' said Rose, fearfully.

'Are you friendly?' said Ellie.

M–A–Y–B–E

'What do you want with us?' I said.

'I thought it was the other way round,' said Cora. The glass ignored her and skated around the board.

T–A–L–K

'We're good at that,' said Gina, attempting a joke. Her hand was vibrating on the glass. 'Especially when we're supposed to be quiet. Ask any of our teachers.'

'I don't think he thinks that's funny,' said Ellie.

'Is he a he?' I said.

YES.

'You don't lark about much in the spirit world then?' said Gina.

NO.

We held our breath for a few more seconds and then the questions – ones Cathy & Claire could never answer – burst past our lips. 'Are you here all the time?' I asked. 'Why don't we fit in with anything any more?'

'Will my mum take me out of Rock Hill?' said Ellie.

'Will Johnny get locked up?' said Gina.

'Does God mind us doing this?' said Rose, and – the rest of us gasped at this – 'Is sex before marriage really a sin?'

Cora's question came out last and echoed round the walls. 'What will I be when I grow up?' she said. That sounded like the sort of question that might be answerable – artist, maybe; designer – but the glass skidded to a halt. It was as if a bucket of live fish had been kicked over – each fish a flickering, tentative question – and now these questions had been released to slither around the shed.

'Stop! It's too much!' cried Rose. 'He can't answer so many.'

My hand was trembling on the glass. 'Just wait a sec,' I said.

'Who are you thinking of having sex with anyway?' said Gina to Rose. 'I didn't think you were allowed.'

'Shush,' I said, but the glass had started to move again.

H–E–R–S–E–L–F

'What?' said Ellie. 'What does that mean? Oh . . . I see.'

'I didn't think that was allowed either,' said Gina.

Rose's redness glowed even in the dimness of the shed. She snatched her hand away from the glass – Cora later swore she'd heard a crack, the breaking of contact – and started for the door.

'Don't go!' I said, turning furiously to Gina. 'Look what you've done now!'

'I didn't realize the spirit would answer my question to Rose.'

'Rose, masturbation isn't sex,' said Cora. 'Well it is, but –'

'You should have told us,' I said. 'Why didn't you say –'

Low sobs rose up from Rose's stomach. For a second I thought she might actually be sick. She pulled open the shed door and suddenly illuminated all our shocked faces. 'How could I tell you about *that*,' Rose yelled. 'I don't even want to think about that. It's all right for you to have boyfriends and wet dreams and be on Abigail's side. You don't have to confess. My mum was right about you lot after all –'

'Stop it, Rose,' said Ellie. 'You don't mean that.'

'I do. I *do*. I'm going home. And I'm not doing the spirits again. How could I ever have thought that they'd help . . .'

However much we tried we couldn't persuade Rose to come and have another go on the Ouija board. She clammed up completely, refusing to talk to any of us – even Gina – and started attending Catholic assembly, which was as good as saying 'stuff you'. Gina cornered Rose – shivering in her bra and knickers – in the changing rooms and reminded her of the rule: 'You have to tell, Rose, what was it that freaked you so much?' But Rose was shut tight; she just carried on lacing her trainers and ducked underneath Gina's arm. Her snub hit us hard. We still looked around for her in the park, the shed, the High Street; expecting to see her tamed curls, her school bag swinging as she rushed into focus out of the blur of blue uniforms. I thought we should ask the spirits for help, but Ellie was against it. That's what drove her away, she said, we're not ready for them. Bits of us are, said Cora, that's the problem.

'I think she felt them too strongly,' said Ellie. 'Isn't it funny how all the teachers love her now?'

'Goody-two-shoes,' said Gina. 'She was always a bit like that.'

'Her mum'll probably give her a chastity belt,' I said. 'A great big iron thing around her bum so she can't play with herself.'

'Alice!' said Ellie. 'There's no need to be mean.'

'I know. I just feel weird about it all.'

'One more letdown,' said Gina, clawing at a scab on her knee.

'We're just jealous,' said Cora.

'I'm not,' said Gina.

'Yes, you are,' said Cora. 'At least she's got her church. Who would any of us go to if we left the group?'

# You're In or You're Out

As if the scene in the changing rooms and going to Catholic assembly wasn't enough, Rose made it even clearer that she was out of the group by sitting with the 'A' Stream girls in English. Mr McGeady didn't notice until about halfway through the lesson and did a doubletake while scanning the usual clusters – Taz's gang, us, the sports teams, the drama groupies, the science buffs who hated English and sat sullenly wrapped in resentment, the heavy-metal boys with Black Sabbath T-shirts poking out from underneath their collars. The class was split by music and sport; Bay City Rollers fans mocked by rock chicks, netball steered clear of hockey, we even had one solitary punk (heading for expulsion, everyone said). Mr McGeady's head zigzagged back twice when his eye snagged on Rose, in the front row; not sprawled across her desk, not chattering, her tie in a nice neat knot. We wore big knots, with the flap as short and fat as possible and the long, snaky ends tucked into our shirts; the 'A' Stream had once proposed that this was a violation of school-uniform rules. They didn't think much of Abigail either.

'She's a terrible girl,' said Rachel Williamson – top of the class and well on her way to being our least favourite person of all time. 'Just evil. And then she gets the others involved in whatever she's up to in those woods and ends up destroying the whole village.'

Rose was gazing up at Rachel admiringly and Rachel tossed us a look of triumphant disgust.

'Did you see that?' hissed Cora.

'What can she have told them about us?' I said.

'Probably that we've been murdering kittens and casting spells in their entrails and that it's all my fault.' Gina shrugged down further into her seat and directed a laser beam of hate at Rachel Williamson's back. Mr McGeady walked through it without even a flinch.

'Mmm,' he said, pacing around the class, nosing out copies of *Shoot* and *Jackie* from under desks. 'Do you think it was entirely Abigail's fault, what happened in Salem?'

'She started it,' said Rachel.

'She started it,' imitated Gina, in singsong.

'Georgina, please!' said Mr McGeady.

'Of course it wasn't,' said Taz. 'She didn't have sex with her*self*, did she? I tell you, this stuff gets on my tits. As soon as there's a bit of upset the whole village is in there having a go. If they were pissed off they should have said so, not wait around for someone like Abigail to hang their problems on.'

Mr McGeady was looking at Taz curiously. 'Richard, please don't swear in my classroom,' he murmured.

'It's true though, isn't it, sir?' said Cora. 'What about Proctor? He's the one who was married. Why do they have to make out it's the girls who are evil?'

'One moment of weakness,' muttered Mr McGeady. Rose had a laser locked on him now and the wash of colour had gone from his face. 'That's all it takes. Took, I mean. For Proctor.'

'You what, sir?' said Gina.

'Well, the girls didn't have any moments of weakness as far as I can see,' said Cora.

'None of it makes sense,' said Taz. 'No one has to stay there. If I was Proctor I'd be off like a shot. Get away from all that crap.'

'Richard!' Mr McGeady was sharp this time. 'Outside! With me. Now.' His hand was hard on Taz's shoulder. 'The rest of

53

you can write a paragraph entitled "If I was Abigail". In silence. Exercise your imaginations for a change. Richard . . . ?'

He opened the door and a smell of floor polish wafted in, smothering the usual racks-of-trainers-meat-and-cabbage smell that seemed to be lodged in the bricks of the school. Someone split open an orange and doused the room in citrus. The urge to escape into the clean wide corridor, away from the classroom, from having to think, was so compelling that Gina actually stood up and leant in that direction. Ellie pulled her down; we wrote.

'If I was Abigail,' wrote Ellie, 'I'd find an adult I could talk to about what happened in the woods and tell them the truth. It would have to be someone I could trust, which might be hard, but I'd have to do it because that's the only answer. Also, I would have to forget about John Proctor. That might be hard too.'

'If I was Abigail,' wrote Gina, 'I'd get right away from there. But not before I'd had it out with that John Proctor. And all those others standing in the church pews thinking they're better than her. Maybe that was what she was doing, really. But a girl like Abigail couldn't even *breathe* without upsetting someone, could she?'

'If I was Abigail,' wrote Cora, 'I'd be off in the woods with Tituba.'

I wrote nothing. I eyeballed the others' work but still nothing; there was too much confusion in my head to find a sentence. What had gone so wrong for Abigail? Was it her? Was it Salem? Were the times just changing too fast for anyone to keep up? I imagined asking the Ouija board and the answer coming clearly through the smooth swipes of the glass.

'Rose's probably written that Abigail should pray for help from God,' said Gina, just loud enough, and Rose's ears reddened.

We could hear Taz and Mr McGeady's voices rising in the corridor. Eventually they came back into the room just as the bell rang and Mr McGeady had to hold his arms across the door to stop us getting out. 'Class!' he said. 'Homework.

Following on from Richard's contribution, I'd like you to think about why John Proctor didn't leave Salem. Why he struggled so hard to be accepted. You might need to look in the history books.'

His words trailed after us as we streamed down the corridor, heading for the bright light of outside.

'Gina,' said Ellie, 'there's no need to pick on Rose.'

The four of us were slouching around the park, kicking stones. The shed was out of bounds again; Mum had visitors and didn't want us hanging around.

'I know.' Gina dug her heel into the grass, twisted it around. 'I just can't stand seeing her there all prim and prissy and doing it right.'

'I bet she's miserable,' I said.

'She won't mention an urge again until she's about twenty,' said Cora.

'I do feel bad though,' said Ellie. 'That stuff in the shed must have really got to her.'

'She can't pretend she didn't feel anything,' said Cora, 'she was in there with the spirits before we even got started.'

'I bet she will, though,' I said.

It was too late in the year for the park. We were cold, the wind blew up our skirts and through our coats and turned our ears red and the ends of our fingers numb. Cora fumbled with lighting a match and when she eventually succeeded – hunched over, hands cupped – the flame flared to her fringe and we sucked in burnt hair along with cigarette smoke. The sky was grey, pregnant with rain.

'Mum's gone all funny about the shed since that day she nearly caught us,' I said. 'Says we've no business hanging around in there all the time. We should be either in or out, she says, not halfway in between.'

'What's that supposed to mean?' said Ellie.

'Search me.'

'She says now there's only four of us we could sit in my bedroom if we want to.'

'She's noticed then,' said Ellie.

Heavy drops of rain as big as pebbles dropped out of the sky. We ran for a clump of trees but it was too late; we were drenched instantly. Gina shook her head – dark coils splayed out – and sprayed the rest of us. The park was sheeted with water; flashes of lightning forked across the sky and turned everything electric blue for a second; the thunder boomed nearer.

'Will we do the board again?' said Gina urgently, shivering. 'Even without Rose?'

'It might not work without her,' said Ellie.

'The spirits seemed to want to come out though,' I said.

We watched the lightning crackling across the city, giant fiery streaks splitting open the sky.

'When can we do it?' said Gina.

'Soon. I'll sort it, I promise.'

We squelched to the park gates, jostling each other and slipping around; sodden shoes across the flooded playing field. Gina said we could go to hers to dry off, so we slithered down the darkening streets to the Marshall house – a beacon of welcoming light in the deserted street. 'Dad put that lamp up outside the front door last week,' said Gina. 'He said they can all go to bollocks, he's not going to pretend he doesn't exist any more just because Johnny's been set up.'

'Is that what you think happened?' said Ellie.

'I love the way your dad swears,' said Cora. 'They can *go to bollocks*,' she mimicked.

We trailed into the house, kicking our shoes off at the door and shrugging off the wettest layers. Johnny was in the living room, watching telly in the dark.

'Hey, Johnny,' said Ellie. 'How are you?'

'Great, never better.'

'Johnny, this is Ellie you're talking to,' said Gina.

He managed half a smile. 'Yeah. Sorry.' He twisted his mouth just like his dad did, ran his fingers through his tousled hair, and I had a sudden urge to touch him, his hair and fingers joining mine. So did Cora and Ellie by the looks of it; I could see Cora's hands twitching.

'Is it a setup then, Johnny?' said Cora. 'What did happen?'

'Tell them, Johnny,' said Gina. 'Someone else might as well know the truth.'

Johnny hitched himself up from horizontal. He had football shorts on, a deep gouge in his thigh from crashing his bike with a box of matches in his pocket, a fireball that had eaten into his flesh. 'Where's Rose?' he said, but none of us answered. 'Well . . . I was with Rushy out on the wasteground. He had some dope, only a little crumb that he'd nicked off his brother.'

'Rushy?' said Cora. 'The doctor's son?'

'I've never liked that Dr Rushton since he burnt my verrucas out,' I said. 'Mum says he was downright sadistic.'

'Yeah, that's the one. Anyway, I don't even think it was dope because we smoked it and nothing much happened – and then we were walking back and Rushy was going on about how he'd got hold of some other stuff and did I want to see it and he handed me this big black lump and then the police just pounced on us. Like they were hiding in a bush or something.'

'So it was his stuff.'

'Yeah. His brother's actually.'

'Why are you up in court then?'

Johnny twisted on his seat. 'Tell them,' said Gina. Her eyes were narrow and unreadable.

'The Old Bill had their hands on my collar straight away.' He looked at us girls ranged around him, with a hint of accusation, of defence. 'I'm a Marshall, remember.'

'Tell them the rest,' said Gina.

'I said it was mine.' He tossed out the words carelessly; maybe we were meant to think him brave; heroic, even. My mouth gaped. 'I had to,' said Johnny. 'Rushy's parents would *kill* him. Lock him up for ever, send him away to boarding school. And his brother knows all these blokes from Bogarts and all over town and anyway the police had already made up their minds . . .'

'As if our dad doesn't want to threaten Johnny like that,' said Gina, 'but he can't, 'cos he's been in trouble himself and everyone knows it. And he'd never throw us out on the streets, so Rushy had a pretty good case, didn't he?' She spat the words out – fish bones stuck in her throat; Johnny wouldn't look at her.

'Does your dad think it was yours then?' said Ellie. 'The dope?'

'He thinks the police set Johnny up.'

'It sounds a bit like that to me,' said Cora, 'hanging around the wasteground picking up schoolboys. They must have needed an arrest badly.'

'It suits them to do me,' said Johnny, 'nice and neat, doesn't upset anyone too much. Good for their crime figures.'

'But, Johnny, you didn't do it!' I said. 'You can't lie to the police!'

'What's the point in doing anything else?' he said. 'Go on, tell me.'

We sat for a while in silence. Mr Marshall came in, grunted at us and fell into a chair opposite Johnny, staring at his son. Gina went upstairs and beckoned to us to follow, and we did, one by one, making excuses – towels and dry clothes and homework. Our wet clothes had become unbearable and we shrugged them off and foraged around Gina's room for T-shirts, dressing gowns, tracksuit trousers. We could have come up with anything; Gina's room was worse than the shed for mess, but it was warm and smelt of perfume sticks and dry shampoo above the faintly mouldy damp clothes. We held back the dour atmosphere downstairs by sitting with our backs to the door and turning on Gina's crackly radio. Robert Plant was in the middle of 'Stairway to Heaven' and we were immediately entranced, pulling the curtains to and losing ourselves in the weird longings in his voice.

A voice from downstairs. 'Oi, you lot. Less of that racket.' Mr Marshall.

'Oh, go on, take it out on me, I should,' said Gina, sticking two fingers up in the direction of her dad's voice. 'He never used to be bothered about a bit of noise.'

58

'Well I am now.' A growl from outside the door. 'You'll want a bit of peace yourselves, by the time you get to my age.'

We stared at each other as Gina's dad's footsteps thumped down the stairs.

'It'll be the year 2000 by the time we're his age,' said Ellie. We shook our heads in disbelief. Reaching the millennium – unthinkable – who could imagine ever being that old?

# Out of the Tunnel

At the top of the escalator I stop; squint my eyes to try to focus. I'm causing a jam here, an eddy, people flow sure-stepped around me. There's a sign – *Move with the Midlands into the Millennium* – but I'm not sure if I can move at all. The concrete floor of New Street station is polished and slippery; a blur of flower sellers, bright sweets in jars, wafts of coffee scent, clicking heels and people bent into their mobiles. The taxi drives down past the Bull Ring – the Rotunda poking into a cloud; down Digbeth; the Barrel Organ – Cora's old stomping ground – now an Irish theme pub; the coach station still the same, unedifying introduction to Brum. Moving into my territory, my childhood. Groups of Sikhs stand chatting in the street, tangerine turbans luminous and neatly pleated; sharp navy suits meticulously pressed. Muslim girls in lace-edged headscarves and fluorescent trainers. Then on to the High Street with its redbrick churches and vegetable carts. Past the cinema, which is now a bingo hall, where we watched *The Song Remains the Same*, night after night, sinking into the pocked velvet seats and mouthing every word. I feel like I'm hallucinating; getting out of a taxi at the front of the flat, the rich yeasty smell of bread from the bakery mixing with traffic fumes and chip fat.

I'm dizzy; grab a lamppost and swing from it, catching myself before my knees buckle. The lamppost is cool and slightly gritty under my hand, I feel the ridges where it widens; then a body-memory of hanging off these same municipal lampposts playing hide and seek, outside Gina's. Before the fires, before Abigail, before any of it. Red shorts and fat plaits, Gina with scabby knees; the memory as clear as a mirror. The traffic moves past in a haze of sprayed water and steam, someone touches my shoulder – *You all right, bab?* – but is gone before I distinguish a face. I take a tentative step and walk carefully over to the jumbled window of the shop.

Mum is pleased to see me. 'Hiya, love,' she says, cheerily, like I've been away for the weekend or something. I've been planning how I'll sit her down and have a serious talk; work out what's going on with her finances, her health, her state of mind. But she drags me through the shop and up the stairs, chattering, sits me down at the kitchen table, puts the kettle on, starts fussing around trying to find the Rich Tea.

The flat looks as it always did, like she's halfway through a clearout that'll never get finished. I'm here again, marooned at the table, looking around at boxes piled up against walls and under tables, drawers spilling out old clothes; postcards from last week and twenty years ago curled on the windowsills. She doesn't seem anywhere near mad, now; here. My mum in her pale lemon sundress filmed with dust from the shop, who never throws anything away just in case there's a diamond in the dust heap.

'Why did you think I should come back now?' I say. 'I thought something serious must have happened. Your letter . . .'

'Oh, it just felt like the right time,' she says, blithely. Then throws me a sharp look. 'He didn't chuck you out, did he? Because he can't you know. There's laws about these things.'

'He didn't do anything, Mum. I decided to leave. There was just something missing, I suppose.'

'And you think by coming back here you'll find it?'

We sit and drink tea. She has the same teapot, with a knitted cosy that came up from the shop. I tell her I've left my job – waiting for recriminations, like you'd expect from a parent – but she's unconcerned.

'I don't know how you could spend your life doing that anyway,' she says, 'poking around after murders and fires and things. What kind of job is that for a girl?'

'You've got to have proper evidence if people are going to get locked up,' I say, thinking of the lab; instruments and implements and sample bags and charts. 'It wasn't just murders, Mum.'

'Yes, well.' She looks uncomfortable; death spooks her. Once she saw an old lady run over on the zebra crossing outside the flat and for years I'd find her staring at the stripes, shaking her head sadly.

'And as for that husband of yours, he can close himself off, that one, just like your father.'

'How do you mean?' I say. That's something new. She never mentioned my dad when I was a teenager. Not that it was ever said – *don't mention your father* – but his name, his title, was so little used, so quickly brushed away that it fell out of usage, became obsolete, like the kitchen appliances relegated to obscurity in the yard.

She ignores me, goes through to her bedroom and starts fussing on her dressing table, comes teetering back down the corridor, clutching hair dyes; peroxide, pillarbox red. 'Which one do you think I should go for, Alice? I can't decide.'

'They're a bit bright, Mum.'

'Have you seen what the girls are wearing this year?'

Well, yes, I have actually. How could I fail to notice that now, in 1997, everyone's wearing platform heels, flares, diagonal-striped dresses straight out of *Shaft*. I haven't seen an Afghan coat yet, like the one Johnny Marshall had, stinking of patchouli and animal hide. That's when I'll really know time has stood still here and it was just me that went away, tried to suddenly grow up, whatever I ever thought that might mean. The idea never even crossed my mum's mind, I'm sure. Even when I was a teenager she was more trendy than me; her heels stacked higher, turquoise triangles sewn into her jeans. Her wardrobe this year seems to consist of slipdresses that look like underwear, and a cosmetic mountain. She'd go without food to buy a new facecream. Looking at her, I wonder if she has.

'So, what do you think, blonde or red?'

'I think you might be better toning them down a bit, Mum.'

'Oh do you?' she says; her eyes make a triangle between me, the boxes and her reflection in the dusty mirrors.

'Mum, don't get all upset on me, it's me that's just left my husband.'

'Well, why don't we go shopping then? I could do with some new stuff myself, you know, summer gear –'

'Mum!'

'Come on, Alice, it'll do us both good, a mooch round town, a bite to eat.'

'Oh grow up, Mum,' I snap. 'Shopping's not going to fix this.'

'Well, that's rich coming from you,' she snaps back. 'You haven't even had a *baby* yet.'

I cry, she cries; that sorts things out a bit. She's always been great with tears, my mum. 'I'm sorry, love,' she says. 'I just thought doing something normal might help.'

'I don't think there's any such thing as normal right now,' I say. 'It feels a bit manic out there for me. Can't even give a straight answer to why I'm here, let alone anything else.'

'Are you worried about Dan?' she says. Weak, after-rain sunlight lands on her and I can see her facepowder mingling with the dust in the air.

'It's not him,' I say. 'I think he's got a bit on the side anyway.'

'Well that's OK then,' says Mum and we laugh. She fetches half a bottle of gin out of a cardboard box in the corner and pours us both a drink. The tea has gone cold even inside its knitted cosy. 'It's not a time for tea,' says Mum.

'Tell me what's bothering you then, love,' she says. 'Don't get me wrong, I'm glad you're back. I knew it was time.'

'I wish I could be so sure,' I say. 'Oh Mum, it's *everything*.'

Emboldened by gin and the comfort of being with Mum – sitting at that table, our feet in familiar grooves in the lino – I go outside to the shed. Outside the city is quieter, the yard monochrome in the dusk. The twintub has sprouted lush, spongy leaves and the shed seems small and insignificant, a place for compost and seedlings, maybe, woodlice and beetles, not spirits and messages from beyond. Still, I have to brace myself to open the door. Musty smells and cold air fall out, the wooden walls are so rotten my fingers make marks on them. I'm wavering at the entrance, voices echoing in my head, *Alice? Alice . . . Alice!* But my feet are braver than me, they step inside. I know no one has been in here since 1977, Mum said so. 'That was your territory,' she said.

Inside. Humps, bumps; shapes and rubbish. Faded faces pinned around the wall, spiders' webs strung from one curled photo-corner to another. Rose's red hair crinkling out; Cora trying to look fierce with her safety-pinned T-shirt, clothes pegs in her hair. Me in my Levi's jacket; I pounded the streets delivering papers for months to buy that. We look girlish and shy – even Cora – ducking from the camera's direct eye, our hair fine and babyish; awkward with our bodies, trying not to be. All five of us crowded into a booth in Woolies, Gina and Johnny's school photo – Johnny with a plaster over his eyebrow. I don't even have to close my eyes to see the glass flashing. My hands are shaking but I make myself scan the darkest corners. It feels brave to do so, not to run into the flat where the light doesn't flicker and crease, where the dusty air doesn't swirl quite so much. Here I can hide; away from the muddle of the city and the strange, naked feeling of having the rest of my life unscripted, a book of empty pages. I remember us as teenagers projecting on to that blankness – I'll be an actress or an explorer, speak eight languages, adopt orphans and abandoned animals, travel round the world.

There is a pile of books to the side of me, mouldy pages stuck together, the smell of disintegrating paper. A lime green cover, a Penguin Plays copy of *The Crucible* with Alice Tracey inscribed on the inside cover over and over again. I pick it up, flick through it, every page has heavily underlined words, biro tips pressed through the thin pages. 'John, you have a faulty understanding of young girls' and, in the introduction, 'The times, to their eyes, must have been out of joint, and to the common folk must have seemed as insoluble and complicated as ours do today.'

It's quiet outside, dark inside. I can no longer see our faces. But there is noise, if I hardly breathe I can hear it. A night train rumbling through the city in the dark, a strange cry from a bird or maybe a fox. I push open the door of the shed and it's dusky outside, early summer dusk, the shapes and colours all blend into each other. I blink to try and make things clearer – instinctively, as if it's my eyes that are clouded – but this only seems to stir movement in the yard, and I head for the back door fast, hands ahead of me reaching for the light switch. The yard is illuminated suddenly, shifting lumps settle down into piles of soggy newsprint, but I know with the certainty of hindsight that nothing will ever be as clear again as red shorts, scabby knees and a fat plait bouncing on my back as I scramble up a tree after Gina.

# A Thousand Questions

'Did I tell you your Aunty Gladys is pregnant again?' Mum called from her bedroom.

'Yes, Mum.'

'Alice! Come here when I'm talking to you.'

I hoisted myself up from chemistry homework and went to hang around the door to her bedroom. Mum was bored. She yawned, stretched out her legs and admired them in the mirrors that lined our flat – any mirror in the shop came upstairs immediately; tiny circular ones like portholes on windowsills and bathroom shelves, huge chipped ones propped up against the hall walls. At any one time you could see a dozen versions of yourself, and Mum loved it; if she was satisfied with nothing else in her life, her attractiveness was confirmed daily during her graceful progressions up and down the hall; twirling, swishing, on high heels, in flirty skirts.

She was in one of her restless phases. Every few months she would drift into vagueness and irritability and announce plans to revamp the shop or even the flat – stirring up the dust around her – but they would never come to much and before too long she'd appear with a new man. It didn't disturb our relationship much; I was to make myself scarce, that was fine by me. A couple of times I'd found her weeping into a gin bottle in the small hours and I listened and fed her toast and tried to find out what had happened before she got fed up with my questions. She made up for any amount of late-night drama when I was upset; was always firmly and totally on my side, which you could never be sure of with some parents – Ellie's for instance, who always seemed to be talking about some other daughter they'd invented. And I knew I'd never be in danger of being thrown out, no matter what I got involved with, and that was worth all Mum's scattiness and impatience.

Her dressing table was crowded with tubes and jars arranged by size, colour and function. Beauty products she could codify.

'Four kids she'll have,' she yawned. 'Why anyone would want to put themselves through that four times is beyond me.' She made a face in the mirror and still looked pretty, which pleased her.

'She likes babies.'

'Good job, too. That's the difference between us, you see. I'm a Libra – an air sign, a seeker of romance and beauty.' She angled her face in the mirror. 'Gladys is a Virgo, a home-maker. She was always a plodder. When we were children she used to play with teasets.' Mum's face drooped, horrified, and I couldn't help but laugh.

'I like her, and Uncle Gordon.'

'Oh, I like her – of course I do – but I wouldn't want to be her. Goodness me, no. Yes, she's got everything safe and secure but she doesn't have much fun, does she, Alice? Not like we do . . .' I squirmed. I usually did when Mum got this idea in her head that we were all-girls-together. 'I tell you what,' she said, plucking a stray hair from her eyebrow, 'why don't you go and put a frock on and we'll take a walk down the canal to that pub . . . what's it called?' She was holding chiffon scarves against her dress, then tossing them away so the carpet was littered with their flimsy brilliance.

'The Otley,' I said.

'Yes, that's the one. It's a nice evening, Alice –'

'I've got homework. You'll only leave me outside in the cold.'

'Do you good to get some fresh air. Come on, Alice.'

'I'm not wearing a dress.'

'Why not? You can look lovely if you try.'

'No dresses, Mum.'

'OK, OK. Although how you can walk in those awful clogs I'll never know.'

'Most mums would be pleased I'm not wrecking my feet in platforms.'

'Oh, most mums,' she said, 'what's that got to do with me? Come on, chop chop.' She linked her arm through mine. 'I saw a gorgeous man at the bar in there the other week –'

'Mum!'


The man in the bar of the Otley Arms turned out to be good news for the group, as Mum was never at home in the evenings any more. She spent her days wafting around the flat in rollers, trying on clothes or reading letters, which she secreted in her bosom; and disappeared promptly at six o'clock when the bar opened.

'I'm glad she's distracted,' said Cora, 'I've got some things I want to ask this Ouija board.'

'Like what?' said Ellie.

'Why won't Rose even speak to us now? Why is everyone at school treating us like we've been sacrificing babies? Why men are such morons?'

'Johnny and Dad aren't morons,' said Gina.

'What men do you know anyway?' I said.

'My dad's not a moron either,' said Ellie. 'Although Mum sometimes treats him like he is.'

I opened up the board. 'Maybe we should just ask general stuff. I think all those questions were a bit much.'

'Seems to me like we're a bit much sometimes,' said Gina. She was hunched up, feet on the bench, arms wrapped around knees.

'No one likes us asking,' said Ellie. 'My mum gets in a right mood if I ask her anything at the moment. "That's all you ever do," she says. "Questions questions questions." Trouble is, I never get any answers.'

'It's the same at school,' I said. 'What d'you reckon, Gina, shall we try the board?'

'Yeah, yeah, whatever.'

'Don't you want to ask about Johnny?'

'I'm not sure if I want to know.'

Gina was being impenetrable. We'd almost got used to it. Some days she was normal Gina, full of cheek and comment, but on others she had such an air of woe about her that even we felt uncomfortable sitting in the dining room with her, or walking down the school drive. We had to though, otherwise she would spit a rancorous 'Whassamarrer?' at us and it would take us ages to convince her that the group was still with her, still solid. Cora thought it was less to do with Johnny as Mr Marshall, who'd not done much but grunt and smoke since Johnny's arrest. Ellie said she was more upset by Rose leaving than she let on, even though they'd always argued. Well, we all are, aren't we, I said, five's better than four . . .

'Right,' said Cora. 'Fingers on.' Our four hands met and we closed our eyes.

'Hello,' I said. 'Is anyone out there?'

Nothing. We waited. The winter had been warm so far, and in the enclosed dimness of the shed, muffled in layers of jumpers, duffel coats and thick tights, our heads lolled and eyelids drooped. I drifted, thinking of nothing, and felt calm spread down through my body. Ellie's finger slipped off the glass and jerked us back into consciousness – for a moment I thought the whole shed was sliding around, but it was just us, falling into sleep.

'What's making us so sleepy?' said Ellie.

A creak, the glass shifted.

M–E

We sat up sharpish. A wave of cool air passed over us.

'Are you the same spirit?' I said, glancing quickly at the others. They were staring at the board.

M–A–Y–B–E

'Who are you?' said Cora. 'How come you can make us sleepy?' Her voice sounded abrasive, maybe even a tiny bit scared. The glass moved; our fingers were barely touching it.

O–N–E   Q–U–E–S–T–I–O–N

'Who are you?' said Ellie.

The glass was moving around the board smoothly now, efficiently. I lifted my finger a millimetre off the smooth glass and it wavered.

A–N–Y–O–N–E  Y–O–U   L–I–K–E

'Huh?' said Cora.

Our eyes flicked up to each other and back down to the board. We were all breathing hard. I felt we were close to grasping something, something certain that might slip away from us at any second.

A–N–Y–O–N–E   L–I–K–E   Y–O–U

Again, questions burst out of us. We couldn't contain them.

'What's your name?' I asked.

'What do you mean?' said Ellie.

'Are you like us then?' said Cora.

'Do you know about the future?' said Gina. But the glass stopped abruptly, the flow gone, the steady swipes, the answers already a memory.

'Shit!' said Cora. 'We've done it again. Too many questions.'

'Isn't that weird how it made us sleepy?' said Ellie.

'Anyone like us?' I said. 'What's all that about?'

'I wonder if he really can see the future?' said Gina.

It was dark by the time we got outside; we'd spent too long in the shed and everyone had to scrabble to grab bags and find shoes and swap homework in time to catch the buses home. We were trying not to get into any more bother at school, and keeping the peace meant keeping parents sweet, too. Ellie's were the worst, but Cora's were coming down unusually hard. They've just realized I'm not twelve any more, scorned Cora. Gina and I had no such restrictions, so we sat on the doorstep of the shed and gazed at the sky.

'What time will your mum be back?' said Gina.

'Late.'

'I've got a couple of cans in my bag – do you want one?'

'Where d'you get them from?'

'The fridge. Either Dad doesn't notice or he doesn't care.'

'I'm sure he cares, Gina.'

We cracked open the cans and sucked the foaming off the top. Cora reckoned you got pissed quicker if you tapped fag ash in the lager so I sneaked into the flat and nicked a couple of Mum's. We sat there, flicking ash and slurping, dust up our noses and bubbles down our throats.

'Does she bring him back with her?' said Gina. 'The man from the Otley?'

'Sometimes.'

'Do you think he's married?' The thought made us stop for a second.

'Probably.'

The sky was clearing. Scallops of cloud remained high up but we could see the stars now.

'Do you mind?' said Gina. 'About him?'

'I mind when I hear them at it in the kitchen.'

Lager sprayed out of Gina's nose. 'At it? In the kitchen?'

'That's what it sounds like,' I said, wiping her face with my school tie.

'Haven't you sneaked along for a look?'

'No way. She'd kill me. Anyway, it must be like having an audience already with all those mirrors around.'

We smothered our laughter into each other's shoulders; the thought was almost too much to bear.

'But do you mind that he's married?'

'She's my mum. I want her to have someone.'

'Don't you remember your dad at all?' said Gina.

I tried to, sometimes. There were some photos of me with him that Mum didn't like me getting out, and I had some vague notions – I couldn't call them memories – of tension in the flat, arguments behind closed doors; long, wordless stares. Then he was gone and there was only emptiness. Something missing.

'No,' I said.

'Johnny remembers Mum,' said Gina. 'But he never talks about it.'

The moon slid out from behind a cloud, lighting up ruffles at its edges – it looked like a mountain, something you could walk on. We stared. The cans were empty, glistening

71

at our feet and the cigarette butts ground out on the dirt floor of the yard.

'What do you feel like when we're doing it?' said Gina. She meant the Ouija, I didn't need to ask.

'I'm just *there* with the board and the glass and us,' I said.

'I know,' said Gina. Her face was silver in the moonlight; the corners of her eyes glittered.

'But afterwards . . . afterwards it's like . . . we just can't get at it. Like there's some magical answer out there but we're looking in the wrong direction.'

'I wonder if there is an answer at all,' said Gina.

I was about to ask her how she was, *really* was, when she was alone at night, away from the group. How she felt about Johnny and her dad and sex and if she still recognized her face in the mirror. A thousand questions – all there in my head – but she upped and left in one movement, swiftly, as if she'd heard my thoughts and couldn't answer. 'Bye, Alice,' she said, and slipped out of the back gate and down the alley. I could hear her quick steps receding and then mingling with all the others out on the High Street until she was lost to me in the blur.

# Gina's Footsteps

The next morning I decided to go and investigate this spirit properly, see if there were any signs – a footprint maybe, a smell – something physical. The thrill for us of the dim shed – the wavering hands, the flashes of light through the glass – soon faded when I was alone, leaving me queasy and restless and anxious for Mum to come home. When at last I heard her clattering on the cobbles, swearing, messing with her keys, I made a heroic leap from the bed to the door, shot past all the mirrors and shivered at the top of the stairs, waiting.

'Alice, love,' she said, her hot sweet breath on my neck. 'What are you doing up? Are you OK?'

'Feel sick,' I mumbled, 'bad dreams.'

'Oh, baby,' she said. 'Come on, I'll sing you to sleep.'

I held her hand past the mirrors and she tucked me back into bed. 'Hush little darling don't you cry,' she sang, her voice low. She hadn't had to do that since I was about nine years old.

The shed looked harmless enough in daylight. I kept glancing out of the kitchen window at it while I made toast for Mum – she had a headache and was watching Saturday morning telly in bed. The air outside was full of wet and muck swept up on the wind and the shed looked a dump; brown and slimy from rain, ramshackle. The yard was much the same, more labyrinthine than ever – if that was possible

73

– but the shed was completely and boringly normal. Dusty, crowded, damp; smells of rust and rot. The Ouija board and glass were tucked where we'd left them. There were no signs that the spirit had had a bad night at all.

I sat on the step and scratched in the dirt with a stick. The wind was teasing all sorts of rubbish out of the corners of the yard; crisp packets, tin cans, yards of tape from old cassettes – real rubbish, as Mum said when she had to clear it up, holding it away from her nose. As opposed to the unreal rubbish you sell, Aunty Gladys always retorted. I suddenly thought – the words unfurling in my head – that they disapprove of her, the rest of our family. The way she lives, the way we live. Mum never mentioned it; well, only indirectly by turning her nose up at Gladys's Tupperware parties and Gordon's rambling group. But it had never occurred to me before that Mum was the one outside other people's expectations – but then again just about everyone I knew seemed to be misjudged in some way. If only I could make sense of it myself, I thought, then maybe I could stop these things happening.

The wind blew some more. Windows rattled. One down the alley burst off its catches and exploded against the brickwork. A rollered head shot out, her voice zipped past me on the wind, *Just what I need on a Saturday morning, why is there no bloody peace in this world?* I remembered Cora's imitation of her mum saying the same thing, 'There's just no peace in this world with you around, Cora.' What am I supposed to do? Cora had said. Stop existing? Anyway, I haven't had any peace since I worked out what boys are for, she said. I have little pools of calm, said Ellie, when I'm reading, or playing the piano. Gina said she used to think she'd never get any, not with Johnny wanting to playfight all the time, but that was nothing compared with what she was up against now.

I stared at a flurry of dust in the alley where Gina had disappeared the night before. The wind had dropped suddenly but a mini-tornado twirled away from me, in Gina's footsteps. I looked down at the dirt and found I had scratched a star with five points; one long point in the direction of the tornado, another back towards the shed. The spirit *was* around; I just knew it.

Gina and Johnny were slouched on their sofa watching *Tiswas* when I got there. The room was dark and they were still in their pyjamas. Gina was wearing a pair of rainbow-coloured socks with individual toes.

'Hey, Gina,' I said. She was staring at Spit the Dog.

'What?'

'Shush!' said Johnny. His eyes were following the movements of Sally James's cleavage. 'I'm watching telly.'

'It's all you ever do these days,' said Gina.

'What's it to you?'

'Nothing. I couldn't give a toss what you do. But Dad won't like it.'

'Dad isn't even here.'

'Isn't he?' I said, trying to throw some brightness into the room with my cheery voice. It sounded sickly, breakable, like school meringue. 'Where is he?'

'Dunno.'

'Went out last night and hasn't come back.'

*Tiswas* finished. Gina clicked the television off and Johnny clicked it back on to *Skippy*. They were close to a fight.

'Shall we go out?' I said.

'It's pissing down,' said Gina.

I started to tell her about my bad night but it didn't seem right once I came to the lullaby bit, so my story faded out. They didn't seem to notice. 'We could go and look for your dad,' I said.

'You go if you want,' said Johnny, 'but we're staying here.' He was flicking rolled up bits of the *Daily Mirror* at Gina.

'Who says?' said Gina.

'I do.'

'You're in charge then?'

'Might as well be.'

'Just wait till Dad comes back.'

'Oh *him*,' said Johnny. 'What use is *he*?' He scrunched the newspaper up into balls and threw them at the wall.

75

'Don't talk about him like that!'

'Why not?'

'He's our dad. Ow! Johnny, you hit me with that one.'

'It's only newspaper.'

'You shouldn't throw things.'

*'You shouldn't throw things. You shouldn't throw things.'*
Johnny was spinning around the room, throwing words over his shoulder.

'Well, you shouldn't.'

*'Well, you shouldn't.'*

'Stop it, Johnny. Stop running around, stop copying, just stop it.' Tears glittered in the corners of her eyes.

*'Stop it. Stop it.'* His voice whined in mimicry and I flinched to think we could sound like that.

'Dad'll kill you when I tell him. He said you weren't to upset me.'

'Dad can't do anything to me.'

'He can throw you out.'

'No he can't.' Johnny stopped his dervish whirling. For a second he balanced in the air on one leg, one arm out to his side. He wavered, then scissored his limbs in slowly and bent over Gina, his face mean. 'Don't you see?' he hissed. 'If he was that sort of dad, then I'd never be in this mess in the first place.'

'You can't blame your dad for being nice,' I said. 'Anyway, you can still tell them the truth, that the dope was Rushy's brother's. Why should you have to lie for him?'

Johnny deflated instantly and slumped down next to Gina, throwing his arm around her shoulders. She was still scowling but didn't push him off. 'It won't make any difference what I do now,' he said, his voice flat. 'Even if I told the truth they wouldn't believe me, because Rushy's a doctor's son and he'll be going to university.'

'You should never have lied in the first place,' Gina and I said in unison.

Johnny looked at us almost pityingly. 'Do you really think that would have made any difference?' he said.

\*

'What's happening to him?' I said to Gina. We were walking from hers to mine; through the estate, along the weedy canal bank, into the park, up the High Street and down the alley into the shed. School was just the other side of the park; this was our territory.

Gina shrugged. 'He thinks "They're all against me so fuck them",' she said. 'A bit like Dad.'

She'd obviously been practising her swearing, like me, in the mirror: f-u-c-k, FUCK, *fuck*. Only Cora could do it casually; Ellie flinched every time.

'Dad says if ever there was a time for swearing it's now.' Gina sat down on the canal bank, kicking gravel into the oily water. 'In some ways I'm more worried about him than Johnny. He's gone right back into his old ways, how Johnny says he was after Mum died, just sitting around doing nothing. No one can make him smile, not even me, and Sandra's just about given up on him.'

'She's not moving back in then?'

'Last time she came round she just took one look at him sitting there and left. Then she rang up – drunk, I think – yelling at him "Do something, do anything," but Dad just put the receiver down on the table and walked off. Left her screaming into the air. She's called in a couple of times since; isn't too bothered about Johnny, she thinks he's young, it'll pass, but Dad won't have any of that. To him, Johnny getting nicked is a sign –'

'What sort of sign?'

'A bad one,' said Gina, throwing a stone in the water. We watched as the rings echoed out from where it dropped. 'One that says he's failed.'

The canal bank was cold, wet seeped through our clothes, so we headed for the shed where at least the wind couldn't get to us.

'Maybe the spirit is a sign for us,' I said. 'I went down there this morning to see if there's any traces of him being around when we're not there.'

'Did you find anything?'

'Not really. I just wish we could make sense of it.'

'Me too. Of everything. I'm glad you came round, Alice. I needed to get out of there. If only to stop Johnny getting at me.'

'You can come to mine any time. Mum won't mind. She's got a lovelife now. Sometimes she looks at me as if she's not sure what I'm doing in the flat.'

Gina laughed. 'Hi, Mum. Remember me.'

'Yeah, it's a bit like that.' We were nearing the High Street, could hear the rumbles, smell fumes, hot newsprint, burnt onions. 'Does Johnny get at you a lot?' I said. It bothered me, him lashing out.

'Yeah. It's weird. We can be messing about and it's just play and then he goes all mean. Well, you saw it. Him and Dad have always clashed, but this drugs thing just makes it a nightmare to be in the same room as them.'

'Yeah.'

'Maybe that's what we need.' Gina started jogging – we often did this on the High Street, it pleased us, to be agile, to weave through the overburdened shoppers.

'What? To get mean?' I swung round a lamppost and dodged in front of her.

'No, a lovelife, prat.' She was running fast, hair streaming back, body a fuzz of moving denim. An old man she was closing in on shouted 'Oi, watch it, you,' and Gina side-stepped him just in time. 'Soz,' she said. Someone clapped.

'Maybe?' I panted, as we skidded to a halt at the entrance to the alley, hands on knees, sweat slipping down our cheeks. 'Gina, I *know* we need a lovelife.'

78

# Gypsies, Tramps and Thieves

Mum gives me her room at the flat. She says it's too big for her now, she's fed up of waking up to an empty space next to her every morning. I attempt to clear clutter off windowsills, shelves and tables; cotton reels and newspaper clippings, bits of driftwood, a jar full of rusty nails, but nothing looks much different even when I've got two full binbags to sneak down the stairs. I'm restless; have to find something to fill my time, still feel more comfortable dashing around Sainsbury's grabbing two-for-the-price-of-one than dawdling, using up the day. So I volunteer at the Citizens Advice on the High Street – they're keen to have me; are impressed with my experience of dealing with the police and the public. They put up a poster in the window: 'Forensics Expert Alice Tracey Available for Specialist Advice'. From my desk I can see out on to the street; watch the bodies moving past. It feels like I'm spying sometimes, on the clumps of blue school uniforms dodging past shoppers; the jumble of buses and lorries and cars inching their way in and out of the city; sometimes a gap through to the other side of the street and a flash of red hair, a tan suede platform boot.

Dan phoned a couple of nights ago, his voice sounding distant and thin. We heard the ring but the phone was buried under a pile of magazines and by the time we found it the flat had been turned over and we were giggling like schoolgirls.

'Sorry, Dan, I couldn't find the phone,' I said.

'Couldn't find the phone?' he said. 'You don't have a place for the phone?'

A picture of him in my head, sitting at his desk with all his papers and files perpendicular, his view over the spruce garden; then looking around the flat: Mum's address book a tea caddy stuffed with scraps of paper; weeds from the yard creeping up the walls, waving around under the kitchen window.

He told me he's selling the house in the village and I remember back to when we first moved in; there were blackberry bushes at the bottom of the garden, densely entangled, the branches as thick as your arm. I let it grow, quite liked the idea of this little bit of wilderness near by, although Dan and I agreed that the house should be neat. He complained continually when the travellers were living there, their battered buses nudging into the bushes, their benders growing up from the earth floor. 'If only we'd cleared that patch,' he said. 'It might have put them off if we could watch what they're up to.' I doubted it somehow, they looked to me like they were well used to disapproving looks, played up to them, sculpted their hair into wild shapes and patched their raggedy clothes with purple and silver. And they were just living, as far as I could tell. I watched the smoke twist out of their chimneys and threw balls back over for the kids. Sometimes we'd hear music thudding out at night and Dan would bristle, rant about illegal parties and how we should call the police – it was the early nineties and the papers were full of stories about drug-crazed madmen. It rattled Dan; he demanded that the kids turn their pockets out when the VW badge off his car went missing and I felt for him, for the world he understood being gone; in the past.

The kids' pockets yielded nothing but tat; sucked-on sweets, matches, bits of string, dirt and earth and pennies. I took a day off work and fed a hosepipe through the hedge and down on to the travellers' patch – no one else in the village would give them water. They were having to fetch it from the church in jerrycans and buckets and squash bottles – two-year-old kids with a squash bottle full of water from the churchyard tap. I'd hang a white pillowcase out of the

80

back bedroom window when I was going to turn on the water and Dan puzzled for months over how they were getting supplies. It never crossed his mind that it could be his water that was washing their pots, their kids' backsides.

'I'd like some specialist advice, please.' A voice breaks through my thoughts and I look up from my untouched paperwork. For a moment I think that the strength of my memories has conjured up the firetruck owner who helped me hide the hose. It's not him but I do know those eyes, that hair, that gap in his teeth.

'Hi, Alice,' he says, sitting down on the chair in front of my desk. He stretches out his legs; yawns, smiles. The first time I've seen Johnny Marshall in twenty years. 'Alice,' he says, 'I'm in a bit of trouble. Thought you might be able to help.'

He's wearing a squashed felt hat and about four layers of T-shirts, shirts, jumper; his jacket is on the back of the chair. Outside the window of the advice centre are three dogs – lurchers or whippets – gypsy dogs, my mum would call them. All waiting patiently, their chins resting on their paws.

'Are they yours?' I say and Johnny nods. One of the dogs lifts its head, sniffs, and darts off around the corner. 'Hadn't you better tie them up?' I say.

'Nah,' says Johnny. 'He'll be back.' He takes his hat off and ruffles his hair. 'My dogs don't need to be on strings.'

A bit of trouble, said Johnny. Johnny, who I last saw when I was fifteen, puzzling me with his adolescent scowls and brief sunshine smiles, who still unsettles me now; only for a second do I think I might be able to disguise it, sit coolly at my desk, my voice professional.

'What is it you're after, Johnny? Isn't Gordenson your brief?'

You hear things, you see, in this business. Names come up, acquire a certain infamy. Whispered on telephones, in corridors and courtrooms: Johnny Marshall this, Johnny Marshall that. The first day I came here a colleague talked about the Marshall case – the name snagging my attention from across a noisy room – and I soon found out it was Johnny they were talking about. Johnny on the wrong side of the law, said Mum when I told her, how come that doesn't surprise me? Johnny, one of the few traces of my youth I've come across on my return to the city. Everyone else has gone – vanished – every one of the group, Taz, Robbie. Rock Hill's been amalgamated. The city is even more crowded – a few new-built flats crammed on to the end of a street, cars piled up on pavements outside the terraces, not even an inch in between them. But there's still parks and canals. The flat and the yard and my mum. And Johnny Marshall.

'What've you been doing anyway, Alice? Left town, didn't you?'

'Yes. So what happened with Gordenson? Didn't you pay him?'

'What are you saying about me, Alice . . . ?' His eyes twinkle. Can he will himself to do that, I wonder, like a wink, or a raised eyebrow?

'Tell me what you want, Johnny.'

'It'll take a bit of explaining.' He shifts about, looks around him. My colleagues are buried in files, talking on the telephone; but I know they're listening, intrigued. So does Johnny.

'Come to the pub.'

'I can't, I'm working.'

'Always so responsible.'

'Yes.'

'Tonight then?'

'Tomorrow, lunchtime.'

'OK. I'll meet you in the Bridge. Midday.' He gets up, long legs loping towards the door. I think about the Bridge. With its beer-glass windows and rumours of leylines. I don't think I ever went in there after all, but I remember the longing, the yearning to be part of it.

He turns at the door. 'Don't forget, Alice,' he says.

'I won't,' I say. 'You can rely on me.'

'I hope so,' says Johnny. His eyes lock on to mine. It's him that breaks contact. 'I hope so,' he says.

Back at the flat Mum is in a flap because she's lost some vital piece of paperwork. The accountant – who works next door, at a typewriter marooned in a sea of brown files and handwritten calculations – has been in and sent Mum into a panic. I'm glad I'm here; I hate to imagine her trying to find it on her own.

'Don't worry, Mum,' I say, 'it'll be here somewhere.'

So we spend the afternoon leafing through old papers. It's a hot summer's day, summer 1997 and Bob Dylan's *Greatest Hits* is number one. 'The Times They Are A-Changing' undulates across the road from the record shop and in through the open windows along with the hum of traffic. Out there tarmac is pooling in windless corners, kids want popsicles and adults want cold beer. I find my birth certificate – I've never seen it before – and Mum finds a bag full of old Christmas cards and reads every single one out loud.

'Great Uncle Frank,' she says, 'd'you remember him? He had all sorts of stories from the war if you got him in the right mood. Me and Gladys used to swoon over the pictures of them all in their smart uniforms. And here's one from my old friend, Pat, she was a laugh . . . Oh look, Alice, a photo of your friend – it must have come with a Christmas card.'

She passes me a small square photo of a girl on a beach, footsteps leading up to her bare legs, a tray of jewellery around her neck. Gina. Gina Marshall staring out at me from beneath her black fringe and her floppy hat, silver and turquoise around her wrists and neck, hanging from her ears and pinned on to the cork board. On the back it says, *Greece, 1978. Happy Christmas!*

'I've never seen this before,' I say.

'It must have come after you left,' says Mum. 'Look! Here's one from Australia. Did I ever tell you about that schoolfriend of mine who moved over there?'

Dylan has finished. There's a gap before the next tune. When it percolates through the rumbling and humming and buzzing and yells and cooling tarmac I can't help but smile. It's Jarvis. 'Disco 2000', he's singing. Won't it be strange when we're all fully grown?

# Witchhunt

School was almost a relief after the spooky business of the spirit. Gina and I had sniffed around the shed, trying to find evidence under rotting planks, in the musty smells that rose up. There was nothing; nothing except a feeling.

School had some regularity then, at least. We scratched and yawned through assembly – Wills-Masterson prowling across the stage, hectoring, her shrill voice penetrating every daydream, then drifted from class to class. The clap of wooden desks, the distant clang of pans from the kitchens, the coughing and pencil gnawing were background constants; steady, lulling. It was only when we caught the odd sidelong glance from groups of girls – arranging their flicked fringes carefully over their eyes – that I realized we weren't a part of it, at least not in the same way as they were. But when a gang of third-year boys we'd never even spoken to rounded a corner and shied, holding their fingers up in the shape of a cross on seeing us, we had to find out what was being said.

Gina asked Taz who professed to know nothing, although his neck flushed red. 'Come on,' said Gina, grabbing his wrist. 'Don't lie to me, Taz.'

'It's nothing,' he said, twisting himself away. 'Stupid gossip. Just some nonsense about your powers.' Taz paused. 'And that the Dick-Master is on to you.'

'What powers?' said Gina. 'Who says?'

But he was gone, grabbed by Robbie and dragged into some long-running game involving dragons and heroes and deadly weaponry. In the corner of the playground Rose's red hair snagged on my eyes.

'Well, they're right,' said Cora, 'we have got powers, haven't we?'

There had been some good news though. Ellie's mum – calmed by her daughter's regular good marks – had given her a reprieve and said she could finish her 'O' Levels at Rock Hill, the inevitable condition being that she didn't wear makeup or have her ears pierced in the meantime. Cora said this showed how bizarrely adults' minds worked – as if wearing makeup could affect your brain. She had recently scandalized the entire school by turning up wearing a studded dogcollar and her makeup was way past the frosted lids and sparkly lipgloss the rest of us were experimenting with; that Ellie's mum objected to so fervidly.

Everyone in our year – from the most casual scruff to perfectly turned-out princesses – was trying to personalize their school uniform. A year or two earlier it hadn't mattered much, the five of us were only distinguishable by an inch and the colour of our hair. But now Cora's skirts got shorter every week, Gina looked wilder by the day and even Ellie had had her hair permed into a tightly curled mop that sat at an odd angle on top of her head. Certain clothing could be adjusted and still stay within school rules – tie-knots, shoes, socks, jewellery, badges, sleeves rolled up or worn short – small and constant changes rippled through the sea of blue uniforms. The teachers, however, seemed to have settled on a fixed style of clothing suitable to their subject: Wills-Masterson the boss in her bosom-first suits, Mr Franks the art teacher in paint-splattered smocks, geography teachers in Crimplene trousers and walking shoes. This matching of clothes to profession and personality bothered us; the choice seemed too weighted, somehow. Even Mr McGeady dressed to fit his role, with his colourful eccentricities, silk handkerchiefs to match his tie, straw hats and cricket whites. So no wonder my pencil dropped from my fingers when he walked into English one murky afternoon – it barely seemed to get light some days – wearing black from head to toe. Gina's elbows slipped off her desk and her chin crunched down.

'Sir, what's happened to your clothes?'

'Been to a funeral, sir?'

'You look like a spy.'

He clapped his hands. 'Enough! Open your books now. We have work to do.'

There was something in his manner that had altered too: he was sterner, and vaguer, as if his old personality had got left behind in the wardrobe with the bow-ties and bright jumpers. Now he wore black shoes, slightly flared black trousers. Black polo-neck sweater tucked into his trousers, thin black belt. Cora thought he looked fantastic and she told him so; but I didn't agree, nor did Ellie. Gina said she couldn't care less.

'I liked the other clothes you wore, sir,' I said, when he was handing back homework. 'Why have you gone all *dark*?'

'It's a reflection of my opinion of the universe,' he said, without a flicker of sarcasm, his lips thinned.

'What can have happened?' whispered Ellie.

'God knows,' said Cora.

Gina was repeating what he'd said, *a reflection of my opinion of the universe*. She looked close to being impressed. Across the room Rose stared out of the window, her eyes fixed on a leafless tree.

'Right, class,' said Mr McGeady. 'Today we're going to discuss some of the essays you've written on *The Crucible*, which range from utterly dire to surprisingly good. Some of you have really thought about the subject matter and related it to our contemporary lives, some of you have done good historical work and some of you –' he paused again '– have even managed to make good use of the English language. Remarkable. Georgina? If you could get us going, please.'

Gina started. 'What? Me?'

'Yes please,' said Mr McGeady, briskly. 'Remind us of the essay topic, first.'

86

Gina stood up tentatively. 'John Proctor. We had to write about why John Proctor doesn't leave Salem.'

'And how did you approach this subject?' Mr McGeady's voice was encouraging and Gina stood up straighter, glancing at him as if to make sure.

'Well, I started off with those words you gave us. "Calumny" means "malicious misrepresentation" or "false charge" – when someone makes out you're something that you're not or puts you in a bad light or says you've done something that you haven't.' She was rushing her words; Mr McGeady slowed her with his hands. 'Yes,' said Gina, understanding. 'In the play – in the introduction bit – it says, *In Proctor's presence a fool felt his foolishness instantly – and Proctor is always marked for calumny therefore.*'

'Sounds like Johnny,' hissed Cora.

'Or her dad,' I said.

Mr McGeady glared at us. 'Carry on, Georgina.'

'Anyway, you'd think if Proctor was being misrepresented so badly he'd just get out of there. But there wasn't anywhere to go. In those days leaving the village would have been like going to the other side of the world. So he struggles to find a way to fit in. But he couldn't avoid it. He had this way about him that got people's backs up . . .' She trailed off. 'Is that enough, sir?'

'Yes. Excellent. Any comments?'

'Avoid what?' said Rachel Williamson. 'I don't know what you mean.'

'Trouble,' said Gina. 'Everyone in power, you know, the church and the courts, they resented him because he made them feel their foolishness, like it says.' Gina was steady now, the class silent. 'Don't you see?' she said. 'If anyone was going to get it when the witchhunt came to town, it was John Proctor.'

Mr McGeady sat behind his desk, apparently deep in thought. He flicked through his notebook and chewed his lip. We shifted uneasily in our seats. It just wasn't like him to not pay any attention to us; people were starting to whisper, elastic bands twanged, Rose got one straight on the back of her neck.

'Sir?'

'Yes, Alice?'

'The lesson . . .'

'Oh. Right. Yes. Where were we?' His internal meter seemed to have stalled completely.

'Essays, sir.'

'Hmm. Well how about you, Cora? Tell us about your essay.'

'You want me to talk about *this*?' said Cora.

'Yes please, Cora.'

'But I made a mistake. I didn't do the Proctor stuff. I wrote about act one.'

'What you wrote was most illuminating,' said Mr McGeady.

We looked at each other in confusion. He seemed to have got his homeworks mixed up. We'd finished with the act one stuff ages ago.

'Come on, Cora,' said Gina. 'Looks like it's your turn whatever.'

'I bet she wrote about that lot and their witchery,' said a voice from the back row. We jerked round quickly but all we could see was a row of fuzzy heads, tucked into chests.

'Nah,' said Taz. 'Got to be sex.'

'If it's Cora, it's sex,' said Robbie.

'What are people saying about us?' said Ellie to Gina.

Gina didn't move; her eyes were fixed unflinchingly on the back row.

'It's about the play actually,' said Cora, disdainful. 'I wrote an essay about an aspect of act one that interested me.'

'Yeah,' said Taz. 'And I bet it's the sex in act one. Teenage girls and older men. Bound to interest her.'

'Oh shut up and listen,' said Cora. She had her mouth open ready when suddenly Mr McGeady's black shape was there, in front of us. He moved like a tear in the light towards the back of the class.

'Out!' shouted Mr McGeady at Taz. 'Out of my class now! I'll deal with you later,' Mr McGeady said, with real menace in his voice. 'Cora, I do apologize. Sincerely. I really do. I thought this class was ready to tackle the subject maturely but I was wrong, again.' He stomped to his desk. 'Now read. Act two. Read in silence and prepare to answer questions. There'll be a test after the Christmas break.'

'Sir?' It was Ellie, tentative.

'Silence!'

From the back of the class came the quietest whisper. 'So it was about sex then.'

Cora charged straight out of English, down the slippery corridor and out of the swinging doors without looking back. We ran after her, shoes squeaking in our haste to keep up. 'Cora, what's the matter? Where are you going?' 'Haven't you got French now?' 'We'll all be late.'

Cora stopped and whipped round. 'I'm not going,' she said. 'You lot can do what you like.'

'Where are you going then?' said Gina.

'To the park.'

'Someone'll see you.'

'Well, I'll go and walk the streets then.' She said it with peculiar vehemence.

Ellie fluttered around next to her. 'Come on, Cora,' she pleaded. 'Don't let it get to you.'

'I'm going.'

'We can sneak out of a hole in the fence,' said Gina.

'And go where?' said Ellie, desperate. 'It won't work. We'll get caught.'

'Come on,' I said. 'We can go to the shed, if we go in the back way and keep quiet.'

'Yes!' said Gina.

'OK,' said Cora, non-committal. 'Are you coming, Ellie?'

She couldn't cop out now and followed us to the fence, dragging her feet.

# Going Haywire

In the shed we sat around for a while. Cora hunkered in a corner, teasing out long strands of her hair and twisting them round her fingers. I was just starting to wonder if Ellie was right, that this was just not worth getting into more trouble for, when Cora cracked.

'What the hell is going on with that McGeady?' she said, glowering at us each in turn. 'First he asks me to explain my essay and then he goes and blows up just as I'm about to get going. How does he expect us to talk about sex anyway when the boys start scratching their groins just at the thought of it? And as for that stupid Taz –'

'Taz isn't stupid,' said Gina, 'he just doesn't know where to put himself. A couple of hairs on their chests and everything goes haywire.'

'So it was about sex then?' I asked.

'He's baffling me,' said Gina.

'Taz isn't the only one who's a bit muddled, let's face it,' said Ellie.

'I meant McGeady,' said Gina. 'Did you hear the rumour that his wife's left him?'

'Really?' I said.

'The rest of us don't mix up hormones with English,' said Cora.

'You did,' said Gina.

'That's awful,' said Ellie. 'I wonder what's happened with his children?'

'No I didn't,' said Cora. 'I wrote about the play.'

'You know you confuse the hell out of the boys,' said Gina. 'Anyway, McGeady said that one of the reasons for reading this stuff is to give us – what was it? – insight. They can't help it if their only insight into Abigail is wondering what her tits look like.'

Cora hooted with laughter. 'Oh you, Gina,' she said, affectionately.

'Come on then, tell us.'

Cora smoothed out the wrinkled pages of her essay. 'Well, I kept wondering what was going on in Abigail's head. I mean she can't have meant to start what she did. She can't have intended that all those people get hanged and the whole village turned inside out . . .'

'Rose would say she was evil,' said Ellie.

'That the devil was at work in Salem.' Gina made devilish horns by waggling her fingers behind her ears. We laughed. Everything was softer now – our faces, the light. We shuffled into corners, propped ourselves up on mouldy cushions, kicked off our shoes – Cora dangled hers from her foot. A sweet smell of baking wafted down from the kitchen into the shed.

'Where's that coming from?' said Ellie. 'Your mum doesn't usually make cakes.'

'It's all down to the man in the Otley Arms,' I said. 'He keeps Mum sweet in more ways than one . . .'

'Think about it though,' said Cora, calm now. 'About Abigail. It wasn't that she chose not to keep quiet and good and cover up all her flesh and lower her head for the priests; she just couldn't. Her head kept rising up and her mouth kept answering back but she only got whipped for that so all the turmoil was trapped under the surface. And then she discovered she could turn it into power.'

'By having sex with John Proctor?'

'Or dancing naked in the woods.'

'Sort of. It's about those feelings anyway. Growing and

growing in you until they get so big they're going to have to burst out sooner or later.'

'Growing in *you*? I thought we were talking about Abigail.'

'We are.'

'Sounds a bit familiar though . . .'

'Yeah.'

'Did you get a good mark for the essay then?'

'How come Mr McGeady lost his rag so badly?'

'God knows,' said Gina. 'My dad's just the same. He'll be sitting there staring at *Midlands Today* and then all of a sudden he'll jump up and start raving on about how he was in the factory by the time he was our age.'

'My mum says Dad's going through his midlife crisis,' said Ellie, 'whatever that is. As far as I can work out it just means he can't find anything.'

'Well, we're in a permanent crisis then,' I said, 'trying to find something among this lot.'

The door of the shed flew open.

Ellie screamed.

'Hello, girls,' said Mum, holding out a tray of fairy cakes. 'I thought you might like to try these.' She placed the tray on the bench and sailed back through the yard without another word, carving her path through the rubbish, as surefooted as a cat, hips swaying slightly. We were gobsmacked.

'The real question is,' I said, staring at the space my mum had vacated, 'what has the man in the Otley Arms done to my mother?'

Mum's oddly serene mood – she didn't say a word to me about us being in the shed in schooltime – lasted until lunchtime on Saturday when she answered the phone and her composure evaporated as she spoke. 'Right . . . I see . . . you'll let me know then . . .' Mum slammed the receiver down and clamped her hands over her freshly curled hair. We'd spent the entire morning trying on clothes for her 'date', as she insisted on calling it, so she was still in her dressing gown when the doorbell rang.

I rushed down the stairs and through the shop, rapidly planning what I would say to him – the things that no one else dared, I hoped – but couldn't quite shake off the image of Mum's hopes perked by the sound of the bell; her dash for the mirror.

I opened the door ready to fire. There stood Gina and Johnny shivering in the sleety rain.

'Oh. Hi,' I said.

'I thought you said we'd be welcome here,' said Johnny, turning away.

'No, no,' I said. 'I didn't mean it like that. I was just expecting someone else.'

'Oh yeah?' said Johnny.

For some reason I felt tinged with guilt and had to physically shake it off. 'No, don't go. Come in.' I coaxed them into the shop and launched into a convoluted explanation about Mum and the man in the Otley Arms, expecting them to laugh at my plans to tear a strip off him, and then opening the door to find them. But they just stood there, heads bent down, arms hanging off their shoulders. Gina hadn't said a word.

'Are you OK, Gina?' I said, belatedly.

'Does she look OK?' said Johnny.

'Of course she's not,' said Mum, appearing at the bottom of the stairs. She was dressed soberly, had her shop overall on. 'Take her upstairs, Alice. You can stay here and help me, young man. On days like this the best we can do is try and be useful.'

I nudged Gina upstairs. She sat down on Mum's chair. 'Do you want a drink,' I said, 'anything to eat?'

'Don't fuss,' said Gina. 'I'm fine, really.'

'But . . .'

'Can't I just come round here, Alice? Do we always have to *talk*?'

Down in the shop, things weren't much better. Johnny was standing at the window, staring out at the High Street through a wash of rain.

'Wouldn't be so bad if I had some cash,' he muttered, bitterly, without turning his head. 'I could get out of his road then.' I knew what his mates would be up to; playing space

93

invaders in the café, fighting over a packet of chips, sliding around on the greasy pavements, hanging out in bus shelters, park toilets, under dripping trees. 'But *he* hasn't got any money to give us, has he?' said Johnny.

'What's happened, Johnny?' I said.

He turned and blinked at me. 'Nothing,' he said.

We stared past the window, which was cluttered with fringed lampshades and boxes of 78s, out at the street. Horizontal rain; old ladies in plastic bonnets, thin dogs and fat-bellied blokes in T-shirts dodging from one pub to the next. A customer came in and leafed through a book of children's poems. Johnny sighed. I felt so awkward and inadequate in the face of his misery that I started to clear out a packing case that had been under the counter for months. There wasn't much in it and I pulled stuff out randomly, trying to think of something casual and appropriate to say to Johnny. Cora would find the right words – they'd just come to her – but I wasn't Cora. I delved deeper into my packing case.

'Here,' said Johnny, holding an envelope out to me. 'Someone just put this under the door.' *Dearest Sally* was written on the front in small, even letters.

Mum's sixth sense must have kicked in because she appeared at the bottom of the stairs instantaneously and whisked the letter out of my hand. 'When did this get here?' she said. 'Who delivered it?'

'Just some bloke,' said Johnny.

Mum rushed to the door and scanned the High Street frantically. 'Damn!' she said, flicking the raindrops out of her hair. 'I've missed him.'

'Why don't you read the letter, Mum?' I said.

'Yes, yes,' she said. 'And stop gawping, you two. Get on with something.'

We emptied the packing case. All that was left was some tissue paper at the bottom. Most of the stuff was rubbish apart from a few coins and some broken bits of a figurine, which Johnny and I tried to piece together. Mum read the letter, drifting around the crowded shop, light on her feet again, easily avoiding jutting chair legs and loose carpet tiles.

Bits of the figurine were missing – a hand, his hat – so I turned the packing case upside down to shake any bits out of the bottom. The tissue paper fell to the floor with a thud.

'Careful, Alice,' said Mum.

'There's something inside this tissue paper,' I said.

'Oh, how beautiful,' said Mum, picking out a wooden box inlaid with mother-of-pearl. 'I'll use it to keep my letters in.'

We never did find the missing pieces.

Johnny had the box in his hands and was admiring it, turning it around, watching the light glance off the mother-of-pearl, when Gina appeared.

'I'm off,' she said, her eyes lost under her hair. 'Thanks, Mrs T.'

'Any time,' said Mum.

'Bye, Gina,' I said.

Johnny followed her out into the pale light of the street. The orange streetlamps were coming on already and Johnny circled round one in a neat movement, hanging off the upright from one arm. Gina trudged ahead of him.

'Strange,' said Mum. 'I've never known your Gina so quiet.'

'I'm worried,' I said.

'Don't be,' said Mum. 'Worrying's the one thing that won't change anything.' She hovered on the edge of a table, twisting her hips to brush it clear of dust. I could tell she wanted to talk about *him*.

'Not now, Mum.'

'He really loves me, Alice. He says so.' She held the letter in her arms.

'I'm going after Gina,' I said.

I was behind them, but not much; I'd a fair idea of which way they'd go. The park would be chained up by now, so it was backstreets all the way. A couple of times I thought I'd caught up with them – two shadowy figures fading into dusk – but however fast I ran they always stayed out of hailing distance or turned out to be strangers carrying shopping or being

95

dragged by a dog. At the top of their street I stopped and panted, peered down to see if the light was on outside the Marshall house. It wasn't, but there were two figures outside. Johnny. Johnny and his dad, arguing. I slid down to crouch behind a wall.

'You'd better tell me where they are, boy. And don't give me any of that "I don't know" crap because your sister saw you rifling through the bags.'

'She never told you that.'

'She didn't have to. I worked it out all by myself.'

Mr Marshall half turned – as if he expected Johnny to back down, bow out – but Johnny followed him with his body, breathed on his neck. He was nearly as tall as his dad, and faster, more lithe. I wished I was brave enough to run down the street and grab him, turn Johnny's challenge in a different direction, tip the dominoes another way.

'I don't blame you for getting out of my sight,' said Mr Marshall, pulling back his shoulders, 'but you shouldn't have taken Gina with you. I've been worried sick about her.'

'Yes. Well. You wouldn't worry about me, would you?'

'Just tell me where the jackets are. How much trouble do you want to be in?'

'Oh yeah. And you can talk to me about that. At least I'm trying to sell them. Not letting them sit there and go to *rot*.'

Silence. A thousand scenarios flashed through my head. Johnny walking off. Gina rushing out and dragging them inside. Mr Marshall relenting, putting a fatherly arm around his son. I didn't dare look round the wall and wondered for a second if they had gone inside, if the electric tension that ebbed up the street was all coming from me. But no, they were standing there, a battle of wills between their twitching bodies.

'Like you,' said Johnny, his voice low. Low, but audible. Audible to me; to his father and to his sister, Gina, whose profile I could see, sitting at her bedroom window, her jaw falling away from the rest of her face.

# Girl Power

*Like you.* I dream I'm there again, behind the wall, listening. The unmistakable heat in Johnny's voice slicing through twenty years and waking me up with a jerk. Mum's bedroom, the flat. Today he'll tell me what he wants from me.

Mum looks up at me vaguely when I go through for breakfast. Some days she seems barely able to work out who I am; on others she acts like I've never been away. Today she screws her eyes to focus on me, bothered by the way I look now that I've left my work suits behind.

'Pyjamas,' she says. 'All your clothes look like pyjamas, Alice.' Even my tame but asymmetrical collection of earrings bother her. 'Why can't you wear a pair that match?' she cries, like it's the end of the world.

'They're only earrings, Mum. People have their bellybuttons pierced now, their tongues.'

'Yes, well,' she says. 'At least then they look like something.'

I put on jeans, sandals, a loose shirt – not much different from when I was fifteen. Even my hair's the same; I've grown out my fringe, cut off the permed curls and am back to long and straight, centre-parted, Glints-instead-of-henna. But when I get out on the street, down the dank stairs from the flat, I realize it's all wrong. It's midsummer; England is hot, damp, lush. The girls are wearing practically nothing, the air moves freely round their legs, their ad-perfect hair swings and bounces. I'm trapped in soggy jeans that chafe my thighs, sweat pricks round my hairline and drips down my neck. I rush back upstairs to find a dress, something flimsy. But I have nothing, only ancient sprigged dresses or my mum's fitted jackets and flared fifties skirts. Too small. For the first time in twenty years I have no idea what I should wear.

'What is it, Alice?'

'I've nothing to wear.'

I'm sitting on the floor, clothes strewn around me. Mum starts picking through them, shaking T-shirts and smoothing them out, arranging them on the bed so that they look like those cardboard cutout clothes with little flaps to fold over a cardboard doll's shoulders. *Outdoor girl. That special occasion.*

'It's never bothered you much before . . .'

'I'm meeting someone.'

She holds a shirt up to the light, finds a mark on it and throws it on to the laundry pile. 'Well, we'll have to go shopping then. I did say so, didn't I?'

'Yes, Mum.'

'Come on then. I saw a dress that'll do you lovely just the other day. The shop's only round the corner. And tie your hair up, Alice, show off your neck. Men like a woman's hair tied up, I read it in a magazine.' She beams at herself in the mirror, pats her hair.

'Spare me *The Rules*, Mum. Anyway, who said I was meeting a man?'

'Alice, you don't need to say.'


The crinkly cotton of my new dress swirls around my legs as I walk down to the Bridge. The High Street is hazy in the summer heat, faces just a few feet away are blurred, moving past as a slick of sweat, coiling the air. This is how I remember the city, always moving and changing and flowing with people and cars and bikes streaming around it and I still feel the urge to put my hand up and say STOP, for it all to fall into focus at my command.

The pub is cool and dark; I am reading the paper and sipping beer when Johnny comes in. He flashes me a grin, buys a pint.

'Shall we sit outside?' he says. 'Nice day.'

'Yes, beautiful.'

'Just like you, Alice.'

'Leave it out, Johnny.'

'You're looking good though.'

'Thanks.' Thanks, Mum.

'What about me? Think I've weathered well?' He does a twirl, his hair fans out. He is wearing tattered jeans, a leather waistcoat, silver around his neck and wrists.

'Always the peacock, Johnny.'

He sits down, puts his feet up on the rail next to the murky canal. 'Yeah, I think I got the vain genes in our family.' He drains his pint. 'This weather makes you thirsty, doesn't it? Fancy another, Alice?'

'I have to go back to work.'

'Oh go on,' he says. His face is close to mine. 'Relax for once. Spend the afternoon with me.'

A nanosecond. 'OK. OK, Johnny.'

Music drifts out of the open pub door. 'Champagne Supernova', Oasis in every pub this summer, on every radio, car stereo. I should ask Johnny what he wants me for; I need to find out about Gina. But we have all day, we can stay here all day – England has relaxed that much at least, and I find that I can too. For a few minutes, half an hour, I can just be. The sun is shining, hot on our necks; a breeze ripples across the canal and disappears into the willow trees. We eat crusty rolls with sharp cheese; swig beer half a pint at a time. Kids roll past, on bikes, skates, boards; there are shouts in the distance, it feels like the seaside. Brummie seaside, a pub by the cut.

'A penny for them,' says Johnny. My eyes are closed, my face turned up to the sun.

'What happened to Gina?' I say. 'I've always wondered where she went after . . . you know . . .' Words run dry in my mouth. Johnny is quiet. I listen to the breeze brush wavelets across the canal.

'She went travelling,' he says. 'And what with me moving around a lot as well, we lost touch.' Another pause. 'She's OK though.'

99

'How do you know?'

'Because she's Gina.'

'I'd like to know that for sure,' I say.

'She is,' says Johnny. 'Trust me.'

Johnny goes to buy more beer. He's used to this, obviously, lounging in the sun and drinking on a weekday afternoon, when everyone else is working. It's an exception for me, but not for Johnny. I doubt if he's done a day of paid-taxed-legit work in his life. But here he comes, hands around two pints, teeth clamped around bags of crisps and a grin widening around them. He stumbles on a bollard but recovers himself, barely spills a drop. He opens his mouth, the crisps drop on the table. We clink our glasses and drink.

I dream of the city, alive. Peeling itself up from the plateau, blocks of flats dropping off the edges as a fire fans out from the middle, and I'm lost in it, tearing along half-familiar roads while the fire nips at my heels. I'm woken by the gap of silence and wish I had a dream book, even a rubbishy one.

In the mirror my face is rosy from the sun and I search for signs that I have changed, that my day of sitting, soaking, sunning myself has lifted the corners of my mouth, brightened my eyes. I think it might have, but don't trust the mirror. Or myself. Bad sign, as Dan would say. Such a familiar feeling though; I wonder if that's why I stayed away so long, because I knew that being here would make me feel so out of joint. Dan's other question would be, 'Why not? You're a perfectly sensible person, Alice. Why on earth don't you trust yourself?' He would have scoffed at the idea of a dream book, too.

All that time. All that time when I never sat in the sun drinking beer on a weekday, throwing crisps for the ducks and then laughing as the water sprayed my legs. I couldn't risk it, didn't trust myself to detour. Anyway, I tell myself sternly, I had a career, contributed to society. The voice comes from inside me but I'm not interested today. I shake my head, untangle curls. I'm bored of the stern voice. I tie in a ribbon, paint colours on to my face. I wonder where the stern voice came from; it was before Dan, I think, Dan was never so unsubtle as to tell me what to do – he was a suggester, a persuader. Standing in the garden with his friends from work, loosening their dark ties and shrugging off their jackets in the golden evening light, so sure that the world's blessings were theirs by right, these tall and healthy young men; clean-clothed, well fed and educated. Dan would put his arm around me and walk me around the garden, examining flowers and shoots, the only wrinkle on his horizon the thin lines of smoke rising in the evening sky behind the blackberry bushes. 'I do think we should try and get them moved,' he'd say. 'Don't you agree, Alice?'

I wear shorts. I want to feel the air on my skin, to smell of summer.

'My,' says Mum, sitting at the kitchen table. She has picked flowers from our weedy yard: dandelions, poppies, cornflowers. 'You look lovely, Alice. You could pass for a teenager in those clothes.' I sip coffee, black, its bitterness cutting through the fuzz in my head.

'So?' she says. 'Good afternoon?' She hovers, won't sit down; has to know what I've been doing.

'Lovely, thanks.'

'I haven't seen you so drunk in years –'

'I wasn't drunk.'

'It did make me smile though, you coming in all dishevelled like that. You've got grass stains all over your new dress. Didn't they have any seats in this pub you went to?'

Dishevelled? I think. Did I really get dishevelled?

'And your talk, Alice . . . All about the summer and the smells and how the city has little pockets of greenery and freshness and life. You kept telling me that, that there's life all around us. How we miss it even when it's right under our noses. Like the summer, you said. We get this fantastic gift of heat and light and abundance and we hardly even notice it half the time. You quite inspired me, Alice.' She wafts her arm around the kitchen, which is full of lavender, buttercups.

101

'You found all those in the yard?' I say. 'I wonder what else is out there.'

The yard smells fertile, the earth is warm and moist, the grass sticky and fluorescently green. Life has grown over the junk; mosses and lichens spread out. And where there's a scrap of soil, grasses bend under the weight of seed, thistles sprout purple flowers overnight. I watch a bee feed, spy a toad snoozing under some sodden carpet. I keep expecting to see the cat, high-wiring along the fence, or dozing in the sunny patches where the clover grows.

'He'll be long gone,' says Mum. She is watching me curiously from the back door. A mist swirls from the coffee in her hand.

'What?'

'The cat. The one that used to hang around this yard.'

'Did I say something about a cat?'

'I'll leave you to it, love.'

While I've been gone our yard's become a haven – a hollow – in the scraped-clean row of backyards; concreted, paved, weeds napalmed, animals evicted. They've come here to make nests in old teapots, forage in Mum's rubbish; like we did as girls, finding a refuge. I'm at the door of the shed; it smells of earth, deep earth, where the soil is black and oily. I walk around, touching the benches, running my fingers over the windowsill. Inches of dust are released and float lazily round the shed. I've tacked up the photos of Gina alongside our girlhood ones, and also a couple of me, under the Leylandii in the garden, with Mum on my wedding day, staring past the camera.

The board is there, a dusty glass. They are small, faded.

'Hey, Alice.'

I stifle a scream.

It's Johnny. 'I can't stop. I just came by to give you this,' he says, peering at the other photos around the walls of the shed. 'It's from years ago.' It's Gina standing somewhere hot, the desert maybe, mountains rising behind her, her feet buried in shimmer off the ground. 'You need one of you now,' says Johnny. 'You don't look like any of these.'

'You're not going to tell me today either then?' I say. We made a deal yesterday: drink today, show tomorrow. So easy with Johnny to let everything else go; talk about the trees and the sunshine and the people coming and going.

He prevaricates, sits down on the bench and pats the dust for me to join him. 'I've got a few things to do.'

'No more of that, Johnny,' I say. 'You've got to tell me what this is all about.'

He stands up, shrugs. 'All right. But tomorrow. Meet you outside the Bridge.'

'OK. Go off and do your things then.'

'Shame,' he says. 'I've got fond memories of this shed.'

I step out of the shed, close the door. Slip through the yard to the back gate. The sun is bright, blinding. Johnny strides ahead towards the street, the High Street that still unsettles me every time I walk down it. There's a girl crossing the road in punk gear, Siouxsie hair and black fishnet tights. I nearly call out to her before I realize she can't be more than nineteen. In Smith's window there's a poster of five girls, all platform heels and miniskirts and mock-witchy faces, and I stop dead. I stare at the accompanying caption in orange lettering, while the morning crowds swerve to avoid me.

GIRL POWER!!!

GRRRRR!!!

# Firestorm

Before I'd had time to properly digest the implications of Johnny and his dad arguing in the street – let alone Gina's strange absence, in spirit if not in body – it was Monday and there was the fire. The big fire; the fire that banished the previous ones to insignificance. Paltry fires; garden clippings, campfires for toasting marshmallows, domestic barbeques. Small fires, functional fires, controlled and controllable – we could imagine Wills-Masterson staring nostalgically at the neat grey circles of ash still dotted around the school grounds and then turning round to glare at the firestorm that the sixth-form block now was.

There were no sixth formers in it. We made feeble jokes about how a fire in a school might as well be in the sixth-form block because there was never anyone there. They were all on work experience or home study or in the pub. It was better than thinking of the alternative, that there could be charred bodies inside, that the smell of smoke and ash and burning plastic might be accompanied by the popping fat of the sixth formers; the people we aspired to be.

Nothing could have hurt Wills-Masterson more. She was excessively proud of her sixth form – Rock Hill had pupils that did 'A' Levels, went on to university. School newsletters were full of ex-pupils' achievements – *you can be like this*, was the subtext, beneath pictures of smiling graduands, *if you toe the line*. For her it meant that Rock Hill was a real school, like the grammar schools she'd taught in as a young woman and never tired of talking about.

You could only feel for her now. The fire alarms had started clanging just after lunch. The whole school rushed out into the playground and then lined up; shocked, uneasy. It was all we could do, stay in line, not make things worse. Even the boys stayed quiet during this, our real-life drama. Wills-Masterson and the teachers were busy, talking to the firemen, running back to the office for telephone calls, checking lists; all we had to do was watch, become hypnotized by the fire.

I was trying to remember what the sixth-form block had been like. I'd been there a few times, to pass on messages; big rooms full of lounging teenagers, drinking coffee, arguing, some glued together in dark corners. But as fast as I was building up the picture it was being burnt down. Flames poured out of windows and snaked up the walls like rapid-growing ivy. Red ivy. Orange and white and blue ivy. Proliferating and propagating and joining together until the whole of what-was-the-sixth-form-block grew into a giant blood-orange triffid climbing up into the sky to consume the clouds, drawing in the air we were breathing.

Ellie coughed. She was wracked with coughs and had to sit on the floor while we pounded her back and wiped her streaming eyes. Then the triffid at last began to die – not, it seemed, because of the action of the firemen's hoses, but of its own accord. At the top of its growth it hovered briefly, then collapsed in on itself. The firemen pounced and claimed their victory spoils of charred, smoking beams. The fire could be put out, but the sixth-form block was gone.

A low cloud of smoke hung over us, as we shuffled and coughed and scratched. Wills-Masterson was supervising the head count personally, in her hand a long ruler that glanced off our heads. By the time she got to us, ranks had broken. Boys were over with the firemen, pestering for a look inside the fire engines, play-vanquishing the fire themselves with huge hoses they could barely lift. Our form teacher, Mr Wilson – strands of his stringy beard straying over his shoulders in the wind – marshalled us together quickly and handed over the register. We were counted.

'Twenty-nine,' said Wills-Masterson. 'Who's missing?'

'Jennifer Peters has the flu,' said Mr Wilson. 'She's been off all week.'

'Who else?' The headmistress's finger ran down the register, but before she got to 'M' someone spoke up.

'I know who's not here.' It was Rose. 'Gina Marshall.'

Wills-Masterson's crêpey skin darkened. She snapped the register shut and practically threw it at Mr Wilson. We were dismissed.

Cora caught up with Rose halfway down the drive. 'I want a word with you,' she said, grabbing her collar.

'Leave me alone,' said Rose.

'Why d'you have to do that?' I said. 'Don't you think Gina has got enough problems?'

'I only said she wasn't there.'

'You might as well have said it was her that started it,' said Cora. 'You know what Wills-Masterson thinks of the Marshalls.'

'Yeah, and now Kenny's been expelled there's only Gina left to pick on,' I said.

'Are you being bothered, Rose?' said Rachel Williamson in a syrupy voice. She didn't lower herself to speak to us directly.

Rose shook her head. 'I can handle it,' she said, to the gravel.

'Are you sure about that?' said Cora. She towered over Rose; had grown three inches since we last looked.

'Leave it, Cora,' said Ellie.

We had to pull on Cora's arm to shift her. 'At least you'll have something to confess this week,' she spat.

'I don't think we need to worry too much,' said Rachel, over her shoulder. 'If I was you I'd be more concerned about what's happened to your *friend*.'

Rachel was right, we couldn't pretend otherwise. Where was Gina?

First place to try was the Marshall house. No one in, but we did bump into Johnny coming back up the street and railed at him with so many questions that in the end he made us sit down on the kerb and explain properly.

'You know those fires round school?'

'Well, Gina didn't light them –'

'But she sort of hung around them –'

'Anyway, now the sixth-form block's been burnt down –'

'God, you should have seen it, Johnny –'

We were gabbling, all speaking at once, but the story was out. He'd say it in a minute, 'Oh, Gina's been with Dad all day, they'll be back soon.' But he said nothing, just slouched around scuffing his trainers. When he did eventually speak there was a waver in his voice; he tried to clear it but it was still there. 'Who did light the fires?' he said.

'Your cousin, we think. Or at least that's what Gina said,' said Ellie.

'But he can't have set the whole sixth-form block on fire,' said Cora.

'It must have been a fault or something,' I said. 'Wiring. Electrics.'

'But it doesn't look good that Gina wasn't there . . .' It was Ellie's voice, saying what we were all thinking.

'Well, Johnny? Where is she?'

Johnny twisted inside his clothes. The wind must have changed direction because we could smell the fire now, dampened-ash smell, it stuck in the top of my throat.

'Johnny?'

'Sheranofflasnight.' He was talking into his chest. I felt a creak inside of me; knew what was coming.

'You what?' said Ellie.

'She ran off last night. Me and Dad were arguing and she just cracked. Stormed out of the house. Dad's been out looking for her ever since. So have I.' Johnny's voice was cracking now; we stopped pestering enough to notice how tired he was, how dirty and frantic.

Cora took hold of his elbow and we pushed him down the street to the house, made him tea, ran a bath. His arms flopped as we tried to get him up the stairs, his head lolled to one side, but then he'd jerk up and say he had to go. But his legs wouldn't take him, they buckled, and we steered him into his bedroom where he collapsed into unsteady sleep.

'Funny,' said Cora, as we walked slowly back up the twi-lit road, 'how he seemed like such a little boy.' The street-lamps flickered, orange light fizzing.

'I felt like I was his mum,' said Ellie, 'you know, wanted to tell him that everything would be OK.'

'Yeah,' said Cora. 'Fancy me feeling like a mother.'

I didn't feel like his mother. I was ablaze. The sight of Johnny's white shoulders when he came out of the bathroom, the rest of his arms brown, his slim, smooth back, wet curls resting on his neck had triggered an ache inside of me that was so sharp, so delicious that I was surprised I could walk, even toss my head nonchalantly in agreement with the others. I wanted to run back and slip into bed beside him, to hold him as he slept and for him to wake and smile on seeing me. I was amazed that I hadn't. I really had to concentrate to make myself listen to Ellie, to put the words together into a sentence that I could follow. What was she saying? Something about . . . Gina.

'Alice, are you listening? What are we going to do about Gina?'

We searched. For hours. All the places we went that Johnny and Mr Marshall might not know – the canal bank, the far reaches of the park, the railway embankment, the alleys behind the shops where we sometimes found throwaway makeup. We even sneaked into the school grounds and were briefly mesmerized by a few final, glowing coals where the sixth-form block had been. Once we thought we saw Mr Marshall in the distance – a stooped figure in an overgrown coat shouting out at something – but he turned out to be a tramp, alcoholically mad, and we were embarrassed by our first impression.

Thinking we'd seen Gina and Johnny's dad jerked Ellie back into some kind of reality. 'My parents!' she said, wildly. 'Oh shit. I'm really in for it now.' We scrambled to a phone box and implored the operator to let us make reverse charge calls.

'Dad!' said Ellie. 'It's-me-I'm-OK-I'm-sorry-we-were-looking-for-Gina.'

'Ellie?' Her dad's voice was severe. 'You just come home right now. I'd come and fetch you if I thought I could leave your mother.' There were gasps in the background – staged, Cora reckoned, but they had the desired affect on Ellie.

'I have to go,' she whispered, dropping the phone. 'Good luck with finding Gina, let me know . . .' and she was gone.

Cora and I stepped out of the phone box into the still smoky night air.

'Are you going to ring your mum?' said Cora.

'Not much point, she'll be out by now.'

'Will she be worried?'

'I shouldn't think so, she pretty much leaves me alone.'

'Lucky you.'

'Cora, it was you who said parents don't always have to know about staying out at night.' I'd forgotten all about that but something about the way she stood there twisting strands of hair reminded me.

'I hardly ever stay out now.'

'How come?'

'Them.' *Them*. Cora's parents. Alien lifeforms.

'But where did you used to go? Could Gina be there?'

'I doubt it.'

'Come on then, let's go and look.'

'No. I'll go. You go home. I'll see you tomorrow.'

'But –'

'No.'

There was no point in arguing, no one had ever won an argument with Cora as far as I knew. And there was something in her eyes too, a warning, which told me maybe I didn't really want to go.

'Bye then,' I said.

'Bye.'

I watched her walk off, her tall figure lengthening with the shadows. 'Take care,' I shouted, and she raised a hand in acknowledgement. I turned and headed up the dark backstreets towards home. By the time I reached the alley behind the shop tiredness had crept up over me. I lifted my heavy arm to unlatch the gate and lost half a second to unconsciousness. I stumbled through the yard, forcing a path through the junk, disturbing the cat, who slithered up the fence and posed motionless, the moon her backdrop, eyes as big as an alien.

Seconds after I got through the door I fell into bed. Outside the cat yowled and the moon glinted on the roof of the shed.

# Aftermath

'Alice? Wake up. It's time to get up for school.'

I groaned, pulled the cover over to the edge of the bed with me.

'Sounds like you've had as bad a night as me,' said Mum. 'Here, I've brought you some tea.'

She sat down on the edge of my bed underneath my poster of Bob Dylan and handed me a cup. We sipped silently, both thirsty.

'I couldn't settle at all, kept waking up thinking there was a storm outside,' said Mum, smoothing her nightie. 'I tossed and turned and that cat was yowling and the flat felt like it was full of spooks. Did you hear anything move around, Alice? Honestly if I didn't know better . . .' She was ruffling herself into consciousness with the chat. I still wished sleep would suck me down. 'And then I went to get a drink and had this peculiar feeling that something was going on in the yard, like those children's stories where the toys all come to life then get interrupted and collapse half off a shelf or in a doorway. I could have sworn I saw a light coming from the shed, but when I looked closely it had gone.'

I choked on my tea. 'The shed!'

'Yes, a light coming from the shed. Isn't that strange? You girls haven't left anything in there, have you? Alice? Where are you going? And why do you smell of *smoke* . . . ?'

111

I was already halfway down the stairs. Mum ran down after me, her fluffy slippers flapping. I was cursing myself. How come I hadn't thought of it last night? We didn't even check the shed. All that running around in the dark and Ellie getting into trouble and Gina could have been in the shed all the time. Why didn't I just think?

A clattering in the yard brought me to.

'Who was that?' said Mum. There was some scuffling in the alley but we didn't reach the gate in time to see anyone.

'Was it Gina?' I said.

'No,' said Mum, a splash of pink in the brown-green of the yard. 'I think it might have been Rose, you can't mistake that hair.'

'I can't see Rose coming anywhere near the shed.'

'Alice, what is going on?' Mum had hold of my arm as I was backing towards the shed. I told her briefly, dragging her reluctantly through the yard. 'You mean Georgina could have slept all night in our shed! Goodness, the poor girl. Well, what are you hanging around for? Let's have a look.' Mum flung the door open. I almost clapped. *My* mum wasn't scared of any stupid spirits.

Nothing came out except a rush of darkness and a familiar musty smell, tinged with something else – bodies, perhaps. But there was no one in there, no one visible anyway. I poked in corners looking for something – evidence – but it was Mum that found it, the candle stub, a few dead matches.

'Have you girls been using candles in here?' she said.

'No, Mum.'

'Then I think you'd better go and phone Georgina's dad. Perhaps we did have a visitor last night.'

'Mr Marshall?'

His voice was hoarse, but steady. 'Is that you, Alice? Yes, she's back.'

'Thank God for that,' I breathed; a rush of relief, like my whole body had been holding something tight and at last I could let it out. 'Only we found a candle stub in our shed and realized that Gina could have been in there.'

'Well, she's back now. Thanks for helping to look last night.'

112

'Can I come over? I want to see her.'

'You should go to school.' Mum and Mr Marshall said exactly the same words. Mum was standing behind me, rubbing my shoulders as I tried to talk and wipe my wet face. 'Maybe later, I'll see how she is.'

'OK.' I could feel strength returning to my legs, muscles and bones clicking back into place. But then my knees buckled. My chin grated on the mouthpiece of the phone.

'Mr Marshall, does she know about the fire?'

There was no answer, the line had gone dead.

At school, ash still hung in the air and we were reduced to two. I was late and Ellie didn't show at all. So the group was just down to me and Cora, and we tried our best to be invisible. Rachel Williamson was itching to taunt us, we could tell, but Rose seemed to be keeping her out of our way.

'Mum thought she saw Rose in our yard this morning,' I said.

'Nah. You know your mum, she sees spooks even when we don't.'

'Rose must be a little bit worried about Gina.'

'And Ellie,' said Cora.

Ellie hardly ever missed school. She wasn't allowed to be ill. In our class the only person who was still talking to us was Taz – the whole of the rest of the school were now convinced the fire in the sixth-form block had something to do with our shrinking group.

'Not much of an arson team are you?' Taz said. 'What did you do, breathe fire to get it going?'

'Hey, watch what you say,' said Cora, nudging him, shoulder to shoulder, 'that'll be the next rumour going round here.'

'Knock it off, Taz. We're worried,' I said.

'Ah, but never let them know that.'

'He's right,' said Cora. She sat up straight, wiggled her hips and blew a kiss straight at Rachel, who blushed furiously and clung on even tighter to Rose's arm.

'Where's Ellie then?' said Taz.

113

We filled him in about the previous night, and Ellie's mum's reaction.

He frowned. 'She's not going to take Ellie away from Rock Hill for good?'

'Almost certainly, now,' said Cora.

'But that's terrible,' said Taz. For a moment he looked no older than about five. 'For you, of course . . . what with Gina and everything . . .' He smiled quickly. 'Anyway, I'm with you girls, whatever.'

'Thanks, Taz.'

Me and Cora pasted on smiles as Taz walked off. On the other side of the room Rose looked close to tears.

We survived the rest of the day by blending into walls, sinking into desks and ignoring the eyes that followed us everywhere. The whole school was subdued, but there was tattle in the thump of shoes on stairs, voices hissing behind doors – we were headline news: even the dinner ladies knew about us; they whispered into their aprons as they doled out our puke pie. Cora didn't even pick hers up off the counter. I tried to eat mine but the potatoes turned to glue in my mouth.

'Let's get out of here,' said Cora, straining towards the door. 'I can't stand it a minute longer.'

'Not today,' I said. 'Everyone'll notice we've gone.'

'How are we going to get through the afternoon?' Cora stirred custard gloomily, lifting up spoonfuls and letting the sloppy yellowness slide back into the bowl with a gloop.

'Just be grateful the morning's over,' I said.

'Yeah, thank fuck for that,' said Cora.

The word bounced round the table – *fuck, fuck, fuck* – people's ears twitched and food dropped off their forks. We left, a tiny triumph, followed by swivelling heads. They wanted something from us; the rumours made everyone hungry and once we'd gone they had nothing to feed on but school dinners.

How long can an afternoon last? Cora was better off than me because she had double art and could lose herself in the smell of oil paint, the rough canvases, stretched and reused a hundred times. Even so, she swore she could count to ten between the ticks of the clock. But that was bliss compared to double physics. I knew it would be bad and took in a Mars bar to ward off the tedium. I cut it into ten pieces, a piece every twelve minutes – even I should be able to last that long, I thought, having swallowed the first piece almost whole in my eagerness for distraction. The second piece I let sit in my mouth and dissolve and trickle chocolatey liquid toffee down my throat. Two minutes gone. If I could make this toffee last another two minutes it would only be eight minutes until the next piece. But eight minutes was better than twelve. I sucked, eyes closed, lost in liquid sweetness.

'Alice? Alice, I do so think my pupils should keep their eyes open in class. It does so help with one's concentration.' Miss 'matchstick legs' Robinson's voice buzzed in my right ear and for a second I was tempted to swat it away. I swallowed my toffee rapidly – two minutes straight down my oesophagus.

'Yes, miss?'

'Bridge expansion. Enlighten the class on two ways that the construction of bridges takes into account the effects of the weather.'

'Huh?' I flicked through a textbook.

'And do so without referring to the literature.' She whipped away the melting Mars bar and dropped it – thunk – into the bin.

It was pure torture, and there were still eighty-two minutes to go.

Outside the school gates and away from the gossiping clumps of blue uniform Cora and I could at last breathe properly.

'Let's go to Gina's,' said Cora, 'or shall we try Ellie's first?'

'Ellie's,' I said. 'We need to know how much trouble she's in.'

'Yeah, we already know how much trouble Gina's in.'

Two of us could move quickly, down back alleys, across playing fields, frost melting under our shoes; through blocks of garages where half-hearted repairs had stalled in the late-afternoon sun. When there were five of us it had always

115

taken ages to get anywhere. Rose didn't like running, Gina got distracted; there was always some argument going on. From the back of Ellie's house we could see that her bedroom curtains were closed and we stopped for a moment to catch our breath and let the sweat evaporate in the quickly cooling air. Ice was re-forming in the shadows.

'You talk,' said Cora. 'Her mum can't stand me.'

'OK, but try and smile.'

I rang the doorbell and we waited. No answer. The telly was on – *Blue Peter*, we could hear the hornpipe chirping – and Mr Allen's car was in the drive. I rang again. There were muffled voices and then a fuzzy shadow behind the glass door. Mrs Allen opened it and stood, hands on pinny-ed hips. 'Yes?'

'Hi, Mrs Allen,' I started, best friendly voice. 'We just came to see how Ellie is. Has she got a cold or something?'

'I don't keep Elinor off school for colds.'

'No, no, of course not . . . what's the matter then? Nothing serious is it?' Cora was vibrating next to me.

'Nothing that changing schools won't sort out.'

'But you can't do that!' Cora burst in.

'Oh can't I? Who says so, young lady? You? And why should I take any notice of you when it comes to my daughter?' Cora's vibration changed key. She was seething.

'But she's doing so well, Mrs Allen. She's the best in our class at English, and she's started her 'O' Level options, it would be crazy to take her out now.' An argument no adult could resist, surely?

'I'll be the judge of what's crazy or not,' snapped Mrs Allen and she slammed the door in our faces. She opened it again before we'd unfrozen. 'And don't you come around here any more. I don't want you seeing her. Is that clear?'

Before we could answer the door slammed again. But she must have heard it, the cry, in unison: 'But she's our *friend*.'

Cora shivered and seethed. We retreated to a lamppost just outside Ellie's gate and stood in the pool of light. I thought we should move away from their house but Cora said that the old bag couldn't do anything to us on the street

116

and she lit a cigarette, puffing defiantly and blowing streams of smoke out of our circle of light where it melted into darkness. We were hoping Ellie might come to an upstairs window or something, but when a figure did loom at the top of the stairs, it wasn't her.

'It's her dad,' said Cora. 'He's signalling. Come on.' Cora grabbed my arm and we ran around the back of the house.

Mr Allen was waiting at the back gate, shifting from one foot to the other. 'Here,' he said, giving us an envelope. 'This is from Ellie. Now run along, before we're all in trouble.'

'She can't keep Ellie off school for ever, you know,' said Cora.

I nudged her. 'Cora, he's trying to help.'

She ignored me and looked straight at Mr Allen. 'Well. Don't you get any say in all this?' His face slid a little bit and we jumped on this slight weakening. 'There's nothing to worry about really, Ellie gets on fine at school, everybody likes her –'

'And she likes it. She does, Mr Allen. She doesn't want to go anywhere else.'

'Imagine how you'd feel if she was really unhappy at another school.'

Ellie had told us that her mother's entire argument against Rock Hill and us was 'I know what's best for my child', which had always struck us as a monstrous piece of adult arrogance.

Mr Allen's body sagged slightly; but then the light in the bathroom behind him went off and he shot indoors; a frightened rabbit.

'Damn!' said Cora. 'We nearly had him.'

'Still, that's who Ellie has to work on.'

'Yeah.'

Mr Allen stood, back-lit in the kitchen window, shoo-ing at us furiously.

Dear Gang,
You're at the door talking to my mum now but I know she won't let you in. I've never seen her so mad as she

117

was last night. Seems like she heard about the fire and went down to school to meet me but we'd already gone. Anyway, she flipped. She really thinks we had something to do with the fire. I told her her imagination was running away with her and she said, See! My Ellie wouldn't talk to her mother like that. So you can see how things are.

I'm going to try and get Dad to slip you this note. I'm locked inside, can't even get out into the garden because she's decided I really must be ill and has had me in bed all day and washed every single item of clothing I own! So if I turn up at yours in pyjamas you'll know why, ha ha.

Leave notes under the stone by the back gate, if you can. I miss you.

Ellie xxxx

P.S. How's Gina?

'Good question,' I said, as Cora and I sat reading Ellie's note with the last of the candle stub, shivering as the night frost gripped the shed. 'How is Gina?'

The candle stuttered and faded, and we sat in the cold darkness wondering what the spirit would say about it all, if we were brave – or foolish – enough to ask him.

# Dissembling

I'm in the shed when the letter comes. A morning when the flat and the High Street are quiet, even rarer now than when I was a teenager. The shed is so buried in junk and weeds that you'd miss it if you didn't know it was there. I squeeze my way through and sit in the dimness. Gina is on all the walls – I think of getting a map to see if I can trace the places she's been. France, Greece, Morocco; those are my guesses so far. Johnny thinks he may have a few more photos somewhere, folded into an envelope, between the leaves of a book. Wherever Johnny keeps the bits of his life that he's hung on to.

A ring on the doorbell and Mum's stirrings and mutterings float through to me. A bird warbles near by, a bus lumbers past, the low hum of the city starts to build up. Then a few minutes later I hear her call me, a snag in her voice, *Alice?* A bill, maybe. Final demands.

'Are you OK, Mum?' I say.

She is sitting with her back to me at the kitchen table, her rollers still in. The exposed back of her neck looks strangely vulnerable.

'Your father's dead,' she says.

The letter is from an uncle I never knew I had. There is a parcel too. They – my relatives – found some things of Mum's while sorting through his stuff: trinkets, wedding photographs and, oddly, some newspaper cuttings of me when I was in the

119

school swimming team, long after he left us, and a tiny tooth in a small silver box.

'Is this mine?' I say.

'I guess so,' says Mum. 'Unless he had any other children.'

'Do you think he might have?'

'No,' she says, looking up at me. 'I don't think he did.'

He's buried in a cemetery just down the road from here. I sit down opposite Mum and watch her face, wondering if I can ask yet, all the questions that have been swimming around for years, now suddenly and urgently nipping the surface. But she's ahead of me. White and shocked, her voice a pale sigh, but ahead of me.

'I had no idea he was still in the city,' she says. 'When he left it felt like we'd stopped existing for him. Like his past never happened.'

He kept some of her things, had an interest in me; her whole picture of him, the one she held in her head for years, has suddenly blurred. His break wasn't so clean, so definite.

'He could have walked past here,' she says. 'Past the shop.'

Maybe he did, I think. We'll never know now. Perhaps he even peered in through the cluttered windows and saw her, painting her nails, sighing, lifting her head to catch a man outside snatching his face away from her sight.

I go back down to the shed again and look at the pictures of the group around the walls. Cora? Who knows where she is? Gina? Away, far away.

Ellie I do know about, we've exchanged letters for years and she used to visit me in the house occasionally. She was working for Oxfam overseas by then, dirt poor, and Dan would get her fed and settled, the luxury of a clean shirt and a full belly, then start talking, his voice low and reasonable. 'You're digging wells and giving reading lessons, Ellie, but their own governments don't care about these people. How are they ever going to be responsible for themselves if we keep clearing up their mess?'

'Capitalism relies on charity,' said Ellie. 'Don't ever think I approve of the system.'

'Our government doesn't care about some of our people,' I said, knowing my loose tongue could be blamed on wine and Ellie; the issue shelved by me and Dan when we were alone again. 'The swimming baths wouldn't let the travellers' kids in the other week,' I said to Ellie. 'And the worse thing is that they lied about the reasons, fluffed on about floats going missing and the drinks machine being broken.'

'The damage was quite serious, you know,' said Dan, low-voiced to me, flashing a quick smile at Ellie. 'Now, who wants another drink?'

I told Ellie about my hosepipe and the next day we went down to the site. It was pouring, piles of muddy boots were stacked outside each bus and bender, a swelling river of water flowed down the main drag. Ellie bent her head into a few of the benders and exchanged words, about rubbish disposal and education rights, casting a professional eye around the site, pointing out the shit pit and communal cooking area. One bus had a bath in it, I discovered. On the days when I hung out my pillowcase they would fill it, boiling pots of water over the fire, everyone taking their turn for a scrub, the kids squealing with pleasure, the first to notice the white flag out of my window. I smiled at the story but kept my distance, wasn't ready to talk just then. Kept my hose a secret and watched from a distance. Maybe I thought if I lifted the flap of one of their benders, their home under a hump of tarp, that I wouldn't make it back through the blackberry bushes and up the long slope of lawn to the house. That I'd never make it home.

I have to meet Johnny outside the Bridge. My dad is dead.

'Where are we going then, Johnny?' I say. 'You'd better fill me in.'

'I'd love to,' says Johnny. His eyes crinkle at the corners; I manage a swift smile. 'Tell you what,' he says. 'Let's go and have breakfast in that café and I'll tell you. I'm starving, me.' He circles his hand over his stomach.

'Starving,' I say.

'You're such a cynic these days,' says Johnny.

We walk along the High Street, heading out of the city. Traffic, people, shops. Congeries of houses and flats – new blocks squeezed in between Victorian terraces, towerblocks poking up behind squat, settled semis. Sometimes it's hard to remember that I ever left. A stack of time, which is side-lined now, but then it was this life that I cut myself off from. It had to happen, I now know, me coming home. Something about what happened here – what *is* happening here – branded me; branded all of us.

'Did you ever want to leave, Johnny?' I say. 'Move some-where different?'

'I've always moved, me,' he says. 'Coming and going, you know.'

'To other cities?' We are nearing the canal entrance. It used to be a hole in the fence; now there's steps and white-painted fencing.

'No.'

'Where then?'

'Just around. You'll see.'

Once I would have pestered him – tell me, Johnny, tell me – beat my fists on his chest until he grabbed my wrists and wrestled me quiet, mimicking my voice's plea. Oh it's noth-ing, he'd say, once I'd stilled and I'd yell in frustration. Now we walk down the towpath – the trees have grown over, making a dim green tunnel – and it is him who stops, has to say something.

'It's drugs, Alice. I expect you've guessed.'

'Is that all?' I say. I realize I must have been thinking much worse. 'It was a big scandal when we were fifteen, but nowa-days it's the kids who don't know about drugs who're the weirdos.'

Johnny looks sideways at me. 'They're still illegal, you know.'

'And everywhere,' I say. 'If you knew how many pow-ders and pills came into my lab.'

'Well, yeah.'

We walk on over damp leaves, a whiff of dankness rises up with each step.

122

'There's a few complications . . .' says Johnny.

'Try me,' I say.

He wants to joke again, brush it off, but we've gone past that. We come to a gate. The field beyond it has an old van in it – smashed windows, flat tyres – and some tarpaulins curved over bent branches: a bender. I watch Johnny open the gate and realize that this is what he means about coming and going; this is how he's been living – outside, *on* the outside. I feel at once how this suits him, the looseness of this kind of life; its flimsiness – home a scrap of tarp, packs of dogs at his heels; how he'd feel wrong in any other clothes, a suit, a uniform. Bits of tat lie about the field; bikes with no wheels, an old cattle trough, scrap metal and woodpiles. Smoke meanders up from a small fire, dogs rush over – not barking, they know Johnny.

'There's a girl involved,' says Johnny. 'Come and meet her.'

The girl is small, young; a hazy blob of colour across the field.

'Her name's Corinne,' says Johnny. He is striding, eager to get to her. 'She's a real traveller, born in a tepee, never lived in a house.'

'Corinne,' I say.

She's coming into focus; dark hair, bright eyes, a glow on her skin from living outside. She is bending, picking up a pot off the fire. As she moves upwards one hand goes to her back, she straightens herself from the hips up.

'She's pregnant,' I say. My feet are moving more slowly; the grass has gone sticky, the air thick.

'Yeah,' says Johnny. 'That's part of the problem.'

'Hi,' she says. She's in front of us now, in my face. She smells of woodsmoke and fresh sweat; robust, unmistakable. 'You must be Alice. I expect you're wondering what this is all about,' she says. 'Knowing Johnny he'll have told you sod all.'

'That's about it,' I say.

'I'm glad he brought you over,' she says. Johnny is fussing one of the dogs, playing with it, slapping it around the jaws. 'We could really do with some help,' she says, taking my arm, leading me over to the igloo-shaped bender.

'Corinne, I don't even know what happened yet,' I say.

I look over at Johnny; he's talking to the dog – go on boy, fetch the stick, that's it, bring it here now. Each throw takes him further from us. I need to ask him what he's told her – if she thinks I'm a lawyer or something, someone who can represent her. Maybe Johnny thinks I can too.

'Shame he fell out with that other bloke,' says Corinne. 'I was almost beginning to think lawyers could be human.'

'Corinne, I'm not a lawyer.'

'You know how it all works though, don't you?'

She lifts a flap of tarpaulin and beckons me through, kicking off her boots and I do too. Johnny is off down the cut, I can hear him whistling to the dogs.

'He won't talk about it,' says Corinne. 'He just wants it sorted. Even if it means getting sent down. Mind you, I don't think he could cope with being inside again. I told him,' she says, 'yeah, of course the law's an ass, we'll probably get stuffed. But there's a difference between getting stuffed and getting really stuffed and if he doesn't want to get really stuffed he'd better get someone on his side.' A look of exasperation pulls her face. 'I told him, someone'll just come down here and get you at this rate. Handcuffs, black Maria, bye bye, Johnny.'

Inside it's dark, warm, a lived-in smell. She lights candles as she speaks and spheres of soft light bloom around us. The hut is made of latticed branches, tarpaulin stretched over the frame. She has hung scarves around, there are cushions, stools, books, a drum. It feels like a den to me; Corinne's home. In the centre is a stove with a pipe going out through the roof. A kettle rattles on the top. She sees me looking around.

'D'you like my bender?' she says. 'Home sweet home.'

'It's nice,' I say. It is. 'Who lives in the van out there?'

'No one,' she says. 'I used to. God, he hasn't told you anything, has he?'

So Corinne tells me about Johnny. He squelches along the towpath, dogs panting around him, rain in a mist around his head and she tells me. 'I've known him since I was a kid,' she says. 'He turned up everywhere, on all the sites we lived on. Dealing, you know, but partying too, into it all. He was never into anything heavy. Was always welcome on the sites, not like some of them who came down handing out smack like sweeties. But the quantities did get bigger and it was harder to hide and more of a risk to travel around with. We get stopped by the police all the time,' she says. 'Try crossing a county border in a van like that . . .'

It's the van that's the problem, she tells me. Johnny built a compartment into it, under the gearbox or something, and used it to hide his stuff. But then he got caught. 'A road-block somewhere and they found a couple of nine-bars on him and thought there must be more,' says Corinne. 'Eventually they followed him to my van and that's why it's all shredded to fuck and I can't live there any more. I wouldn't mind so much but –' she looks up, meets my eyes '– it would help when the baby comes.'

The baby. We are quiet. I sip fruity tea, let the blackcurrant steam flow up my nose and down my throat. The fire hisses and crackles, wood pigeons coo in the trees – they are wild here, only a mile or two from Mum's flat. I keep expecting her to look vulnerable, to start crying, but she is still, breathing gently.

'I'm surprised they haven't impounded the van,' I say. 'It's evidence, surely?'

'They haven't found a way to move it yet,' says Corinne, a touch of a smile growing. 'Johnny took the engine out and they can't get a truck down the towpath.'

'When is he up in court?'

'Not long. Two or three weeks.' She pauses. 'And it's not just him they're charging. It's me.'

'How come?' I say.

'My van, my drugs,' she says, quietly. 'Alice, if we don't get some help quickly my baby could be born inside.'

# A Single Question

Cora had stayed at mine, and I woke in the morning and watched her still sleeping, her toes brushing mine as she twitched, dreaming – I tried to imagine what, but her face gave nothing away. We tried to slip out early so we could bunk off school and go to Gina's, but Mum stopped us at the door – asked no questions – and made us put on warm clothes before leaving. We were both shivering, had been cold all night, since sitting up too late in the shed, frost creeping into the warped wood all around us. When we left the flat we were bundled up like little kids. We ran a bit, got hot, felt better.

'Your mum's great,' said Cora, as we left the main road for the estate. 'Whenever I try to talk to mine about anything close to the truth their faces fill up with such horror I think, Bollocks, it's easier just to lie.'

Gina's house (*Johnny*'s house) was boiling – every fire thudding out heat. Once inside I started to drip and flush and thought I might melt clean away at the sight of Johnny in shorts and a T-shirt lounging on the sofa.

'Hi girls,' he said. 'Thanks for sorting me out the other night. I was knackered.'

'No sweat,' said Cora. She winked at him.

'Yeah, no sweat,' I said, desperately nonchalant. Johnny reached over to wipe away the beads leaking out of my forehead with his T-shirt. I smelt his hot body.

126

'Where's Gina?' said Cora.

'Upstairs.'

'How is she?'

Johnny shrugged. 'Go and ask her. It sure takes the heat off me, anyway.'

I backed to the bottom of the stairs, on a rolling boil.

'Gina? It's us.'

She was in bed, covers up to her neck, pale, her hair scraped back. 'Hi.'

'Are you OK?'

'Ish.'

'Did you hear about the fire?'

'Yeah. I bet school is hell.'

'When are you coming back?'

'Dunno,' said Gina. Nothing else. A fan heater pumped out waves of heat but Gina pulled her dressing gown round her shoulders. 'Where's Ellie?' she said.

'Incarcerated,' said Cora.

'Oh.'

Cars rumbled past. Johnny changed the TV channel downstairs, the chatty voices loud against our silence.

'Listen, Gina –'

'What?'

'It's not that we want to bug you or anything, but they're going to want to know where you were –'

'What's it to you?'

'Don't be like that.'

'Like what?'

'Like *that*.'

Cora went to the window. She pulled back the curtain and let in a shaft of light, which Gina dodged.

'Shut that,' she snapped, creasing her eyes.

'Yes, ma'am,' said Cora. 'And would your ladyship like anything else?'

'I'd like you to get lost.'

'Well, if that's the thanks we get,' said Cora, huffily.

'Why should I thank you?' said Gina.

'*Gina*. Stop being like that with us,' I said. 'You can't stay

127

in bed for ever.' Gina shuffled down in the bed and rolled away from us.

'Gina, for God's sake, listen. Wills-Masterson is bound to ask where you were on the morning of the fire. So you'd better start thinking, because the minute you show your face back at Rock Hill you're going to be straight in that office.' It was a scene we all knew well. Shoes sinking into the blue carpet. The heavy desk, trophies glinting in glass cabinets.

Gina's voice came out of the blankets, sulky and scared. 'I was in the shed.'

'All that time?'

'Most of it. Dad and Johnny had been rowing all weekend and by Sunday night I'd had enough. I just ran out of the house . . .' Gina sniffed hard, looked at me for the first time.

Mr Marshall's head peered around the door, drooping with guilt. Gina gave him the blackest of looks and he flinched.

'It's not his fault, Gina,' I said.

'Your dad should be able to make things better,' she said. I thought I heard a small strangled noise outside the door.

'Tell us, Gina,' I said. 'If we know what happened we can defend ourselves.'

'Well, I spent the night just roaming about and at dawn I crept up the alley and into the shed. I heard you leave for school, but then it went completely quiet, no noise from the High Street or anywhere and I had . . . I had this feeling that the spirit was around so I decided to ask him about Dad –'

'You got the Ouija board out on your own?' said Cora.

'I just started talking – asking questions, about how all this mess was going to be sorted out. I was pacing around, kicking up the dirt, angry, you know. It was so weird in there, so clammy and quiet, I just knew the spirit was there. So I did it. I got the board out.'

'Oh, Gina . . .'

'I asked it one question. I put my finger on the glass and said, "What should I do?" And do you know what it said?' Gina looked up at us, the blackness of her eyes expanding to fill her whole sockets.

'S–A–V–E   Y–O–U–R–S–E–L–F.'

For the rest of the day Gina's bedroom was the centre of fevered speculation. What could the spirit mean? Should we try and find out more? Ellie's advice would have been to leave well alone – we knew that – but she was gone now, and we missed her presence, her steadiness. There was also the urgent question of what we were going to say at school, once the inevitable inquisition started.

'You can't tell Dracula you were in the shed when the fire started,' I said to Gina. 'Not with all those stupid rumours going around school.'

'Imagine their faces if we tried to tell them about the spirit,' said Cora.

'If we let them mix up the fires with our spirit we're done for, for sure,' I said.

'What if she did believe us?' said Cora. 'And thought that we're really demons or something, who can start a fire by thought-power.' She placed an index finger on each temple. 'Zzz . . . *Zap* the whole school.'

We stared at each other, a triangle of eyes and implications.

'Thanks for coming, you two,' said Gina.

'No sweat.'

'Just say it wasn't you and stick to that,' I said. 'They've no proof, never have had. If you ask me it couldn't have been Marshall and his lot either. How could a bunch of kids start a fire as big as that?'

'Anyone could,' said Gina. 'That's the thing about fires, they spread.'

'Well, in that case it wasn't intentional, was it? And anyway, we're not trying to save them.'

'Save yourself,' said Gina. 'I wonder if that was what the spirit meant.'

The light was dimming outside. There was a last burst of birdsong out of the trees and then the sun sank, dropping so fast it made us dizzy. We watched the city lights come on; streetlights, lamps in windows, car beams, and in the distance the blinking from the post office tower, orange motorway lights in great stripes across the city. Gina had her arms around our waists, she didn't seem to want to let us go. Her head dropped on to my shoulder. 'I wish Rose was here,' she murmured.

'You mean Ellie,' said Cora.

I watched Gina struggle to open her eyes, they flickered in the mirror opposite us. 'Do I?' she said. 'Oh, yes, I wish Ellie was here.'

Christmas was subdued that year. Mum announced we were going to Aunty Gladys's; she didn't seem to want to be anywhere near the flat. I spent the entire holiday wandering on the frosted beach until I was too cold to think and memorizing every word of 'Bohemian Rhapsody'. I made a few phone calls to Gina but didn't dare ask to speak to Johnny, who filled my dreams with heat and colour, making the wind-blown beach seem even more pale and lonely. Gladys and Gordon looked at me with worried eyes but Mum said it was just a phase and protected me from their prying. I thanked her telepathically and tried to phone Cora. She was always out.

The first day of school dawned grey and cold. Slate grey; heavy clouds squeezing us on to the slime-grey pavements. Cora challenged the greyness with streaks of pink in her hair and Gina and I clung on to either side of her, her five-inch platform heels and raised chin sweeping us forward. She chattered the whole way; about clothes and bad-taste Christmas presents and the top ten – whatever was happening we still always knew who was number one (Queen; for ever). By the time we got to school we could almost believe that we were normal teenagers and this was a normal boring school morning.

'Whatever that might mean,' said Gina.

'Worrying about homework and boys, I think,' said Cora.

'I was never normal then,' said Gina.

'Nor me,' said Cora, as we crossed the lunar expanse of playground, 'unless you count getting out of homework and into the lads' trousers –'

'And stop pretending you don't think about it, Alice.'

'Yeah, and you've probably done your homework too.'

They were right, on both counts. Thoughts of Johnny had invaded my whole body; he was with me every second. *Johnny breathes, Johnny moves, Johnny sleeps and dreams*. I had also spent the last days of the holiday catching up with homework in a vain attempt to stave off longing with something practical. I wanted to write his name everywhere, on my bag, my pencil case, prick his name out with a compass on my arm and fill it in with Indian ink; like the boys did with their greatest loves: the Villa, BCFC.

Inside school it was quiet, slightly damp. Two girls sidled past us, their backs to the wall. They were friends of Gina's, from the estate, but avoided looking her in the face.

'Hey, Clare!' said Gina.

'Oh, hey, Gina,' said Clare, stopping reluctantly.

'There's no need to pretend you don't know me. I didn't do anything, you know.'

'I never said you did.'

'Walk into assembly with us then.'

'Yeah . . . I've just got to fetch something. Catch you later,' and Clare fled, skating down the corridor and round the corner in seconds.

Gina's knees gave way, she tipped backwards on to the wall and slid down, taking a wadge of damp wallpaper with her.

'I'll come in with you,' said Taz, running up behind us, his familiar grin a bright light. 'Great hair, Cora.'

The hall was a rustling, twitching, muttering sea of blue. News of our arrival spread like a wave – they're here. Cora did a small bow; piano chords signalled the beginning of a hymn. Taz tried to make us laugh by deliberately singing off key but we had to suppress it, swallow hard, because it felt too brazen – even to us. The whole point was that we *hadn't* done anything, we knew nothing about the fire. The attention made Cora stiffen, her earrings jangled; but I was more worried about Gina, whose lip was curling under Dracula's unwavering glare. 'Let us pray,' she said. We bent our heads, but could still feel it. Dracula obviously had nothing to pray about.

131

'Now.' Wills-Masterson clapped her hands. 'Today we're going to talk about contrition.' Not once did she take her eyes off Gina, who stared back, refusing to so much as blink.

I signed H-a-n-g i-n t-h-e-r-e to Gina, my hands moving quickly – it was strictly forbidden to talk like this in assembly. Y-a-w-n y-a-w-n signed Cora. Teachers prowled up and down the side of the hall watching for dancing hands, chewing gum, vandalism, drooping heads.

On stage Wills-Masterson was building up to something and everyone knew it had to be the fire. 'So, I hope you can all see that a wrongdoing is not finished with until it is attoned for, publicly, and to the proper authorities.' She stood, hands on hips, white-blond hair back-lit from the stage lights and stared out at us.

Everyone else in the hall was mesmerized, except for Mr McGeady, who was concentrating on his knees. They really believe this, I thought, they think it's real. Only a few of us – foolishly, perhaps – dismissed Wills-Masterson as having lost the plot over the fire. We snatched wary glances at each other and started to shuffle out of the hall.

Gina hissed in my ear. 'She's wrong and he's right,' she said.

'Who?' I hissed back. Gina nodded to her hands and signed the rest of her sentence. S-a-v-e y-o-u-r-s-e-l-f.

Mr McGeady was still in black and in no mood for messing. We were sympathetic – first day of school rumour was that not only had his wife left him but she'd taken their two small children with her. Anyway, being in English gave us something else to think about; especially when we were faced with a written test on act two of *The Crucible*.

'What are you all looking so surprised about?' said Mr McGeady. 'I said I'd test you, didn't I? Down to your papers please. In silence.'

I had no problem with tests if I'd done the work. There was something comforting about the whole process – studying the textbooks, the answers all sitting there neatly on the page. Turning an exam paper over and straight away thinking *I know that one*. It wasn't quite as easy in English as it was in biology or chemistry, but there were some rules – answer the question, remember to quote.

Question 1. 'What indications are given of the domestic estrangement between John and Elizabeth Proctor? What kind of wife is she?'

This was going to be fine. I sneaked a look at Taz and he gave me a thumbs-up. I started to write about the Proctor's strained marriage and then realized – with a flash of resentment – that the question asked about indications. That was more difficult. And then it came to me, remembering Gina's dad slamming doors, shouldering his way around the house when things went wrong. The farmhouse outside Salem village; Elizabeth Proctor preparing food, John Proctor pretending to like it, the stilted conversation, her muted accusation – 'You come so late I thought you'd gone to Salem.' The sadness of the two of them struggling with their failures rose in my throat. I wrote furiously, as did Cora and Gina on either side of me. Why did this seem so important?

Question 2. 'Why does John Proctor dislike Abigail's uncle, the Reverend Parris?'

I could even remember a quote for that one. Proctor said, 'I see no light of God in that man.' So, a leader that gave no guidance, only hellfire and damnation; that was familiar enough.

Question 3. 'What crucial decision does Proctor make at the end of act two?'

Well, he decides to confess, doesn't he? He had no other choice, unless he gave up on the village, ran away into the wilderness. Confess that he did have sex with Abigail and that's why his wife was accused of witchcraft, because Abigail wanted rid of her. So he admitted to the first wrongdoing to prevent a much greater one. He had to. What else could he do when his wife was taken away in chains?

The last question was totally unexpected. Not even on *The Crucible* really, which seemed like cheating to me.

Question 4. 'What does "domestic estrangement" mean to you? Write a paragraph of creative work on this topic.'

Only five minutes to go. I had to write quickly. 'Domestic estrangement is when people who are living together have gaps between them, spaces that can't be filled by work or new curtains or babies. They might fill the spaces with polite talk or even blazing rows but they might as well be speaking a different language because the words won't cross the gap.'

The bell rang. The papers were collected. We filed out in silence.

'Nosy bastard,' said Cora. 'What's it got to do with him what our domestic arrangements are?'

'He wasn't asking that,' said Gina, 'he was just asking us to think about it. You know, literature as a reflection of life and all that.'

'You're very fond of literature all of a sudden.'

'I didn't believe the question at first,' I said. 'Then this paragraph just jumped straight out of my pen.'

'Maybe the spirit wrote it,' said Cora.

We stared at each other. Gina shivered but she was hot, we all were; blood pumping on to our flushing cheeks. What the hell was going on? The spirit getting mixed up with our English lessons and Cora's domestically estranged parents and Mr McGeady's weird metamorphosis. Not to mention the fire.

'They can't be taking this seriously,' I said. 'It's just not possible, that Gina is really going to get blamed for the fire.'

# Us Against the World

'No way,' said Cora, a week or so later. 'No way are we going to let them get us down tonight.'

If one thing had been made clear to us since we returned to school, it was that the fire had not been forgotten, and it was getting to us all.

Gina kicked stones all the way down the drive. 'Why the fuck not?' she said, mutinously, the exact same tone as her dad. Or Johnny.

'Oh come on, you can't have forgotten?' Cora said. 'It's the Mop tonight, idiot. I thought the whole school had heard about the new bellbottoms Melanie's going to wear?' Cora was doing impressions of the girls in front of the mirror, dancing around in shall-I-shan't-I poses. 'Oh yes, and Rose's going with Rachel. Her dad's going to come and fetch them from the waltzers at ten o'clock.'

'It's hardly even started by ten o'clock.'

'Yep.'

'Well, I can't miss that,' said Gina. 'I'm going to get changed. See you back here in an hour?'

'We should go and try and sneak Ellie out,' I said.

'Yeah, OK. An hour then.'

'OK.'

The Mop! I'd always loved it, even when I was little and Mum took me, flirting with the fairground boys and coming home with goldfish in plastic bags; outsize teddies pressed on her by the men on the rifle range. The Green transformed by the fair; a real, travelling fair with stalls and candyfloss and strings of coloured lights and rides that made you giddy and sick with laughter.

For the last three years the group had gone together; five girls, arms linked, causing havoc with the crowds. Plunging ourselves into the whirl of burnt sugar; clanking, slamming rides; black-eyed gypsy boys. ('They're not really gypsy boys,' said Cora, 'I've seen them up town, selling flowers on the market.' 'Oh, let them believe it for a night,' said Rose, her face shining. 'Why not?') She could have been a gypsy herself that night, hair loosened from its band, red-braided waistcoat. Clothes were important at the Mop. We remembered what we'd worn the year before and measured our grownupness against it. Cora would be spiking up her fringe this year, Gina would be in jeans and a baggy jumper, I was somewhere in between and scrutinized my wardrobe.

'Alice!' Mum came in behind me. 'Staring at your clothes won't change what's in there, love. Now are you going to get to the fair tonight or what?'

Yes, yes, but tonight might be the night that Johnny sees me.

Ellie's house didn't look inviting, the curtains were closed, the gates chained. Fortunately, I'd managed a ten-second conversation earlier on, before Ellie's mum grabbed the phone off her. None of us dared to go and knock on the door – not because we were scared of Mrs Allen, as Cora said, but because it would only mean trouble for Ellie; but Gina found the note quickly. *Can't get out now but will try later. Look out for me and save me a toffee apple, love Ellie xxxxx.*

'Poor Ellie,' I said, 'what can it be like locked up in there all day?'

'Crap, for sure,' said Gina.

'She's got to let her out sometime.'

'Yeah, but when?'

The Mop was calling us. Even from Ellie's house, which was a good mile and a half away, we could hear faint music, thumps and bangs, the odd firework whistled up into the sky. We ran, steadily covering ground until the smells of frying onions and diesel from the generators stopped us in our tracks. Gina wiped her face, Cora pulled at her high-riding skirt.

'Is Johnny coming?' I said, unable to swallow the words down any more.

'Dunno,' said Gina, unhelpfully. 'Look, there's Taz.'

'Is Ellie coming?' said Taz.

'Dunno.'

A group of lads from our class appeared in Led Zeppelin T-shirts, trying to swagger; one even had a leather jacket. They were all growing their hair; some lucky with thick, long tresses, some frustrated by wispiness or frizz. Taz and his gang had feather cuts and baggy trousers with envelope pockets – two-tone, some of them – and jumpers with sparkly stars on them, stripes around their waists.

'What do you look like?' said Gina, sauntering round them, counting buttons on waistbands, kicking at platform soles.

'It's all to make you smile,' said Taz. 'Fancy going on the waltzers?'

I'd settled on my newly tie-dyed grandad shirt and quilted jacket – hippie-ish, but not dull, I hoped – the jacket was a gorgeous plum colour with a paisley trim; even Cora had admired it.

Waltzers, Ferris wheels, dodgems – we soared, the hair on our arms erect with excitement and chill; screamed as the earth jumped up to meet us, hair streaked back. Then the hall of mirrors, squealing as our bodies swelled and elongated, our faces squashed and sucked-in. Bumper cars, coconut shies, rifle ranges – we challenged each other, claimed badges and balloons and kiss-me hats. Robbie was so excited he took up the offer – grabbed my waist and then lost his confidence and pecked the air. He tried to kiss Cora too, and would have given Gina a go if she'd stayed still long enough, but she couldn't be contained, darting through the crowds like a swallow and then appearing flushed and panting with a juicy titbit of news wriggling between her lips.

137

'You'll never guess!' she breathed, as we were pumping the slot machine with windfall coins. 'Rose and Rachel are here and they're in Bay City Rollers gear!'

'The tartan trousers?'

'Rose? She can't stand the Bay City Rollers. Rose's the ballady type – you know, "Bridge over Troubled Water", that sort of thing.' Cora howled a line of the song and we laughed.

'She liked "Bye Bye Baby",' I said. 'I remember her singing it down Silver Blades, skating around in rapture.'

'Come on then, let's check it out,' said Taz. 'Any sign of Ellie yet?'

Rose and Rachel were trying to win giant tartan teddies by throwing hoops over stakes.

'Hey,' said Gina, 'like the gear, Rose. Who's your favourite – Quiet Woody? Moody Les?'

'Just ignore them, Rose,' said Rachel.

'What about you, Rach?' said Taz. 'Are you trying to win an Eric bear?'

'It's Rachel to you.'

'Oh, excuse me.'

'Haven't seen you on any of the rides, Rose,' said Cora. Rose loved the rides, being whirled around. First-on-last-off, that was her, at the Mop. 'What's the matter, lost your bottle this year?'

'I just don't feel like it, all right,' said Rose. She flung a hoop too hard and hit the canvas at the back of the stall.

'We prefer the stalls, actually,' said Rachel.

'You can come with us if you want.' I couldn't help saying it. It just seemed so sad, seeing Rose there, in her fancy-dress outfit, wandering aimlessly from hoopla to skittles when she could have been flying around the sky. The tinny fairground music playing from the stall stuttered. Rachel shifted from foot to foot.

'Girls!' There was a shout from behind and the skin on the back of my neck prickled. Johnny put one arm round Cora and one round me. She leant into him and bright green streaks of jealousy shot up and down my veins. 'Have you been on the Ferris wheel yet?' he said. 'It's wild, much bigger than last year. Come on.' Johnny danced off, pulling me and Cora with him.

As Johnny wheeled me round the corner I caught sight of Rachel throwing a hoop. It snagged a stake.

'There,' said Rachel, as loud as she could. 'We've won a teddy. Won't that be something to remember the Mop by?'

From there on it was magic; pure, bright, clear magic. I could have sung, I probably did. And it wasn't just me. Ellie arrived, gasping for breath. 'I've just run a four-minute mile,' she said.

'How did you get away?' said Gina.

'Down the drainpipe. They're glued to *When the Boat Comes In*, so I should be safe for an hour or so.'

'Let's not waste any time then,' said Taz, grabbing her hand.

Gina and Cora nudged each other. I slid on the gravelly ground – I couldn't seem to keep my balance – and was rescued by Johnny.

'Fancy the dodgems?' he said. 'Come on, me and you against Cora and my sis.'

'*You will be exterminated*,' said Gina.

I laughed the loudest, happiest laugh of the whole fair.

The moon came up late, casting its eerie fluorescent glow over the remains of the Mop. It was nearly over and I thought I might cry. The rides had finished, lights were being switched off, fairground workers hung around the food stalls munching hotdogs and slurping tea. We were ankle deep in chip wrappers, popcorn cones, burst balloons, discarded trinkets. Taz and Ellie had gone long ago – he'd offered to walk her home, she'd said yes with a nervous-excited quiver.

Johnny had disappeared.

'What are you doing now?' I said to Gina, trying to be casual. I scanned the fair for signs of him. There were some hunched shapes round the back of a trailer, lads squatting in a circle. 'Is that your brother?' I said. 'What are they doing?'

Cora and Gina exchanged glances. 'Skinning up by the looks of it,' said Cora.

'What? Dope?' I could just make out Johnny's curly head bent down, his face lit up for a second by a match flare. 'But he's in such trouble already.'

'He couldn't care less about that,' said Gina. 'He couldn't care less about anything.'

Cora was heading in their direction, and I followed, slid down on my haunches behind the boys and let the wetness from the tarpaulin seep through my clothes. Couldn't care less about anything? That wasn't true, surely. How could the boy with sparklers in his eyes, the boy who I'd just laughed with until my sides ached, not care? Gina was still upset, that's all, he was her brother for God's sake. You can't just say 'He couldn't care less' about your brother and leave it at that. I say that about Mum sometimes – oh, she couldn't care less what the neighbours think – but that doesn't mean she doesn't care at all, does it?

'Alice? You still with us?' It was Cora. I looked up to a circle of grinning faces. Cora's was wreathed in smoke, Gina was rocking blissfully. 'Do you want some?' said Cora.

'Nice smoke, Johnny,' someone said.

'Almost as good as Rushy's brother's stuff,' said Johnny. His eyes were glazed, even more beautiful than before. 'Shame the Old Bill have got it.' Everyone laughed; I felt a cold shaft of shock in my chest.

'What about it, Alice?' said Gina.

'Since when have you two smoked?' Cora gave an airy shrug. Giggles erupted up her throat.

'Since now if you ask me,' said Robbie.

Gina was giggling too. 'Oh Alice, you should see your face. You look like we've betrayed your deepest secret.'

'Sad Alice,' said Robbie, pulling a glum clown face.

'She doesn't have to,' said Johnny, casually licking Rizlas and joining them together. His fingers were delicate and deft. A joint appeared between his fingers and he lit it with a flourish.

'Pass it here then,' I said.

After Johnny passed me the joint – my fingers touching his for a second – I took two long sucks and passed it back to him, daring to hold his eyes while I did so. He was beautiful.

140

The dying fair was beautiful. Behind Johnny strings of lights danced fuzzily between canopies and tents. It looked like a medieval carnival, pennants fluttering from domed canvas, smoke rising from glowing coals, the heat drawing us in. I took another joint from Johnny and brushed his wrist with my fingers.

'Blue,' said Gina, staring at her jeans.

I don't know how long we sat there. I thought I'd seen a bloke come up and talk to Cora. She might have gone off with him. The noises of the fair died down, followed by shouts and scuffles as the pubs emptied. Lights went out, one by one. We were huddled in the darkness against the wheels of a trailer, the stilled rides ghostly around us, like abandoned toys. I walked back with Gina and Johnny to their house and we warmed our hands around coffee mugs, sipping and shivering. They were talking about something – the court case – it was the next day apparently.

'Bet Rushy'll have half his family there,' Johnny said. 'Right laugh it's going to be for me on my own.'

'You know how Dad feels about that place,' said Gina. 'And I can't risk skiving school.'

'I'll come,' I said.

Johnny walked me home through the silent streets and when he left he kissed me, swiftly, on the cheek. 'See you tomorrow then,' he said. 'You'll be my lucky charm,' and then he vanished into the orange haze of mist and street-lamp.

I waltzed to my room, Johnny my handsome ghost partner, and slept on a soft cloud suspended above my bed. By morning it was a duvet again, and I was curled underneath it.

'Earth calling Alice,' said Mum, after the third time I'd fallen back to sleep. 'Are you going to school today or what?'

Not school. Court. The word intruded on my dream world and forced me awake. Court. Johnny. Reality.

It had rained in the night and I trudged under watery sunlight to the law courts. It was miles, through Moseley village and out to Balsall Heath, Highgate, the solid chunks of the city centre clustering ahead of me. But I needed to move; to think. My stomach was all nervy spasms; I felt sick with the prospect of being inadequate. A bus crunched past me and sprayed oily puddle-water all over my clean jeans. My hair was squashed and tangled; spots were mushrooming under my skin. My shoes were leaking and I hated every-one in the street – shopkeepers lurking under dripping awn-ings, glazed commuters in their cars, the lollipop lady whose coat repelled water at ten feet. No one else was walking. Some lucky charm.

Nearer the courts there were a few people around, loitering outside the ruched redbrick towers in ill-fitting suits, smoking in doorways. They looked hunted – trapped – and I felt imme-diately sympathetic. The lawyers, stalking the corridors, flick-ing their raven's-wing gowns, were in control, as bossy and efficient and sure of their authority as Dracula in full flow. It struck me that they needed their clients – no lawbreakers, no lawyers – and that there was something basic about this. No kids, no teachers, no school. It felt like such an adult sort of place, where being a kid didn't count for much. Had all these people been bothered by enigmatic spirits when they were teen-agers, I wondered. Were they labelled as in or out before they'd even found a label for themselves?

A breath on my neck. Johnny. 'Hi, gorgeous, you made it then.'

'Looks like it.' I was trying to be cool. The rain had stopped and the sun was glimmering just behind the thin cloud. My wet clothes started to steam.

'You don't have to stay,' said Johnny.

'No, no, it's OK.'

'What's up then?'

'Nothing. I just hope . . . I hope I don't let you down.'

'You're here, aren't you?' A shaft of sunlight broke through the clammy sky. Johnny took my arm. I was dazed, spark-ling. Light bounced off the spires of the law courts and a pale rainbow appeared; a sign, a magic thing.

'Look, Johnny, it's a rainbow!'

'No, darlin', it's another lucky charm.'

The waiting area for the court was packed with anxious bodies. 'Your dad should be here with you,' I said.

Johnny was sanguine. 'I'm OK. I've got you.'

My heart thudded. 'But he's your dad.'

'Alice, you've never even seen your dad.'

'That's different.'

'Yeah. Maybe.'

Johnny was holding my hand. A group of suited men in one corner caught my eye and I recognized one of them as Rushy's father, my doctor.

'Ah, Jonathan; Alice,' he said, striding over, his wide-striped shirt making my eyes go fuzzy. He smelt of Imperial Leather and Brylcream. Mum'd had boyfriends who colonized our bathroom with these things, and I'd sniffed at them suspiciously when I was younger. He smiled widely, stretching his face. I didn't trust him, this man who burnt out verrucas, gave Mum pills. I moved closer to Johnny.

'Where's Rushy?' said Johnny.

'Andrew's at school. His lawyers will deal with matters today.'

'I thought we had to stand up and be questioned.' Johnny had gone red. His voice sounded rough and whiny next to this man's assured speech. But I loved his voice. When it said *darlin'*. I moved out from half behind him.

Rushy's dad was still talking. 'It's nothing to worry about. We're trying to get the case adjourned.'

'I'd have thought you'd want it out of the way,' said Johnny.

'Oh, I do, I do. But there's more evidence to collect – all in your favour, dear boy, about the police operation – and we need more time for that.'

'What evidence?' I said. 'What's the police operation got to do with whose dope it was?'

The stretched face contracted. 'It's OK, Alice,' said Johnny. 'I always said it was a setup.'

'Quite. I'll just check with the lawyers on the new court date and then you two can be off.' He backed off, his eyes fixed on Johnny, flicking to me.

143

'He's a smarm,' I said. 'Don't trust him, Johnny.'

'I don't.'

The room was stuffy, we twitched under damp clothes. Rushy's dad gestured over to us a few times, held his hand up indicating five. We waited.

'I can't stand these places,' said Johnny, pulling at his collar.

'Gina said you'd hate it.'

The clock ticked. Gavels thumped behind closed doors. I began to panic that I'd said the wrong thing – Johnny was scratching the backs of his hands, jiggling his knees.

'It's not that Gina says much about you,' I said. That sounded wrong, too. 'Just that you get . . . well . . . itchy . . .'

'It's all right, darlin',' said Johnny. 'I should have known better than to go out with one of my sister's friends.'

I felt a warm glow curl inside me. 'We going out then?'

'If you want to, Alice.' He said my name like it was a sweet, a pear drop on his tongue.

Mr Rushton came over. 'It'll be a few weeks yet. I'll let you know, OK?'

We sprinted for the exit, for the weak gold sunlight, which was creeping in through the cracks under the door.

Johnny sang all the way back. 'Stairway to Heaven' on his knees on the top floor of the bus he crooned to me, making the old ladies chuckle, shoulders shaking while they pursed their lips.

'Shouldn't you be in school?' said one.

'Day off,' said Johnny, 'all the plumbing's out at our place. Can't have a school without anywhere to *pee*, can we?'

'What school is it?' said another. 'I'll report you if you're lying.'

But we were down the stairs, clatter clatter. My cheeks bursting with laughter, Johnny still singing. 'Freedom, free-dom, freedom, *freedom*.'

We landed on the pavement in a heap, Johnny's face between my breasts. 'Sorry,' he said, lifting his head away.

'It's OK,' I whispered, my voice dwindled by the thud in my throat.

The park was too near school, so we sidestepped down

the backstreets to the cut. Johnny was impressed that I knew the route; I pretended I thought everyone did.

'Oh no,' said Johnny. 'Most of the lads don't even know this way.'

'You mean they go all the way round by the main road?' I said, taking longer leaps, crunching both feet down together in the stubbly grass. Johnny jumped after me. 'Silly lads.'

'Do you know how to get back to the estate from here?'

'Over the pipe bridge and through the lock-ups.'

'How about the High Street?'

'Through the drainage channel by that big oak tree and then along the alleys at the back of Mum's shop.'

'Clever Alice,' said Johnny. Bare willow branches grazed the still water of the cut. A few first snowdrops quivered at the side of the towpath.

'What shall we do now?' he said.

I wasn't expecting that. 'Dunno,' I said. The thud in my throat changed from one of anticipation to panic. I'd scratched my leg coming down the embankment and the blood trickling down was suddenly unbearable. Johnny was peeling the bark off a stick. 'We could walk down the cut to the tunnel,' I said, in a rush. There was countryside at the other end of the tunnel, hills and woods.

'Too far,' said Johnny. He skimmed a couple of stones. Three bounces, I could do better than that.

'We could . . .' I swivelled my head around. Canal, towpath, trees. 'We could climb that tree.'

'What, the big beech?'

'Yes.'

'Been up it a hundred times.'

'A hundred, hey,' I said. The thud was getting irritating, I felt a bit sick. I sat down next to Johnny, picked out a flat stone from the gravel and flicked it over the canal. Five bounces.

'Nice one!' said Johnny. 'Hey, you've cut your leg.' He licked his fingers and bent over to clean my leg with a corner of his T-shirt. His neck was slightly damp and his hair curled and stuck to it. I watched my fingers play with the

145

curls and wondered if I'd passed this obscure testing. Johnny jolted. I froze, my fingers still indenting the soft skin of his neck. I let the pressure off and forced myself to breathe. The air was still; Johnny lifted his head and grinned, kissed my knee on the way up. 'That went right through me,' he said.

'Did it?' I said. My voice had a curl to it, a new tone.

I'd wanted to kiss him for so long I thought I really was going to be sick unless it happened soon. The still air seemed thick, glutinous, cold slabs of it slapping my face whenever I moved; the lapping and trickling of water niggled. I wanted it all tuned in, focused. Johnny's face was close, I could feel the heat from his skin, his damp breath. Between us was warmth and thickness and closeness but underneath I still felt a tinge of panic – I should be saying something, I should be doing something – but I pushed it down, let my fingers spider across his skin. We kissed, I sighed; at last.

We lay in the spiky reeds, faded to parchment over the winter, flattened to the form of our bodies, the sky wide above us. I put my arms out and waved them up and down, making angel shapes. When Johnny sat up, his absence pulled me with him. But I was relieved, he wasn't going to push. Johnny didn't need to push. I felt like I had after the first levitation – exhilarated, a little lost – without the words to explain it. This was better though, because I could use my lips, my hands. I pushed Johnny's shoulders and his head fell back into my lap. Lying there, between the water and the urban wilderness, I kissed him from above, my eyes his sky now.

'Come up and see me,' Johnny sang. The city had crowded in on us since we'd moved from our den on the canalside, body shapes in the reeds and our names carved into a tree stump: JOHNNY & ALICE 4 EVER. We nearly got run over by a number eleven bus and then bumped straight into Sandra coming out of the hairdresser's, her big hair replaced by a sleek bob.

'Hello, Johnny,' she said. 'How's your father?'

Johnny's body stiffened. 'Well, he's still here, if that's what you mean,' he said.

146

Sandra sighed. 'I'm going away,' she said. 'You have to, don't you? When there's nothing left in a place for you?' She stared at us, brushed an invisible hair out of her face.

Johnny just looked down. Sandra leant over to touch him, but baulked and clattered off. The rain had started again, dark splodges appeared on the pavement. We'd stopped in the middle of the street. A large, bearded man scowled at us when we didn't shift for him. Johnny brushed my lips with his and the scowl deepened.

'Got to get away from these prying eyes,' said Johnny. 'Can we go back to yours?'

'In a bit,' I said. 'Mum'll be out soon.'

'Pretend we've got a bubble round us, right,' said Johnny.

'OK,' I said. There was a bubble inside me threatening to burst open. 'Anyone else allowed in?'

'No one,' said Johnny. 'It's us against the world.'

# A Story of My Own

I dream of school; juniors. Of wetting my knickers in assembly, a hot pool spreading out from underneath my crossed legs. Then I'm at Rock Hill walking across the playground and I'm not wearing any knickers. The wind is worrying my skirt and crowds of kids stand around laughing, their faces loom out at me. Then they scatter; someone is advancing from the netball courts. It looks like Wills-Masterson – stooping slightly forward, handbag on arm like a shield – but there's something not quite right about her, something even more menacing. I try to hold my skirt down as the shape advances, but I haven't got enough arms, the wind is quicker, sneakier than me. I need to piss again and know I will if I move, try to run; straight down on to the grey tarmac, the liquid spreading towards a pair of glossy, pointed shoes . . .

'Alice! Alice, wake up. You're dreaming again.'

I open my eyes. Mum's face fades in. 'You OK?' she says. 'I am now.'

'That was a bad one, Alice.' She hands me tea, nudges me to sit up. 'What were you dreaming about anyway?'

I swing my legs out of the bed. 'You're not going to believe this, Mum,' I say. 'But I think I dreamt that Mrs Wills-Masterson turned into Margaret Thatcher.'

Johnny comes round and sits in the kitchen. His dogs sniff round the yard, carefully examining it by smell. There's chocolate in the air today; blown over from Cadbury's; mixed with diesel and baking bread and a tang of metal at the back of your throat, from the welding shop down the alley. Johnny wants to talk about Corinne and the van; he shuffles around casting glances, expecting me to get us started. Instead Mum tells him my dream, she thinks it's hilarious.

'It's just perfect, don't you think?' she says. 'I don't know why I never thought of that before. I remember when I first saw that Mrs Thatcher on the telly my hackles rose straight away, all of their own accord.'

'I remember how much that headmistress wound you all up,' says Johnny.

'Thatcher, Thatcher, milk-snatcher,' I say. 'Everyone's nightmare headmistress.'

I ring the office and tell them I'm not coming in – Johnny and Mum exchange a look – and then I go out, leaving them sitting there with half a pot of tea. It's hot again, busy, the High Street thick with people and I slip in with them, buy trinkets, clips for my hair, a pair of bright bootlaces for Corinne. People call me 'love' and 'bab' and let me pat their babies. It was never like this in the village. I didn't feel as if I could fling an arm out in front of a child if they stepped off the pavement; chat in the baker's was stilted and brief. Dan didn't see the point in trying. 'You go in there for bread, not conversation,' he'd say.

I realize that's what I've come out here for, to think about Dan. Dan the Man, Dan *my* man. Mr Fix-it. Suit, mobile, laptop, fax in the bedroom. He liked the click and whirr of it, said it was sexy, all that business he could manage from his bed. He liked the fact that I am – was – a scientist too; said we balanced each other, public and private sector, a finger in each pie. While he was out pitching for more business I got on with my job in the forensic lab, sifting evidence, analysing and testing; signed cards for colleagues' birthdays and weddings; went to leaving parties and congratulated others when they moved on.

Dan found me staring out of the kitchen window at the back of our house, a plate of congealed food in my hand.

'What's up?' he said, brisk and bristling with the closure of a deal.

'I don't know . . . I just don't know how it all fits together,' I said, watching his face for a flinch, a twitch of recognition. The words slid off him, dropped into a gap.

'Come on, Alice,' he said. 'This is the eighties. We can do anything we want.' I watched him grasp his life, stepping sure-footed into the throng of commuters each morning, briskly dispensing with paperwork, changing direction neatly, cleanly, like à skier, his flank of mountainside flexing slightly to reveal new vistas, new possibilities.

That was before the travellers came to stay. Dan always said they were the sign, the advance wave of a turning tide. But some did come through the village a few years earlier, when Dan was riding his wave, expansion plans and team-building trips and bonuses every few months. He was confident then, nothing threatened him, so when the caravan of buses and vans and kids swarming around on bikes first rumbled through the village it was a curiosity, he was sure they wouldn't stay.

'Well they can't, can they?' he said. 'All the land's private around here.'

'Someone might let them use a patch,' I said.

'Why would anyone want to do that?'

The travellers bothered him, their lifestyle. 'Who'd actually choose to live in an old bus like that?' he said, coming back from the pub tipsy, chatty, a slight sheen of sweat glistening on his skin. 'There was this bloke out the other morning out lighting a fire. Freezing it was and I said "Run out of gas, have you?" and he said "No, just felt like cooking outside this morning." He'd rather be outside with a cold wind up his arse messing about with bits of stick than inside his caravan with a gas ring! I mean, what problem have these people got with houses anyway?'

I looked around ours, soft-lit, spacious, stereo lights dancing in the corner.

Dan flopped down on the sofa next to me, nudging my shoulder. 'And those old caravans aren't worth another few hundred quid every week, are they?' he said.

Ellie said that lots of runaways ended up on the road, home-less kids, drifters. I often wondered if I'd see Gina, although she'd have been in her twenties by then. I imagined what I'd say to her if I met her walking up the lane, a bundle of sticks on her back and layers of coloured skirts. I gave one of the women a lift once, she was walking back from the next village along, rain splashing off her forehead. I asked her about her life and she seemed surprised at my interest.

'It can be tough in winter,' she said. 'But in summer there's nothing like it. I just like to keep moving, I suppose.' Her clothes steamed in the heat of the car and she told me they were off again, into Wales for the winter, where there was a bit more space and they wouldn't have to crowd into laybys or strips of common land. 'Near to some water,' she said, 'a bit of wildness.'

I dropped her off by her van and crunched up my drive, barely through the door before I shrugged my suit off; the labels in the collars scratching at my neck. I cut them out that night, one by one.

After they'd gone there were rumours. A local teenager was pregnant by one of them, they'd killed a sheep and roasted it, tearing strips of meat off with their bare hands. A boy from the village on his cross-country run had stumbled on them in the woods and glimpsed a circle of shadows pacing around a spit-ting fire; strange lanterns hung from the trees.

'It was Halloween,' I said, 'and the one I met was a vegan.'

'I'm not sure you should have given her a lift,' said Dan. He was watching my hands and face as I moved around the kitchen stacking food in cupboards.

'What harm could it do?' I said.

'Nothing, I suppose,' said Dan, leaning against the freshly plastered and painted wall of our kitchen. 'Are you sure you like this colour, Alice? Because we can always change it.'

Dan decorated like some people change clothes; from the minute we moved in, the house was his project. He talked about air conditioning, electronic controls for lights and curtains. In charge and in touch with everything by switch, button and keypad. I thought of the caravans wobbling off down the road out of town, music wheeling out of the front vehicle, and looked down at my hands as they rearranged the freezer.

I sit here in an anonymous café on the High Street. I watch the faces, backwards and forwards, in and out, and when I stand up I slip into the flow, the crush out on the hot street. Taking me past Smith's and the grocer's and the record shop and the draper's with frilly pink knickers hanging in the window. There's babble all around me, *Mail, get your Mail*, and horns honking and the beep of the pedestrian crossing. Snatches of conversation, *I told her, but would she listen?*, the clunk of the cashpoint, *You're not going back to that dump!* I step aside for a man with a stick, nudge an abandoned trolley out of my path and for a few seconds every movement is right; lights change, the traffic stops, we cross the road, the traffic moves on.

As I approach the back gate I know someone is there and I know that it's Johnny. I hitch the latch, already speaking. 'Johnny, I'm sorry,' I say. 'I know you wanted to sort some things out this morning but –'

'It's OK, Alice,' he says. He's leaning against the shed, the dogs settled at his feet, tongues lolled out and panting steadily. 'Everyone's got their stuff going on.'

'I will help if I can,' I say.

'Thanks,' says Johnny. He pushes himself upright and the dogs stir, instantly alert, twirling around his legs in antici-pation. 'I found this for your collection.'

He hands it to me, another photograph. Gina at some kind of festival, twirling a stick between her fingers, silver sun glancing off it as it spins in the air. All around her are unicycles and squeeze-boxes and juggling clubs and drums; she is in some sort of a circus. I pin it up next to the other pictures in the shed, and run my eyes along the collection, trying to resist the temp-tation to fill in the gaps with a story of my own.

When I remember to look up, Johnny has gone.

Pinned to the shed there's a note. *Be back in a while with Corinne.* I go upstairs and put on my new, summery clothes, flimsy and light and colourful, and I wonder how I ever tolerated those suits and tights and pinching shoes. Dan liked them: my jackets neatly tucked at the waist. We'd brush each other's collars before we went out of the door. I wander back into the yard thinking of me, a teenager, trying to pin down the strangeness of our lives by asking questions, expecting answers in a line, a, b, c. Maybe that was just me. I remember how this yard pulsed with life, the power of it, my head full of outrage and confusion and longing. It pulses now, a green glimmer on a puddle, a cluster of buttercups glossy yellow.

I go next door to buy a paper, filled with vague pleasure about the day ahead. Something has lifted or shifted and it's to do with Johnny, his acceptance of me. The way I can say *Later, Johnny* and he goes *Fine*. I scan the papers, deciding which one to buy but the headline in the local rag snags me and puts me off all of them.

### TRAVELLER PLAGUE HITS SUBURBS
Into our streets they come, the so-called New Age Travellers. But what is new about disruption, rubbish, drugs and indiscipline?

I think of Corinne, blowing on her hands, her red rag of a skirt caught up in the wind, ruffling a dog's ears and chattering. Every step a bounce, hands whirring round her face as she talks. A shaft of anger jerks through me, setting off a waver deep down. Part of me is scared for Corinne, I realize, scared of what might happen to her. Like I was for Gina.

Johnny and Corinne arrive geared up for a day out, time out, as Corinne says. 'Some old mates have turned up.' Their fate, the court case, sidelined for a while. She spins round the hallway watching herself in the mirrors, laughing, as excited as a kid at the fair. 'Got any clothes you don't want?' she says.

'Yes,' I say. 'There's cupboards full of my old stuff.'

'Told you,' she says to Johnny. 'Let's have a look.'

When we go out she is wearing my jeans – open at the waist, but still neat round the arse, as she says. My tie-dyed shirt, an old waistcoat that came from a jumble sale in the first place. I remember it; a Scout hut smelling of mothballs and old shoes. She even found my clogs, red ones on which I'd painted silver flowers with nail varnish.

'I remember them,' says Johnny. He is quiet as Corinne chatters us down the road. 'Clear as yesterday.'

'Is it?' I say.

He stops. Cuts a curve out of the air with his hand echoing my shoulder, waist, hip. 'How could I forget, Alice?' he says. 'It'd be like forgetting my own name.'

The Bridge is packed. Corinne leaps with excitement and runs off into the crowd.

'She's happy,' I say. 'You're good to her, Johnny.' It's a leading question.

'Look, Alice,' he says, turning towards me. 'Don't worry about me in all this, just get her off, hey?'

I'm still stunned by Johnny's memories of me. One of those moments, a doubletake, an instant reflection, where how you imagine yourself and how others remember you jar. For a second I see myself as he did, striding up to the law courts in the rain, slipping my arm through his and keeping hold of it, facing wigs and gavels and stripy shirts together.

Across the room Corinne is showing off her clogs. Johnny passes me a pint and I take a long swig, the cool thick liquid slipping down my throat. The sky is clear.

'Just got to catch up with a few folk,' says Johnny. 'OK?'

'Course.'

Corinne joins me out on the towpath; we people watch. Noisy voices rise up from the general hum – chattering, arguing, exclaiming. I haven't heard such a racket since the school playground; my other life was quiet. Civilized, some would say. Not wild, like this lot. Mostly I watch Johnny, sitting on a bench, legs splayed, telling a tale. The canal bank is a mess of colour, clinking glasses, noise and chatter. People peel off layers, sun their shoulders, lie back on the grassy bank releasing groans of pleasure. Corinne laughs, she loves this.

'Where do they all live?' I ask. 'How do you find each other?' None of these people have addresses, phone numbers, they're not attached in that way.

'Word gets about,' she says. 'That's the beauty of travelling, you'll always bump into someone.'

We watch a gang of lads arrive, dumping their sports bags in a pile. They wear tracksuits, trainers, sweatshirts; all with names on: Adidas, Reebok, Hilfiger.

'Maybe they wear those so they can remember who they are,' giggles Corinne. 'Imagine if I called my baby Nike –'

'I'm not sure Johnny would think much of that,' I say.

Corinne stares at me. 'What's it got to do with Johnny?'

I escape to the toilet to hide my red face, watch the blood pricking in my pores and splash it down with water.

On the way back outside Johnny corners me. 'How about if you talk to the court?' he says. 'None of this was Corinne's fault, it's only because she knows me that she's in trouble.'

I want to say yes, of course, to wave a magic wand and make it all right for them both. 'I'll try,' I say. 'I will try, Johnny.'

'It's dead simple,' says Johnny. 'I'm guilty, she's innocent. Only they won't take that from me, they think I'm trying to pull some kind of weird con-trick so as I'll get off as well.' As he moves off he glances back at me, a raggety thread of conscience spinning between us. 'Just tell them, Alice,' he mouths.

Corinne is talking to the sporty boys, they're all leaning in to listen to her. That much has changed; when me and Johnny were younger you were rock or pop; reggae or soul; a different species if you liked different music or wore different clothes or came from another town. Now it seems possible to cross the lines, to try living another way. A voice winds over from the jukebox, a song I recognize but I can't quite pin down, and I wonder how these decisions really get made. An impulse – I'm going to India, I'm going on the road, I'm going to change my life – the reasons filled in later, stringing events into narrative, words into explanation. I remember how I tested theories at work; measuring, tabulating, cross-checking. 'Every contact leaves a trace', the forensic scientist's mantra gilt-framed on the wall. A tyre mark, a scrap of clothing – I would build the story up from these traces; draw a conclusion. Except in arson, of course. A successful crime of arson destroys its own evidence. I never managed to apply the methods in my personal life even then, although I was willing to build my life up from a degree, a husband, a house. Someone somewhere told me that's what I should do.

I find that I'm singing along: 'Why not leave? Why not go away?'

'That's the question, isn't it?' A voice next to me. 'Why not?' A man has appeared out of nowhere. He has serious, steady eyes.

'What?' I say. 'Do a Reggie Perrin? I must admit, it sounds tempting –'

'Why don't you then?'

'Well . . .' His questions irritate me slightly. Who is this person, this voice from nowhere? But I still feel compelled to answer. 'There's my mum for a start,' I say, 'and . . .' I can't think of anything else, except that I'm too old for it, that it's the sort of thing you do when you're a teenager. That I should be sorted out by now.

He's a mind reader. 'You shouldn't worry about that,' he says. 'Our whole society is adolescent. Take that group in the corner. They're all in their thirties, with kids and careers, but they still want to be young and funky and somewhere deep down they know that their future's no more certain than these travellers. It's all a process. You don't get to one point and stop.' I stare out at the wind-ruffled water. 'Think about it,' he says, then disappears into the blackness of the pub.

I stare at the space he was in, his voice, his command echoing around my head and then lie back on the grass, clutch fistfuls of it, feeling suddenly dizzy, queasy, the sun spinning wildly in the sky above me. Corinne and Johnny and the stranger in my head; Mum and Mr McGeady and a spirit or two, still lurking, waiting to be called.

I jerk up suddenly, my eyes still dazed, and leave the pub; stumble along the High Street to the graveyard. There's a stone engraved with his name, the dates he lived, In Memoriam. The stone is clean and the grass clipped back, but it's not smothered with flowers, notes, mementoes, as some of the others are. It's blank; a space, like my knowledge of him, my father. There are other people in the graveyard, drifting around, staring at the place where their loved ones are not, and everyone is alone, alone with their memories. But I have none, so I walk past his stone again and leave. Maybe next time I'll bring flowers.

A man is standing at the entrance to the graveyard. I only notice him because he's wearing odd, old-fashioned clothes – a deerstalker hat, riding boots past his knees. I expect to exchange glances like I have with the other mourners, in deference to the grief we suppose each other must be feeling, but he turns his face away, rather sharply. As I hurry off I fancy that he changes his mind, leans forward as I pass, wanting to speak. But I've had enough of speaking with strangers, of letting other voices crowd my head. I steady myself, look at the sky until I can see the sun distinct from the blue, until the only voice left that I'm hearing is a silent note, steady and clear, thrumming through my body like sound travelling underwater. And the music from the juke-box is still in my head, muffled, half-recognized, telling the stories of our lives.

# Mutiny

Another day of school over and we met up and headed in silence for the shed. Gina was morose, Cora preoccupied, and I felt guilty about the occasional blasts of euphoria that burst through my skin of anxiety. I skipped occasionally, returning quickly to a shamble, hoping the others hadn't noticed. I *did* care about Gina, and I couldn't understand why she – and us – were being hounded. But then again I didn't understand why I felt the wrong shape without Johnny near by, why my body leant towards wherever I thought he might be. I didn't understand levitation, or Ouija boards, or why more things seemed possible at dusk. The exciting things were as incomprehensible as the frightening ones, the distinctions fudged; nothing was obvious except that I wanted Johnny. Thinking about anything else caused my mind to cloud over, sinking Gina, Cora, fires, spirits, witches, scapegoats and Dracula into a jumble as messy and entangled as any that surrounded the shed. Will it ever become clear, I thought, a path open up, shining and unequivocal, like the yellow brick road?

The yard was dark and quiet and cold. We fetched candles and hot tea from the flat and pinned up some old cloth over the shed window to try and warm the place up. The cat appeared, circled around us twitching his tail and then settled on a shelf to watch, his huge amber eyes glinting.

'Come on, Gina,' said Cora. 'What's worse today than yesterday?'

Gina's hands were cupped around a candle. They were transparent, bones and knuckles showing through her skin. Her face flickered in the yellowy light.

'Don't worry about it,' I said, trying to sound confident. My voice was all wrong, too chirpy, like a newsreader smiling through some terrible announcement. 'Dracula's got no evidence against you. The only people that know you had anything to do with the fires are us, and we're not telling.'

'And Rose,' said Gina.

'She won't say anything,' said Cora.

'How d'you know?' said Gina.

'Because I'll fill her face in if she does. Pious little sneak. I wouldn't be surprised if she's said something already.'

'She wouldn't.'

The candle stuttered, struggling against a draught. The cold pressed down on us.

'Well, someone has,' said Gina. 'Wilson stopped me after class this afternoon, told me that a report's been made. A person with dark curly hair was seen round the back of the sixth-form block on the morning of the fire.'

Cold trickled through my stomach. Shadows stalked the walls behind us: Cora's head; her hooped earrings elongating into ovals; Gina's hands, still cupped around the flame, became a forest of fingers, twitching. The cat arched its back and slunk out, the ghost of a great creature slipping into the darkness.

'Ask the spirit if you don't believe me,' Gina burst out. 'I was in *here*, with him.'

'Of course we believe you,' said Cora.

'They've still got no proof,' I said. 'There's got to be a way round this.'

Gina seemed to be sinking into the bench. She looked like her dad, as he sat at the kitchen table, saying 'Don't give up on me', and I couldn't bear it, felt her slipping away. There was nothing I could do.

'There's only one thing for it,' said Cora. 'We're going to have to ask the spirit.' The glass shimmered in the candlelight.

'One question, right? Let's keep it simple,' said Cora. 'We'll just say, "How can we help Gina?"'

I could feel the tingling immediately, the edginess, as we reached out – three hands now – to the glass. The wavering candlelight and the importance of the question sobered us; Cora breathed heavily, Gina looked solemn. I felt tight-chested, the pit of my stomach clenched in a new, untranslatable way and Johnny's grin flashed into my head with such clarity that, for a moment, I was sure *he* was the spirit. This was too mad to tell even Gina or Cora. Anyway, Johnny didn't want them to know about us. I want something that's just mine, he had said. That I don't have to share with the rest of the world. His words had set off a slow fizzing inside of me and I nodded mutely.

'Ready?' said Cora.

'Right. Spirit? Are you there?'

There was a clatter: the cat jumping on to the roof of the shed, his claws scraping. I could see a thud at the base of Gina's throat. The glass shifted.

YES.

The noise of traffic from the High Street stopped dead, the cat on the roof stilled mid-pounce. A flush was creeping up Cora's neck, but she was shivering, we all were; us and the light and the glass vibrating.

'It's not moving,' Gina whispered.

'It will,' I said.

'Shush,' said Cora. The glass shifted; we all felt it.

'How can we help Gina?' I said, in a rush. The glass was moving before I'd finished.

A–S–K   W–H–Y

'Ask why?' snapped Gina. 'If I thought there was any *reason* for all this I'd be out there sorting it, not sitting here talking to a bloody spirit.'

'Wait,' said Cora. 'It's moving again.'

The glass skimmed across the board.

A–S–K   T–H–E–M   W–H–Y

The candle burnt to nothing in front of us. It was getting colder – I thought of the snowdrops freezing on the canal bank

– we could hear ice tiptoeing over the roof, rising up in puddles.

Something cracked outside – the cat? – and Gina straightened her back with a jerk. 'That's it!' she said. 'He means ask Them why. School. Turn the tables. Ask them why would I light the fires. They've got to give a reason, haven't they? I mean, what do I get out of burning down half the school?'

*Ask them why.* Gina changed after that. Her mouth slid over to one side of her face, fixed into a permanent scowl. She stared people out; said 'So?' and 'Yeah?' and 'Really?' Her hair turned wiry, electric, standing up in black question marks around her face. I don't think I ever saw her comb it again. Her clothes – always casual and loose – melded into one shade of sludge. I wore tie-dyed purple grandad shirts, Cora fishnets and leather; Gina wore a sack. She looked like a ragamuffin, Stig of the dump. Her mouth turned up a fraction when I said it, while we were hanging around the rec waiting for Cora.

'Well, I come from a dump, anyway,' she said.

'Your house isn't a dump,' I said.

'Have you been down our way lately?' said Gina.

Any excuse would do. Johnny had been strangely elusive since our day together. 'It's not that I don't want to see you,' he said, on the phone, 'but there's other things happening and you're best out of it.' Something told me if I fussed too much, demanded to know what was going on, it would only close him up more and that was no good. I had to be someone he could trust. 'One day it'll all be over,' he said. *It,* I thought. Does he mean us?

'Let's go now,' I said to Gina. 'I'd like to see your dad, Johnny . . .'

'You're mad,' she said, tapping her temple with one long finger. 'Who'd want to see them? All they do is eat chips and glower at each other while the footy's on. Johnny hasn't even got a suit to wear for when his case comes up again.'

'Case? Why? Has he got a date for it?'

'Dunno.' Gina snatched at a clump of grass. It had just started to grow again, out of the slushy mud.

'Gina, you do –'

She put a piece of grass between her thumbs and blew.
'Gina, tell me.'

The shriek from the grass was piercing. Birds burst out of the trees, kids' heads swivelled.

'You should go with him, Gina, he's your brother.'

'If I need telling what to do I'll go back into school.'

Cora had been kept in after lessons for defacing the portraits in the hall next to Dracula's office. Gina was the culprit, but we were alternating between taking the rap for her since she'd grown to fit her rebel label otherwise she'd get expelled for sure. The previous week I'd been in detention three times; four times in one week meant instant suspension. But Gina was like a tornado around school, there was no way of stopping her. She ripped coat pegs from the wall, tore up posters (Rachel Williamson had done one on citizen responsibility; Gina shredded it), chewed gum with loud smacks all the way through assembly. If she was caught she just faced out the teachers with 'Why?' – smack, smack – 'Why would I do that?' There was real hate in the air now, real venom. I wrote frantic notes to Ellie. *What can we do about Gina? What's she going to do if she gets expelled?*

Cora sauntered over to us in the rec. She didn't seem to care about much either, but she was more casual about it.

'Johnny's up in court again soon,' I said.

'You're very interested in Johnny, aren't you?' said Cora.

'I can't believe you're not. Jesus, the guy's in trouble.' Cora and Gina looked at least a little bit guilty, and I swooped on my small advantage. 'You two couldn't give a toss about anyone else, these days. I bet neither of you have been in touch with Ellie.' I knew they hadn't; Ellie had complained about it in one of her notes to me. *I bet Gina and Cora never even think of me, shut up here with nothing but schoolbooks for company.* Ellie's mum's tactic – she's ill, she can work from home.

Cora brushed imaginary dust off her skirt.

Gina spat out the grass she was chewing. 'OK,' she said. 'Let's go and see that brother of mine.'

The Marshall house did look a bit dumpish. Mucky

windows, an old car on bricks outside. We went in. Johnny was rooted to the sofa. He didn't look up.

'Where's Dad?'

'Out.'

'Oh.' Gina went into the kitchen. Cora asked to use the phone.

'I hear you've got a date through for court,' I said, sounding like an embarrassing aunty. But what else could I do? I couldn't ignore it, pretend it wasn't happening, settle down to watch *Scooby Do*. I glanced sideways at him. His chin was on his chest, knees jiggling. 'Are you all right about it?' I said, my shoulder millimetres away from his. 'Are you scared?'

Johnny's head twisted towards me. He looked hard into my eyes. 'Scared? Nah. Probably just get a fine, a telling-off. But you can come along again if you like. Be nice to have something worth looking at when I'm up in front of the beak.' His eyes were smiling, like they had on the canal bank. A smile just for me.

I flushed, managed to smile back. Keep letting them know you're interested, that's what Cathy & Claire say. But how could he not know, with me sitting there practically panting, my heart thudding?

'Anyone for a cuppa?' Gina called from the kitchen.

'Yes please,' I stuttered.

'That would be nice,' said Johnny, still holding my eyes. 'Very nice indeed.'

I sat back on the sofa, close enough to feel Johnny's breathing as his chest rose and fell. All I needed was Johnny to smile and everything clicked into place. If only I could carry on feeling like this maybe I could tidy the mess we were all in, untangle all the knots. I glowed, sat as close to him as I dared.

'Tea,' said Gina.

'I'll be there in an hour,' said Cora, still on the phone.

'D'you want one, Cora?' said Gina.

'No ta. So you all right for next week then, Johnny?'

Things weren't so bad. We were friends, we'd help each other, get Gina through this. We just had to stick with her, that's all. And, as for Johnny, how could anyone think Johnny was a bad person? The magistrate would see that straight away.

'Rushy's brief thinks I'll get off with a caution,' said Johnny.

'I said he should have got his own brief,' said Gina.

I could see us in court. Me, brave and supportive. Johnny blurting out the truth, 'I didn't want my friend to get into trouble,' and the magistrate reassuring him, 'I understand, son, but in matters of the law it's always best to be honest, let the courts do the rest.' Cheers from me. A wave and a blown kiss from Johnny.

'Might have been an idea,' said Cora.

'It's just a procedure. Routine, that's what Rushy's brother says.'

'Rushy's brother's the one who can get all the good dope, isn't he?' said Cora. 'I wouldn't mind meeting him.'

'He probably wouldn't mind meeting you,' said Johnny. Cora's breasts swelled inside her too-small school blouse. I felt cold shock slice my lungs.

Cora laughed. 'Another time, OK?' she said, slinging her bag over her shoulders.

'I can get it for you if you want,' said Johnny.

'I think I'd rather get to know Rushy's brother,' said Cora.

'I'm sure you would.' Johnny winked. At Cora. The shock spread down to my stomach and legs. I was frozen to the sofa.

'Anyway, I'm off,' said Cora. 'See you tomorrow.'

'Don't do anything I wouldn't,' said Johnny.

'Would I?' said Cora. She tipped her head, mock-innocent. For a second I hated her. And her cleavage.

'Anyone want a sandwich?' said Gina.

'No ta,' said Johnny. He got up suddenly and followed Cora out of the door.

'No thanks,' I said. The room was cold and shabby. A brown sludge, like Gina's clothes. There was a smell of burnt dust from the boiler. Gina sat down with her peanut butter sandwich and I fled before she could see the tears leaking out of the corners of my screwed-up eyes.

At home that night I sat in front of the mirror in Mum's room trying to push my breasts up with one of her bras. Then I found an old school blouse and fastened it – straining – over the lace.

164

It looked terrible but I still tried a few poses, a tip of the head like Cora's.

'Oo er,' said Mum, appearing at the door. I snatched up a T-shirt.

'What's up with you?' said Mum.

'Get lost.'

'Alice, you're lovely, OK.' She swished up and down the corridor playing with her own reflection. 'How could a daughter of mine not be?'

This was my cue to join in the parade and we would laugh and be friends. Us against the world. I sat and said nothing.

'Oh go on, talk to me, Alice,' said Mum. 'I've only had one customer in the shop all day, and he was a dirty old man trying to get me up the stepladders. But then this came through the door.' She had a letter in her hand. 'It's from him,' she said. I could feel the glow from her face and see how it changed her; every movement more gracious, every utterance brighter. 'I'm starting to actually believe this is someone who really cares, Alice.'

'Mmm,' I said. I didn't believe it, but Mum was away with the fairies.

'Anyway, I wanted to put it in my box – you know, the one with all his other letters in – and it's gone missing, mysteriously. Will you look through your stuff please? I can't think where it's got to.'

A letter, a smile, tiny moments of clarity. I went to bed and – before I'd even fallen asleep – conjured up me and Johnny walking in the sunset, him lifting me up and spinning me around, my legs and arms tracing arcs in the air and my skin glowing like Mum's. Then I fell asleep and dreamt that I was lost in a jungle of motorways, roads, factories and flashing lights; but in there somewhere was a box – glowing, tumescent – and if I found it everything would fall into place. I could make everything all right.

# A Song You Never Forget

Some post arrives from Dan. It is junk mail mostly but a few other things: medical card, P45, some old letters from Ellie. I reread them, sitting in Mum's bedroom where the sun is coming through the net curtains in a haze. Corinne arrives and sits with me while I read about child immunization and sinking wells. There's a few photographs of Ellie crowded by children, and I show them to Corinne.

'Who's this?' she says, passing me a picture of a black-haired girl on a mountainside, a horseshoe of icy peaks behind, mountain kids all around; straggle-haired. Four layers of jumper and bare feet.

'That's Gina,' I say. I remember it now, the photo sent to Ellie and then on to me. Gina teaching in the Himalayas. English.

'You've got to help Johnny,' says Corinne, staring at the photograph. That's what she's come here for. The High Street rumbles below us, we watch the tops of lorries go past, buses' roofs splattered with pigeon droppings. 'They'll be OK with me; being pregnant and everything, but Johnny, well, no one gives the benefit of the doubt to blokes like him. But you know that. You've seen it all before.'

I realize she must be talking about me and Johnny as teenagers. 'How come you know so much about us?' I say.

Corinne looks a little puzzled. 'Must have just seeped

through, I suppose,' she says. 'Maybe when you've known someone so long their life just becomes part of yours.'

'Corinne,' I say, 'you're not even twenty yet.'

The sun is warm, the noises of the High Street sleepily familiar. Corinne lies back on the bed and her breathing slows. 'You will help him?' she murmurs, her lids closed, her belly rising and falling.

'I'll try,' I say.

'Johnny's sure you can do it,' she says.

'I will,' I say. 'Somehow.'

Somehow. At the office they say I should get him a lawyer. But Johnny says he's done with lawyers. There are some technicalities over the evidence that could delay things a bit. We could petition for a new date perhaps, there's a small chance. I've heard there might be a more sympathetic judge on the circuit soon, one who doesn't think no fixed abode equals scum of the earth. But there's no obvious way to sort it, no direct route. Dan would say forget it, Alice, lost cause, but I'm not listening to his voice any more. It feels stubborn to ignore him, to ignore all of them; reckless. I wasn't brought up to ignore what I'm told. But then I think *Why not?* and no answer comes.

'You can use this address if you need to,' I say to Corinne. 'Mum doesn't mind.'

At first I thought Mum might disapprove of the travellers, the clothes, the lifestyle, but she surprised me by liking Corinne; her spirit, she said. Treats the coming baby like it's practically her grandchild and tells Corinne not to worry, Alice will sort it out, what with her education and all.

'I'm not ashamed of living in a bender,' says Corinne. 'Why should I lie?'

I go down to the shed and add the new photograph to the others. There are quite a few now, and I have to shift some boxes so I can get to the far wall, lean back on them to look at the pictures. Gina doesn't seem any different, only the backdrops have changed. She still wears jeans and old shirts, her tangle of hair escaping from a scarf. She still screws her eyes up at the camera, looks slightly irritated that someone

167

might want to capture this moment. Yet she sent us photos. Me in the early days, Ellie a bit later. I wonder if there are other scraps of her life around, sent to Cora, or even Rose.

A crash. The boxes behind me collapse and spill out and I stagger into the debris of old pennies and paperclips and boxes of earrings we made from beads and feathers, some idea about selling them, I vaguely remember. And a bundle of letters, Rose's writing at the top, I recognize it immediately; fat, curvy *a*s and *c*s, and little full moons for dots above *i*s and *j*s: 'received from Jayne M. 10 November 1976'. And underneath, in an excited scrawl, *Dear Rose, wow, exciting news about Taz, gosh, is there any boy in your school that doesn't fancy you? Let me know when you've snogged him, I'm dying to know what it's like.* Taz and Rose? I think. What was she telling people that for? I skim the rest of the letters – each one from a different girl, Rose's Catholic penpals – she must have hidden them in the shed. All shocked-thrilled responses to Rose's stories of Taz and Robbie and Johnny and even Kenny Marshall. *You let him put his hand up your jumper? He wanted to stroke your knickers? Oh Rose, you didn't . . .*

No; almost certainly not. But she wanted someone to think that she did.


I have to go, to meet Johnny in the Bridge. He can't sit still in the office, keeps glancing round at the street as if someone might come in any minute and feel his collar. The High Street is as busy as ever; old ladies with headscarves and battered, checked shopping bags, nimble kids with bulging pockets. A tramp on the bench outside the church, crooning to his trolley; shouts and curses and squealing brakes and smells of bread from the bakery and vans thudding piles of newsprint in the street. I walk past the record shop where as girls we would scour the secondhand LPs; I found *Hard Nose on the Highway*, Gina a scratched copy of *Blood on the Tracks* from which we transcribed every word. I swear she took that album cover to bed with her. Now it is CDs, shiny and expensive, but the track that's playing is one from back then, 'Whole Lotta Love'.

The man behind the counter is fingering guitar chords in the air, staring at me; I realize my head is bouncing along – an instinct, imprinted behaviour. 'Now there's a song you never forget,' he says. 'Top of the charts, they are. And ol' Dylan. We must have been doing something right, heh?'

In the pub Johnny is relaxed, in his element, saying 'Hiya, all right mate' to everyone, people buying him drinks and asking his advice about sites and engines and what's happening this summer, man.

He grins when I come in, introduces me to people. 'Let's go and sit outside,' he says. 'It's a beautiful day.'

'Did you know Gina was in the Himalayas?' I say. 'She sent a photo to Ellie. It makes me wonder if she might have sent some to the others, you know, Rose and Cora.'

Johnny's eyes cloud for a moment, a stiffening in his face. I'm so aware of him it's absurd, every tiny involuntary movement clocked. 'The Himalayas,' he says. 'Where hasn't she been?'

'Corinne's over at mine,' I say. 'She's told me not to worry about her, to try and help you.'

'She's a good kid,' says Johnny, his eyes soft now, a hint of amusement, affection.

'I thought the baby was yours,' I say. The words are out before I can gulp them back in. Good, I think, I've said it. Johnny stares at me. His body is so close I have to shove my hands hard into my pockets to stop them reaching out to him.

'We're friends, Alice,' he says. 'I'm more like her uncle than anything. But we're close, you know, all of us. Stick together, like.'

He takes my hand. 'And now we've got you.'

'I've not been much help so far,' I say.

'There's always a way,' he says. 'You'll find it.'

He smells of leather and woodsmoke. The sun glints on the canal, diamonds of light and water. I am dazed by it, want to say, Yes! Of course I can fix it, Johnny, and be rewarded with roses and kisses and undivided attention. I want to sit here in the sunshine and have my leg stroked gently. For the first time since coming back I allow myself to look at

169

him, properly, lingeringly. His fingernails are black, his hands rough as I turn them in mine. There are grass stains on his jeans, seeds in his hair. He is brown, wildish, has a gold tooth and a ring in his ear.

'Gypsy Johnny,' I say.

'Something like that,' he says.

I open my mouth to speak – who knows what words, doubts probably, worries – but he can tell and he stops me. Hand over my mouth. Mouth over my mouth. I become a liquid pool, floating out over the water, rippling in the breeze. I am beautiful, flickering.

'Don't say anything,' whispers Johnny. 'Not today. Let's just have today, Alice.'

I am weak. I like being weak. 'OK, just today.'

Johnny grins; he licks my lips.

Someone wolf-whistles, kids snigger from behind a bush. Johnny strokes my arm, takes a gulp of beer and I move my face to meet his. There is the scent of honeysuckle in the air; the elderberries lining the canal are frosted with tiny blossoms; summer snow. A boat chugs past and toots its horn and I feel like I'm in a film, a long shot moving towards a couple on a canal bank, barely a slice of air between their bodies.

Corinne appears and gives an excited skip when she sees Johnny's arm round my shoulders. Johnny goes to the bar for drinks and is on his way back when Pete, one of the fishermen from the canal bank, bursts through the door. Corinne has befriended them; they fetch water and wood and watch out for her, she brews them tea, knows the names of their children and dogs.

Pete is panting, red-faced. 'Quick!' he says, grabbing Corinne by the shoulder. 'They've got a barge with a crane on it down by your bender. I think they're going to try and take away the van.'

My legs are still weak from emotion but I move with everyone else, like a wave, towards the door.

'They won't be able to shift it.'

'They will if the crane's big enough.'

'Bastards.'

'How did they get the barge down the cut anyway? There's been hardly any water in that section for weeks.'

'Must've released some from the lakes.'

'Just so they can get at an old traveller's van?'

'Bastards.'

The van looms forward from the back of my mind. The van with the secret compartment, the van that is evidence against them both. No van no evidence no case. Pete is badgering Corinne about it being her property, how they can't take it away. But she is shaking her head, she knows all about evictions, vehicles and trucks being impounded, *notice to quit* slapped on the side of her home.

'They can do anything they like,' she says.

Johnny is white, grim-mouthed. 'Should have moved it,' he is muttering. 'Should have scrapped it.'

'And get done for destroying evidence?' says Corinne. 'You might as well put your hands in the air.'

We race around the corner. Four blokes – bailiffs with eyes sunk into their faces – are trying to get straps under the van, the dogs are yapping at them, one raises his arm. 'Git!' he snarls, at the dog.

'Look at them,' says one of Johnny's mates, Vinny. 'You'd think they'd be out catching criminals or something.'

'If you hit any of my dogs,' says Corinne, 'I'll have the RSPCA down here so fast you won't get your breath.' She walks over to her bender; one corner of it has been trampled on. 'Who did this?' she demands. 'This is my home. You've no right to treat it like a piece of tat.'

The men look at her, bemused. They can't quite connect these events, what their eyes are telling them. Home. Pregnant. Rights. The dogs lie down at Corinne's feet, grumbling, their eyes tracing the bailiffs. The crowd from the pub is an audience too, everyone's watching and the bailiffs know it, cast uneasy glances at us. We spread out along the towpath; Bri the barman has a notebook.

'We've got to move this van,' says one of the men, waving a piece of paper. 'Come on you lot, out of the way.' They've got one strap under it.

171

'Public right of way this,' says Bri. 'Can't move us along from here.'

Pete fetches some bait out of a pocket and attaches it to a hook. The men stare at the wriggling maggots, stupefied.

'You can't fish here!' says one.

Pete prepares his rod, puts his seat down between the men and the barge. The crane arm is right over his head. He whistles. The rest of us loiter between the bailiffs and the crane; Corinne puts one of the dogs on a lead, walks it up and down. I notice Vinny disappearing into a hedgerow, raise my eyes in question, Johnny shushes me. We saunter arm in arm and for a few seconds I am wildly happy, exhilarated by this gentle defiance. Rebel by smiling, by strolling in the sunshine, it seems so clearly a better way. The back way. The way that no one else even knows is there.

The bailiffs are conferring. Corinne potters around her camp, puts a brew on, edges the men back.

'You shouldn't be here,' they say to her, eventually.

The strap has sagged, the van settles back down into the mud. Corinne doesn't even answer them, she is feeding the dogs and the bailiffs appear uncomfortable, as if they have strayed into her front garden.

'Tea?' she says, politely.

Two shake their heads and scowl but one cannot sustain this bad grace. 'No thanks,' he says.

'Are you sure?' she says, holding the teapot ready. 'It's freshly made.'

I have to bury my head in Johnny's chest so as not to laugh, this burlesque scene of dog walking and tea making and English manners becoming too much. The bailiffs glare at me and I smile back. They gather their bags and leave.

'Oi!' yells Bri, as we watch their shrinking figures move down the towpath. 'You've forgotten your crane.'

'We'll be back,' they call.

Back in the pub I try to hold on to the brief feeling of exhilaration but brows soon wrinkle, heads shake.

'They're on to me now,' says Corinne. 'It only winds them up.' Her fingers thread through her hair, her head sags for a moment and a flash of pure fury sparks through me.

My head is swirling with questions, they leap out of my mouth. I'm activated – something I can actually do at last. Would getting rid of the van ourselves be any help? Who owns the field? Can we get them on our side?

'It's owned by a local bloke,' says Corinne. 'I've seen him a couple of times. He's OK as long as I keep the dogs under control and keep promising to move on.'

'I'll go and see him,' I say. 'He might not like the bailiffs on his land.' I am energized, my head is clear.

'Nice one, Alice,' says Johnny.

'I can get a fishing rota going,' says Pete, 'so there'll always be someone around.'

'Make sure they've all got permits,' I say. 'We want this legal.'

'Everything legal?' says Johnny.

'Well, as near as we can,' I say. 'Why?'

Johnny's eyes swivel to the bar, where Vinny's Adam's apple twitches as he empties another glass. Vinny looks dishevelled, triumphant, brushes soft green moss from his trousers. 'Well?' says Johnny.

'Mission accomplished,' says Vinny. 'I've drained Corinne's section of canal from the bottom lock. That barge will float for now, but the minute they put anything heavy on it, like a *van*, for instance, she'll be on the bottom. Take a monsoon to shift her.'

'Won't they just let more water in from the lakes?' says Bri.

'Not without draining the higher sections,' says Johnny. 'And that'll upset people further up, they'll get complaints.'

'Perhaps I'd better go and see the Waterways too,' I say.

# A Trial Examined

'Right,' said Mr McGeady. 'Act three, we're really getting to the nitty-gritty now. The trial. Have any of you actually read this act or would that be too much for a mere teacher to expect?'

Rachel Williamson sat up straight, wiggled her shoulders. 'Of course I have, sir,' she said. 'You did ask us to.'

'Good *girl*, Rachel.'

We loved English even more than ever; it was bliss to be in a classroom where the teacher didn't sit us separately and thought it safe to let us speak. Mr McGeady acted exaggeratedly polite when we came in, was especially nice to Gina, and always asked after Ellie, which pretty much gave him ten out of ten in our books. All the other teachers in the school were about minus twenty; Dracula had slipped right off the scale.

'You can tell us what happens then,' said Mr McGeady to Rachel.

She smiled. 'You mean give a précis.' She said *précis* as if she was presenting the word to the class, on a platter, like a birthday cake. Gina nearly retched.

'A summary will do,' said Mr McGeady. 'Come on, chop chop. I want to concentrate on the authority of this trial.'

That was a nudge in our direction. He'd started dropping hints to us all the time; Cora had sussed it out first. Sometimes they were about the play, but sometimes he seemed to be trying to get at something else and that had to be our trial; what else could it be?

'You're not on trial,' Gina had said.

'We might as well be,' said Cora.

'Guilty by association,' I said. 'That happens in the play, doesn't it?'

'Yeah, but I'm not guilty,' said Gina.

'Neither were they,' I said. 'Were they?'

It was all pretty confusing and all we had to help us through was an elusive spirit and our equally mystifying fruitcake of an English teacher. *Ask them why* the spirit had said, which had so far only propelled Gina into her private anarchies; and now this, from Mr McGeady. Cora was doodling elaborate patterns down her margin. Gina was staring at Mr McGeady. I tried to concentrate.

'Mary Warren signs a paper saying she never saw any spirits,' droned Rachel, chancing a glance at us on the word *never*. Rose was next to her, buried in hair. Gina stuck her tongue out and Rachel stopped, looked expectantly at Mr McGeady, who asked her if she'd finished. 'But then she backtracks later,' continued Rachel, 'when Abigail comes in.'

Abigail. I was getting really worried by Abigail, pushing everything so far. It had all started with her falling in love, after all, and I was beginning to realize what that could do. Love and jealousy mixed up with a few forays into the spirit world. It was all very disconcerting.

I couldn't help feeling sorry for her though – Abigail – Mr McGeady had done too good a job in igniting my imagination about life in Salem. The thought of her working for the Proctors, living in their house, skivvying under the stern eye of Elizabeth and going liquid every time John Proctor walked by. Snatched kisses under the dark eaves of the barn, scanning the fields for his stride, sneaking glances at the silent table. Lying in bed with visions of him vivid in her head and then meeting him later; cold, stern, condemning. Quite enough to twist a girl's head even without Tituba's spells. And she didn't do the killing. She and her friends just got caught, doing nothing worse

175

than we do, in the shed, with the spirit. *How can a group of girls get to be so scary?*

'And this is where Abigail gets really frightening,' Rachel was saying. Cora's doodle had extended across the page. Gina was gouging holes in the desk. 'After Mary has admitted that she hasn't seen any spirits or the devil then Abigail and the rest of the girls go . . . well, they go hysterical –'

'Hysterical,' muttered Gina.

'– and start pretending they've seen birds in the rafters and copying Mary Warren's sentences –'

'Yellow birds,' said Gina.

'Yes, yellow,' said Rachel. She was looking anxiously between Gina and Mr McGeady. 'Anyway, I don't understand this bit, sir. Because all the judges and priests and stuff believe the girls, even though it's obvious that they're just putting it on.'

'Obvious,' said Gina.

'Obvious,' said Cora. Rose put her hands over her ears.

Rachel glared. 'And now *they're* being stupid and you don't do anything, sir. Sometimes I really do wonder!' She sat down with a thump and crossed her arms over her chest. Behind us we could hear suppressed laughter from the boys.

'Well, I'm sure it's only my class you have to put up with it in,' Mr McGeady said, patting Rachel's shoulder. 'Interesting point, though. Are the girls "putting it on"?'

'Of course they are,' said Rachel. 'What else could they be doing?'

'What else, indeed.'

I wasn't going to say anything about that. Neither were Gina or Cora; their heads were down too.

'Any takers?' said Mr McGeady. 'Yes, William?'

'I think it's clear that the author intends ambivalence over the girls' state of mind,' said the Brain – William Bullmer – who didn't usually bother much with discussions in English and had had to stop selling us his essays because no one was clever enough to disguise them adequately. 'One only has to look at the acting instructions. *Overwhelmed by the girls' utter conviction; the girls run to one wall, shielding their eyes.* There are plenty of interpretations of this scene

176

but I don't think it can be that the girls are merely stupid.'

Cora let out a great hoot of laughter. 'Nice one, Brain,' she said.

'I didn't say Abigail was stupid,' said Rachel.

'No, you said we were,' said Gina.

'There can be many interpretations, Gina,' said Cora. 'Remember that.'

'This class is just degenerating,' said Rachel.

'Is it?' said Mr McGeady. 'I thought it was going rather well. One of the great lessons in life, Rachel, is that there is always another take on events apart from your own. Many, in fact. Some people never learn it. I didn't really learn it until recently.'

'Well. And I thought this was supposed to be a lesson in English,' said Rachel, folding her arms again.

Mr McGeady sneezed – or laughed, we couldn't be sure – there could even have been tears in his eyes. 'Quite, Rachel,' he said, mopping his face and patting her on the shoulder. 'I do apologize.'

Mr McGeady was right next to Rose's desk. She flinched as he passed and shuffled her chair away from him, into the aisle. That's not put on, I thought, she really doesn't like him. Buzzing signalled the end of the class.

'Saved by the bell,' said Mr McGeady, and he started to pack up his papers. 'Next lesson, authority and lying. Read and think, my little cherubs. Read and think.'

It was cold outside. Our breath came out in cloudy puffs. The playground was dotted with bundled-up teenagers but we weren't allowed inside. Wills-Masterson's latest dictate: no one indoors at break or lunchtime. She even sent teachers to check the toilets and the far reaches of the art room and science labs, just to make sure no one was hiding out with a bunsen burner, trying to keep warm. Condemned to freeze; no wonder everyone hated us. We breathed on our hands, skidded on soupy ice, went for a ciggy behind the bike sheds.

'I don't know how much more of this I can stand,' said Gina. 'I think I might just leave.'

'Leave what?' I said.

'School. The country. Then at least you could get back to normal.'

'Oh yeah, and what's normal then?' said Cora. 'You think we can rewind the last few months?'

'What about your 'O' Levels?' I said.

'Stuff my 'O' Levels. How am I supposed to work anyway?' said Gina. 'Living in a house full of crooks.'

'They're not crooks!' I said.

'Don't you believe it,' said Gina. 'All that coming and going and arguing. Stuff coming in and out of the house that doesn't belong to any of us. How am I supposed to concentrate on bloody cosines in the middle of that?'

'Oh for God's sake,' Cora snapped. 'The sooner you realize that this isn't just happening to you the better.' She broke away from our huddle with a crack, and left us shivering in the wind.

Gina lit another No. 6, stared hard at the sky, the ground, anywhere but in my direction. So I split away too, headed back across the ice-wet playground and through the swing doors into the blissful sanctuary of chemistry.


After school I slipped down the dark icy streets to Ellie's. Ellie's mum's evening out, coast clear. When I got there Ellie was garrisoned by piles of books.

'Hi,' she said. 'Someone remembered then.'

'Your mum at Guides?'

'Yes. She keeps trying to get me to go along, such *nice* girls, they are.'

'Nice girls.' I sat down. The books at eye level had intimidating titles like *Twentieth Century Political Thought*, *International Relations since World War II*. 'How come we've ended up as the baddies, Ellie?'

'Dunno. Mum thinks it all started when I wouldn't go to Guides. And because of the group, of course.'

'What does she think we did, bully you into being our friend?'

'Something like that.'

We made tea, and I told her about Cora and Gina bickering and Mr McGeady getting weirder.

'I'm fed up with those two,' said Ellie. 'I don't suppose it ever occurs to them that I'm the one that's being punished here.'

'They're kind of wrapped up at the moment,' I said. Sitting in Ellie's house, this sounded feeble. She was pale, her hair stringy and hastily scraped back. As far as I knew the only time she'd been out since the fire was a couple of sneaked hours at the Mop. 'Been out lately?' I said.

'Oh yeah, Taz comes and whisks me off disco dancing every night.'

'Ellie . . .'

'She won't let me, Alice. I mean she really won't. The only way I'm going to get out of this house is to leave. I've got ten months and fourteen days to plan my escape.' She pulled out a calendar from under her writing pad. It had days marked off and fractions scribbled by the side.

'What happens in ten months and fourteen days?' I said.

'I'm sixteen. Legally free.'

Ellie had it all worked out. Instead of sneaking out of windows, like Cora might have, scraping her fishnets on the drainpipe, or arguing with the impossible, like me, she'd quietly made plans. On her sixteenth birthday she was out – gone – and there would be nothing her parents could do about it. She was going to do her 'O' levels early – easy, she said, I could do them next week, I've had so much time to study – and apply to sixth-form college somewhere else. She had money – presents for birthday and Christmas – none of her relatives thought it odd that she was saving. That's how stupid they all are, she said, they think a fifteen-year-old girl cares more about the future than having nice clothes and going out. But Ellie, I said, you're planning your future. No I'm not, she said. I'm planning how to get out. She'd get more money, too, from addressing envelopes, sewing up cheap skirts for the market traders to sell. Ellie had plans and no one seemed to mind what they were as long as they didn't involve us. I was impressed; more than that – baffled. Where

179

had this Ellie come from? She'd always seemed slightly behind the rest of us, up until now.

'What about Taz?' I said. There was no point in acting like she was still part of the group – what group, I thought, with a chill.

'We write. He comes round when she's out.'

We chatted a bit more, about schoolwork, what might happen with Gina. I wanted to tell her about Johnny but something stopped me – an instinct? – and her mum would be back soon, Ellie was already glancing at her watch.

'What are all these books, anyway?' I said. 'You're not studying politics, are you?'

'Self-education,' said Ellie. 'They've left me to it, so the least I'm going to do is study what I want to.'

'Yes, but *politics*?' It wasn't even an option at school. The closest was economics at 'A' Level. And history, I suppose; if you could get past the kings and queens.

'It's important, Alice. Stops you getting too wrapped up. You should think about it, think about yourself, Alice, how *you* want to live, not spend your time fretting over Gina and Cora.'

There wasn't a lot I could say to that; so I kissed her and left. 'Take care, Ellie, and good luck.'

'I'll be fine. Don't forget me now.'

I trudged home. The city was wrapped in freezing fog, tufts glued to walls and fences and tarmac; it insinuated its way under the loose flap of my shoe sole, down the back of my neck. The flat was empty; the yard full of dark, formless lumps. I ran up the stairs quickly and bolted the door behind me, dodged all the mirrors, slipped under my bedclothes and lay there, listening to my breathing and waiting for a gap in the noise in my head so that I might eventually sleep.

# Russian Dolls

Rock Hill. Monday morning. The remains of the group –
Gina, Cora and me – summoned to see Dracula. Her office
smelt of wood polish and chemicalish flowers, although the
huge vase of blood-orange lilies between us and her seemed
real enough. They looked like they might bite us, snap off a
finger or two if you went too close. Venus flytrap lilies. Car-
nivorous lilies. Lilies with teeth.

Dracula was hectoring us. Précis, to use one of righteous
Rachel's words: having finished their investigations at last, the
police could find no evidence of faulty wiring or other struc-
tural cause for the fire; all that was left was the arson theory.
Georgina Marshall was believed to be involved with previous
fires around school grounds. Alice Tracey and Cora Kirk also
had knowledge of the fires. Georgina Marshall was absent from
school on the day of the fire but a witness saw a person matching her description around the back of the sixth-form block in
the hour prior to the fire being discovered. Georgina Marshall
could not, or would not, account for her whereabouts on the
said day. Therefore, not only was Georgina a sinner beyond
redemption but she was protected by her two friends who, if
they didn't buck up their ideas very soon, would also be held
responsible for this shameful act of wanton destruction.

'How can we be?' said Cora. 'I was in French when it
started. Ask Monsieur. And Alice was in history.'

'So you deny any involvement?'

'Of course we do. So does Gina.'

'Where was she then? Can anyone corroborate her story?' Dracula moved closer to us, her arms moving robotically. 'Or lack of it.'

'She's the cat's mother,' Gina hissed between closed teeth.

'Have you got something to say, Georgina?'

'Look, I didn't do it, right? I've told you that a thousand times. You're picking on me because of our Kenny. It's victimization this.' Gina glared.

Dracula staggered slightly, like a metal pole kicked at its base. 'I just want the truth,' she said.

'The truth is it wasn't me.'

'Where were you then?' Dracula was advancing again, her heels forcing her to lean forward as she strutted. I could feel a vibration of laughter rising in Cora, hoped it wouldn't spread to me. Gina dug holes in the carpet with her heel. Dracula was bent over her, breathing in short snorts, waiting. 'Well?'

'I'm not saying,' said Gina, monotone. She flinched at a blast from Dracula's nostrils. 'It's none of your business.'

'I think it is, young lady.'

'No it's not. I didn't start the fire; any of the fires. You've no evidence, not even any reason to think it's me apart from the fact that you don't like me.'

'*Tell me where you were.*'

Gina's face was flushing, but she wasn't going to back down, I could see that. Cora's laughter vibration changed to pride, I felt it, and stood up straighter. She couldn't beat us. Dracula's breath flickered.

'No,' said Gina, quietly. 'I won't.'

'Mrs Wills-Masterson,' said Cora, in a not very convincing polite voice. 'Just suppose that Gina didn't light the fires. If that's true then where she was on that day isn't really anything to do with you, is it?'

'*She should have been in school.*' Dracula was steaming. Drips of sweat trickled down her hairline, mixing with face-powder. It smelt sickly sweet and we could see the cracks it was supposed to cover up.

182

'Yes, but that's a different matter,' I said. 'Nothing to do with the fires.'

'The deputies usually deal with unauthorized absences, don't they?' said Cora. 'Should Gina go and see them?'

Dracula raised her arm above Cora's head, and I realized with a jolt that's what she wanted to do – cow us, frighten us, hit us even.

'Don't even think about hitting me,' said Cora, her vibrations transformed to quivers of anger, quick and dangerous.

Dracula's hand wavered, then returned to her side. She turned her back on us and growled, 'Leave. Go on. For now. But don't think for a moment that I've finished with you.'

'If you're going to question me again I want the police here,' said Gina, calmly, talking to Dracula's back. 'I want to hear what their evidence against me is. You can't carry on harassing us like this for no reason.' We headed for the door. 'And another thing,' she said, once the door was open, escape in sight. 'If you still think I did it, ask yourself why. Why would I do it? What good does it do me if your school burns down?'

The toilets had just been cleaned, disinfectant hung as thick as fog. I felt suddenly sick. The moment of triumph over Dracula seemed fleeting to me, but Cora was high.

'Brilliant,' she said. 'Did you see the way she was sweating?' She peered at herself in the mirror. Gina was flaky; shaking. Cora opened her mouth to stretch the skin around her eyes, started to paint on colour. 'Don't worry, Gina,' she said. 'It'll be OK now. She'll have to back down.'

'Are you sure, Cora?' I said. She was applying lipstick; scarlet, not-for-school.

'Sure as I can be. Anyway, we can't have her threatening to beat us, can we?'

'I don't think she would have done.'

'Best not take the chance.' Cora stuffed her makeup back into her school bag. It was packed with clothes, a pair of heels almost as high as Dracula's poked out. 'Anyway, I've got to be off. See you tomorrow.'

'Cora, where are you going? It's not even lunchtime.'

183

She checked her appearance one more time and, satisfied, tapped her finger on the side of her nose as she left.

Gina and I stared at each other's reflections in the mirror, mutely, her eyes glaring, fierce and furious and brimming. I patted her shoulders, pulled her hair back from her face and smoothed it, like Mum did to me after a bad dream.

My voice started to make noises, saying anything. 'You did great in there, Gina, asking her why. And you were right about the police. If she really thinks we did it we should be down the cop shop . . .' Gina's knees sagged. My bright-frantic face was talking at hers in the mirror. What did Gina look like? Angry? Scared? My voice rattled on. 'And acting like you're not bothered – I don't know how you and Cora do it. You know, I think if we grovelled enough Dracula might just forget this whole thing . . .'

Gina groaned, slid down on to the cold tile floor and braced her head with her arms. I rubbed her shoulders.

'It's OK, Gina. It'll be fine. We'll sort it out somehow.' I was lying though, had no confidence in my words. My stomach dropped further and further.

Eventually she spoke, her voice rough, dredged from deep down in her. 'You don't understand, Alice,' she said. 'I do care what she thinks. I don't want her to hate me. I want to go through school like any other person. Like Rachel *Williamson*. It's Cora that couldn't give a shit what happens. Not me.'

I carried on speaking, background noise, like a voice off the radio. Told her that everyone admired her for saying what she thought, not worrying what she looked like, for trying and laughing and not being cowed. Rose misses you, I said. She does, Taz told me. He says she's bored and boring because she's good all the time. She doesn't miss us, Gina, she misses you. My voice swirled round us both as we crouched on the hard cold floor. I talked on and on like Mum does when I'm really upset; she tells me about my mad uncles and the mangy cat she once had and isn't James Bolam just gorgeous. I told Gina about the time my second cousin met Robert Plant in a pub, and sang the whole of

184

'Changes' while I rocked her in my arms. Eventually she stopped crying and gathered herself together by staring grimly at her face in the mirror and sealing it back in place with a wash in the chipped sink.

'Thanks, Alice,' she said. Her eyes were black, red-rimmed. 'Don't mention this to anyone, OK?'

'Course not.'

'Looks like Ellie's not the only one who's got plans to make,' said Gina. I'd told her and Cora about Ellie getting out but this was Gina's first comment about it. In the mirror I watched her back straighten and her chin tilt up.

'What do you mean?' I said.

'Plans for being out of here,' she said.

It was dark when I finally crept into the shed. I took candles, a torch; told myself I was only a few steps from the flat, TV, normality. It was calm in there; cool, dark. I leant back, breathed slowly, felt my stomach relax. Outside the day was winding down, cars and people draining off the streets. In there I could let myself unravel, lie down and feel the weight of my body on the floor. Sometimes it seemed like the only certain thing; physicality, muscles, skin, bones. Whatever happened to *me* I could never leave this body. Even if I tried to leave it I felt that I'd just come out the same – but smaller – like Russian dolls. Not Gina, her layers were different. I'd seen that earlier on in the school toilets, a layer peeling off in front of my eyes. It had never happened before, in all the years I'd known her, and I was fairly sure no one else had seen it either. You only had to see how raw and sore she was underneath the tough layer to know it didn't come off that often.

I opened my eyes; darkness had settled over me. The traffic had dwindled to a distant hum. Without really thinking I reached for the Ouija board and glass and set them on the bench, lit a candle, sat and waited.

'I don't know what to do,' I said, my words disappearing like bubbles into the darkness. The glass was trembling on the board. The imps twitched their limbs in the yellow candlelight,

185

the sun smiled, the moon winked. 'What makes this come alive?' I whispered.

Y–O–U

A rustle behind me. My stomach flipped over.

'Where are you?'

H–E–R–E

I could feel questions churning upwards in me but I had to word it right. The candle burned darker, orangey, and I thought of Gina, raw.

'How can I get us out of this? Help Gina? She's going to leave otherwise and God knows what will happen to her . . .' It was the first time I'd acknowledged it to myself – the possibility of losing Gina – and it made me ache inside, like an old torn muscle ripped again. The candle wavered in a draught, leant sideways, towards me.

The glass was already moving.

U–S–E   M–E

# On the Cusp

What sort of flowers do you buy for a man you never knew? I stand stranded in the florist's, scent rising from the giant tin buckets of lilies and carnations.

In the end the girl takes pity on me. 'For a bloke is it?' she says. 'How about a pot of marigolds? He can plant them out in the garden then.'

So I end up buying a trowel as well, and dig a little hole next to my father's gravestone. I feel disconnected from this ritual of visiting and placing and glancing at other mourners; but I don't know what else to do. There are only these rituals. When the marigolds are planted I am pleased. That they're so bright. That they're in the ground and will grow roots, give off seed.

'Hello, Alice.' A voice from behind me. I know it's him straight away. The man with the boots and deerstalker hat. I probably knew at the time, last time I came here but couldn't connect it; my unknown father's grave and my old English teacher from Rock Hill. I should have done; the change of image alone was enough to have given him away.

'Mr McGeady,' I say, without turning round.

'Roger, please.'

'Your father would have liked them,' he says. 'The marigolds.'

'You knew him?' The words fall out of my mouth so heavy with incredulity that I look to the ground to see if they've made a mark, a dent in the soil.

'Yes,' says Mr McGeady. 'Come and sit down and I'll tell you.'

We walk over to a bench. The tweeds are a reasonable disguise, but his walk gives him away, the way he turns his toes out and bangs his arms rhythmically against his sides. He used to walk around the classroom like that, as if his agitation might stir our sluggishness.

'You've changed your image again,' I say. 'Why do you do that?'

'Why did I or why do I?'

'Both.'

My father followed my life, I now learn. He did go away after he left us but then he came back and he kept up with my progress, bits of my life tacked together; the newspaper cuttings, the swimming team.

'Is that allowed,' I say, 'when me and Mum knew nothing about it?' Mr McGeady flushes, deep red, digs his shoes into the gravel. 'It wasn't official, was it?' I say. 'You just did it anyway.'

'It was when . . . you know, the fires and everything started that your father came to see the headmistress,' he says. He is looking straight at me now. I get the feeling that the speech is rehearsed. 'She gave him short shrift but I . . . well, he was so keen to find out about you and all this trouble was brewing and it seemed a good idea to have someone on your side. Even if he was invisible. We became friends, Alice. Your father was my friend for twenty years.'

'But why did he want to know when he didn't want to see?' I say. I'm aware of a terrible tear inside, and look around the graveyard at the grieving visitors with new compassion, feel that I could lurch towards them, all clumsy condolences and clutching hands.

'I think he was frightened, Alice,' Mr McGeady says, 'although no one can really know what his life was like. Frightened that he wouldn't fulfil your expectations. He always used to talk about when you were a little girl, wondered if you remembered anything of him. I tried to persuade him to get in touch; nearly told you myself a couple of times . . .'

Do I remember anything? Maybe; hissed arguments reflected in the mirrors, friction seeping under my bedroom door. We all have these memories, don't we? They're part of our lives.

'But I didn't have any expectations,' I say.

'I think that might have been worse.'

'You're separated though, aren't you?' I say. 'How would you feel if you never saw your kids?'

'I didn't,' says Mr McGeady. 'For far too long.'

The rumours were true, then. His wife did leave him and she did take the kids.

'I was going through it myself,' he says. 'When you and the others were taking all that stick. Waking up to an empty house, falling over kids' toys when there were no kids any more. Before that, life was a kind of dream for me, I could do anything I liked – but then my dream lost all its colour.'

And his clothes too – *a reflection of my opinion of the universe* – I remember that. 'But why couldn't you see them?' I say. 'Didn't you have access?'

'Custody battle,' he says, shortly. 'I lost. You wouldn't think the courts had any right to stop me seeing them, would you? But they did, as it turned out.'

He comes here every day, that's how much he misses my father. 'I hoped you'd come back,' he says. 'I wasn't brave enough to talk to you the first time. I was about to, but I missed a beat and you were gone.'

'I have to go now.' I stand up. Hold out my hand. He grasps it and hangs on, shaking, looking at me, shaking again. Another ritual.

'I'd like to tell you about him,' says Mr McGeady.

'I'll think about it,' I say.

'I know his brother – your uncle – as well. I think you should go and see them. Make some contact.'

'I think that's up to me,' I say.

'He was proud of you. That you were so, so –' he is searching for a word '– *solid*.' Another image of me, an impression dissonant with my own. I turn to leave but he still has hold of my hand. 'They came back as well,' he says. 'My kids. She moved away but when they got old enough they found

189

me. Just looked through the telephone book, there's not many McGeadys. She couldn't take away their name. I see them quite often now. Things are better. Hence . . .' He waves his hands up and down his body. The clothes; the eccentric, long-lost dad. Only they found him before he died.

I walk back. I'm late and have to hurry, my feet skimming the pavements, darting in between traffic, a true city girl. Dan was always amazed at that, my fearlessness on busy streets, my instinct for an adequate gap between cars. I never lost it, despite being away for so long, so something must have endured, something was solid.

I think of Mr McGeady going through a custody battle – when we were in the middle of our trial – and then reinventing himself for his children, like a clown, wearing clothes that the kids will be comfortable with, a code, a marker we all understand. Now he wants to be a harmless old fool, someone who can never hurt them again. If he dresses like that he can be that, re-creating himself, an act of his imagination.

The man who owns Corinne's field appears startled when I arrive, striding up the neatly edged drive to his house.

'Alice,' I say, holding out my hand. 'Alice Tracey. I wonder if I could have a word about your field.'

'Sorry?' he says, lifting his glasses and peering at me. The rake he was holding clatters to the floor. His face tenses. 'You don't live there, do you?'

'Not me,' I say. 'A friend. That's what I've come to talk to you about.'

He was OK once I'd explained. Pleased to help. That's what he said when I left. 'I'm pleased to help you, Alice. The lass has never been any bother to me and I certainly don't want those thugs on my land.'

Corinne is a child to him. An elf, or a fairy, a creature from another existence who passes through his life. I shake his hand, his wife's. She walks with me to the gate, wants to know more details. She is sturdy and sensible, concerned about Corinne being alone down there, about the baby.

'It's odd,' she says, 'that he's decided to be nice about this. Only last week he was talking about how we could get her to leave.'

'I'm glad,' I say.

'So am I.'

Corinne's on the towpath waiting for me. 'Any luck?' she says.

'You won't get any bother from him,' I say. 'He seems to be quite benevolent towards you, although neither me nor his wife can work out quite why.'

'Great.' She looks anxious though, despite her team of fishermen – silhouettes in quilted shirts and wading boots – lining the bank. 'If only we could get rid of that van some-how, without the Old Bill having any grounds to suspect me or Johnny of scrapping it,' she says. 'Then we'd be in the clear. Me and the baby.'

'What about Johnny?' I say.

'If he's lucky. If it's his day in court.'

We're on our way to the Waterways office, trudging up the canal, our breath curling out of our noses and condens-ing as the day heats up. Corinne is sweating slightly, her stomach growing; swelling in the night, underneath the smooth cover of belly and blanket. The Waterways office is a few miles away, over fields and through woods, but Corinne wants to walk. Says she can think better when she's moving, things become clearer to her.

'I've decided I'm leaving the city,' she says, as we pass under the spiralled red brick of a bridge, a cyclist weaving past us. 'Once this is all over. You lived in the country, didn't you?'

'Yes,' I say.

'Johnny thinks you'll go back, you know. To whatever you had before.'

'I don't think so.'

'That's what I said,' says Corinne. 'Although we did won-der what it was that made you come back here in the first place. But you couldn't have just left it all, could you?'

'Gina did,' I say.

'You're not Gina.'

I pause, stare blankly at the water. 'It was lots of things,' I say. 'My husband wanted to move to America; I was worried about Mum; my career had become unsatisfying; it all seemed . . . empty.'

Corinne can't possibly realize how odd this sounds to me. Because I *wanted* to empty my life when I left here. I wanted it streamlined, with boundaries, neat edges. That's the first thing that Ellie said when she came to visit me, newly married. 'You know what's going to happen, don't you?' she said. 'You've got it all under control.' Ellie's home was Greenham Common then, she'd come to us to recuperate, get over a cold that had plagued her for months. She was weary from arguing with soldiers and police, needed to sleep and eat and be warm. But within days she was talking of bolt cutters and decorating the razor wire with ribbons. When she left I gave her a sleeping bag, duckdown, the warmest in the shop, and she squeezed my arm and touched my cheek, her hand lingering. I missed her even before she had gone.

Me and Corinne are on a ridge. On one side is the city, green sliding into grey and humming gently, as if a huge flying saucer has landed on the plateau and sprouted roots, grown electric tendrils, streets and houses geometric notches on its surface. The other side has locks stepping down into the valley, a giant's staircase. Standing on the edge of the canal on the edge of the city I think about the trigger, because Corinne is right, there was just one thing that tipped me over, made the decision impossible not to take.

'It was one Monday morning,' I say. 'Dashing about, trying to find some documents and write a note for Dan and sort out some food and prepare for court. The TV was on in the background, breakfast telly. A woman going on about the demands of modern life. I was standing there with my arms full of crockery thinking "What does she know?" when the voice snagged on me and I stopped dead. It was her; Rose O'Connor. The last time I'd seen her she'd been crying into her hair in biology, and there she was presenting morning telly for Granada. The perfect job for Rose – chatty, genial;

a little bit of glamour. I watched her; so composed and controlled and everything else stopped.'

I think about that moment – a gap when I caught sight of myself, the person I'd turned out to be. Suddenly the room wasn't tidy and organized any more, it was crammed with shelved emotions, discarded feelings. In a flash the itch under my suit became unbearable. I undressed right there, made a pyre in the garden and burnt the lot of them. I'd spent all those years thinking there was no other sort of life for me and suddenly it was all reversed.

'There was nothing left to do but come home,' I say.

We stand for a moment, on the cusp, looking at the muddied waters; the dogs swirling around our feet, a heron poised in the bushes.

'So you didn't come back just to find Johnny, then?' says Corinne.

'No,' I say.

I'd tried my best to forget about Johnny. Forget how I lay liquid in bed in the flat with the moon outside and the cat howling and the spirit up to its tricks; rearranging the yard, flipping the world inside out. How my heart missed a beat at the mention of his name. But it was a memory that never quite went away, the one that swam to the top, emerging from the blur. He's just the same now, a bit wrinkled, more worn; like a photograph that has been tucked away in a purse, fingered occasionally. All that time I tried to forget about love.

# A Lie, a Warning

Cora appeared in school with a bag full of nicked lipsticks from the Rimmel counter at Woolies. Hint of Pink and Perfect Pearl tipped out on to the scarred desktop.

'That's the new shade, that is, only out last week.'

'I'll have that mauvy one, my sister'll love that.'

'Can you get nail varnish to match?'

I stood at the edge and watched them pocket the money.

'You should come with us next time,' said Gina. 'Plenty of cash in this.'

'Funny how those girls didn't want to know us last week,' I said.

'Commerce crosses all barriers, that's what my Uncle Dennis says,' said Gina.

'It's not that,' said Cora. 'Vanity's just stronger than any of their other so-called principles.' Her words were acid drops, more scathing than ever.

'I don't know why you're listening to Uncle Dennis all of a sudden,' I said, as we walked off down the corridor to English. 'His idea of retail is under a pub table.'

'Bit like a school desk then,' said Gina, rattling the coins in her pocket.

'But Gina, you want to keep away from all that.'

'Says who?' said Gina.

Uncle Dennis was Kenny Marshall's dad, which brought

me gloomily back full circle. If only Marshall and his mates hadn't lit those bloody fires in the first place then none of this would have happened and I could be concentrating on other things.

'Hurry up, Alice,' said Cora.

I had slowed down, my soles stuttering on the lino. I didn't want to go into English, to face all that mad stuff about witches and trials and lies and slandering. And Mr McGeady, with his dark clothes and dark face, casting us glances like a fishing line, always disappointed when we didn't bite.

Cora was waiting by the classroom door. 'Come on,' she said. 'And cheer up. It can't be any more weird than real life.'

Mr McGeady eyed us carefully, ushered us to our seats. The whole class was subdued. English was no longer a lesson we could relax in, and even the most judgemental of our classmates couldn't entirely blame that on us. We were still studying the trial; everyone had read the ending, they knew what was coming. Proctor had, after much agonizing, confessed his adultery, but had been undermined by his wife, whom everyone was sure would never lie, and her faint 'No, sir,' when asked, 'Is your husband a lecher?' Mr McGeady thundered out the lines *'Has John Proctor ever committed the crime of lechery? Answer my question! Is your husband a lecher?'*

*'No, sir,'* said Rose, chosen as Elizabeth Proctor that day. Her faltering voice caused me a physical twinge. Gina, too, I think.

*'Remove her, Marshal,'* said Mr McGeady as Danforth the magistrate.

*'Elizabeth, tell the truth!'* said Robbie as Proctor.

*'She has spoken. Remove her!'*

*'Elizabeth, I have confessed it!'* said Robbie, desperately. The acting instructions said *crying out* and Robbie did, quieting the rustles and shuffles, stilling us all. The shock on Rose's face was worse though, as if she really was Elizabeth, and felt with a slap on her heart the impact of that one and only lie.

195

'Good, very good,' said Mr McGeady. 'Some people consider that the whole play turns on that lie, that if Elizabeth had told the truth about her husband and Abigail then the witchhunt would have been over . . .' He stopped. Gina was drawing elaborate spirals in her margins, Cora zeroed in on a cuticle.

'Why didn't she then?' said Taz. 'Look at all that trouble she caused by trying to protect him.'

'Elizabeth Proctor was confronted with a situation she was ill equipped to deal with,' said Mr McGeady. 'She was torn, and vacillated – a perfectly normal response. However, the real question is, would it have made any difference if she had told the truth? If we take a look at what happened next . . .' We flicked through our *Crucible*s. Gina and Cora were yawning, feet jiggled under desks. The sky was grey with rain, but moving slightly, you could see it if you watched carefully. It made me dizzy, my head was on one side, following the massed cloud.

I was brought back to the classroom by Rose's cry. 'No,' she gasped raggedly, her book held up in front of her like she was reading in church. 'Mary Warren turns on Proctor, accuses *him* of being the devil. Nothing could have stopped the witchhunt. It had all gone too far.' I pulled my eyes away from the cloud and saw Rose getting up from her seat, Rachel Williamson trying to pull her back. But Rose twisted away and rushed to the door; we heard her shoes squeaking fast away. The door swung to and fro a few times then eased shut.

'Leave her,' said Mr McGeady. 'I'll make sure she's all right.'
'But . . .' said Rachel, her backside hovering above her seat.
'Leave her.'

After that, McGeady's pet subject of the court's authority just didn't grab our attention. 'Think about it,' he said. 'What gives a court the authority to judge and condemn others? In the case of this play it supposedly comes from God, but as this increasingly appears to conflict with any sense of justice or innate rightness, then . . .' But we weren't listening, our senses were tuned into any tiny shuffle or sniff from the corridor that might indicate that Rose was back. 'Of course in this country, now,' Mr McGeady continued valiantly, 'we are brought up to believe that the law is arranged to protect the individual and ensure that everyone is treated equally, but not so in Salem, 1792.'

'Not in England, 1977, either, if your name's Marshall,' muttered Gina.

After English I slipped off to the cloakroom, skiving French. I was fed up with them, Gina and Cora, but they didn't seem bothered, watched me slouch off down the corridor, eyed each other and shrugged. The warm fug – trainers, steaming coats, mud and grass cursorily wiped at the door – was oddly comforting. I pulled my legs up on a bench, rested my back on the wire mesh partition and hauled a coat over me. The school went quiet, lesson time. The odd drumming of footsteps up and down stairs, muffled thumps from the gym, someone practising a violin in a distant room, the same phrase, over and over again. I was lulled, may even have dozed off. I'm either struggling to stay conscious or totally hyper at the moment, I thought; or electric-liquid, when I'm with Johnny . . .

'Alice?' A voice next to me. The coat was heavy on my head. 'It's OK. You're not in trouble.' Mr McGeady. I peeled off the coat.

'Can I have that in writing?' I said.

'I'll have a word with Monsieur.'

'Oh yeah, and that's going to stop him reporting me. We only have to whisper too loud in this place at the moment and we're for it.'

'You'd be surprised who's out there for you, Alice.'

A couple of lads from the second form came tearing round the corner, skidded to a halt and stared at us, bug-eyed. 'Soz,' they said, before backing off.

'Whoops,' said Mr McGeady.

'Now it's your reputation that'll be up the spout,' I said.

'Oh, I shouldn't think that'll make much difference,' he said.

197

'Huh?'

Mr McGeady ignored me. He sat for a while, gestured with his hand, opened and closed his mouth. I sneaked a look at my watch – ten minutes till lunchtime, he'd have to hurry up if he was going to say anything, I was starving. Mr McGeady; Mr Opinion, sitting there in the acrid cloakroom, tongue-tied.

'Did you find Rose?' I said, eventually, when the shuffling and twitching next to me got too much; he was worse than Johnny for sitting still.

'Her mother came for her.'

'What was up with her?'

'She's having some difficulties right now –' He almost relaxed into chat, I could see the signs, but then he suddenly clamped his mouth shut, flushed red from the neck up. I noticed pimples around his collar, felt the ones on my shoulder blades throb.

'Difficulties?' I said, standing up, watching him shrink beneath my questioning. 'She left us with all the difficulties.'

'Oh, Alice,' sighed Mr McGeady. 'I hope you're up to this. Because I really do think that you're the only one who can sort it out now.'

He took me out for lunch, to a café on the High Street with misted-up windows. I had egg and chips, brown sauce. His voice was heavy with warning as he told me about Wills-Masterson and the deputies, how they would get rid of Gina one way or another. He talked about the atmosphere in the staff room since the fires started, since Wills-Masterson arrived at Rock Hill. There's a sense that everything's out of control, he said, endless rumours about your group – he looked at me sideways when he mentioned us; edgily. And now no one trusts anyone else – his speech was faltering – it's almost as if there has to be a purge.

Egg congealed in my mouth. 'Sir,' I said, 'what do you mean "a purge"?'

'A way of starting again,' he said. 'The headmistress feels that some of the pupils are out to get her and that this just shouldn't happen.'

'Well it does,' I said. 'And she's got the wrong people.'

'I know,' he said, staring out of a smeared circle in the window. 'But there were some questions from the city authorities after Kenny Marshall got expelled, she's had to answer to them and she . . . she . . . feels affronted.' He seemed relieved to get the word out. 'I'm afraid nothing short of abject servility will help now.'

He pulled his glasses off his nose. 'Do you think you can persuade Georgina to apologize, Alice?'

'Can you see it, sir?' I said. 'Gina doesn't really do grovelling.'

'You must understand that the headmistress is, well, a little obsessed by this. Believe me, Alice, I don't like the smell of this authority any more than you do. It's the easiest answer, to blame you girls for the fire. But, to put it bluntly, she's likely to expel you all the way she's talking. It's as if she thinks there's a conspiracy against her or something –'

'Expel us for what?' I said. 'We haven't done anything.'

'Oh, you know – truancy, smoking, Cora's clothes, Georgina's attitude. I have to tell you this, Alice, there's rumours of some kind of dossier being kept.'

'They're not the real reasons, and you know it.' I wanted to bang the table, grab his collar at this injustice – I nearly did – but it felt important to appear mature, as if that could somehow make a difference. He looked at me earnestly and I realized with a flash of triumph that it had worked. After all, it was me he had taken aside to talk to. It was me who he thought could sort it out.

'Real reasons or not, Alice,' said Mr McGeady, gravely, 'unless Georgina can bring herself to, as you so aptly put it, grovel; then according to the school rules – and Mrs Wills-Masterson will have checked out the details, cleared it with the governors, you can be sure of that – it's perfectly within her rights to use those rules to expel you all.'

# Betrayal

'What's the big deal if you do get expelled anyway?' said Johnny. We were lying on my mother's sun-dappled bed. He'd appeared as I was walking to school that morning. 'Hi, Alice,' he said, swooping down to kiss me.

'Oh. Hi.'

'What's up?' he said. 'Not pleased to see me?'

'Yes. Yes. But . . .' We'd stopped dead in the street.

'But what, Alice?'

'Last time I saw you . . . you went off after Cora, you didn't even say goodbye to me . . .' I was struggling for words, hated sounding so feeble.

Johnny's face split into a grin. 'Darlin', I just had to ask her something. I didn't expect you to be gone when I came back.'

So I never made it to school. Mum was out and we slipped back to the flat and on to the bed. A slight breeze lapped through the open window, along with the roar of the High Street. I was desperate to touch him, had to clamp my arms to my sides, breathe steadily to keep my concentration.

I pushed myself up on one elbow. 'I don't want to get expelled because I'm in the middle of my 'O' Levels for a start . . .' I said, trailing off again. Johnny hadn't been put in for any exams, and his future – if you listened to all the voices around us – was looking grim.

'You could do them at college,' said Johnny. 'Or at home, like Ellie.'

'She's so disciplined though,' I said. 'I'm not sure I'd learn very well sitting on my own with a pile of books.'

'College then.'

'But I don't want to leave school.'

'Doesn't sound like you've got much choice to me.'

Johnny was dead certain that Gina wouldn't apologize – not if you ask her straight out anyway, he said. You'll have to find another way round, and I haven't managed that in fifteen years. It did seem unlikely, but I'd promised Mr McGeady that I'd try and there was something about the solution that appealed to me. It was neat, quick – back to normal in a few minutes – and we had pushed our luck at school, caused Dracula a lot of grief. Yeah, it was as good as admitting guilt – a lie – but if Mr McGeady was right, as he insisted, and the whole situation was careering out of control, here was a way we could all get out of it.

'I tell you what I want to know,' said Johnny, rolling over to face me.

'What?' The space between us was cavernous. I wanted to scoop it out of the way, like snow.

'How do married people ever get anything done when they've got a great big bed like this to play in?'

The space shifted, melted; slid away. We were drawn together by the vacuum. I pressed his skin with my fingertips. His fingers were on my skin, too, we were drawing patterns through each other's bodies. It was going to happen soon, I knew it, I'd been permanently hungry for days, couldn't be filled by food any longer. I'd even been to the Brook Advisory, got myself some pills and a pile of condoms – enough to last a year, as far as I could work out.

Johnny's skin was getting more taut under my touch. My fingers found the dent in his thigh from the gravel-sparked matches. I was lost in it all, letting my hands free. But some part of me, some instinct must have been on alert because when Mum put her key in the lock down at the bottom of the stairs it registered fast.

'Mum!' I said. We bolted up. Johnny was panting. He tried to move and groaned.

'Shit. This is painful, Alice.'

'But what can I do?'

'Let's go somewhere else.'

'Where?' We hustled to the door of Mum's room, darted into the kitchen.

'Alice?' came a call up the stairs.

'In here, Mum,' I called, my skin flushing and prickling.

Johnny was at the window. 'The shed,' he said, urgently.

Mum breezed in, glanced at us, touched her hair. 'Didn't expect to see you here,' she said. 'Another free period?'

'I'm finished except for exams now, Mrs T,' said Johnny.

'Lucky you,' said Mum. 'Well, I'm beat. I think I'll have a lie down. See you later, kids.'

I watched her clip down the corridor, hundreds of her criss-crossed reflections heading for the bed, which must surely still have the shape of our bodies scalloped in the bedclothes. The door shut behind her. I heard the swish of the curtains.

'Come on,' Johnny breathed in my ear. 'The shed.'

It was over quickly; we had to stand up. The only bit I liked was Johnny's long low groan. We couldn't lie down, spend any time; but it wasn't just that. The fizz abandoned my body – so fickle a feeling – and this made me angry. How come I'd wake – start upright – in the night and have to rub the longing out of me, but now he was here, I just felt stiff and sore and wanted to cry?

Johnny liked it though. He grinned as he zipped his fly. 'Phew, Alice, I needed that.' He could have been talking about a cup of tea, an orange slice at half time. 'You OK?'

'Fine.'

'Shame your mum came back.'

'Yes.'

'Oh well, plenty more time, hey.'

I smiled weakly. There was a block of fuzzy green light coming through one of the windows. It landed on Johnny, who was pulling his fingers through his hair.

'This is where you used to do that stuff, isn't it?' said Johnny. 'You and Gina and Cora.'

'And Ellie and Rose,' I said. The light was slipping off him, swallowed by the dirt floor. 'What do you mean "used to"?'

His eyes clouded. 'Oh, I thought it was all finished with, that's all. Don't be shitty with me, Alice. Come and sit down.'

I sat a few inches along from him. Then my shoulders began to shake, rattling the bench. Betrayed by my body. Again.

'Hey . . . What's up?'

'Nothing.'

He put his arm round my waist. My head slotted under his shoulder blade.

'Nothing?'

'Oh, you know, school and Gina and everything.'

Johnny lifted my face, cupped it in both hands. 'Alice, listen to me, don't worry about Gina, OK?'

'How can I not?'

'She can look after herself. Really.' He was gentle, reassuring. A dream. I felt strength return to my limbs. Plenty more time, he'd said. No need to worry, plenty more time.

'Anyway, you can always ask your spirit if you're really stuck,' said Johnny.

'You what?'

'Nothing. Listen, I've got to go.'

'Right.'

'Don't forget my court date on Friday.'

My brain felt thick and unyielding. 'What? Oh yeah.'

'Bye then.' He kissed my forehead.

'Bye.'


When I got back to the flat later that day Mum sniffed around me, her eyes narrowed. 'What are you doing, Mum?' I said, slinging my bag into the corner of the room, flopping down on the sofa, hoping that my actions camouflaged the cold shock I felt when I realized she might have somehow twigged about me and Johnny.

'It's what you're doing that I'm bothered about,' she said.

I couldn't believe it; this was the sort of thing other people's

203

parents said. Ellie's; Cora's a few years previously. 'Mum, I can look after myself. Don't start treating me like a kid just when I'm just stopping being one.'

'What? Skiving off school, upsetting the teachers, that's grown-up? You never speak to me properly any more, Alice; I'm worried. Your last report was the worst one you've ever had.'

'Oh yeah, and you're Mrs Intellectual.'

'Alice, don't speak to me like that.' I turned to leave the room but she wasn't finished with me yet. 'Wait a minute, I haven't finished with you. Have you looked for that box yet?'

'What box?'

'You know what I'm talking about. The mother-of-pearl one I found in the shop. That I keep my letters in.'

'You had it last time I saw it.'

'Alice, why would I steal my own box?'

'Are you accusing me of stealing?'

'No, I'm asking you if you've seen it. Don't twist my words.'

'No.'

'No?'

'No! I haven't bloody well seen it. Clear enough? No. No. No. I don't know.'

'There's no need for that.'

'What do you want, blood?'

'No, I want my daughter back.'

'And I want my mother. The one who trusts me.'

That was it for a day. We didn't speak. Mum could do a huff a million times better than me and had a huge range of silent recriminations – sad-eyed stares, plates of unfinished food snatched from in front of me.

I arrived at school late, in a foul mood, skipped as many lessons as I could, ignored everyone including Mr Wilson, who then followed me down the corridor and frogmarched me into detention. 'Your attitude isn't doing you any good, young lady,' he said, as if I needed reminding.

My insides still ached for Johnny but I was angry with him too, for his self-satisfaction; for disappearing just when I needed him to stay.

I left school as soon as I could and crept up the stairs hoping to make it to my bedroom without encountering Mum. No such luck, she was sitting at the kitchen table with a box of tissues. I stomped into the living room and glowered on the sofa. She sat down next to me and switched the TV on. We watched *Magpie*, *Crossroads*, in silence, unable to move, barely able to breathe until we'd somehow got over this. I wasn't going to crack, it was only a question of when Mum did.

Finally she switched off the TV with a snap of exasperation and knelt down in front of me. 'Alice, don't let's fall out,' she said. 'Why don't we go to your Aunty Gladys's for a few days? I've spoken to your teachers, they agree a break would do you good.'

I thought of Gladys's clean airy house on the coast, her chubby smiling babies, the wide beach, dogs charging like bullets into the sea after a stick.

'That would be nice, just for a bit.'

'I'll ring her then.'

'OK.'


We were halfway to Weymouth when I remembered Johnny's trial. Mum was singing as she drove, her hair streaming back, Jackie-O sunglasses blanking half her face. I screamed. 'Stop!'

The countryside zipped past, my scream with it. I was white, I knew I was because all the blood in my body was swirling round my stomach. 'What's up, love?'

'We have to go back.'

'Don't be silly.'

'We *have* to.'

'What on earth for?'

'Johnny. Johnny's . . . I promised him . . .' I couldn't get the words out, they had sharp edges, cut my throat on the way up. *Court. Drugs. Setup.*

Mum patted me sympathetically. 'Give him a ring when we get there, love. Arrange to see him when we get back. Hey, we could look for some new clothes for you while we're at Gladys's. There's that really good shop, remember, where we got you those lovely culottes.'

She drove on blithely while I wondered how soon I would die.

'Johnny? It's Alice.'

'Hi, darlin'. Fancy coming over? Dad and Gina are out. Dad stormed off actually.'

'You've not been arguing again?'

'Yeah. It's bad. I'll tell you when you get here.'

'I can't.'

'Can't what?'

'Can't come over.'

'Why not?'

'I'm in Weymouth.'

'*Weymouth?*'

Tears formed sheets down my face. I couldn't speak.

'But it's my trial tomorrow.'

'I know. I can't get back. I haven't got any money for the train.' No noise at the other end of the line, not even breathing. 'Johnny?'

Nothing.

'Johnny, I even tried to steal some money from Mum, honestly, I've really tried. I begged the man at the station, said I'd owe it to him, but he just laughed –'

A crack, like a stone hitting ice. 'It's OK, Alice,' said Johnny, his voice clipped. 'I don't suppose you coming will make any difference anyway.'

# Another One Starts the Next Day

At the Waterways office they are harassed, dismissive. We have to wait to see someone. I think this is a good sign. Corinne is not so sure, she doesn't trust officials. As we stand in the queue I mull over all my reasons for coming back, and how even this – the past – seems to be changing now.

'Has Johnny talked much about Gina to you?' I say.

'Not much,' says Corinne, 'and always sadly. Why? Was it her you came back for?'

'I knew she wouldn't be here,' I say. 'But I do feel less estranged from it all than when I first came back, somehow, with those photos that keep turning up. I thought about trying to find Cora, but then I got embroiled with you and Johnny and set off on a different tack completely.'

'Yeah. You never know how things will turn out,' she says, resting her hands on the rise under her breasts. 'Take this baby. The whole time around when it was conceived was –' she shrugs '– a mess. And then Johnny got busted and it felt like the end of the world. It was the end of one world, but then another one starts the next day. You came along, for a start.'

'I can't promise anything, Corinne, about the case.'

'No one can,' she says.

People come in to the office and complain: there's no water in the canal, their boats are grounded. They don't pay their licence fees for this. Corinne thinks the chaos will be blamed on her – an easy scapegoat – but I smell incompetence, confusion. When we finally get to see the weary official it's clear to me that nothing will happen for a while, not as far as moving the van goes, anyway. I'm confident enough to promise Corinne that.

She smiles. 'I thought you said you couldn't promise anything,' she says.

'Believe me,' I say, 'I've worked in enough offices to be able to tell.'

We walk back in silence, companionably. Boots crunching on gravel, limbs swinging over gates. Back at the flat, Johnny joins us.

'So what's next?' he says.

'Dates,' I say. 'When are you in court?'

'Next Thursday,' says Johnny. 'We just have to show up and sign, although we'll probably be kept hanging around there all day. It's just so they know we haven't absconded. While they try to gather their evidence.'

'What other evidence is there,' I say, 'apart from the van?'

'What they found in there,' says Johnny. 'Before I'd even had a bloody smoke of it.' He's putting up a front, trying to joke.

Mum laughs from the corner of the kitchen – her hands on kettle and cups – and we all turn to stare at her.

'It's true though, isn't it?' she says. 'That's what life's like. Gone before you even get your hands on it. Yesterday I was a little girl – I was, really – a small girl with ribbons and a ration card. Skipping up this High Street, fetching errands for your grandfather. Then I stop paying attention for a while and find myself here.'

'I'd still feel better if I'd at least have tried the stuff,' says Johnny.

'You and me both,' says Mum.

Mum is wary when I tell her I've been to the graveyard. 'What for?' she says. 'I'd have thought you'd be even more angry with him now you know he was here all the time.'

'I never was angry with him, Mum. I didn't feel anything much. It was all that I knew – me and you and the flat and

208

the shop – I didn't need anything else. It's only later that you try and make sense of it all, discover holes you never knew about before. That's why I went, I think, to see if I did feel anything. When I was a kid I just thought myself lucky. You were the best parent by miles, out of all my friends.'

'Oh, I don't know,' she says. 'What about that nice Mr Marshall? Does your Johnny still see him?'

My Johnny. 'No. They fell out years ago. No one seems to know where he is.'

'Now, he'd be someone worth seeking out,' she says.

She's not surprised by me meeting Mr McGeady. 'Two of a kind him and your father,' she says. 'I always had my suspicions about that McGeady. Bit too fond of young girls for a teacher, if you ask me. Did I ever tell you about that time I met your friend's mother in the High Street? What was her name, the one with the red hair, who used to be on telly here –'

'Rose was on telly *here*?' I say. 'No, Mum, you did not tell me –'

'Oh yes, she did the weather for years. But I didn't watch it, not after her mother was so off with me. We were never best friends or anything but we used to exchange nods at parents' evenings and I know she was very churchy and everything but there was no need for her attitude, like I was the sort of person she just didn't speak to.'

'Mum, when was this? What did she say?'

'After you left sometime. I just asked her how Rose was getting on and she said "Very well, no thanks to you" and I said "Me?" and she sort of huffed and said "That school anyway, that English teacher" and she gave me such a look I nearly walked off. But she was away with it, as if she just had to speak to someone, anyone who was remotely connected . . .'

My hands grip the edge of the kitchen table; the cups are rattling slightly on it; liquid rings vibrate through coffee.

'Say what, Mum?'

'Oh, this whole tirade,' says Mum. 'All about that McGeady and how he shouldn't have been given the job at Rock Hill. How she should have been told Rose was in his class and how would I feel if my niece got pregnant at seventeen, although she didn't suppose I'd actually be bothered that much but hers was a *good* family. Glaring at me saying, "What do you think the priest thought of us after that?" As if I was supposed to answer her questions! Well, I left, Alice, stuck my head up in the air as far as I could and swung my bag on my shoulder and wiggled my hips as I walked off.' Mum giggles at the memory. 'You know I don't badmouth people normally, Alice, but I tell you, she was one stuck-up cow.'

'Her niece,' I say. 'Rose's cousin . . .' I'm trying to remember, any vague whiff of scandal, but we were always kept away from Rose's family, any infamy among them was strictly internal. There certainly wasn't any baby, even they wouldn't have been able to hide that.

'What school did her cousin go to?' says Mum. 'Because if it was the one McGeady taught at before Rock Hill then I think we can work out the rest.'

'Mum, she had about twenty cousins. But he did lose custody of his kids,' I say. 'It was all going on at the same time they threatened to expel us.'

'Well,' says Mum, 'a court wouldn't have done that for no reason.'

'He did try to help us –' I say.

'Meddling,' she says, shortly. 'It's not even as if he was any good at it.'

She's chuffed though, that I said she was the best parent, feels secure enough to talk about her marriage a little. I wonder if she might have been to the graveyard too, standing there awkwardly among the other mourners.

'We were so young,' she says, sitting down and sighing. 'He was a drifter, but I wasn't much better to tell you the truth. I used to look at men in the street and wonder if they were the one for me. Because I was convinced, you know, that there was *one*. And I knew your father wasn't him by then.'

'Was there one, Mum?' I say.

But she doesn't answer. Goes to the kitchen window and stares out at the yard, a cast of dust blanketing the lumps and bumps. She makes a noise but it's drowned out by a sudden gurgle from the hot-water pipes. Yes, it could have been. Or no. Or a name. She could have been saying a name. She is still wearing the same dressing gown she had when I was a kid, with sprigs of pink flowers, faded and smudged, the cloth as soft as a duster. I could be sitting here in school uniform. We have the same teapot, the same scratched yellow plastic tablecloth.

I stand at the window with her and stare at the yard – shapes and heaps and mounds, nothing distinguishable now, the shed almost buried under brambles – and want to sweep it all clean. Spray and wipe and sort and tidy, until it's all back where it should be; boxed and labelled and filed and finished with.

'We should sort out that yard,' I say, through my teeth.

Mum puts her arm round my shoulders. I can see the skin sagging around her armpits. 'Maybe,' she says. 'Or maybe we should just leave it be.'

I go into the office and move pieces of paper around my desk. Johnny comes by, kicking his heels, but there's nothing new to say – it's all waiting now. Waiting for the court case, waiting for the result, the one loose end that does need tying up before any of us can move on. He shifts about on his seat and I shuffle papers and in the end I have to say, 'What is it, Johnny? Is there something else you think I should know?'

'It's nothing,' he says. 'Not to do with the case. Only you mentioned something to Corinne about Cora –'

'You know where she is?' I say.

'If you really want to find her try Selina's in Selly Oak,' he says. He's looking at me curiously, like it's him gauging every flicker of my eyelids now, every twitch of my mouth.

'Selina's,' I say. 'OK. Johnny, I'm going to have to get some of this work out of the way now . . .' I want to work, to fill up waiting time.

'Just thought you'd like to know.'

I go home early and find Mum sitting on the sofa hugging a cushion and staring into space. 'Are you OK?' I say.

'Fine,' she says, her eyes drifting past mine. She follows me into the kitchen and interferes with me cooking tea – stirring soup that doesn't need stirring, turning over toast that isn't done.

'Just sit down, Mum,' I say, but she can't. She boils a kettle and decides to scramble eggs but drops them on the floor and smears the runniness all over the kitchen. '*Mum!*' I say.

'There's no need to get irritable,' she says.

'I'm not.'

'You are.'

'Mum, I'm making tea.'

'Excuse me, but this is my kitchen.'

'Mum . . .'

'Did you feel anything, Alice?' she says, egg white dripping from her hands. 'At the graveyard?' Behind me the toast burns and the soup binds itself to the bottom of the pan.

'Well,' I say, 'there's still this gap in my life, but it's got more shape, if you know what I mean. I know the size of it now, which makes it easier to deal with, somehow . . .'

She relaxes, visibly. Shakes the slop off her hands and goes to the sink to rinse them. 'I think you'd better go over to the chippy for tea tonight,' she says.

# Use Me

When we got back from Weymouth there was nothing on the hall mat except bills and a cryptic note from Cora saying *Are you ready for your UB40?*

'Looks like we're out then,' I said, showing it to Mum.

'Out?' she said.

'Expelled,' I said. 'What else could it mean?'

'Well, we'll see about that,' she said, with a look on her face that I'd only ever seen the like of once before, when Aunty Gladys had a cancer scare and the doctor tried to brush her off.

'Mum, don't make a fuss.'

'Alice, if you think I'm going to keep quiet about this then you're plain wrong.'

'It's not just me.'

'I know. And I shall plead the others' cases if I can, I promise. Now, have you kept up with your schoolwork? Fetch me your latest report. What are your results going to be like this year? Come on, Alice, get busy. The resistance starts here.'

Fighting talk, but the strain of the last few months was taking its toll; the rings under her eyes were dark, skin frayed around her fingernails. When I found my reports she looked at them as if their very existence made her head ache; the comments a code she had to crack.

I was grateful to her, but couldn't muster much enthusiasm.

213

Cora and Gina were right in that respect – once Wills-Masterson had elected us to take the rap, we might as well sing nursery rhymes in our defence. Mum buried herself in piles of my reports, muttering, the thin sheets of paper escaping from her fingers and littering the floor.

I tried to phone Johnny but there was no answer; thought about going round there, couldn't imagine what I'd say. I'd made a promise to be in court and then not shown up; what words could make up for that? There was a hard lump growing in my stomach, creeping up my oesophagus.

'Hello?' It was Gina's voice. I'd been sitting listening to their phone ring, given up hope of it being answered. A lump of undigested bread sat in my throat.

'Is Johnny there?' I said, knowing my voice wasn't disguised enough.

'No. He's . . . gone away. Who wants him?' I didn't say anything. Watched my wrist shaking and the carpet swirls swelling around my feet. 'Hello? Are you still there? Who is this?'

The phone slipped from my hand as I ran to the bathroom to throw up my tea.

I had to go to the shed. It seemed the only thing to do, sitting in the bathroom dizzied by the white tiles spinning around me, unsure as to which ones were walls and which ones floor. Eventually I managed to determine which way up the world was by concentrating on the shell shapes Mum had stencilled around the walls. I knew they faced upwards, so if I matched my head to one of them I would end up vertical. It worked. The room snapped back into shape around me. I breathed, beat back the nausea.

Shells, shed, Spirit. *Use me.*

It was my only hope.

I cleared up the bathroom and went in to say goodnight to Mum. She was rubbing the side of her face, holding report papers at arm's length. 'You'll have to get glasses, Mum, your arms won't grow any longer.'

She smiled. 'Feeling better?'

'A bit. Dodgy kebab or something.'

'Poor love. Sleep well then.'

'Night, Mum.' I padded to the door.

'Hey, Alice.' I turned. Mum was holding a sheaf of papers, transparent with the lamp behind them. 'These are good, you know. Better than I ever got. I'm proud of you, right? Whatever happens.'

'Right.'

That day it didn't seem enough, and I sensed that somehow she knew it.

Outside. Pitch black. No moon, very little noise, a damper on the traffic that night. No rustles or squeaks. I pulled open the shed door, lit the candle I'd hidden in my dressing-gown pocket. The globe of yellow light took me to the middle of the shed, where the board was. As I fetched out the glass and got myself ready I felt determination creep over me like a glaze. The glass trembled, the globe of light squeezed and relaxed. He was here.

'I need help,' I said.

I   K–N–O–W

Tears were sliding out of my eyes, but I didn't feel them, didn't notice them until they splashed on the board. The little imps danced.

'Has Johnny run away?' I said, the words ragged. The glass felt heavy under my fingers. My hand twitched and the glass moved an inch and then stopped. I sat breathing with the darkness draped around me.

NO.

'Where is he then?'

I–N–S–I–D–E

'Inside?' I heard a hiss of relief from my mouth. He must be safe then. He hasn't run away. A wave of nausea passed through me again as I wondered if he'd ever forgive me for missing the court date. My finger slipped off the glass and it rattled. Yes. Ask about Gina.

'But what can I do?' I said. 'She really is going to expel us this time.'

T–O–L–D   Y–O–U

215

U–S–E   M–E

'Told me what? Told me we'd get expelled?' Sparks of irritation made my mouth twitch. The glass zipped around the board, swiftly; urgently even, my finger barely in contact. There was an idea floating around my brain somewhere but I couldn't grasp it. Too slippery. My sweaty hands had made the glass too slippery. It was moving without me questioning.

U–S–E   M–E
S–A–Y   S–O–R–R–Y
U–S–E   M–E


'Where you been then?' said Cora and Gina the next morning at school. They seemed taller, their mouths drooped more. Cora's looked like it should have had a cigarette sliding out of the side.

'Weymouth,' I said. 'To see my aunty.'

'Very nice,' said Cora.

'Yes, very nice,' said Gina.

At least they were walking down the corridor with me, even if they did seem to be passing secret messages to each other with flicks of their wrists, tosses of their hair. 'Tell me what's been happening then?' I said, trying to fall in with their swagger, stumbling along behind.

'I don't know, Gina,' said Cora. 'What has been happening?'

'I don't know, Cora. I'm sure there must have been something.'

'I got your note, about Dracula and all that, but what about Johnny?' I said, his name falling too fast off my tongue. Maybe he got probation; a fine. I'd help him with the money. It'd be OK.

They strolled to the door, I was sure I could never walk like that. I ran to catch up with them, feeling more and more like the dumb little sister. Fluorescent lights flickered above us. I felt my oesophagus working the wrong way again.

'Johnny?' said Gina. 'Yes, I forgot you missed all that as well. Johnny's gone.'

216

'Gone where?' I stuttered. I was looking at my feet. They were still moving somehow.

'Down,' said Cora. I swear she was smacking her lips with relish. 'They sent him down.'

'Yep,' said Gina. 'As soon as he mentioned the name Marshall they were on to him like a ton of bricks. Sent him to Borstal, or whatever they call it now. Said people like him needed to be taught a lesson, made an example of, or the drug problem would just get out of hand.' Cora and Gina exchanged a how-could-they-be-so-stupid glance.

'Did anyone go along?' I said. Oh no, I thought. Oh no no no.

'No. No one. Dad's still too mad with him for selling *his* nicked leather jackets. I mean, can you believe those two?'

'So how do you know what happened?' I said. Hoping they were wrong, clinging on to a vanishing dream that this might not be true.

'Rushy told us,' said Gina. 'In graphic detail.'

'Yeah,' said Cora, circling Gina from behind with her arms and clasping her wrists. 'The full works, he got. Handcuffs, black Maria, bye bye Johnny.'

An insect banged repeatedly into the buzzing light above us. Gina and Cora were scrapping with each other, laughing, teeth and eyes flashing, lurching around in front of me, their faces looming out.

'And as for Dracula,' said Gina.

'She's lost it,' said Cora. 'She still stares at us as if we should fall at her feet and beg for forgiveness.' Gina's face flinched. 'And McGeady's still giving us these looks like we're supposed to know something.'

'We've got a "final audience" with her on Thursday,' said Gina. 'But I think we're supposed to sneak in weeping about our sins before then.'

'Yeah, really,' said Cora.

'What are you going to do when we're kicked out?' said Gina to me. 'Three more days of school, three more days of sorrow, three more days of *this old dump*,' she sang with venom.

The lino under my feet buckled and swam. I clutched on to a flexing wall.

'You can come nicking with us,' said Cora. 'I want to get some of those false eyelashes – the really huge ones that they used to wear in the sixties. They've got them in Rackhams.'

'Rackhams is easy,' said Gina. Her tone was just as if we were in the park trying out cartwheels and handstands a few years previously.

I grabbed both their arms – shook them violently. 'Stop it. Stop it, you two. How can you just joke about it like that? I don't want to leave school. You're talking like you've just given up.'

They looked at me pityingly.

'We're only telling you what's been happening,' said Gina.

'Get real, Alice,' said Cora. 'We're out of here.'

The bell rang for classes. Bodies rushed around us and Cora and Gina were swept up in them. Johnny was gone. For the first time I wished I'd told them about us, so I could talk about it, claim something, some extra loss. But you can't do that when your love's a secret. You have to bear it alone. And I doubted that they'd listen anyway. Gina's shell was tightly in place, fixed and varnished, not even a hairline crack. It seemed to get even shinier when I was around. Nothing I said or did all day penetrated, she rebuffed every attempt at real contact as casually as swatting a fly. It didn't stop me trying. She couldn't close off every part of her, I would get through with vibrations, through the air she was breathing; *somehow*. I watched the corners of her eyes when I asked if she thought there was any way to stop Dracula getting rid of us, Dracula winning. They wrinkled for a second, then smoothed out as she shrugged. 'Nah. Can't wait to get out anyway.'

In the end there was nothing left to do but to try Rose. I found her walking around the sports field, arm in arm with Rachel Williamson. 'Rose, can I have a word?'

'Alice!' She was shocked that I'd approached her, wouldn't meet my eyes for more than a second or two.

'In private,' I said. 'Please, Rose.'

Rachel pulled Rose closer. 'You don't have to,' she said.

'Who asked you?' I said.

'I won't be long,' said Rose, disentangling herself. 'Wait here, hey?'

We walked off into the woods. There were still a few burnt rings in the undergrowth – from another age, it seemed – and daffodils were coming up, edging the playing field with yellow. Rose was hanging back a few steps, casting glances over her shoulder.

'What's up?' I said. 'Bothered she won't be your friend any more?'

Rose glared at me. 'You really think that's all I've got to worry about, don't you?' she said.

'Well, you're hardly about to get kicked out of school.'

'It's not my fault,' she said, her eyes brimming. 'I didn't mean –' Rachel was moving towards us and Rose stopped, swallowed hard. 'Look Alice, I don't want you all to get thrown out. And I'm really sorry about Johnny being sent to Borstal, that must be awful for Gina. But there's nothing I can do.'

'Talk to Gina,' I said. A few drops of rain bounced off the tree canopy and stirred up the ash at our feet. 'She's closed up totally. I know she doesn't want to leave, doesn't want to end up nicking lipsticks all her life. You used to be close . . . I thought maybe you could get through somehow.' The rain came down harder, Rachel was calling.

'Believe me, Alice. Anything I say will only make it worse.' She stifled a sob; turned away and started to run.

'Rose, please!' I called after her.

But she'd joined Rachel, there were two wet figures running for shelter. Just before the school entrance Rose stopped, swiped the rain from her face and stared at me – almost like she was trying to send a message. Then she vanished into the blackness of the science corridor.

219

# Fake It

I wrote to the Borstal that night, the first of many letters, never replied to. Young offenders' institution. Juvenile prison. Boot camp. Nick. I could hardly bear to think about it. Johnny dressed in some anonymous uniform, up before it was light, drills in the yard, inedible food, locks, bolts; violence saturating the very bricks. I didn't know where I'd got these ideas from, an extra light had turned on in my consciousness; I could see it all so clearly, feel the rough thin bedclothes, smell shit and sick and disinfectant and fear. In my bag I found some postcards I'd written to Johnny in Weymouth, and never sent in case Gina picked them up off the mat. Holiday postcards of blue sea and white chalky cliffs with messages of suppressed longing. *It's lovely here but I wish you were too.* Simple words with decorations, flourishes and shadings, all my passion in the detail. Dear Johnny. Lots of LOVE XXXX. I put them in with my guilt- and tear-soaked letter, a breath of the time before, when I traced my decorations on his skin.

'Of course, his previous didn't help,' said Gina, the next day, when I asked her about the decision; desperate for information, details.

'What previous?'

'Oh, stealing; cars, you know.'

'You mean nicking, like you and Cora do.'

'Oh, Alice, everyone does that.'

Yes, maybe; sweets from the corner shop, the odd lipstick. Crowding in so the assistants were harassed, shoving penny chews and tester makeup in your pocket – everyone did that, but not so many graduated to full-scale theft like Cora and Gina. They were selling their stuff around school. I'd heard Cora say she'd got twenty quid for a leather jacket. *Twenty quid.* An absolute fortune. And who did Cora know who had twenty quid to spend on a leather jacket?

I had to stop them, I had to stop what had happened to Johnny happening to them.

We were supposed to be in English but the thought of McGeady was just too much. Instead we hid in the biology lab; the class was on a field trip. Gina sat on a desk kicking her heels and sang 'two more days of school'. Cora singed the ends of her bootlaces with a bunsen burner, sending trails of smoke up to the ceiling.

'Listen,' I said, 'I've had an idea.'

Neither of them looked at me. Cora got a mirror out of her bag and started shaping her eyebrows. I winced at every pluck.

'Why don't we ask the spirit what to do?' I said. 'Just to see. There might be something we haven't thought of.'

'The spirit?' said Gina.

'The spirit?' said Cora. But they'd looked up, I'd got their attention.

'Oh, you mean that stuff in the shed,' said Gina. 'You still into that?'

'We could just ask,' I said. I swear my heart stopped, but I fixed my face in casual mode.

'OK,' said Gina, grabbing her Army & Navy rucksack and jumping off the desk. No harm in asking.' *Sex Pistols* had joined *Dylan* and *Led Zeppelin* on the bag.

'Yeah, why not?' said Cora.

'When?' I said.

'I'm busy tonight,' said Cora. 'Tomorrow lunchtime.'

'OK.'

'Come on then,' said Gina. 'Let's get on with this.' We were crowded into the shed – too big for it really, our elbows and knees colliding, Cora's hair getting mussed up with spiders' webs and dust. She wasn't impressed, her eyes said I'm-just-tolerating-this. Anxiety spread down my arms and legs, to my fingers and toes then crackled out into the atmosphere. 'And stop banging into things, Alice, we're jammed in enough as it is.'

'No room for a spirit if you ask me,' said Cora.

'What?'

'Joke, Alice.'

The board was out, the glass in place. I'd got it all ready earlier – couldn't afford anything to go wrong. 'Ready?' I said.

'Wait a minute,' said Cora. 'What are we going to ask it?'

'Well, we could ask . . . I mean we could see . . . if there's anything we can do about tomorrow.' I was sitting opposite the window with a block of hazy light resting on me. Gina and Cora were in the darkness; I could only see flashes from them – earrings, nails, Cora's newly acquired gold tooth.

'You mean when Dracula kicks us out of school?'

'If she kicks us out of school,' I said. 'We might be able to stop it.'

'Yeah? And how's that?' They'd leant back from the board, crossed legs, swung one leg each; irritatingly, in unison. I wondered why they'd bothered to come at all.

'Well, I don't know, do I?' I said. 'That's what we're here to ask.'

'Keep your hair on, Alice,' said Gina.

I was sweating. The creatures on the board were dancing in front of my eyes. Cora tapped her fingers in a drum roll.

'OK, fingers on,' I said.

We waited. Something moved in the sky behind me: I felt my back go cold as the sun was cut off. Nothing happened, I could feel absolutely nothing and knew with horrible gut-emptying certainty that it wouldn't; not today. The spirit wasn't coming. The light was the same, the traffic noise didn't dim, there was no softening in the air. Cora started to hum, click out a tune on her teeth. Gina's eyes stared at me out of the darkness opposite.

'Not much happening, Alice.'

'No. We'd better think of a question.'

'Go on then.'

'Spirit, are you there?' I said. My finger trembled on the glass and it rattled. Gina glanced at me expectantly.

YES.

'That's more like it,' said Cora.

'What's going to happen tomorrow?' said Gina. Now my eyes had adjusted to the shed's darkness I could see that she was very intent, very still, her bravado dissolved in the fading light.

B–A–D

Cora's forehead wrinkled, Gina's body sagged. They were looking up from the board to me and back again.

'How bad?' I said.

The glass scratched and scraped around the board. Our eyes followed it.

F–O–R   F–U–T–U–R–E

'We know it's going to be bad,' said Cora. 'That's hardly news.'

'I think he means there'll be consequences,' I said.

'Oh,' said Gina.

Shivers were passing through my body, I couldn't believe the others didn't notice.

'Ask then, Alice,' said Gina, her eyes wide and expectant.

'You want me to?'

'Yes.'

'Cora?'

'Go on then.'

I took a deep breath. 'Spirit help us,' I said. 'What can we do tomorrow?'

A slight creak. A roar from traffic outside.

S–A–Y   S–O–R–R–Y

'Huh?' said Gina. 'Say sorry to who? For what?'

I clamped my teeth together to stop them chattering.

A–P–O–L–O–G–I–Z–E

The glass moved slowly. Sweat was pricking round my collar.

D–R–A–C–U–L–

A squeal of airbrakes outside. Shouting, an argument.

My finger slipped off the glass. It stopped moving, half-way to the A.

For a few seconds there was silence. No one breathed. Then distant, strangely piercing screaming from the High Street. *Look what you've done! Just look at what you've done!* I wiped my hand on my jeans, but sweat appeared again straight away, slicked across my palm.

'You pushed it!' said Cora. She stood up above me. 'Alice, you were pushing the glass!'

I tried to speak, protest, but the lies got stuck in my throat.

'You bloody cow,' said Gina. Her face throbbed, full of blood.

'Right, that is it,' said Cora. 'I told you ages ago she couldn't be trusted.'

'What do you mean?' I said. My voice sounded distant too. They were gathering their things, throwing needle-sharp looks at me.

'With anything. There's something in you that just *wobbles*, Alice.'

'How could you do this to us?' said Gina. They were at the door, leaving me. 'And anyway,' she said as she stepped out of the shed, dusk blurring her shape. 'I would never have said sorry, you should know that, Alice. Because if I did, if I apologized for something I didn't do, well, I wouldn't be *me* any more, would I? And that's more important than school.'

'Come on, Gina,' said Cora. 'Let's get out of here.'

Even Ellie's mum couldn't refuse to let me through the door when she saw the state I was in; shivering and shaking and completely drowned by a freak downpour that had fallen out of the sky, right on to me. 'Ellie's working,' she said. My foot slithered over the doorstep. 'OK,' she said. 'She's in the back room.'

Ellie looked up from her books. The skin under her eyes was smudged purple. She rubbed them and blinked at me. 'Alice? What's happened?'

I sat down with a squelch on a chair next to Ellie and let the tears fall out.

'I was only trying to help,' I said, later, dry-eyed, dry-mouthed. All the liquid was gone from me; my skin felt papery, my throat sore.

I know,' said Ellie. Her eyes were kind and she patted my arm, but it was more like I was a skittery animal than a best friend. I remembered when there were the five of us, when we could lift each other's worries by linking arms, sticking our heads in the air and singing them away. I'd only have to see Ellie or Gina and I'd feel better, because they were like me, they understood.

'I can see her point though,' said Ellie. She rushed on quickly, before I had time to protest. 'Look, I know you're upset, Alice, and I know you wanted to do the right thing, but can't you see what you were asking of Gina?'

'Two words,' I said. '*I'm sorry*. And it would all be over. It's not much to ask to stop her ending up in Borstal like Johnny.'

'Yes, but . . .' Ellie fell silent for a moment, softly exasperated. A copy of *The Crucible* lay open on her desk. 'Don't you see? It's like John Proctor,' she said. 'He doesn't – he can't – sign the confession of witchcraft in the end even though he knows the whole process is a sham. Because he can't have his name put to it. Part of him wants to – to get it all over with, to give them what they want, someone who'll stand up and take the blame – but he just can't do it in the end. That's what Gina would have been like, even if she had believed the spirit was telling her to say sorry. She would have got in that room and –'

We could both see it. Us standing in Dracula's office, the carpet creeping over our shoes. Me mentally urging Gina on, thinking only of the result, the end to all our troubles. Gina glancing at me and then at Wills-Masterson and then at Cora and then saying, No! I can't do it. I can't say sorry because I'm not.

'But he died, Ellie,' I said. 'Proctor. That was the end of him.'

'Have some faith, Alice,' said Ellie. 'Gina won't die.'

We talked a bit more, about Ellie's plans. She had it all sorted. 'O' Levels then sixth-form college, then a year working abroad, then a degree in politics, economics, something like that. Her desk was covered in leaflets – CND, animal rights. 'I've stopped eating meat,' she said. 'Have you ever thought about it, Alice?'

'Er, no.'

I felt uncomfortable, my damp clothes itched. 'Working abroad? Where will you go?'

'I'm not sure yet. Anywhere. I'm sick of trying to fit in here. England's just like school, you're either a hundred per cent in or a hundred per cent out. I might try Israel. A kibbutz.'

'A what?'

'A kibbutz. Haven't you heard of them? It's a totally different way of living, everything's communal, even bringing up the children.'

'I can see why that might appeal,' I said.

'It's not just that, Alice,' she said. 'It's based on principles.'

At the door she stopped to tidy her hair in the hall mirror and I couldn't help staring at her. Her face was the same as it had always been – pretty, kind, soft – except for smudges of late-night study; but her body was different. It was squarer, leaner. I wondered if the old Ellie had ever really existed. If this person with purpose was always there, waiting to come out, for the right time. I wondered what she must have thought of us.

'Thanks, Ellie,' I said.

'Don't be too hard on yourself, Alice. It's not your fault.'

'Oh, but it is.'

'It's not,' she said, grasping my shoulder, shaking me a little. 'It's Wills-Masterson and her regime that's caused this. Plain and simple. It's just like in politics – they get hold of a bit of power and it goes straight to their heads. But times have changed; people – even teenagers – won't sit back and take it any more. Dracula just hasn't woken up to that.'

'It doesn't feel simple.'

'Well it is. And Alice . . .' I walked out to the gate, stood under the orange light of the streetlamp, needlepoints of rain pricking through my hair. 'I'm sorry about Johnny. I really am.'

I couldn't sleep so I read all night. Read to block out the awful realization that I'd failed; failed both of them. So I read everything I had. *The Water Gypsies*, *Stig of the Dump*, old copies of *Jackie* and the *Beano* annual. The Bash Street Kids didn't seem funny any more, somehow. By four a.m. there was nothing left except *The Crucible*, discarded in a corner of the room. I thought I might rip it up and throw it into the yard but the next thing I knew, after my hand had reached out for it, the light had started to tinge the sky outside. I felt like a layer of stupidity had been scoured off me, like I'd just watched the drama in Salem happening in front of my eyes. John Proctor finding himself challenging the church and its power when he'd have much preferred to keep well out of it. So what had we done, when faced with *our* challenge? Rose backed off, Ellie was dragged away, Gina stood firm, Cora defied. But what did I do? Fiddled and interfered and got distracted and, finally, failed. What did that say about me?

The morning noise of the city started to gear up outside. As I drifted off into sleep a name echoed around my head. Gina. Gina Marshall.

# A Miraculous Escape

That was twenty years ago. Twenty-one since the fire. I go
into my old bedroom, where Mum now sleeps, and look for
my books but they're not there; *Stig of the Dump* replaced by
*New Woman*. The room is strewn with discarded clothes and
cosmetics, the bin overflowing, cotton wool smeared with
mascara-black, foundation-pink. Mum's bed is a tangle of
bedclothes, nightdresses, magazines. But she's still here –
that girl – her shape, her voice. I lift a piece of wallpaper
loosened by me and underneath find scribbled pencil sig-
natures *GinaRoseAliceCoraEllie*. I go to the windowsill where
I scratched *Johnny 4 Alice 4 ever* and find it, the place where
the point on my compass scored into layers of paint, now
ingrained with dust and muck, come up in relief like a brass
rubbing, clearer than it ever was then. Then you had to angle
your eyes to see the words, could only catch them in certain
lights.

I got married when I was twenty-one. It was winter; the
streets sheets of ice outside the register office, my mum
standing there in her flowery frock, shivering, her mouth
stretched into a smile. We had a house to go to, me and Dan;
jobs. I was pleased to be married, to have a piece of paper
which said I was a different person now, the past was just
that; gone. There was a plan, a map for our lives. 'In five
years . . .' Dan would say, 'In ten . . .' and I'd smile and nod,

the right words would pop out of my mouth in a bubble and I'd watch them bounce gently around the room. The clean spacious rooms of our marital home. We wouldn't even clutter it with words. I floated around those rooms not touching anything, cushioned, suspended. It felt like we'd made a den for ourselves, like children, a starter-home den. We kept the lawn clipped and the paint fresh and told each other if we were going to be late. He had a set to his stride as he crunched the gravel. Determined, ambitious. Grown-up. The law said we were, anyway.

Staring out at the frosted fields behind the house I asked Dan who decided on twenty-one. Who said that at twenty-one we become adults overnight? He said we can't decently leave it any later, even our society can't pretend that twenty-one years isn't long enough to mature. He was born forty. There are photographs of him at thirteen, in his school tie and blazer, looking like he's about to chair a board meeting. He put his arm round my shoulders and for a moment everything seemed certain. I was twenty-one and my life was starting again. Only this time there was a plan, I wouldn't get sidetracked. Even though twenty-one is a little bit of conjury; a number pulled out of a hat, it still seemed fitting; helped me believe it was right. I chose a shape and I tried to live in it. A shape out of an arbitrary number. One way to do it, I suppose.

Mum arrived at our wedding expecting flowers and confetti and speeches and found me and Dan, sleek in grey without so much as a cake. 'No cake?' said Mum. 'You can't have a wedding without a cake. And where are all your friends?' Dan was irritated by even having to have witnesses. Pare things down to the essentials, that was his idea. No frills. It appealed to me then, a streamlined life. We bought the house on the edge of a village that still had a post office, an easy drive to the gym.

It was just about the only thing I ever did that Ellie approved of, that wedding. 'No fuss,' she said. 'All that money that people spend on weddings, it's disgusting, hundreds of pounds on a dress you only wear for one day.'

'What should they spend it on then, Ellie?' said Dan. She was just back from a year abroad, VSO, pained by the contrasts. The only one of the group that came to our wedding. 'It's their money. They can do what they like.'

'Isn't life simple when you're a capitalist?' snapped Ellie.

'The simpler the better,' said Dan.

I thought I was sorting it all out; sorting my life. Putting the past behind me and making something of myself. Houses, careers, cars, a place in the pecking order – as near to the top as possible for Dan. All that space and comfort and money as a cushion, lifting us into a double-glazed bubble from which we could watch the world, refracted two or three times. But it only works if it's what you want. If your heart is in it, if you truly believe in everything that holds it all up. Dan did; still does. But if you don't truly believe in that then your whole life becomes a terrible fake.

I take the bus out to one of the council estates that ring the edge of the city; tell Mum and Corinne and Johnny I've got a job to do. They think it's something to do with the case, that I'm plotting, and they're pleased; glance at each other. Alice will sort it out. Destination Druids Heath – I smile at the name – and I look at the houses, small and square with scrappy gardens, but can't find any clues in them. People's faces are blank. Dogs and kids. Towerblocks and abandoned shopping trolleys. Beyond, a glimpse of green.

There's no answer at the flat, only a mat outside the door, a faded and smudged *Welcome*. I'm disappointed that there's no window, nowhere to peer through, check out the curtains, ornaments, a glimpse of a photograph . . .

'He's away, love.' It's a woman from the flat opposite.

'Away?' I say. A small boy appears between her legs, clutching a toy koala.

'On holiday.'

'But he will be back?'

'Oh yes. Can't be too soon for me. Doesn't feel right in this block without him here.' She ruffles the boy's hair. 'My Jason misses him too.'

'Right. Thanks.'
'Any message?'
'No. I'll call back.'

It's lively in the Bridge. A midweek buzz coming out of nowhere and I find I can enjoy it, like an unexpected present. Some of Johnny's mates have arrived, fresh from a trip to Amsterdam or Copenhagen or somewhere, full of stories and news of people spread afar. Corinne is sitting on a seat, cross-legged, her stomach spilling out, and people say, 'Hey! A baby, that's wonderful.' They're talking about leaving, going to Spain before the weather gets cold.

I head for the bar. Johnny grabs my waist as I go by. I must look shocked because he says, 'Sorry, Alice, sometimes the caveman in me just takes over.'

'It's OK,' I say. 'I used to feel like that about you.'

'You did?' I feel that his eyes can scour off a layer of my skin, trigger words that I never meant to say.

'Yes. I just wanted to grab you and never let you go.'

'You should have,' says Johnny fiercely. His face is close to mine. 'Why didn't you?'

'Johnny, I was only fifteen. I didn't know anything.'

'Maybe you did,' he says. 'Maybe you just forgot it all later.'

He's leaning on the bar, unusually relaxed, and I have an urge to pull him closer, tap the buried power in me that might draw out his sweetness, his love. I'm smiling at the thought of me, the forensics expert, the scientist and sensible one sitting in a pub in the middle of the day, the middle of the week, surrounded by what the newspapers call scum, trying to reach my buried power. But I must have some; have had some. What else could it have been going on in the shed, with the board, and the spirit?

Sunlight flares on his beer glass. 'I found your dad,' I say to Johnny. It just slips out, a fish through the net. 'In the telephone book. He's been here all the time. I went to his flat.' The fish is out, swimming away. I'll never catch it now. Johnny stiffens, says nothing, but I feel a flinch in him. 'He wasn't there, though. Gone on holiday.' Johnny is stone-faced

231

next to me; his fingers tighten around his glass. 'It was Mr McGeady who put me on to it,' I say, as fast as I can, before I lose my nerve. 'His kids tracked him down by looking in the phone book. And finding my dad too, it just made me realize that there's a time, you know, when you have to do these things.'

The pub is noisy but I can hear nothing except Johnny's breathing, a little faster than normal, a touch panicky. 'What happened between you two?' I say. 'I mean I know you argued, but . . .'

Johnny stares at the wall opposite, eyes fixed on a painting of hunting dogs. I can't read him, who he is angry with. There's anger though, I can taste it in the air as it hits the back of my throat.

'When I came out of Borstal they were gone, both of them,' he says, still staring at the dogs. 'The house was empty. No note no address no fuck all.' I don't dare touch him, my fingers would burn. 'That's when I went on the road, pack on my back, away from everything. And I bloody loved it. It's my life, being free, going where I like, outside of all of it. They forced me out, Alice; and I'll never go back in.' He turns to me, presses the words on to my skin with his hot breath. 'That's why I can't go down. I can't come out of prison and walk back to nothing again. But you're right, there is a time, and when this is all over I'm going to stop running,' he says, fiercely.

'Running from what?' I say. I can feel emotions churning around inside him. Perhaps I can read them if I tune in properly.

'You know,' he says. 'You were there.'

The house on the estate. An outside light. The back way through the gardens on to the railway so you didn't have to walk down the street.

'You and those other girls, you were always there,' says Johnny. 'But it all went –' he clicks two fingers, a snap next to my ear '– like that. One minute Sandra was there and Dad was a laugh and the house was full and then it was just gone. They were gone. Everything vanished. I just turned and ran, from all the things that weren't there any more.'

232

'And you never tried to find them again?' I say.

His eyes cloud for a second, he speaks through his teeth. 'I miss Gina,' he says, 'I've always missed her. But I couldn't stand to see him. Sitting there just taking it, doing nothing but brood. It was no good, Alice. I had to get away. He was such a hypocrite about me getting into trouble, and you know how much hypocrisy winds you up when you're fifteen. The bastard never even wrote to me while I was inside. Him – who knows what it's like to sit locked in a cell, what it's like not to exist any more.' He pauses, takes a breath. 'You didn't forget me though, did you, my lovely Alice?'

'What was it like in there, Johnny?' I say. My heart is beating hard, up into my throat. 'Only I've always wondered if there was anything I could have done, you know, at the time –'

'You?' He is staring at me.

'Yes.' I feel limp. A piece of seaweed dragged by the tide. 'I should have turned up that day. Should have been there for you.' I close my eyes at the shame of the memory, try to blend the hum in my head with the hum of talking, music, beer hissing into glasses.

The hum is broken by Johnny's laugh. I hear it rumble in his stomach first, then the laugh jumps out. People look round, Bri glances over and gives us a thumbs-up. They notice happiness in here, like to see it.

Johnny puts his arm around me. 'Alice,' he says, 'the Old Bill put me in the nick, them and Andrew Rushton's lot. I'm glad you weren't there actually. It wasn't a pretty sight when they tried to take me down.'

Rushy. I take a puff on a joint that's going round – best hash oil, from the 'Dam, so I'm told – and it unlocks something, opens a hole that was sealed up; in comes Andrew Rushton, in Technicolor. The surgery, smelling of disinfectant and chemicals. Rushy, tacking on to the gangs that Johnny hung around with; buying packets of Embassy and crashing them all out, nervously touching his spots.

'What happened to him?' I say.

'Rich-boy Rushy?' Johnny says. 'In and out of rehab for the last fifteen years.'

233

'That's terrible,' I say. 'Have you seen him?'

'Now and again,' says Johnny. 'When I first came out of Borstal he'd run a mile at the mention of my name. Then he stopped caring. Robbed his own dad's surgery a few years back, I heard. The family moved out of town.'

I think of their house, squat and solid, well-pointed bricks, topiary in the garden. I think of the doctor – bristling and bustling and bossing the lawyers around – getting what he wanted for his boy, while me and Johnny squirmed on our seats, powerless. I think of Rushy, addicted, like the kids who come into the Citizens Advice trying to scratch and scrabble their way out of trouble, annihilating their memories with drugs. Did Rushy blame himself for what happened to Johnny? Feel so guilty that he had to destroy himself? For being weak and going along with his parents? For somehow blanking what was important. Like I did.

'Just shows you what guilt can do,' I say, lightly. Experimentally.

'Nah,' says Johnny. 'It just shows you what drugs can do. They can get anyone. His father might have been able to shield him from the law, but anyone can get addicted; even a doctor's son.'

And now my life – the one that I've spurned, since being back here – seems like a miraculous escape. From crime, drugs, prostitution; all those things that could have happened. Death, disability, madness. That I touched them, got burnt and drew my hand back – I'd like to think purposefully, but it wasn't, it was more like being cowed. *This is what happens if you break the rules.* So I didn't any more. I lived a life that was socially approved. Ellie was the one with purpose, with passion. Get obsessed and stay obsessed. Make a decision and then get on with it. Sounds easy, huh? But how can it be, sitting in a refugee camp band-aiding the messes of war and history? That's not an easy life. I think of her coming to my house and sleeping for a week, staring in my wardrobe, uncomprehending. Wearing one of Dan's sweatshirts as she watched documentaries about inner-city riots, leaning forward to try and catch the sense of it. But

234

she wasn't going to end up a junkie; on the game. It was one way to get through the eighties – leave the country. Do good.

But what about Rose? Rose with her Colgate smile staring at me out of the TV screen. Remade, madeover, completely transformed from the vacillating schoolgirl I knew. Now I find out that she was here all the time, on *Midlands Today*, the weathergirl. Ask Rose O'Connor, people said, when there were weddings or parties or they were thinking about a barbeque. Rose knows if it'll be bright or not. The move to Granada was a career step, she wanted out of the weather, the papers said, into chat shows, morning telly. Recipes and real-life tales. All those lives to dip into; squeaky clean and shining, nothing dark before lunchtime, unless the message is unequivocal, the redemption clear. They say she has a happy home, the papers. A good family. So she must have known, deep down. She didn't want that sort of life; she'd have this, instead. Like choosing an outfit – ready to wear – with the certainty that it'll suit you for the rest of your life.

The people in the pub swirl around me. 'So are you satisfied now?' says Johnny. 'Will you let things be?' He's not angry with me, I don't think. But he's still stiff, his voice clipped.

'I can't,' I say. 'Not until I find out what happened to Gina.'

# Calumny

I tried to skive off school after my disaster in the shed, but Mum wasn't having any of it.

'Time off?' she said. 'When I'm prostrating myself in front of that battleaxe to allow you to stay on? Forget it, Alice. And mind you behave when you're in that office. Look sorry even if you can't say it. Your future's more important than your pride.'

'But, Mum –'

'No way. Come on, up out of that bed. And don't even think about sloping off to your park or your shed. I'll ring to make sure you're there. Get busy, Alice, I've got a lot to get through today.'

Too sunk in my own gloom to be bothered with Mum's day, I still couldn't help noticing how bright she looked at breakfast. She danced around the table, choreographing toast and cereal to 'Don't Go Breaking My Heart', which chirped irritatingly out of the radio.

'OK then, what is it?' I said, through clenched teeth.

'You don't have to be interested.'

'All right.' I chewed a toast crust. Mum let out a small gasp of exasperation. 'All right then, tell me,' I said.

'No, no. Don't you concern yourself about me.' She had her back to me, was reapplying shimmery lipstick, patting her freshly rollered hair.

236

'Come on, Mum. Where are you going? Why are you dressed up?'

She twirled round, beaming. 'For a business meeting, with Robert.' She was absurdly happy about it.

'A business meeting? About what? Who's Robert?' The pit of my stomach froze. She's going to sell the shop, I thought. For some reason this terrified me, almost as much as the thought of Wills-Masterson. Gina and Cora.

'Oh, some deal he's doing. Says the feminine touch should help him through the last stages. Don't you think it was nice of him to ask me?'

'Delightful,' I said. 'But who is he?'

'Alice, you really haven't been paying attention around here, have you? He's my man from the Otley Arms.'

Outside the sky was heavy grey. Workmen were resurfacing the road and I breathed in the dark, acrid smoke, let it settle in my lungs. Perhaps I'll die, I thought, then they'll see how unfair they've been. The only honourable way out of this, to die young and misunderstood.

'Alice.' Mr McGeady stepped out from behind a tree.

'Oh. Hi.'

'I've been waiting for you.' He seemed a bit frantic. His hair stood out in clumps and his black clothes were glazed, like school skirts that had fidgeted on too many wooden chairs.

'Really.'

'You know what today is, don't you?'

'Thursday.'

'*Alice.*' He was following me up the school drive.

Anger lifted my head. 'Thursday the tenth.'

'Alice, this is really important.'

I spun round instantly so that everything was frozen in the swirl, for a second. 'Leave me alone, right?' I said. 'I tried your suggestion, and it failed. Abysmally. So just leave me alone.'

No one else spoke to me all morning, unless you count Taz giving me the Vulcan death grip and then running away manically laughing. I wished it had worked. Dragging my weight around the corridors from room to room took all my energy;

237

everyone else rushed, in groups of three, four, five. Chatting and laughing and yelling and swirling into one big noise and movement. Cora and Gina were around, but we blanked each other, could sense when we might meet around corners and veered off; instinctively sat in the one place in the room where we couldn't see each other. Rose kept snagging my vision though, materializing out of a blur of bodies, her voice rising above the babble, as if she was trying to reach me. I kept my head down. The clock ticked nearer to midday. Each time I looked at my watch it seemed to have jumped twenty minutes, chunks of time vanished until I was late, late for an appointment with Dracula and my destiny.

Cora had excelled herself. Head to toe in ragged black; electric pink hair pinned with neon clothes pegs, shiny lips, nails and a Dangerous Girls T-shirt. She must have transformed herself in the toilets. Her eyelids were bruise-purple from her eyebrows down, eyeliner meeting at her temples, the whole peacock-tail pattern twitching. Dracula was a match for her: patent high heels, metallic jacket buttons with anchors, keys clanking from her shiny belt and hair concrete-gold. I chanced a glance at Gina – my fellow peahen – but she was studying the floor, scowl creases etched deep into her forehead.

We shuffled in. Wills-Masterson stood behind the desk and handed us each a sheet of paper.

'These figures, young ladies,' she said, 'detail the costs so far of replacing the sixth-form block and repairing other incendiary damage around the school grounds. As you can see they are far from insignificant.' She paused for a reaction, grabbed the paper out of Gina's hand and stuck it under her nose. 'The governors and I are agreed that your involvement in this extremely serious matter cannot go unpunished and they are fully behind my decision that this meeting today is your very last chance to show some contrition.' Her chest was puffing up and I wouldn't have been surprised to see the anchors pinging off, bouncing off the glass cabinets. 'Have you anything to say?' Her eyes swept over the three of us, halted on me.

'I'm sorry,' I said, almost involuntarily. I was; for the costs, for the trouble to the school, for Gina not speaking to me, for Johnny being in Borstal. My eyes pricked. Cora clicked her teeth.

'And you two?' said Dracula, minesweeping the others. Gina sniffed, Cora bored holes in the window behind with her great purple eyes. 'I hope you realize my only alternative is to expel you from this school?'

A clock ticked, a door slammed, Dracula hovered.

Cora's voice was steady, low; as reasonable as I'd ever heard it. 'That's bullshit, actually,' she said, looking straight at Wills-Masterson. 'There's plenty of things you could do. Like leaving us alone. Like forgetting this ridiculous witchhunt. Maybe find out who really did it. You could even accept that accidents happen.' She waved her hand in the air, changed her voice tone to sickly sweet. 'Any number of things.' Wills-Masterson fizzed.

'Why?' said Gina, a bullet from her mouth. 'Why are we being expelled? You can't expel us for the fire because we didn't have anything to do with it. So why?'

Dracula splayed her hands on the desk in front of her and leant forward, her gold hair like a helmet, glinting. 'You think I don't know, don't you?' she said. 'But you're wrong. The whole school knows what your group has been up to. And as if that wasn't enough –' she advanced round the desk, flicking her finger with each phrase '– truancy. Sale of stolen property around school. Forged absence notes. Violation of school-uniform rules. Poor reports. Discipline problems. Persistent lateness. Insolence. Smoking on school property. Bullying. Bad –'

She was cut off by Cora, who whipped herself around and headed for the door. 'Bullying?' she said. 'I'm not listening to this. There's only one bully around here that I can see.'

'You come back here, young lady!'

'I don't have to,' said Cora, stepping to the door. 'I'm expelled, aren't I?'

Cora opened the office door and disappeared down the corridor in a spiky haze of black and pink. When I turned back round to face the headmistress, Gina had vanished too.

She paced, I waited. I couldn't make my feet move. I kept thinking of Mum, her morning optimism, prompted by so little, a friendly word, an unexpected invitation. Wills-Masterson leant forwards slightly, as if into the wind, shouldering it out of the way. I wished I'd stormed off with Gina and Cora, and was at that very moment smoking in the park with them, triumphantly. No need to be furtive any more. But Alice Tracey was still sinking into the carpet in Mrs Wills-Masterson's office, reminding herself to breathe.

'I take it you're not leaving with your friends?'

I shook my head. I wasn't sure I could walk, let alone face Gina and Cora.

'Well. We've got some things to discuss then.' She handed me a slim folder. Evidence: the forged notes I'd written for Ellie and Gina, detention records, attendance records. An affidavit from Mr Wilson that he'd seen me on the street when I should have been in school. *With a boy.* My heart sank to my shoes; I should have left with the others, maintained a scrap of dignity.

'However, your case is slightly different, Alice,' said Dracula. 'Your reports are good, all the teachers seem to think you're university material.' I looked at Dracula's trophy photos on the wall. 'And secondly, you have some people on your side. Your case has been strongly pleaded, and not only by your mother.'

'Mr McGeady,' I said.

'No,' said Dracula. 'It wasn't him. He's hardly a shining example despite what you girls think. But we won't go into his weaknesses just now.'

*One moment of weakness. That's all it takes.* The words flashed through my consciousness but I pushed them away, tried to concentrate on the moment. I thought of our different parents. Mr Marshall. Mum. Ellie's mum. Cora's stiff-faced father.

'Cora probably hasn't even told her parents,' I said. The sound of my voice was a surprise. 'And Gina's dad, well, he's got a few problems.'

240

'Don't make excuses for them, Alice. Nothing will wash with me after the way those two have behaved.'

'But –' The headmistress cut in. I wasn't sure what I was going to say anyway.

'Alice. If you want to save yourself and your future I'd stay quiet now. Remember we know what you've been up to. In that shed. With that board. You've been playing with fire, young lady, but from this moment on it stops.'

Rose. Bloody Rose O'Connor. It had to be. I was out of the office and in the slippery corridor. Move, feet, *move*. Get me out of here. The door was getting closer, my legs were working at last. Keep at it. Keep going. Bloody Rose, she'd *told* them. That was why Wills-Masterson was so convinced we had something to do with the fires. She thought we'd somehow conjured the fire, to wind her up, to taunt her. Trees rushed past me, someone called out. Ignore them, legs, *move*. But then why let me off? After all, I started it, it was all done in our shed. My feet slowed, weighed down by the thoughts in my head. Because I don't use the power. Don't flaunt it, like Cora; or wear it as skin, like Gina. The only time I did try to use it I failed so badly that I lost the trust of my best friend. But Rose failed too, if she was trying to stop the Ouija drawing Gina away, if she thought what was happening was the spirit's fault. Because Gina's gone now, gone from both of us.

My knees collapsed. I grabbed hold of a lamppost and hung on. The street lurched around me, buses at perilous angles, pigeons pecking holes in the sky. A face coming sideways at me. Him again. Mr McGeady.

'Alice? Are you OK?'

I clawed up the lamppost. Glowered.

'I saw you leave,' he said. 'And the others.' Flecks of spit came out of his mouth when he spoke. His neckline was peppered with shaving nicks.

'Where have they gone?' I said.

'Oh, they were too quick for me.' An attempt at a smile. Sweat dripped from his temples.

I looked hard at him; he was, he was trembling.

241

'Listen, Alice, I think you should know that . . . well you shouldn't take this too personally. The headmistress isn't used to, you know, being challenged. I think it's a bit . . . messy for her. There have been problems with the governors, the authority, she felt she had to assert herself –'

'Why are you telling me this?'

'Well . . . I hoped that you might understand it better, one day.'

'What I understand is that she can do what she likes, whether it's fair or right or not.'

'Alice, there's no need for this –'

'It was you Rose told,' I said. 'Wasn't it?'

'Rose's very troubled, Alice. Try not to be so hard on her.'

'Troubled?' I said. 'Show me someone who isn't.'

It seemed like that, that day. Mr McGeady with his strange changes and furtive air. Get a grip, I kept wanting to say, I thought you were supposed to be sorted by the time you're in your thirties. I watched people's faces in the street. The bus driver battling with his steering wheel, wresting the bus past roadworks. Mothers herding fractious children – *I'm hungry I'm tired I'm bored* – trying to talk trying to think trying to clear some space. A girl in tears in a shop doorway, a workman rubbing his shoulders and wincing. I put my head down and ran, ran my way through it. Up the street down the alley and into the shed, where it was dark and cool and the noise might die down.

The cat was there, curled up on an old coat. He opened one eye and stretched out a paw. I stroked him, sat down, let my chest rise and fall in sync with his. It seemed important that he was here, at this time, when everyone else was gone. The last of the light through the window was brown, filtered by dirt and smears and handprints.

'Alice?' Mum's voice was gentle, concerned.

'How did you find me?'

'This has been your refuge since you were a little girl, Alice. I always look in the shed first.'

'Has it?' A pause. Mum's breathing. Quiet rumbling and darkness. 'I didn't get expelled.'

242

'Good.' Her hand was round my shoulder, mine was resting on the cat.

'But I lost my friends.'

'Not for ever.'

'I'm not sure, Mum. I can't seem to get it right, whatever I do.'

'You tried to help, Alice.'

'I made it worse. I wanted to make it better. But I just made it worse.' A tear splashed from my cheek on to the cat. He peered at me, licked the fur where my tear had melted.

'You will, Alice,' said Mum. 'One day you will.'

# Echoes Down the Corridor

That was the last time I saw Gina and Cora, silhouettes echoing down the corridor at Rock Hill. Cora spiky black and
pink; Gina with a trail of curdled air behind her. Gina vanished within days; went to her aunt's or something, I heard.
The sister of her mother – she'd never even mentioned an
aunty to me. The house was, as Johnny said, empty. I went
to look at it a few times; walls and a roof, some dusty shrubs,
no lights. A shell. Cora I glimpsed, during that summer. In
the High Street suddenly Cora's face was in front of mine.
From a bus window, the other side of the revolving doors at
Rackhams. She averted her eyes even quicker than me, drew
her long fringe over her face. She wore black – fishnet tights,
spindly jumpers. There was a sharp wind and I thought she
must be freezing, but Cora had never seemed to notice stuff
like that.

Sitting in the park next to the old school building I let it
all wash over me. Just sit here and don't think about it but
let the feelings come and go, like visiting a house you used
to live in and standing in every room, feeling your life bouncing back in waves. There are groups of kids around the park,
some are smoking, some are strutting, some preening and
some are on their own, under a tree with a book or a
Walkman. So; Cora and Gina got expelled, excluded they
call it now, which somehow sounds worse. The message –

you're unacceptable, you're out. Is it any wonder they never came back? Or at least Gina doesn't seem to have; in the photos *she*'s the Russian doll, the same wherever she is, indelible Gina. I sat there alone in my English lessons with the people I loved excluded and expelled and locked away, yet unable to uncouple myself from the production line of lessons and exams and a place in the pecking order, the prize for toeing the line. It was easiest just to blame it all on Rose. I discovered how to humiliate her. Rose was struggling and I could make her cry, with a look; we both knew it.

Mr McGeady chided me. 'Why are you so cruel to Rose, Alice?' he said. 'There's no need for it.'

I glared, said nothing. You've forgotten, I thought. You've forgotten what she did.

Dracula left not long after she expelled Cora and Gina. Transferred, they said, but the rumours were of a purge by the governors. Need for new blood, or something. It left me raging for the whole summer; no one wanted to come near me. Mum would leave trays outside my room, throw in piles of clean clothes and snap the door shut again quickly. And then a year of lonely sullenness before I finally did my 'O' Levels, my English Literature essay on *The Crucible* a torrent of adolescent scorn at the stupidity of *them*, which finished with a quote from the author's own notes at the end of the play: 'The legend has it that Abigail turned up later as a prostitute in Boston. Twenty years after the first execution, the government awarded compensation to the victims still living, and to the families of the dead.' *So*, I scrawled across the page in red marker pen, *so what was the bloody point in it all?*

Mr McGeady tried to persuade me to choose English as one of my 'A' Levels but I refused, said I was going to do science; something concrete. He left Rock Hill too – wanted to take me for a farewell drink but that meant a chat, and I'd had enough of Mr McGeady's chats. So eventually there was only Rose left, and I couldn't get away from her fast enough. Her eyes bothered me, following me around, her mouth opening and closing like a fish. Just say something, I thought. Out with it. But she never did. Rose, whose stream of chatter had rippled through our lives for so long, was dammed. Damned; by me.

'Sorry, Rose,' I say, aloud, in the park. Her only mistake was sticking with us after the queue for the nit nurse. If she'd been an inch shorter she'd have been with Rachel right from the start. And whatever she did she must have thought it the right thing at the time. Like me. A group of girls walk past me, bunched together, whispering; their world tight and enclosed and impenetrable, almost as if they have to have this inwardness before they can step out of it.

It's hot; dust hangs in the air, dandelion fairies float past – I try to catch them so I can make a wish – cars move on the streets all around, floating on the slick of mirror that is the road. A wave – of how I couldn't bear to be on these streets, to walk down these roads, every alley a memory, every lamp-post's pool of light a place where I'd loitered, with Gina and Johnny, Cora and Ellie. I screamed at Mum that we had to leave, banging on the door of her room in the night, my ghostly nightdress reflected in the mirrors, twenty of me screaming, 'Mum, Mum, we have to get out of here.' I kept dreaming it, you see, *Save yourself*.

'It's OK, Alice,' she'd say, folding me back into bed, smoothing my face with her hands. 'You'll be OK.' A lorry grumbled past, a goods train rattled in the distance. I tensed at the noise, my stomach a knot.

'Of course I'm OK,' I said. 'There's nothing wrong with me that getting out of this damn city won't sort out.'

I wanted out of the flat as well. I couldn't stand it; the noise, the mess, the confusion. Demonstrations passed under our windows; CND, anti-nuclear, and I thought of Ellie in another city, part of the protest on another High Street. I lay awake listening to airbrakes hissing in the middle of the night, traffic lights flashing through the curtains. Red, amber, green. Trying to get to sleep to red, amber, green; woken by the milk cart's whining as soon as I did. Mum abandoned domesticity completely – apart from her clothes – and the kitchen slumped into dinginess. Green fuzz on coffee cups, sour milk, whiffs of sewage from the sink hole. Like a student flat without the roach ends. It wouldn't have surprised me to see Mum smoking a joint, the way she was acting.

'I thought it was supposed to be me swooning and sighing like that,' I said.

'Yes,' said Mum, 'it is.' She would come in from her nights out with the man-at-the-Otley and hang around me, breathing Campari and sticky lipstick over my neck. 'How's the studying, Alice?'

'Fine.'

'Well, talk to me a bit then.' She sat down, skirts billowing after her, wanting to talk about Robert. 'Look – Robert bought me this, Robert's taking me away for the weekend, Robert said he loves me, Alice.'

'Robert's married,' I said, bending my head into the pool of light from my lamp. The words buzzed on the page of my book; Mum scowled.

'Sorry, Mum,' I said, 'but it's true.'

'So are lots of things, Alice,' she said.

She took me to see him once, maybe even twice. A glowering teenager in oversized jumpers frowning at their snatched pleasure. It might even have been the Bridge she took me to, asking me to be nice, 'Try a smile, Alice.' The Bridge where I go now, to meet Johnny and Corinne and the rest of the travellers; to plot and drink and smoke and laugh. She didn't take me to the Otley, I know that. Perhaps she wanted that one place to herself anyway. I would have done, if I were her.

I walk through the park down to the railway embankment, treading the familiar path, sure-footed. I don't know where I'm going but I do, sort of, because wherever I come out, on a street or snicket, allotments, garages, churchyard, factory lot or a bridge over the canal I'll know it; can orientate myself quickly, the rest of the city clicking into place as I scan around me for landmarks. But back then all these spaces had to be avoided, there was nowhere I could go that didn't mean something, even the flat and most of all the shed. I felt like the city was scowling at me, every street corner, every one of the thousands of trees.

'Are you ever getting out of that bed?' said Mum, trying to pull the sheet from underneath me, dragging blankets off.

'I can't,' I said, spellbound, foetal in the middle of the mattress.

Eventually we agreed that I could go and live with Gladys, do my 'A' Levels at a college down there. I wanted Mum to come with me but she wouldn't.

'I'm not leaving,' she said.

'Because of *him*, I suppose,' I said.

'He's got nothing to do with this.'

The week before I left I dragged myself off the bed and cleaned. 'Don't touch the shop,' said Mum. 'That's for me in my old age.' As if she was saving those shelves of dusty biscuit tins, boxes of wooden soldiers, candle-shaped lamps for when it was proper to have a really good sortout. When she was ready for that. There was other stuff down there too, boxes of letters, photographs, bits of lace, a locket. Her life was in those boxes.

'You act like you're not coming back,' she said. She touched the scarf I'd tied round my head, pulled out a lock of hair.

'Don't be daft, Mum. You can come and see me, anyway.'

It took me three days to get to the bottom step of the flat – brushing and scrubbing and sorting, a cloud of dust around me. I sat down and looked out at the yard. The sun was setting over the city, blood-orange brooding over the whole broiling noisy mess of it. Dusk blurred all the edges in the yard, the crates of unsorted junk that offended me most. It would take years to clear this up, I thought. I'll just have to turn my back; leave what's lurking behind. The last of the sun glinted on broken glass, mirrors, and flared finally on the windows of the shed before sinking beyond the jagged fence. I pulled my scarf off, shook my hair free, sat down in the darkness and cried for all the things that I couldn't put in a box.

At the back of the park there used to be a gate through to the railway embankment, a short cut to the canal. There's a fence now but I climb over it. I want to get to the pipe bridge because if you stand on the top of the arc you can see over the roofs of the estate down to Gina and Johnny's old house, and behind that the city towers jutting out of leafy skirts. When we were kids we used to do dares on this bridge, see who could run over it fastest, over the spikes without snagging clothes or slipping a foot. I always had to be careful, watch each footstep; Gina was the nimblest, the most fearless. She wasn't scared of the drainage tunnel where Rose said the witches lived, even when we found an old boot outside it, buttons up the ankles and a small curved heel. Even before my breakdown – I suppose I have to call it that now, there's no other word, even though it still sticks in my throat, like Mum who for years called divorce the 'D' word – I'd get a small flutter of fear from walking past the pipe bridge. I'm there now. It's in front of me, black and slippery and spiky. I settle on to the grass and watch the sun cut through the spikes and fall on to my skin.

I settled at Gladys's. The beach, the sea and space all calmed me. I signed up at college and stayed anonymous, wore corduroy in drab colours. Brown, black, sludge-green maybe. There was a careers office that used road signs as their symbolism – arrows pointing in different directions, signposts at the corners and stations where you had to collect qualifications and experience. It all seemed terribly significant to me – the options laid out by someone else, and all I had to do was choose which path and stick to it; if I stayed focused on that everything would be OK.

Mum and Gladys were still anxious, whispering around the kitchen table late at night. 'She's doing OK but she still worries about her friends,' I heard Gladys say, from the top of the stairs. 'Johnny, is it? And Gina?'

Mum swirled her drink around, ice-cubes clinking; she clicked her tongue. 'If she'd spent more time worrying about herself instead of them she'd have never got into this mess in the first place.'

I still had nightmares. The city swallowing me up. Stepping on to the edge of it and being dragged into the jumble. I would get up and walk to the sea shore, let the wind scour me until I was sure I was awake, away from it, the clean lines of beach and sea my confirmation.

They both tried to get me into brighter clothes – plum jumpers, furry suede boots with braid up the side – but I wasn't interested. Those clothes weren't for me. Then I went to university where only silly, frivolous women got dressed up. It was dungaree time, boiler suits even. One woman I knew made all her clothes from prickly grey blankets; no one wore flimsy things, like they do now, showed any flesh. I dressed neatly, like my lecturers with their wire-rimmed glasses and lab coats over neat pleats; I thought I'd be OK if I blended in.

From the day I got there I was thought of as sensible, everyone remarked upon it. Sensible Alice who studies hard and has a good career in science ahead of her, that's how my flatmates talked about me. She eats properly and stays fit and healthy; doesn't join sit-ins or demonstrations or occupy the bursar's office. Alice only goes to parties at week-ends; she won't throw it all in for the love of a rogue. They said it slightly patronizingly, as if they really believed that love had not or would not ever hit me, that if you're sensi-ble you're immune. Their just-got-out-of-bed eyes in the kitchen said it, as I was eating breakfast, amid their stretches and yawns and sated passions that loosened them and made them want to talk, about it, their love.

'You've got a boyfriend though, Alice,' they'd say. 'What's he like?'

'He's OK.'

'Just OK?'

'Yes. Good in bed. He's a five times a night man.'

'Oh, Alice. You're so dry.' They didn't believe me.

'But do you love him?'

'I love his dick.'

That was enough to shut them up, to take them out of the kitchen, out of my face. When I told my boyfriend of the conversation he was pleased that my flatmates might think him a stud and it was true that we did have lively sex. But we weren't in love. 'How do people work in these places,'

250

we scorned, 'trying to teach class after class of students weighed down by their broken hearts?'

'Imagine living your life in the middle of that.'

'Must arrest your development.'

We were going to get out and do things in the world, me and that boyfriend, not hang around at university where the longing could get to you any time. He was an engineering student, an early nerd, who could build circuit boards and write machine code. He wouldn't approve of me now; irrationally walking out on my life, wilfully following an instinct; but he did at the time.

'You're so smart, Alice,' he would say, as he watched me in the lab, surrounded by my experiments. 'You set things up and you test them and you build up a picture from there.'

'Do you want to test what happens if I do this?' I said, drawing my finger up the inside of his thigh.

'I know what happens if you do that.'

Most of the time, though, I was sensible Alice. My flatmates knew they could rely on me for a shoulder to cry on, a sympathetic ear, a bowl of soup, loan of a tenner. Occasionally they would decide – like Mum had – that I was too set in my ways, and dress me up in thigh-length boots or a bodice or punky makeup but no one was really comfortable with the result, and I would always change back into jeans. It seemed that everyone wanted to slot me in somewhere – all those groups with their stalls in the student union – wanting me to pin myself down, sign up. The girls in my flat relished it all, changed their allegiances as blithely as their clothes and gawped at me in amazement if I was behind on the current phase. 'Oh no, Alice. That was ages ago. I'm into Art now, darling.' The politicos were the most insistent – the doom merchants, as my flatmates called them – with their posters of mushroom clouds and dark entreaties to protest and survive. Protest and survive? I thought. Surviving will do fine, just now.

And then I met Dan, who knew exactly where he was going, what he wanted. Me, for starters. He came up to me one day when I was struggling with my bags out of the library, dizzied by the traffic in front of me. 'Are you OK?' he said. 'It's Alice, isn't it?'

Cars blurred my path ahead. 'Yes,' I said, rubbing my eyes, the strap of my bag sliding off my shoulder. For a second I thought I might black out. 'Fine. It's just a bit . . . busy around here today.'

'Want to go to Scotland?' he said.

We went to the hills and walked. 'The only bit of wilderness we have left on this island,' he said. He was prepared. Had maps and a compass, spare rations and a survival blanket. At the top of Ben Nevis with the satellite hills rippling into the distance he told me his story – his parents drinking, the family business collapsing, Dan unable to stop it. I sketched a little about school, about Gina, the outlines as vague as the hills in the distance.

He nodded. 'We'll be OK, Alice,' he said, eyes on the horizon. 'We know the pitfalls now. I'll look after you.'

Only Ellie visited me at university; once she brought Taz with her – grinning and joking about the witches' reunion. Ellie ignored this, touched his hair absently. I was amazed by their closeness. 'Simple,' said Taz, when I asked him how he'd done it, worked out how to live. 'I love her.' He grinned again. 'And I do what I'm told.' We went on a demo Ellie wanted to support, Reclaim the Night, and then to a bar, underground somewhere, and got drunk in the blackness.

Ellie tried to talk to me about Rose, but I wouldn't listen. I couldn't, my brain just wouldn't take it in. 'Why are you telling me about her?' I said, shaking my head.

'You need to know,' said Ellie. 'How torn she was, between us and her family. It wasn't easy for anyone; Rose lost as much as the rest of us.'

'She didn't lose Johnny,' I said, my head lolling. I pulled it up in time to see Ellie going out of the door, trailing Taz. He mouthed over, 'Take care, Alice.'

After that I swore I'd never mention Johnny to anyone. I stopped drinking because I couldn't trust myself when pissed, couldn't make the split in my life work. I read books instead – not fiction; never. Look what had happened when

I muddled up truth and fiction. No, I read *Issues in Contemporary Chemical Analysis*. *Whodunnit? Modern Techniques Available to the Forensic Scientist*. They told me how to find the truth. I set myself goals, made action plans, went on work experience while everyone else was off smoking spliff and talking revolution. Just like Ellie when her mother took her out of school. I went into forensics because it was solid. I investigated real things – soil, paint, tyre marks – and then used that evidence to judge a situation. It seemed good to me, to be able to judge with some real data behind the decision. I was fascinated by the methodology, the principles behind it. But towards the end I got buried under the weight of it all. So many facts, so much data. And nothing can be totally and utterly and irrefutably proved; not even science. Evidence can be lost, tampered with. There's always more than one way of looking at a fact. I'd be standing there in court hearing myself speak about reasonable doubt, making brutal calculations of probability. Calculations that matter. That people's lives depend on.

The pipe bridge is in front of me, the sun sinking behind the spikes now. Sun-dogs blur my eyes and there are shouts behind me, kids on bikes zip past, stirring up dust, one of them flings her bike down and is up and over the pipe bridge, triumphant on the other side, black curls springing out from her head. A moment, a glitch, when it's all happening at once. Gina over the pipe bridge, me in the shed. Gina in the toilets at Rock Hill giving in to fear for a few minutes but then shouldering it, straightening her back. Me meddling then running, thinking I could leave it all behind, but how could I when it's all happening at once? The shadow of a spike lands on me like an arrow and I stand up and watch my feet as they start to move over the slippery hot paint.

# The Hall of Mirrors

'At least he doesn't mind her staying in his field,' I say to Mum. 'That's one thing I got sorted. His wife was surprised, said he'd been moaning on about it.'

'He?' says Mum. 'Who's he?'

'The man who owns the field Corinne's bender is in,' I say. 'You haven't been listening to a word I've said, have you?'

She waves her hand around her head. She looks vague today, unsecured. With her ancient dressing gown thinned to nothing in places, her hair climbing up her head, transparent. I watch her drifting down the corridor, echoes floating in the cloudy mirrors, stopping halfway and coming back to me.

'What was I doing, Alice? I forgot what I was doing.'

'Are you all right, Mum?'

'Bad dreams,' she says. 'Bad dreams about Corinne.'

She's worried, I realize, belatedly. Like she was when I couldn't get out of bed during the day but hammered, ghostly, on her door at night. She talked in speech-bubble sentences. 'Think of your future, Alice. I know it's hard but what's done is done.' The way parents talk to children when they don't know the answer. When they're not sure themselves but have to say something.

'We're all relying on you, Alice,' she says. 'Corinne and Johnny are up in court tomorrow.'

'It's only a hearing, Mum. No need for you to worry.'

'Yes, well,' she says. 'I'll make some tea.'

I watch her waver down the corridor. Her wrists shake sometimes now, her jaw strays a little between words. Standing in the doorway I can see myself panned down; reflections of reflections zigzagging down to the open door where Mum is. I am solid, bare legs straight, hair pulled off my face. My eyes are clear and I don't shake; I am still.

They all think I can do something. They're counting on it. As if I can reach out of this reality through to somewhere else and tweak, twitch, flick. Make a change that will change everything. And I wish I could. I swim through my dreams thinking I'll find a clue here – in this rock crevice – here – in this hidden chest, in the long-forgotten attic.

Mum comes back a bit calmer – the chink of spoons on teacups, the hot stream from the kettle – she peers at herself, licks a finger and wipes an eyebrow straight, brings herself into focus. 'I don't know what it is about that Corinne that gets to me,' she says. 'I just want her to be all right, I suppose.'

'She will be,' I say, automatically.

Mum sits down next to me, flicks the TV on, squeezes my arm. 'Thanks, Alice,' she says.

It's morning telly. Leela or Leeza or Ralph or Ranulph bringing drama direct to our living room. Mum is engrossed immediately. I pull myself away and head down to the kitchen, to clear up; to think.

Johnny is blasé about the court case – says they've still got to get the van off the towpath to really prove anything – but I'm guessing that this is just a front, to calm Corinne, whose arms rarely stray from a protective circle around her belly these days. She's not panicking but she is anxious; it seeps out, into Johnny's stride, Mum's dreams. I stare out into the yard, at the humps and lumps and buried messes, the largest one of which is the shed. The window is open – it's hot today, the hottest day of the summer yet, hot as 1976, the summer before the fires, the summer before the crucible that changed everything. Mum wanders by, flapping a magazine around her face, stares at the yard, goes through and opens a window at the front but the air doesn't shift, the noises and smells of the High Street linger in our corridor, our kitchen, our yard.

'We could do with a fan or something,' says Mum, 'something to shift this air. I wonder if there's an old one down in the shop?'

'I'll go and buy one,' I say. 'I'll go now.'

Selly Oak is a simmering strip of traffic, squashed between the curry houses and supermarkets. Cars in the bus lane and buses in the middle of the road, kids on bikes bouncing between bollards. I walk down from Battery Park, the fan banging against my bare legs, over the oily canal, past the heavily tagged playground squeezed in between electricity sub-station and railway, the university's high clockface hanging in the hazy sky like a yellow moon, its tower faded into the city dust.

Selina's. A name over a shopfront, blinds down, a plastic palm tree in the hallway behind the open door. It's cooler in there, fans whirr, snatching the cigarette smoke that rises from the receptionist's shiny fingernails. 'Yes?' she says, licking a finger and flicking over the page of her glossy mag.

'I'm looking for Cora,' I say. 'Cora Kirk.'

She presses buttons on a phone, whispers into it. A man comes in, raises his eyebrows at the receptionist and she spreads on a smile and nods him through a doorway hung with strips of plastic. The layout of the place is exactly like our shop. I know where the stairs are, the size of the rooms upstairs, even how much of a yard they have out the back. Thousands and thousands of these terraces all over Birmingham, climbing up and down the bumpy landscape; houses, flats, hardware stores and launderettes. Secondhand shops, massage parlours.

The receptionist is describing me into the phone. 'Long straight hair,' she says, 'about your age, your height –'

'Not quite as tall,' I say. 'Tell her it's Alice.'

We don't stay at the massage parlour. Cora's says there's someone she wants me to meet and drives me off in her big comfy car. She's wearing black, her hair sleek, her nails French-polished and she drives confidently, elbow out of the window. I feel grimy by comparison, sweat drying on my face, legs grubby below my shorts.

'How long have you worked there?' I say, raking my hair back with my fingers.

'I own the place,' says Cora, flicking indicators on and off, flashing a car in front of her to go. 'I still have a few clients though. My regulars, the ones who've been coming to me for years.'

'What's it like?' I blurt out. 'I mean . . .'

We're at a junction; hot air and exhaust fumes still all around us. The leather of the car seat is stuck to my bare legs.

Cora clicks the car smoothly into gear and we get some breeze again, the corners of her eyes crinkle and she flashes me a look straight out of 4b, her and Gina giggling over some transgression. 'You wouldn't believe the half of it, Alice,' she says, and something is unblocked between us, a gap in the traffic; we both move into it.

I talk about Dan and Mum and Johnny and Corinne. The story seems an impossible tangle to me but Cora just nods, asks after Johnny and Mum. She tells me about her daughter – a quiet glow on her face – and how she took over the business when the old man died. The old man that took Cora in after her parents threw her out.

'I always told him I'd run the place one day,' she says. 'I said, "Women sell the sex so why shouldn't they run the business?" The way he looked at me, Alice, you'd think I was the new barbarian.'

'It's true though,' I say.

'Course it is,' says Cora.

Over lunch we get a bit rowdy, Cora in storytelling mood, the waitresses leaning away from us as they pour drinks. Cora rattles her silvered wrists at them and talks loudly about her clients. 'This one, right, I send him into the corner of the room and yell at him if he dares move,' she says. 'Easiest money on the planet. I don't even have to take my clothes off.' She leans back and scans the room. People snatch their faces away from her, pasta dropping off their forks. 'If there's one thing I've learnt,' she says, 'it's not to be scared of what people think. I

257

mean, who knows what all these folk get up to behind closed doors? Why do they think they can put themselves above me?'

I sneeze into the froth on my coffee at the face of some old trout sitting behind Cora and the head waiter comes over, stern-faced.

'What's the matter? Isn't my money good enough for you?' says Cora, flashing her gold Visa card at him. The expression on her face says more though. It says *go to bollocks*.

We drive to Cora's house. 'Sadie should be back from college by now,' she says. 'She'll be up in the attic with her friends.'

'How?' I say. 'I mean . . . when?'

'That summer, after we were expelled,' says Cora. 'That's why my parents kicked me out. I got pregnant and they said no abortion no living at home, so I left.' She shrugs. 'I had to get out one way or another.'

The house is full of paintings and dogs. I want to linger with both but Cora rushes me up the stairs and prods a broomstick handle on the attic hatch. It opens and we climb up a ladder to Sadie's lair, five or six young women lying around on cushions, swinging their feet in the air. I'm introduced and they say hello politely. Sadie couples herself to her mum and they all cluster around chattering, breaking into a dance routine halfway through a sentence, miming into the mirrors that line one wall and then stopping on an offbeat, limbs frozen, collapsing into giggles at the images they project.

Cora and I go back downstairs and I tell her about Ellie and my photos of Gina – she's heard nothing, but doesn't think that's surprising.

'None of us wanted to be found for a while,' she says. 'I just hope Sadie at least keeps in touch with me when she decides she needs to lose herself.'

'What does she think,' I say, 'about your business and all that?'

'I've never lied about what I do,' says Cora.

Sadie is standing in the doorway, her friends around her. They arrived silently. 'Have you seen Mum's paintings?' she says. 'They're good, aren't they?'

'Wonderful,' I say.

Sadie sits down on the arm of my chair and stares into my face as she speaks. 'I know all about it, you know, how it happened,' she says. 'It's not as if people can just burn up their past, is it?'

'No, no, of course not.'

'And my mum's great. All my friends think so . . .' The group of girls at the door are nodding vigorously, leaning in for emphasis.

'They know they can ask her things and get a straight answer. Mind you –' she giggles, glimpses of girlhood flickering through the grown-up demeanour '– I don't know if their parents feel the same way . . .'

The girls troop back upstairs, all platform heels and barely covered flesh. 'Scary, aren't they?' says Cora.

'So,' says Mum, after I tell her about Sadie and her friends. 'Sounds like she's done a good job bringing the girl up, your Cora.' The fan is blowing into her face and she pulls on her blouse, directs the cool air down her body.

My Cora. Mum used to think of the group like that, us belonging to each other. Alice and her friends, they're inseparable, she'd say. I feel like I've got five daughters sometimes. I wonder if she missed them all as much as I did; if she had to screw her eyes up to stop the tears falling out when she woke in the mornings. But Mum was always good with change. Let it all wash around her and stayed in the flat with her mirrors and her memories and the accumulations of the years. As if at some point she'd decided that life was never going to match her dreams, so she split them apart. Drew a line down the middle. Live with a head full of fancy and leave the unsortable as it is. And occasionally, when reality coincided with the dreams, she could dress in her finery and trip down the High Street, cinematically beautiful, casting a smile over her shoulder, holding her hat against the breeze.

'Did you know anything about it?' says Mum. 'About Cora?'

'No,' I say. 'Not really.'

'She's done OK though,' says Mum. 'Could have been a lot worse. Did you see that story in the papers about that young lass who started hanging out with prostitutes and ended up dead behind the Dome? They said she was fascinated by it; by that kind of life.'

'Don't, Mum –'

'Well, it's not a career you'd choose for your daughters, is it? But your Cora seems to have made it work, in her own way. I mean, one mistake doesn't have to ruin your whole life, does it?'

Mum is getting up, sighing like she's just finished watching a good weepy film, with a proper ending and everything. Both of us should be getting on. Outside the street is busy, we can hear the newspaper hawkers already. *Evening Mail. Get your Mail.* Buses honk. Fumes rise in giant brown rings past our window. The TV is chattering – a recipe, summer salads, new ways with fish – and I think of Rose. Her broad bright face appearing in the living room of my old house as I flicked the TV on.

'You're dreaming again, Alice,' says Mum. 'Isn't there some stuff you should be getting on with?'

There is, and the next morning I know what. I have to go out to do it, out into the world, into the great magical bewildering mishmash outside of myself; only if I'm in it do I have a chance of influencing it. Out on to the street where the sun is a silver disc high in the sky. There is a strange, penetrating light, sparks in the air, like a flashbulb has just gone off. People's hair is fire-tinged, their clothes transparent. Wind is channelled up the High Street, between the tall rows of buildings, escaping down alleyways and entries, swerving round corners, rattling leaves, buffeting old ladies. I slide through it all. Past the grocer with his brown overalls and brown paperbags, head swivelling as I skim by. Past Woolworth's sweet-jewelled window; a crust of children stuck to the glass. Two girls run out clutching tester lipsticks and then the manager, shaking his fist. He'll never catch them. They know all the escape routes. I'm moving faster now, moonwalking. Past the park and the children's shouts, through the sticky, leaf-mashed mud to the fence with two bars pulled apart. My boots are clotted with mud but still feel light, I slip through the child-sized gap like a genie and am there, by the smoke-misted canal, breath streaming dragon-like out of my nostrils.

A pause, where I can feel everything. Smell the sweetly rotting leaves, the moss and crumbling clay; faint whiffs of sewage and distant smoke from a narrowboat's chimney. It reminds me of the shed. Another hidden place, magical place, with its own smells and secrets. On this stretch of the canal the trees grow right over the narrow strip of stained water, their leaves falling down on to the surface. I stand, and they fall on me. I am rooted for a moment, the mud on my boots mingling with the mud of the towpath. I am steady; not even the merest wobble. It is so still around me that I can hear the webbed feet of the ducks swishing under the water, the crack of a stick way off, murmured voices backing up into the city. And so clear to me now, an idea – a shape – coming to me letter by letter, crystallizing out of the mist. No one will see me, I can blend into a tree trunk, melt into the bushes, slip between cracks in the brickwork. Maybe I was never here at all. I just went to the shops – you saw me there didn't you? In the queue for the veg?

Outside the flat Mum is talking to someone, a man. Strands of hair streak across her face, her skirt is blowing out of control and she has to pin it between her knees. I approach, bags of groceries my alibi.

'Alice!' says Mum, her voice strangely tuned. 'I was wondering where you'd got to.' I hold up my shopping bags as explanation. 'Goodness,' says Mum. 'Are we expecting company?'

The man turns towards me. His face is white, carefully expressionless. 'I just came to see about your friend,' he says. 'The girl who lives on my field. Then I –'

'He found me,' says Mum. I wonder why they have to explain this to me, why it matters.

261

'You see we know each other,' says the man in the Otley Arms.

'Knew,' says Mum. 'It was a long time ago. Don't you recognize him, Alice? Didn't you realize when you went to see him? He certainly knew it was you.'

No, I didn't recognize him. How could I have? He was only ever real to me through her.

'I had no idea you'd still be here,' says the man. Robert.

'What did you think I'd do?' says Mum, so sharply that I stagger a few steps back. 'Cease to exist?'

# The Crucible

'You're too calm,' says Mum, pacing, lighting another cigarette. There are ten or so half-smoked ones in the ashtray.
'It's not natural.'

'You want me to panic with you?' I say. 'Will that help?'

'They should be finished in that court by now. Corinne
said she'd be straight here.'

'Well, she will then.'

'Very helpful, Alice,' she says.

There's no talking to her today. I tried to ask her about
Robert, the man-in-the-Otley who owns Corinne's field, but
all she'd say was, 'Don't wait around for things, Alice. It
gets so you don't know how to do anything else.' A glare; a
look right inside.

And now she's wound up about Corinne – as if Corinne's
her daughter, a small, grumpy part of me says. As if the
baby is her grandchild. I need to escape her wire-tight tension but I can't go far – Johnny and Corinne could arrive
any minute – so it has to be the shed. From the kitchen window it seems small; I narrow my eyes and zoom it down to
nothing, hide my head in the crook of my arm and watch it
flare back to size as my pupils widen.

Down in the yard autumn is seeping into the corners;
damp, mulching moss creeping up walls and even on to the
cloudy window of the shed, so that – with a wink, or a shake

of the head – you could be underwater. It's an old sunken boat, with a greened porthole, where a mermaid might live.

Where a spirit might live.

'You and your spirit,' said Gina, as we stood panting in the alleyway. 'Sometimes I wonder who's playing tricks on who.'

'So what,' said Cora, snatching up bits of her *Crucible* essay, 'I mean what does it matter?'

'It matters to me,' said Ellie. She looked up to me from her school books; we could hear her mother's footsteps advancing, her father tutting at the news next door. 'That I don't end up like them.'

'Oh but he's lovely, your dad,' said Rose. 'They only want you to do well.'

Their voices echo around the shed. Their faces from then are all around me – wide-eyed and euphoric as Ellie's body bobbed up into the air – and I visualize them now. Rose's tooth-perfect smile, girl-next-door face for TV; Ellie tanned and serious; Cora with her chin tilted up, her daughter's arm round her waist. Only Gina is missing now, nothing to fill the gap where she should be in my memory, like a blank space in a photograph album, a yellowed rectangle on a page, the picture slipped out, carelessly attached.

I could ask the board, the Ouija. It's crossed my mind plenty of times since I've been back. Literally – an imp-creature hornpiping through my dreams; a glass sliding off the kitchen table. But these photographs around the shed tell a story of an unpredictable world, full of pitfalls, dead ends, imperceptible currents that move you so you wake up one day with *How did I get here?* the refrain in your head. What might I stir up by asking the simple question, 'Where's Gina?'

There's a noise, a low rumble and for a moment I think I might have set something off without even touching the board. But it's nothing – a noise from the street and it sets me off laughing. Laughing because Rose was right, in her way. It was too scary. It is too scary. Rose with her primary-coloured world, her pristine kitchen-in-a-studio. No grease sliding down the side of the cooker, no mouldy vegetables at the back of the fridge. She knew she didn't want that, had to cut out early on, no matter how much that hurt. She was right. We were all right, in our own ways. Even me.

The door creaks. I spin round, stifling my cry with a hand to my mouth.

'What's up darlin'?' Johnny's silhouette fills the doorway, his smell. 'It's only me.'

'And me,' says Corinne, squeezing round the doorframe. 'Wow, I never realized you could actually get *in* here.' Her eyes sink into the darkness, scanning the bumps and humps and shapes lost in the shadows.

'This is where Alice practises her witchery,' says Johnny. 'Where she talks to her spirits.'

'I –'

'So it was you then,' says Corinne. Her face is calm. Her cheeks have slipped back on to their bones and her body is fluid. 'Someone said a spell for us anyway. Or a prayer. Your mum's gone to get some drinks to celebrate. Come on, you two –'

Johnny and I are still.

'We'll be up in a bit,' I say.

'Right,' says Corinne. Her eyebrows flicker together for a second. 'I'll have a look through this stuff sometime, if you don't mind,' she says, waving an arm around the shed. 'Bound to be something useful in here.'

Johnny grabs me from behind, encircling my waist, his hot breath over my shoulder. 'What did you do?' he says. 'What have you been cooking up down here?'

'You got off?' I say. 'You and Corinne?'

Johnny is clamped around me, his unshaven chin rough on my back. I spin around slowly and bury my head in his neck. It is warm there, and it smells of joy.

I run to the edge of the city. My feet are too twitchy to wait for a bus, my backside wouldn't stay on the seat. Ants in your pants, we used to say when we were kids. You've got ants in your pants you. Gina had them; always. Classrooms were too small for her, she scratched her way through lessons, running for the door the second the bell went. I pound the streets. It's a few miles but that's OK, I'm in a rhythm now. Over this bridge, through that railway cutting, scramble up the bank and through the entry into the street. Parks flash by in seconds, rows of houses a blur of windows and brick. I can't believe I haven't done this for so long. Whipped past a row of shops, raced through the garages, taken a short cut through a block of flats. We made the city ours this way, our fingermarks on lampposts, our footprints on newly laid concrete. The back way was our way.

Low afternoon sun catches on the windows of the block of flats, sparking it into a golden sheet rising unexpectedly out of the grey. I have to shade my eyes to find the entrance, slip into the dark hallway and readjust. I run up the seven or eight floors in a final burst of energy and bang the door, action erasing indecision. I pant. I wait.

'Hello.' He's not sure who I am. 'Are you all right, love?'

He is smaller, too. A little shrunken maybe, but tougher, compacted, not less. A mass of curls for hair, all grey now.

'Hi.' I'm still catching my breath. 'Mr Marshall, I don't know if you remember me, I used to be friends with –'

'Alice!' Something about him changes, a slight relaxation, a swirl of air around his shoulders. 'Of course I remember you. You and my Gina were like that.' He holds up two looped fingers. 'And you were quite sweet on my boy too, if I remember it right. Come on in, I'll put the kettle on.'

I'm surprised by his flat and I'm not sure why. It's neat; mannish. Newspapers, books, a packet of mints next to his glasses.

He chinks around the kitchen, humming. 'Back for a visit, love?' he says. 'How do you take your tea?'

Then I remember him in the kitchen of their house, head clamped in hands, and I wonder if – some part of me at least – has been expecting devastation. A cliché of strewn whisky bottles, bloodshot eyes; a broken man.

He comes back in with a tray, biscuits on a plate. 'Sit down, love,' he says. 'Or were you looking at the photos?'

Photos. My eyes flick to the bookcase and there she is. Somewhere sunny, blindingly bright, leaning on a tiny battered old car, sand all around her. Only a few strands of black hair escaping her bush hat, hand shading her eyes, mouth stretched wide across her face.

'That was a few years ago when she crossed the Nullabor,' he says. 'In a Mini, they did it. Built down the Austin, driven across Australia by my Gina,' he says, full of himself, filled up with her. 'Now isn't that something? Take a look at this one.' He pulls an album from a drawer. 'This is where she's living at the moment, a whole group of them together. Although who knows how long it'll last, she never stays anywhere more than a few months.' He points at a photo of a house by the sea; flyblown, rambling. Beach and sky; people lounging around the porch; kids, dogs. 'That's Pete, he's Gina's boyfriend, nice lad. She could do a lot worse.' Pete is big and red and crisped up by the sun.

'You've been there, then?' I say. My knees have gone, I sit down with a thud.

'Oh yes, love. I try and catch up with her every year. I'd go more often if I could afford it. Leave it all behind, y'do, when you get on that plane.'

He shows me more photos – beaches, deserts, brand-new cities gleaming like Oz. His voice has a tinge of Aussie, a sing-song tone. A lightness that I never heard in England, even in the good times, when Sandra did her Tammy Wynette in the living room and me and Johnny and Gina danced a backing routine. Gina always wanted to get to Australia, he tells me, though it took her a while. Saw a poster of Ayers Rock, glowing red in the blistering sun, and said, I'm going to go there, Dad, work my way over, starting in France. She was only sixteen when she left.

'That's pretty young to head off to the other side of the world,' I say.

'Yes,' he says, the lightness in his voice sinking. 'She couldn't get away fast enough I'm afraid. She'd had enough . . . of all of it really. I wanted her to do her exams at the time but now I'm glad she went. Glad she did it her way. There isn't any other way, is there?'

'But what happened to the house?' I say. 'I wanted to see her but you'd disappeared.'

267

'We were evicted, love. It was a bad time.'

'What about Johnny?' I say. I can't bring myself to accuse him, this gentle man, his quiet pride.

'He made his own choices.'

He opens another drawer and picks out a box. It's *the* box, Mum's box. Dark wood inlaid with mother-of-pearl shells. 'The only thing I have left of him apart from memories,' says Mr Marshall, looking at the box, dejection and – I fancy – a faint streak of indistinguishable hope in his voice. 'He did find us, when he came out of Borstal. But it was a bad day. Gina had just left and I didn't even know where she'd gone to and I'd been drinking and Johnny came in and saw me. He couldn't stand it that I wasn't doing anything, that I just sat and let it all happen. He'd seen it all before, you see. When his mother died. Me sitting around doing nothing and letting everything go. I think he just gave up on me.' Johnny's dad's words fade out into remorse. I want to reach out and touch his grey hair, as Gina might do, to comfort him, to reach his desolation.

'May I look?' I say. 'At the box?'

He hands it over. It is full of letters. My letters to Johnny when he was in Borstal, my slanted handwriting full of love and regret and panic that this will never be fixed, not even for a moment. And under them, Mum's letters from her man in the Otley Arms, saying much the same things. Our lives in a box in a drawer in a flat in a towerblock on the edge of the city.

'I think he meant to take it with him,' says Mr Marshall. 'But he stormed off in such a rush. I like to believe he left it for a reason, though, a sign. An old man's fancy, perhaps, but there you go.'

We drink our tea and I tell him about Johnny; a little, just enough. He smiles at the picture I paint, another hobo, he says, where did those two get their itchy feet? Gina is happy, her dad tells me. She suits a big country. Enough space in Australia for even her to roam around in. She knew she'd be all right there, he says, a place where you make your own kind of life, not like here where you have to take on the whole lot if you want to fit in. Should have taken the kids myself, when they were younger. I never thought it was an option for someone like me. Don't know why, really. She spotted it though, my Gina, knew it was her chance. Imagine if she hadn't seen that poster? Such a small thing to turn a life around.

A poster of a red rock hill in an empty landscape blazing in the sun. Gina would never have missed that. She must have known she could do it, take on the wilderness; we have those choices now.

'She'd have been all right,' I say, certain of this now. 'She'd have found a way.'

He gives me a photograph; of Gina, in the bush, squatting around a fire and stirring it with a stick. And an address. 'Write to her,' he says, 'she'd love to hear from you. Your other friend came – years ago, the one with the red hair. Said she'd fallen out with Gina when you were girls but she wanted to make up. They write, I think. You girls and your fallings out,' he says, shaking his head.

It feels good to have the envelope, with a little bit of her, safe in my pocket. I think of her dramatic gesture – so Gina – setting off to the other side of the world, while I skulked down to Gladys's to lick my wounds. I imagine what she might have done, who she's met. What tales she tells about her childhood growing up on the rain-soaked streets; in the parks and alleyways and sidings of the crowded city. Finding some space in a song, a flash of lightning maybe; the embers of an abandoned fire.

'I'll tell Johnny,' I say, as I'm leaving. 'I'll tell him that the door is open.'

'Ooh no,' says Mum, to Corinne, patting her arm. 'You don't want to suffer any more than you have to, love. Tell them you want drugs, and early on.'

'I never thought I'd hear you say that, Mrs T,' says Johnny.

'We're talking about childbirth, lad, not recreation.' She looks up as I walk in. She's a bit tiddly, unsteady on her unsteady heels. 'Alice! Where have you been? We've been celebrating.' She totters into the kitchen, fetches another bottle, her voice trailing behind her, up and down the corridor. 'I still can't believe it,' she says, 'that van getting burnt up on the towpath. To a shell, they said, nothing else but ashes. Must've been quite a blaze. Johnny reckons that's what tipped the balance in his favour, don't you, love?' She hands me a glass. 'Isn't it wonderful, Alice?' I chink with Mum, Corinne, Johnny.

'To a shell?' I say.

'Someone was on our side,' says Corinne. 'Looking out for us.'

'Yeah,' says Johnny. I can feel him willing me to look at him. 'We've definitely got a friend.'

'Course you have,' says Mum. 'But that still doesn't explain how that van got burnt up precisely when you two were safely in the courtroom and above suspicion.'

'You should have seen them when the bailiffs came in with the news,' says Johnny. 'The look on their faces was almost worth the whole thing.'

'Almost,' says Corinne.

'We got what we wanted,' I say. 'That's what matters.'

Mum looks at me, her eyes squeezed. She opens her mouth. I can feel her puzzlement – it's not like you, Alice, to ask no questions – it rises up in her throat, but stays there, is rinsed away by another burst of chatter from Corinne. We are incurious about this good thing, coming out of nowhere; raise our glasses, don't need to ask why. I like this notion, that rightness, fitness might arrive unnoticed, be welling up behind our backs. Just a little tweaking, here and there, such a tempting idea. But you're not in control of what could be let loose, and it might not take so much. A change, a shift, a balance disturbed. A dance in the woods, perhaps.

'You look pleased with yourself.' It's Johnny, with another glass for me.

'Of course I'm pleased,' I say.

'Corinne's going, you know. To Spain. There's a whole group of them. Be a good life.'

'Plenty of fresh air,' I say. He stares at me – wanting me to understand everything – and I feel about fifteen. My gaze is steady though. 'Are you going too?' I say. He'll go somewhere, I know that much.

270

'Maybe.'

Mum is still talking babies to Corinne. She wants to be there for the birth and Corinne seems pleased. 'Someone who's been through it,' she says. 'Who's got a bit of experience.'

I go into the kitchen and look out over the yard. The sun is sinking off the edge of the city; long, liquid tentacles of red slipping behind the horizon. The shed is small and black, the door hanging off its hinges. It's hard to believe so much happened in there; a tiny, dank place squeezed into the corner of our midden of a yard. A place that my body's too big for now; but then, then it was the one place we did fit, our backs curved into the warped walls, our hair tangled in with the spiders' webs.

'You can come, if you want,' says Johnny.

'Yes,' I say. 'I suppose I can.'

'Or are you going back?' he says. He is leaning in the door-frame, silhouetted. Light fans out from behind him and his stance is echoed in the mirrors. An arm casually on his hip, his hair curling around his shoulders.

'Back to what?' I say.

'To your life. That life. You can still do it, you know, you've not been outside too long yet.'

'I've got other choices now,' I say. 'It's possible. Anything's possible.'

'It always was,' says Johnny.

There's a silence. A space in which a decision could be made. Down the corridor, her swollen belly weaving in between Johnny's angled reflection, comes Corinne. She has arms full of bags and a square, folded shape under her arm.

'I'm going back to the bender,' she says. 'Catch you later, right?'

'Right,' says Johnny.

'Right,' I say.

'I had a look through your shed while you were out, Alice.'

'You're a braver girl than me.'

'There's loads of stuff in there,' says Corinne. 'Tat mostly, but it'll sell for a few pence. And some good stuff. A few diamonds in the dust heap. Should set me up nicely for when

271

'I'm on the road.' She's choosing what she wants out of the hotchpotch. What will be of use to her; her life.

'You pretty much sorted for that then?' says Johnny.

'I'm on my way,' says Corinne. She backs out, all belly and bags through the narrow doorway.

'Here, let me help you,' says Mum. 'What's this you've got?' She slides the board out from under Corinne's arm.

'Is it OK if I take it?' says Corinne, flushing. 'It was buried in all this stuff and I thought –'

'Goodness me,' says Mum. 'Has this been out in that shed all these years?' She looks at me. I nod. 'Well, well,' says Mum.

'I'd like to keep it if that's OK,' says Corinne. Glances bounce between me, Corinne, Mum.

'What is this thing you're making such a fuss about, anyway?' says Johnny. He takes the board off Mum and unfolds it on the kitchen table. 'Ouija?' he says.

Corinne leaves. Mum potters around the flat, clearing up, humming. Me and Johnny drift down to the yard. It's started to rain, lightly, drops of water rolling off sticky leaves and pooling in bits of cracked pottery, shining the spokes of an old bicycle wheel. I go into the shed and pin up Gina's Australian picture with the others, and look at us all, sitting awkwardly inside those bodies, peering into the misty mirrors for clues, asking the Ouija and Cathy & Claire. It doesn't feel any less strange now, this life, a tingling between skin and flesh, a curl of adrenalin.

Johnny is standing in the doorway reading my letters from the box, glancing up at me every now and again. He comes to stand close by me. 'I can't believe I've got these back, after all this time,' he says. 'It's a little bit of magic isn't it?' The air is fragrant with fresh-washed greenery and an unseen bird peals out music, an ounce of creature filling the air with sound.

'It seems like that when you write it down.'